COLDWAKE

GJ Hawkins

For Ruth.

CONTENTS

The Tetrarchy

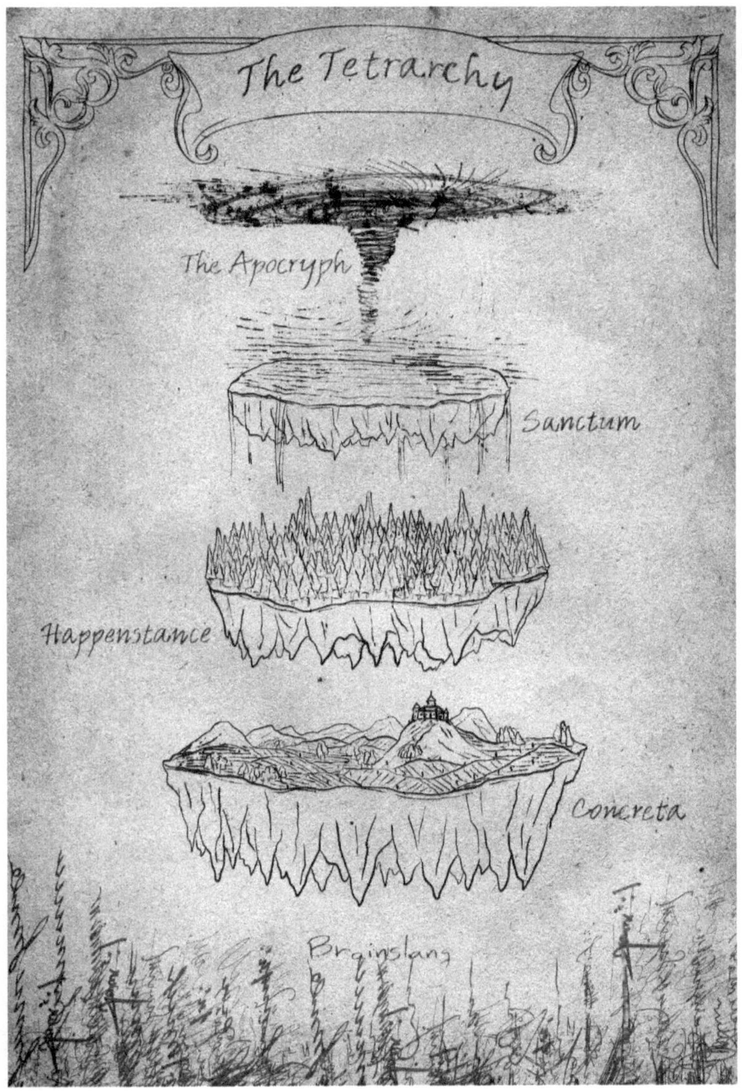

The Vigilant, Marta, planted her boots in the undergrowth, dropped her pack and slumped against a furrowed tree trunk, desperate to regain a sense of control. Across the sky, rainclouds shed momentum gathered over uncharted seas. Leaves drooped, sodden, and the blunt smell of the soil was heavy with moisture. Under camo-trousers and navy vest, Marta's skin prickled.

She had sworn not to do it. She'd written her oath, sealed it, and worn it at her throat these past few months. She had no right and no claim — nothing but dread that her past would meet her gaze with stony eyes.

True to form she did it anyway. Events had carried her too close. When the girl was a galaxy away Marta could, with practice, forget her. When she was a countryside away, Marta could at least ignore her. But when she was mere miles away… no, no-one could expect that of her. But now she was cursing herself for it, for the way she'd allowed herself to think, and the heartache she'd dragged to the surface.

How much, then, had she done? Watched with pride as the girl scaled the rock. Then revealed herself, distantly, and almost killed the poor girl. There were so many sins she was capable of, so many ways she could have touched or intervened, pried or pestered. In reality, all she'd done was concresce on a cliff edge as the girl ate her lunch then, in a panic of regret, force sleep upon her.

Marta dropped her head. Shame crawled across her prickly skin.

Fool.

She had risked more than her emotional equilibrium. If Abbot Barnabas was right, allowing her talents free rein right now could be fatal. Imagine if her rashness had slain them both in this desolate grub-infested hole.

Never had it been so crucial to maintain some self-control.

Never had it been so hard.

And what, really, was the point of hiking laboriously for three days to get into this mess if she was going to casually tic from peak to peak when she got here?

She shivered, pushed the girl from her mind, and steeled herself to hack deeper into the forest to find the boy all the fuss was about. Already, there were things she needed to tell Weakjohn —echoes, auguries, past effects of future causes— but she was afraid to talk over this distance. Was Barnabas right about how dangerous it had become? Were they truly walking on such a knife-edge suddenly? She wanted to howl with frustration.

Doing things the hard way didn't come naturally to Marta. Every instinct she had, honed through years of Vigil training, begged her to see the forest around her as a fluid facade of her own construction, enticed her to be one with her surroundings and master them with a single thought. But to have succumbed once and survived did not mean it was safe to do it again. Against her instinct, she stayed resolutely in the body she had, leaned on the tree, sweated in the heat, stretched out her calves, massaged a thigh.

Even without casting her mind into the flux she could

sense the life around her. She could hear it in the incessant rustling of the undergrowth and the slithers and squawks in the branches. She could smell it in the muggy, swampy odour of the air. It made it so hard to breathe, hard to even think straight, let alone to banish the wild ideas that had taken hold of her.

For deep down she was vibrating. She felt more alive than she had for a decade.

Might there be a future where they knew each other? She had always thought it impossible but now she wasn't so sure. Circumstances *might* be changing. There'd been times of late when she thought all three lives were going to line up.

And if they did? What could she be to the girl? How much was she finally prepared to sacrifice?

A lot, oh my soul, a lot.

But, really, how dare she even dream it?

PART ONE

1. Semele

Martoth, Timoth

— My *what*?

Martoth spat saki.

— Father, said Jessic.

They sat on barrels, shoulders to the taproom wall, heels wedged into the rims, and windburned faces to the screeching and the stomping. The flimsiest of panels separated them from Semele's dense biosphere, and though the sound in their ears was all fiddles and hoots, the *ringing* in their ears was geckos and crickets, the cackling of foxes and the shriek of waterboar. For both girls worked the wild paddies from daybreak to twilight, both knew better than any what crept, what crawled, what bit, what stung, and what ate what.

Of all the teenage rice harvesters operating out of the shanty-village of Border, only the girls were in tonight. Alban and Teppen would be in one of the common houses, and with a hardiness that Martoth still thought absurd, Timoth had stayed out again.

As Martoth's closest friend, Jessic could never pass up an opportunity to patronise:

— You know, like some people have and everything. Some people have *pa*s (I mean here me, obviously). Other people have *ma*s (citing here, dear Timoth). And hey looks like you can join my club.

Ma Mackelay, Timoth's mother, had taken to the dance floor, gripping her heavy skirts with both hands and pacing out her heel-stamps with a practiced dignity, all the while shooting kind but watchful glances at Martoth and her friend.

— In *Laketown*?

Her father's name was known. Martoth had always known it, though she didn't remember sharing it with Jessic. He was a man who, for all she knew, had been on the planet once, sixteen Semele-years ago. And now he was asking questions in the Laketown bars where Jessic's friends hung out.

— What questions?

— No idea. But look, I'm going back to Laketown tomorrow—

— You *what*?

Martoth turned from the revelry to wince at her friend.

— What? I finished my paddy.

The harvest wasn't the issue, and they both knew it. However obtuse Jessic might decide to be, Martoth's unspoken accusation was clear: *You haven't told Timoth!* Martoth was used to squirming at the confidences Jessic chose to share about her implausible romance with Timoth but sometimes she just didn't want to know.

— It's okay, protested Jessic, I'll leave a note.

Martoth would steer clear of Timoth tomorrow night. No sense being near when the dead cow hit. Though maybe, just maybe, Mr Self-obsessed wouldn't even notice. She could almost see him, swaying up a few nights from now, sweating saki, tall and close, with those mad eyes that only seemed to focus when they weren't on her. Twigging. *Hey Martoth, what happened to, you know, Miss Ang?*

The thought appealed. She held it for a second, aware of how palpable her memory was, of his cropped hair, clear dark skin, sloping shoulders, unguarded expression. Her deep fondness for Jessic meant she would stomach all the slightly-too-intimate details, tolerate Jessic's weirdly candid pride in her repertoire of little manipulations, but Martoth never hid from herself her conviction that Timoth would be better off without Jessic buzzing around him, filling his head with half-truths and third-hand gossip recycled from the bars of Laketown. He'd never really left Border; he didn't realise you had to sift the grit for the gold.

Jessic took their empty cups to the bar for a refill and Martoth looked through a lens of encroaching weariness at the community that gave her a home for half the year. She was fiercely proud of them: the sort of people who work so hard by day that the nightly revels demanded, and received, an equal commitment. They screamed and stamped on the dance floor because the gap between them and the bleakness of this universe was as thin as the taproom wall. She could love these people and work for these people. She admired their unrelenting fight to live in the present, not the past. What she could not see for herself, or for any of them, was any kind of future.

Jessic brought the empty cups back together with a full pitcher and set them down on her barrel. Martoth glanced down at them.

— See me off? suggested Jessic.

— Sure.

She slid off her barrel while Jessic poured. With left hands they grasped each other's left arms just above the elbow. *Border!* proposed Martoth, and with their right hands they raised their cups and downed them. The toasts flew by — *Freedom! Clean Clothes! Off-world Stories! Copperknives!*— and another pitcher was obtained. In an economy based on little more than pulling weight, the young ricers were rarely denied. *Death to Leeches! These Awesome Boots! Firm Buttocks!*

They were not going to talk about Timoth so as the saki flowed they inevitably turned back to Martoth's father. Of whom: Jessic's intel was he was some kind of investigator. So questions were just questions. No need to chase that cat into the woods.

— Maybe he could investigate my mother, burped Martoth.

— Guess that's how this whole thing started…

— I mean I don't really care about *him*. Way more interested in her.

Was this even true? Martoth had never thought of it like that but something about Jessic forced you to boil down complexities. In fact, her mother's desertion had left Martoth oddly well endowed in the maternal stakes. She'd always had at least one mother figure in her life wherever she lived. She was never short of care, guidance, or a firm hand and in retrospect she'd had enough raw headcount in the role to sustain Semele's inevitably high mortality rate. But it still stung in a way her father's disappearance didn't. Of her mother, Marta, Teresa had told her what little she knew: She'd sheltered Marta in Porton for six months, from which Martoth had long ago inferred —though Teresa never spelled it out— that the pregnancy was secret. There were some tales of Marta's supposed kindness that Teresa returned to when Martoth pressed for more, but anything else was either unknown or buried deep.

— You're so grasping! I offer you one, you want two! No-one has two. Wait! Are you actually serious? Like… *commission* him? Are you serious? Can you pay him anything?

Martoth's face jerked an inch or two backward and she swayed on her feet.

— Doesn't matter, I'll skin Dad for it.

It got hazy from there. When Martoth woke from first sleep she was still drunk and in the grip of the drowning dream. She could smell the pitcher and cups standing on the barrel above her head while she lay below trying to force the dark weight off her chest. When Semele's clamorous dawn roused her from second sleep, she had no time to replay the night's conversation: her trail through the wilderness demanded all the concentration she could muster.

There were artificial paddies by the village, continually re-imposed on the resistant landscape by the last three generations, though the wild crop remained the major factor in the village's agreements with Laketown and beyond. Martoth was past those and into the forest in a few minutes. It was a full hour before she broke out of the vegetation once more into the shifting lake margins that formed her paddy.

Back thigh-deep in the greening water, she found she was further along than she remembered. A patch was clear and one floating barrow full. She checked it, wedged it shut with one of her set of copperknives, then stooped into her repetitious work, using another knife to strip the stalks beneath the surface, bringing her other hand up from below in its net glove to gather the grains. She worked swiftly by touch, not sight, and moved from stalk to stalk mechanically, mindlessly, relying on skills internalised over the last four hard seasons.

Above the skidding clouds, Semele's sun rose steadily to its midday mark and Martoth stopped for lunch. She'd collected some crabby apples on the way down and stowed them in her pack with some crumbling rice bread. She shrugged off her wet work trousers and draped them on the boulder most likely to catch the passing sunlight, slung her bag over her shoulders, and climbed the tall rock face behind. Reaching the soft moss and bristly grass of her customary lunch spot, she spread the bread and apples on top of her bag and turned to face back over the giant lake.

This late in the season, so established was her daily toil, so familiar this rugged, verdant landscape, that she rarely took a moment to remember the majesty of her situation: blissfully alone before the vast, soggy, soulless unknown. She gazed now across all the crinkled horizon of the uncharted western wilderness and savoured the fact there wasn't another human being in all the vast world in front of her. Not counting Timoth, of course.

In Border she belonged, and derived her sense of security from the close knit of the community around her. Out here it was the simple fact of her solitude. No-one here would harm her or worry her. Because there was nobody here.

And in a way, she reflected, *right here* was as far as humanity had got. She was at the very edge. But she also knew the migrations had not stopped with Semele. In all likelihood the great tribe of humanity was still wandering in the starlit night, still carrying forward the dwindling momentum of the crises and the loss of Earth. So there might be thousands or millions further out than she. On wilder worlds. On blanker maps. But on Semele, each and every day, it was Martoth. And Timoth.

Briefly, something fell into the space between consciousness and daydream, something she thought she saw, but when she narrowed her eyes, stretched her gaze out westward, it disappeared, so she could not be sure of what she'd seen. She was left with some impression that might or might not have been a memory. She believed she'd seen a figure stepping out of some distant trees, an arm passing to their neck, a step or stumble backward, then gone. A sudden fear clutched at her, and the hard lunch ached in her belly. She crouched, pulled a blanket from her bag and wrapped it round her legs, and knelt on one knee as she screwed up her eyes to focus.

The distant trees crowned a rocky bluff that was higher than hers, rising like a prow from the skulking forest to jut into the sky a hundred yards to her west. She knew its granite cliff face was unclimbable, but a mysterious ascent paled beside the greater problem: *there should be no-one here.*

There was nobody there now. She stood back up, looked around at other peaks and platforms in the landscape, alert for human shapes popping in and out of existence, but in spinning around she must have made herself dizzy, because her head began to reel, the green floor capsized and before she knew it, she had blacked out.

Again, the drowning.

So vivid, even in waking, she could taste the cold black water in her mouth.

Martoth clung to the ground, fists bunched around tufts of grass, breathing the thick scent of the earth in her face and the paddy below. Then she pulled her dangling feet away from the edge and willed her muscles to relax.

The drowning dream. They called them *relics*, these dreams that fascinated children of Semele as they played together in halls and hollows, discovering as they grew just how much they shared. They were the soil in which landed the infant seeds of empathy, of tiny hands touching at bedtime, of soft whispers to eyes wide in the early dawn, and of an easy forgiveness for those late to rise and those late to bed. By Martoth's age, sixteen hard seasons, relics were a devil you knew, a familiar trespasser on the less predictable trials of frontier living. Since childhood Martoth was especially susceptible to the drowning. Her tweensleep routine had evolved to accommodate recovery, to allow her to steady her heartbeat, wipe off the cool sweat, massage some life into pallid cheeks and rigid limbs, to seek some scant comfort in Semele's long night.

Now she had suffered it in daylight, she knew she had to get back in the water. Too long dwelling on this intrusion and the fortitude she'd established could slip away from her. If she made it look easy, it wasn't. If concern did not show in her face as she strode out from Border in the early dawn, if her ease of pace suggested confidence, competence, then it was testament only to a determination she was known for in both her homes. It wasn't easy. Not for her, nor for any of the others, Jessic, Timoth, or any of the handful of ricers flung sparsely into the wet wilds of *Semele Incognita*. So she twisted down onto the rock face and descended towards the paddy.

Timoth waded out of the deep paddy. The last light of dusk was ebbing away, and the hillsides seemed to lean in on him from every side. His barrows were full and his back ached. Tomorrow he'd haul them round the sweep of the shore to where he could retrieve them and ferry them upstream. He turned his eyes in the direction of the village far above and imagined he could see over the forested hills to its firelight and lanterns.

Jessic should have cleared her paddy today. Martoth might take another week but then she would be done too. The hard season would stretch longer for Timoth, but he needed time to think anyway, and for all the unpleasant hazards of the deep paddy, at least interruptions were rare.

He found his backpack and changed out of his work trousers, hanging them over a high branch. Sodden trousers were the least of his morning trials and the rain overnight would clean off the scum and any leeches. He pushed his gloves onto the ends of other branches where they looked oddly human, flinging themselves out for an embrace with the dark. How did Jessic and Martoth manage this stuff? He'd ask, tonight if they were coming into the village. Or not — it might seem like prying. An involuntary shiver of arousal worried at him but he shook himself free of it. Was it Jessic's hands he imagined on him, tracing down his spine and round to his front? Or Martoth's? Or… both?

He stared at the gloves in the dark. It bothered him that a tableau like that could seem so human. It seemed like evidence of something deeper in the world, of some of the things he'd begun to suspect these recent weeks. As if the boundary between him and the world around him wasn't quite so crisp as he'd once thought.

Then one last glance out across the paddy and the unstable waters beyond. He had a strange almost-memory, an upside-down mental niggle like deja vu, an idea that he'd lost something in the water today, something that was lying waiting for him in the depths. But if he had, he couldn't recall what or how. Maybe it was the rushes and reeds churning in the breeze but the more he stared, the more he began to see movements in the darkness. He rubbed his eyes and turned back toward the village.

In fresh trousers and dry boots he started the climb. He'd eat with Ma and the others in the common house, ditch his bag and then hang out and sleep in the taproom if there was space. He wouldn't fight off a late-night saki session with the others but he wasn't going to instigate it with everyone else so far ahead of him. The breeze died away as he entered the forest. The going was slow around precipices still slippery from the showers but he reached the village before full-dark.

The taproom was already raucous when he and his mother showed up. The usual suspects were playing a semi-improvised collection of accordions, guitars, a clarino, the weedhorn, cymbals, fiddles. No dancing yet but it was loud with chatter and with kids screaming. A handful of men and women worked the bar but the line between staff and patron was hazy. Many served themselves, others did stints behind the bar just for conversation. Martoth was sitting alone with her back against the book crates, reading something old and off-world, her dirty-blond hair knotted and her top sweat-stained and muddy. Jessic wasn't around. Timoth's mother ruffled his hair and went off to join the aunties.

The tables and benches, even the barrels, were taken, and he wasn't talking to Martoth, so he fetched himself a ricebag and went off to find a drink. Mulkah, the taproom's only permanent member of staff, served him a saki in a burntwood cup and pointed to where Alban was slouching in a fortress of ricebags.

— Did that woman find you, by the way?

— Woman? asked Timoth, surprised.

— I sent her down to the deep paddy? Oh, and I got this for you, Miss Jessic Ang dropped it off this morning.

Mulkah plucked off one of dozens of grey paper scraps that were pinned up behind the bar and passed it to Timoth who held it close to his face, as if distracted, breathing in the air that came off it. Mulkah always called her *Miss Jessic Ang* though he knew how it riled her.

— Woman, you say?

— She didn't find you?

— Mulkah, what are you talking about?

Mulkah paused for a second, a hint of concern in his eyes.

— She came in lunchtime, from Laketown. Asked after you by name. Or by your father's name, I suppose. Didn't eat. I drew her a map.

By this hour the rainflies would be suffocating by the deep paddy. Timoth slept there sometimes but his first night had been horrific, and he was young with healthy lungs. Anyone down there now was bivouacked or dead. He tapped Jessic's note against his forehead thoughtfully and went over to the table where his mother had found a slot.

— Ma, do we know any women from Laketown?

— I reckon your dad knew some, she snorted.

The aunties threw a few names around —Gerane, Alberta, Alban's Grandma...— but the woman was a mystery. Ma gestured at the note in Timoth's hand:

— Love letter?

— Well I assume so.

He shuffled off toward Alban, kicking his ricebag along the floor while he held his saki with one hand and read the note in his other. *Moth*, it said, *Talk to Martoth. Love, Sic. PS. It's different rules in Laketown.*

Jessic could never just go. She had to toss in that shred of a promise too. That perpetual maybe that got Timoth hard as iron.

When he finally fell asleep he lost himself in the murmur of the shifting ricebags. In his mind, the grains were made into an infinite frictionless fluid that he could melt into, a boundless multiplicity that shimmered all around him and that bathed away his preoccupations with Jessic and Martoth and the other distractions of his Semele life.

— This is very fucking unusual.

They were a hundred strong, mustering in the taproom as a pastel dawn slipped in through the narrow windows. A cluster of candle stubs lay cold on the bar where Timoth had seen a hushed conference taking place between first and second sleeps. Mulkah had leaned forward in the gloom, jowls resplendent in the flickering uplight, arms spread wide on the bar. Ma Mackelay had been amongst them, whispering urgently and jabbing her finger on the surface. A few of the Border elders, Jeppa and Big Ian, had crowded near.

It was clear now what the discussion had been about. Mulkah and Jeppa were bustling about, describing the missing woman, explaining a search plan. Even before he'd woken, they'd nominated Timoth to lead one party straight down to the deep paddy, with other groups to follow, combing the forest off to the sides of the trail, carrying provisions to rendezvous at the deep paddy for lunch.

— What I don't get, grumbled Alban, is why're they so worried about Mrs Bloody Laketown. She comes here looking for your dad more'n likely. He's not here. She finds you're a shitty mile into the wild so she doesn't come to see you. She's crashed somewhere on the way back to Laketown.

Timoth had all the ricers. He also had Gilda, youngest of the council, and a few others judged fit enough not to slow them down. He was horrified enough by the idea of just this group descending on his paddy let alone a lunchtime congregation of a hundred. Until today only a handful of Border folk even knew the route. Suddenly his private space was about to become very public. He could not shrug off a nagging unease about how he'd left things yesterday evening, what he might have left lying around.

They trekked out through the village and down through the forest and what usually took him an hour looked set to take them three. Timoth went in front and Martoth followed close behind. Not speaking, for which he was grateful. He didn't like her seeing his paths like this. She was comparing his daily routine to her own. It was such a large part of their day that was so private, so hidden from each other. Alban's too. Maybe Timoth's paddy, the deep one, was a plum job. Maybe she'd resent it. Or maybe hers was an easier ride. Maybe she'd exult, ridicule.

She stayed silent though as they led the group along the trail. He admired the way she walked through this landscape. She trod firmly like she owned everything around her but lightly enough that she didn't disturb what didn't need to be disturbed. The others hit nettles, ant columns, even a viper's nest. They all stuttered to a halt to scramble down the rough spots, but Martoth navigated this bitch of a route better than Timoth had the first time. Only once did she show any interest in the route at all, when Timoth explained a tortuous set of manoeuvres down an eroding earthen cliff face, wet with mud and poor in solid rock stances on the descent.

— You can't go the obvious way, he said. That hanging moss hides a rainfly nest.

— How…? She stared at him. How did you find that out?

— A quite hard way.

It *had* been hard, that first time, knowing that choking was as much of a risk as the bites. Only later had he discovered he could keep them at bay with little more than an angry stare — another one of the awkward mysteries he was pondering in his time alone. It was some kind of knack, he'd once theorised, a way of moving. Except that didn't explain the feeling he got when he did it. The sense of *cheating*.

— This is *it*? Martoth asked as they finally reached the narrow shore of the wild paddy.

He bristled. He'd realised as they reached the paddy just how intimate this place had become to him. The things he'd started exploring, experimenting with. His own theories and feelings. His trousers were hanging up on a tree over there for fuck's sake. Could she at least respect his space?

— No. I mean, she said, perceptive sometimes, I like it. It's beautiful isn't it? But fuck, Timoth, you *sleep* here?

— I've got some canvas sheets and stuff. I can rig things together. Some nights the flies aren't so bad.

— Has Jessic ever seen this?

That was a question so loaded he wasn't going within a mile of it but of course she hadn't. Not really. She knew the way. They'd been down as far as the nearest hills to look out over the deep paddy. She'd not seen how he lived.

— Remind me to show you mine sometime.

— Tease.

Alban helped him check his things, but otherwise Martoth was all over the place, exploring the limits of his domain, climbing his tree, perching on his branch. He watched feeling slightly sick but also transfixed, as she climbed. He couldn't understand quite how she could combine this robust business-like physicality with an equal amount of sinuous sway. He couldn't help take advantage of the moment to let his gaze wander up her infinite buckskin trousers, up to vest, armpits, neck, curls.

— Take some time, Timoth, said Gilda.

Timoth brushed off the condescension and nodded. He turned from the paddy, heading back into the undergrowth, drifting eastward around the waterline to a landing place he used. The sounds of his working life, birdsong, the buzz of insects, the splashes of bobbing ducks, the wind in the rushes, everything proceeded as normal. But, as he came towards the shore a dread settled on him and he knew something was wrong.

Worse was a spiralling feeling of exposure as if something that he had hidden from everyone was coming into the light here and he couldn't escape. The things he had found he could do, the feeling he had when he changed things, when he cheated the world around him... That feeling was here now, in this place. But bigger, more saturated. Someone else was cheating too, but someone much better at it than him.

Then he saw her.

Her body lay touching the water's edge so the leeches were crawling over exposed legs where her camo-trousers had torn. Her neck was snapped and her arms were wrenched to either side. A great deep wound slashed across her back from shoulder to thigh — a wound that Timoth could not understand. It was not blood and flesh, it was more a bubbling melt of fleshy, animal colours, reaching deep into the corpse and spreading somehow out from it. This wound, or whatever it was — this was where the *cheating* was coming from. It was the same sort of trespass that he was capable of, but on a much, much bigger scale. It wasn't fear or revulsion that consumed him now but a breath-taking and debilitating shame.

He couldn't raise a shout. In a mad panic he even considered hiding the body. Maybe he would have, or maybe he would have just dissolved into the undergrowth or waded out into the paddy. But one thing and one thing alone brought him back to himself and sent him running back to the party. When he looked at her white face, looked deep through the agony and the deadness, he saw at last that this woman was not a stranger after all.

2. Knock Knock

Martoth, Timoth

Timoth stormed out in the end, leaving Ma sobbing and Jeppa purple with fury. Let someone else harvest the paddy, he'd told them, though he knew no-one could learn this late in the season. It was ruined for him. What did he care what it would cost Border to leave three weeks of crop to rot in the water?

Ma kept saying it wasn't about him. That woman wanted his father. But Timoth did not believe it. Then, when Timoth kicked open the taproom door, dragging his pack along behind him and still fumbling an arm into his coatsleeve, Martoth had been outside all along, her own pack bound neatly to her bare shoulders, hair tied back, face firm and eyes on the sky. So that was another week's crop destined to die on the stalks.

He'd growled but what could he say? She'd as much right to chase this down as he did. More, even. Much more. But he didn't understand why she would come with him to Laketown. They had no leads in Laketown, only what Jessic could help with. If this woman really was to Martoth what he suspected, some aunt, sister or even her mother, then the answers she sought must begin at her other home in Porton. Why, when all he needed was to be free of all of this chattering, pestering, noise did she suddenly have to dog his every move?

So when they arrived in the first night's shelter they'd spoken less than a dozen words to each other, trekking silently all day under brooding skies. A cold rain started up as they ducked their heads under the lintel and hurried in to slam the windward shutters. Martoth went to look for candles. Timoth improvised some ricebags with the sacking and grain in the stores. He was angry and unhappy but it was something more like shame that muted him. The deep paddy had been his own private dominion; what happened there had to be his fault. What Martoth must be feeling he didn't dare guess but he could hardly blame her if she really did resent him as much as she seemed to.

She settled in one corner, he in another, and they simply let the candles die.

Day two dawned clear and bright, and the first burst of sunlight was enough to thaw their stiff backs and limbs. Martoth had slept badly. He had watched her between his first and second sleeps when the moonlight fell across her face. She jolted frequently as sleepers do when they fall through the dream-void to be caught suddenly in their own bodies. Perhaps it was the drowning dream. But come morning, she was up quickly. Together they stood in the sunshine and looked ahead, picking out the landmarks they had learned before setting out.

The trail crossed gentle slopes, passing in and out of dense vegetation. Occasional footprints in the mud witnessed a runner's passing early in the morning but they saw no-one.

Timoth fell into a deep contemplation as they walked, dwelling on the *cheating* — no longer an insubstantial curiosity and become instead something quite sinister. In the beginning Timoth had thought he'd regressed into a sort of infantile credulity, the sort that convinces children that arranging bedsheets in just such a way wards off monsters, or blinking thrice brings parents to their bedside. But this did not last long. Over months working waist-deep in leech-infested water his strange talent had become too practical to doubt.

More recently he'd come to believe the paddy itself was the source of the strangeness. All the luck that came his way seemed to relate to the paddy. The behaviour of the flies and leeches, the water and the reeds, the buffeting winds — they were all part the paddy's domain and all, therefore, his world.

But now as they hiked up a sunlit hillside, puddles dwindling and the trailside shoots popping unbent, there were hints in the world around him, tiny suggestions that he was a part of it in the same way he'd been a part of the paddy. As he swished his arms through the air at his side, he could almost see a matching ripple playing in the grass a few feet away. When he blew gently into the wind, it seemed to die away and disperse. Later, when Martoth went off behind a tree, he banished a prurient impulse to follow her with his imagination, and instead knelt on the ground and picked a handful of small stones to inspect, hoping to read some hidden truth on their exterior. Minutes later, he realised Martoth had returned and was watching him in silence. He pocketed the stones and walked on.

The breeze stiffened as they climbed to higher ground, making for a distant saddle beyond which lay the Laketown valley. With the saddle in sight, they kept hard on their route and did not let up for lunch but snacked on rice cakes through the day.

He missed Jessic. He missed her unconcerned bluster and

her luminous chatter. Only a week ago they had been together, she pulling him close under a tilting broom-tree and whispering something irrelevant and inconsequential as she kissed him. She was the very opposite of Border, an imposter in the ricers' ranks, daughter of a Laketown industrialist who exiled her for half the year, either for the fortifying influence of hard labour, as Jessic would have it or, as Timoth privately believed, for a little peace and quiet. Timoth missed whatever it was that was beginning to form between them and was stung that she had flown off with only a cursory note when he could imagine any number of more physical goodbyes he would happily have accommodated.

But right now he missed Jessic's accidental ability to mediate between himself and Martoth. Jessic might needle them both in different ways but in doing so she brought them both into a precious overlap where communication was possible.

They went hard and made good progress. They reached the saddle in the late afternoon and discussed whether to press on to reach the town before nightfall. It was a foolish idea and, for Timoth's part at least, it was driven by dread of the difficult hours to be spent together in the shelter, rather than any urgency in their mission. In the end Martoth vetoed it and they pushed open the door of the travellers croft a hundred feet below the saddle ridge. Timoth got a fire going and Martoth found a lamp to set on the table while they emptied out their packs to see what provisions were left and bickered over who would walk down to the well for water.

The door flew open. Martoth froze, a steaming mug of tea halfway to her mouth. Timoth spun round and nearly fell off his stool.

The man who shot in turned in the same fluent movement to slam the door and drop the latch. As he brushed the rain off his coat, Timoth and Martoth recovered their wits enough to say hi.

He was a runner, small in frame, pale skinned, in light shoes and tight trousers soaked through and slick against the skin. When he had his breath back, he raised them a lazy salute and disappeared into the stores at the back, to where the runners' stow boxes were stacked.

By the time he joined them round the table lamp, Timoth had fixed him a mug of tea. He accepted it gratefully but left it sitting on the table while he set out his damp clothes by the fire on a little timber frame. His name was Ben.

— Everyone else is going the other way, he said. You know that, right?

Martoth raised her eyebrows at Timoth. They'd seen no-one.

— No? she said. Is there trouble?

Ben gave her a suspicious look but took her at her word.

— A month ago, he said, streets are safe after dark, and a man knows his walls won't burn down around him as he sleeps. Not so now.

They both raised their heads at this. Timoth's mouth opened to speak but it was Martoth who asked:

— How have we not heard of this?

Ben shook his head.

— I done Laketown-Border twice this fortnight and no time was it tidings of comfort and joy.

— Maybe we have, said Timoth. Remember that religious-sounding stuff that Jeppa and Big Ian were talking about last week… The "smoke without a flame" thing.

— Ha! spat Ben. That's a joke that turned sour.

— You think that's what Jessic is chasing? asked Martoth, turning her eyes away from them all and back to a copper-knife and the rice bread she was buttering.

Timoth shrugged. Border was not a community that would

follow the ebbs and flows of a more cultured town's religious life. Whatever this new movement was he doubted Jessic was any more interested than he was.

— This friend, said Ben with concern, she's new in town?

— She knows the town well enough, said Martoth.

Ben finished with his clothes and came to join them.

— It's not religious, he said. The Allegorians and Jews and the others are as mystified as everyone. The smoke without fire thing was just they don't seem to have any actual leaders. It's always different faces stirring up trouble.

— Our friend recommended us a common house called The Hole, said Timoth uncertainly.

— I know it, he said. You'll be safe there but stay in after dark. I'm carrying a message for a Jessic Ang, actually. I gather I already missed her?

Timoth and Martoth were tripping over each other in their eagerness to take the letter but Ben wouldn't pass it on. Return to sender was the rule and privacy was sacred to a runner.

— She's not related to Mike Ang, is she? asked Ben. Imports business?

— That's right, said Timoth, happy to be in the know for a change. He's out of town.

Ben whistled through his teeth.

— He's a target. It was his warehouse burnt a few nights ago. I hope your friend knows how to take care of herself.

Timoth was convinced she did. Martoth was nowhere near as sure.

After a while the rain abated and Ben decided to press on through the night, so they promised to stow his clothes and after preparing and devouring a scalding hot rice pudding he lit a shuttered lantern and vanished into the night.

Chatting had eased the tension. They sat together sipping tea and pondering Ben's news. Occasionally Timoth would get up to prod at the fire or hang the kettle.

— You think we should be worried?

Her brow creased. They both *were* worried. She was sitting bolt upright and unnaturally still, as if caught in some act of wrongdoing.

— We're not kids anymore, Timoth.

She undid her ponytail, shook her hair free and ran fingers through to drag out the knots the wind had blown in.

— No, he agreed, though he had no idea what she was getting at.

At length they extinguished the table lamp and let the fire die down. As their eyes grew accustomed to the darkening room, a sudden crashing noise erupted from the door.

They jumped in shock. Immediately, there came a louder crash, a drawn-out squeal of timber under stress, and then a persistent hammering.

The flames had dwindled but Timoth could see the door shudder in its frame and he knew what weight must be behind it. The windows were shuttered; there was no seeing out. He felt closed in and vulnerable suddenly.

The door wasn't locked. It didn't even have a lock. Everybody knew travellers crofts were open to all. All you had to do was lift the latch… Whatever had slammed against the door with such violence was surely feral, or crazed or desperate. The crash came again and the shutters rattled and the fire spat sparks into the room. He tried to gauge the height of the thing. It was not hitting the door low — it might be human height.

He grabbed a large broom from the corner and advanced on the door, not sure whether to throw it open or to buttress it. The thing hit again, hard. Behind him, he heard Martoth swear and rush off to close the shutters in the stores.

Another crash, and he heard wood splinter. They'd seen no

Semele buck on the trail, no waterboar, and whatever this was it was bigger than a fox.

Up now, inches from the door, his ears strained for tell-tale sounds, but there were no growls, no barks, no words, just the violent slamming. With each impact the metal latch bounced and he felt the cold air slip in around the frame. With his heart beating in his ears, he turned to Martoth, looking for ideas.

Again, the door slammed and a shock of cold and damp showered his shivering skin. He hung there, clutching the broom in both hands, and poking the butt-end at the door roughly where he felt the beast should be.

Then came a rough scratching at the timber and a sound that Timoth had been dreading without realising it: the metal clatter of something or someone moving the latch.

— *Timoth!* cried Martoth behind him.

She was showing him the blunt knife, glittering in the waning firelight. She showed it and then tossed it at him. He lost it instantly; the room was too dark. But instinctively he imagined its arc, pictured the knife, tumbling and sparkling in a light of his own imagination, and somehow plucked it out of the darkness and jammed it hard into the latch with the heel of his fist. It was a ricer move, he realised. A million times he'd wedged a barrow shut with his work knife with just such a movement. He'd seen Teppen do it a couple of years back when he'd been learning. And he realised now that Martoth did the same as he did, day in, day out. She knew what she was doing when she threw the knife.

The scrabbling stopped but the door slammed hard again. Martoth rushed over to join him.

— *Brace it!* she yelled, grasping his broom and trying to wedge it between the door and the gaps in the flagstones. Drag stuff over!

He came back with two chairs and then a heavy stow box

while she braced a leg against the broom. But the ferocity of the attacks seemed to be waning and they began to hear a guttural wheezing sound from behind the door that convinced them at last that it was some kind of animal. The crashes turned to thuds which became knocks and eventually there was a brushing, scratching sound that hit somewhere round waist height and scraped slowly to floor level. Then the noises stopped entirely.

The fire had died and they were trembling together in the light of the embers.

— Should we look? she whispered.

— Fuck that, was his considered opinion.

So they waited till morning to open the door.

It was a Semele buck, robust and muscular. It would have stood high as Timoth's chest, but it lay now in a stinking bloody mess in front of the door. Its head was broken beyond recognition, skull shattered into a sagging flatness with red, black and grey matter leaking over the stones. Its powerful shoulders were beaten and bloodied. Its antlers lay in pieces over a ten-yard radius. The door was stained brown with blood over the scoring and dents.

— That's a royal breakfast right there, said Timoth, but he felt ill at the sight and neither was seriously contemplating butchering the thing. In the end he used the broom again, first to lever the carcass away from the path and then to brush away the gore.

— We can't just leave it here, she protested.

But it wasn't like she had any other suggestions.

Laketown was reckoned a big town these days, which didn't mean much: less than thirty thousand inhabitants, most of them third-generation colonists. Its pre-eminence amongst the neighbouring settlements had come about unexpectedly through the accident of its location and forgiving climate. It was no sort of capital —there were bigger towns further North in the lowlands of Greater Semele— but it did represent a connection, shaky and remote, with the world beyond Semele. It was where migrants and visitors arrived and where those with itchy feet departed.

Like many of the settlements that had sprung up as humanity spread across the universe, Laketown was a mixture of the contrived and the ridiculous. Its name was a conscious literary reference but was also somehow the name it would have had anyway. By contrast, its streets were often named for intentions that had never matched reality (Carpentry, Weaver Street, Lakeward and The Crescent were anything but) or formed out of a fecund mixture of creativity and nostalgia (Pall Mall, Daytime's Square, Lime Street - Under and Lime Street - Over) or were works of inexplicable exoticism that showed how completely an original thought might abandon its roots in only two or three generations of a modest but growing populace (Okrasia, Ekrasia).

The town rested against the tip of the lake in a deep-sided valley that was prone more to fog than to rain. Sun caught it in the mornings but days turned cool at the first meal. Over at the far end of the lake the smaller towns of Seaton and Porton had more sustained sunlight but harsher wind. Where they lived off their rice crop, cultivated by the shores of the lake, Laketown had a more industrial bent. Nearby quarrying had given the town a stony core underneath the cladding of larchwood that came down from the mountains in even greater quantities than the rock. And the town had iron foundries, glassworks, lumberyards, textile workshops.

It was as the sun dipped and the air turned damp that Timoth and Martoth reached the town. A rutted, packed-earth road dropped steeply down the valley side to a broad gap in the town's patchwork of stone walls. A pair of timber-framed watchtowers faced each other across the gap, but there was no gate. People had been hanging washing in the open areas outside the walls and were now busy gathering it back in. A few traders with stalls around the gateway turned their heads to Martoth and Timoth as they passed. Their eyes were dark and unreadable and somehow made Timoth feel a long way from home.

They found *The Hole* without difficulty, entered its large, airy common room, dumped their packs and slumped on some ricebags.

— So what now? asked Timoth.

— Wait. You're asking me?

He shrugged. They both felt lost. To get anywhere they needed Jessic's help.

She glared.

— Okay, okay, he said, we've got a few things. Mulkah's contacts, Jessic's note.

— You won't let me see the note.

— Forget the note. We've got her dad's business, and we know the sort of stuff she gets off on. She'll be where there's off-world tales and foreign gossip.

— Ask at the bar?

— Right.

Martoth looked at him. He made no move to get up. She swore and rose to her feet to make enquiries.

As soon as Martoth left, he sat up and fished the handful of small stones out of his pocket and spread them on the wooden floorboards. The powerful fuzziness that had wrapped him up when he saw the body, the sense of cheating that had grown familiar during his little experiments with grasses in the deep paddy — it was there inside him now, hung about with a cloying smell of decay. He couldn't shake it. He'd been dwelling on it as they walked, trying to understand what this cheating could be, how he could use it, where it came from. And he thought he'd made some connections.

He focussed on one of the stones on the planked floor and tried to make it move. He knew nothing would happen. This was a control, a baseline. Trying to make it move didn't work. It was not about concentration. Nor was it wishing or commanding or picturing — he tried all of these things just to prove them inert.

Then for the first time he tried consciously something that he'd only managed accidentally in the paddy. Instead of directing his attention upon his object, he focussed on himself and turned his effort towards *becoming* or simply *being* the thing that he wanted. Instead of being Timoth, he would be *Timoth-and-stone*. He wasn't sure how he'd landed on this idea. It was something to do with the body by the paddy and its ugly, boiling wound and the way that everything seemed to blur together, as if the boundaries that separated people and things were vulnerable.

It did not come quickly but when it happened, it happened smoothly and just as he'd intended. He didn't feel very different —the stone didn't play much of a role in Timoth-and-stone— but he was different. There was some way in which what had been the stone was now available to all sorts of capacities and capabilities that Timoth could dimly sense inside himself, some way that the stone was now in his power. But walls of shame pressed in on him and the rotting smell pervaded every shallow breath, and the stone did not move.

— What are you doing?

Martoth was suddenly behind him. Timoth started and let out a gasp he disguised with invective:

— Fuuuuck! You scared the living—

He turned and saw a gravity in her face so he dialled back the banter.

— Wassup? What's wrong?

Martoth stepped over him and slumped down into a ricebag opposite. She peeled her boots off and poked a curious toe at his stones but let them be and lay back to gaze vacantly into The Hole's sooty ceiling. Timoth wriggled a little in his ricebag and fixed his eyes upon her feet.

— Well the shitstorm we've walked into sounds way worse than the shitstorm we walked out of.

— What's happened?

— Not too sure, I didn't really follow everything, but sounds like gangs have been out on the streets at night. And something's broken the off-world stuff. I don't know how that all works. There've been some fights, buildings burnt down, people killed. No-one knows what's going on with Jessic's dad's business but they all say his premises are wrecked. And deserted. And somebody is looking for you and me, and they've left messages in all the coms apparently.

— Well we know someone was looking for me anyway. That's why we're here.

— Why you're here, dick. And that was by name. This is both of us, by *description*.

Martoth pulled out a note.

— "Please watch out for a young couple in from Border. Man: mid-height, tone-dark, decent build. Woman: shorter, off-blonde. Late teens. I have information for them. Weakjohn."

— *Couple*?

Timoth wasn't even sure if his reaction was mock aghast or forced flirtatious, but the word made his skin tingle.

— Oh just whatever. What is off-blonde?

— Nearly blonde I reckon.

— So anyway. Weakjohn is a woman's name apparently, Mister "decent build". Barman described her as some kind of harmless busybody. We can find her in one of the market

halls on Ekrasia.
— Any word of Jessic?
Martoth shook her head.

3. The Gallery

1938

A blast of wind and a shower of icy raindrops shot through the car, then the door slammed and a tall gentleman toppled into the front passenger seat. Anna rolled her face around to watch without peeling her forehead away from the cool glass. Rain rattled the windowpane so savagely she could feel it in her skull. Cold droplets slid down her spine, thunder rocked the skies and a carnival of lightning danced around the car. Amongst fading memories of life with her parents she remembered thunderstorms like this, when dense tobacco skies broke into electric mayhem and strange lights raced across her nursery walls. Those nights, her mother had slept with her in the nursery until the storm subsided. But nothing from home could have prepared her for the thrilling power of such storms here, in the Alps of the Bernese Oberland. Everywhere she looked, enormous deep black mountains were threaded together by the lightning. She was in awe. In some visceral way, she felt connected to everything around her, an instrument in a cosmic orchestra. At each thunderclap the world was playing some universal trill upon her body.

She listened to the roar of the rain and tried to pick out

individual drops. To count them. A hundred — a thousand in each heartbeat? Millions? Squintillions? She could so nearly hear them individually, but then she couldn't — she could hear that there *were* individual raindrops but she couldn't hold them apart in her head, couldn't catch hold of them one at a time. And even when she caught one, louder or harsher than the rest, it was somehow annihilated by the next. This disappointed her. She thought it ought to be possible to hear all of them. How could she hear the entire, cacophonous roar without hearing its parts? Or was there something else out there? Some unseen growling thing knitting together the raindrops in an almighty roar of its own, something she didn't know how to listen for. Yes, she was sure of it. Something dark and noisy and bad.

The tall man paused to compose himself, eyes closed and gloved hands resting on the dashboard. Anna knew better than to disturb him. He breathed deeply in slow, measured breaths which drifted and clung to the windscreen then used his gloves to wipe the rainwater off an elegant wooden cane and then laid it gently against the dashboard between his knees. He removed his hat and smoothed down his thin dark hair, tucking rain-soaked tendrils behind each ear. He took out a white handkerchief and wiped his face and moustache and uttered a heartfelt but genteel curse in one of his beloved dead languages: Luwian, Lycian, Hittite... Anna could recite all their names.

— Uncle Stephen, she ventured. Are you *sure* Pyotr will be there?

— Anna, darling, please not again.

Another freezing blast heralded the arrival of a small, wiry man in the driver's seat. Stephen winced as the fellow shook his rainy clothes dry.

— *Au Galerie des Témoins*, declared Stephen, his tone of authority only delicately there, like froth.

The driver was a local man, clean-shaven with thick dark hair, narrow eyes and strong cheekbones. He was a German speaker but spoke French enough to air his grievances.

— The road is not safe. The rivers will burst their banks.

But Uncle Stephen was equal to insisting: Madame Génoise understood the risks to her ageing car, and, as Anna's legal guardian he was qualified to make the (no doubt life-or-death) decision for both passengers. After some grumbling, the car engine stuttered into life and the driver nodded in grudging satisfaction.

— Electric starter motor, he explained with some pride. He wiggled his thumbs at Stephen in a gesture no one understood but himself.

Anna shifted forward in her seat and spoke.

— Lots of people are going. Aren't they? There will be other people in cars. Won't there?

— They're mostly in Grindelwald already, darling. This is rather last minute. I daresay it's not even crossed Pyotr's mind the difficulties we might have. And really Anna, you know, we'll hardly have set foot in the gallery before it will be time for you to go to bed.

Anna laid a delicate hand on the driver's shoulder and whispered:

— We can drive slowly.

The driver unbent perceptibly and ran a hand over his face to wipe the rain away.

— You can call me Josef, he told her.

— I'm five, she said.

The journey was slow and uncomfortable. The road unravelled in front of them yard by yard. To the front the weak headlights served only to decorate the many-layered curtains of driving rain. To the right Anna could make out the faint luminous blue-black cresting of a churning river that seemed always to encroach onto the road, crashing against the car. The interior was unlit and unheated. Anna felt like she was suspended in dark space as the symphony played around her.

All three were wrapped in several layers in the darkness. Josef and Stephen bickered and more than once they were forced to stop while Josef got out to drag fallen tree branches out of the road. After a while Anna began to fall into and out of a shallow sleep.

And then, with a gasp, Anna realised that for the space of just a few breaths she had become aware of every single droplet of rain as it hit the window, each one individually, each of thousands. Each and any she might have named; each she understood and could have marked it out for its characteristics and flaws and its place in the storm. She gulped in the air of the car in quick breaths. It was as if the passing of time was no longer an obstacle to her perception but more like a painter's canvas, a surface she could see every piece of at once. Suddenly she owned the storm. She was out amongst it and in it and of it. She wanted to cry out but didn't, couldn't.

The car drove on.

As Anna emerged from the car, her mind was pirouetting through the raindrops that fell, more softly now, in the grand dark amphitheatre formed by the mountains and glacier. The gallery was two storeys of granite pierced sparingly by the glitter of gaslit windows, and it seemed to shrug backwards into the gloomy rock behind, offering its pillared portico unwillingly to the world as if through a grave sense of duty.

The car had drawn up onto the packed earth courtyard that lay in front of the gallery. Stephen hurried Anna to the shelter of the portico and made introductions to the doorman. Even through the rain Anna could feel a biting chill from the direction of the glacier that hung above them, a paler shade in the night, a tensed predator just at the edge of vision. This place gave her a feeling she'd never had before, like a stretched spring or a dammed stream. Or maybe an unfinished or unread story.

The doorman was polite but cautious and begged their leave to consult Madame Giroud. Two braziers flickered and hissed at the edge of the portico and Stephen and Anna stood by them for warmth, though the stuttering brightness caused Anna to see all sorts of quivering mirages in the darkness beyond. Stephen laid a hand across her shoulders to keep her from the fire. Inside her coat, she shrank from his touch as if he'd broken her from a private daydream, or caught her misbehaving.

From inside came sounds of conversation, animated but without laughter. Guests in dinner suits and frocks passed by the windows with wineglasses in hand. When the door opened again, accompanied by a front of warmth and louder buzz of voices, it was not the doorman who emerged but Pyotr, with floppy blond-brown hair, a grin, a plate of pastry and meat in one hand and the other extended for hugs.

— Annochka!

Anna ran to him and Stephen hurried past into the warm hallway.

— *Uzhasnaya noch'*, he spat, then stopped and stared awkwardly at his cane as if unsure what to do with it.

— Isn't it immense? replied Pyotr, brimming with excitement. Madame Giroud is having a canopy erected on the balcony so we can watch!

— Excellent! Perhaps, young man, you can convey us to our esteemed hostess. Or failing that, the source of those meaty pastry delicacies.

— Oh, but Dr Harrison, these are for you, said Pyotr, passing the plate to Stephen. And Madame Giroud is in hiding in her study. Robin will let you in. Come Annochka,

I'll show you all the best pictures.

As Anna shrugged off her coat and rushed away with Pyotr, Robin and a younger man appeared and helped Stephen with his hat, cane and coat. Robin greeted Stephen with a relaxed bow and a genuine smile.

— Our driver is waiting by the car, said Stephen. There's only a small bag. This was something of a hurried decision.

— I understand, Dr Harrison, please don't worry. Lisa has both rooms prepared and will help with Miss Wilkes as soon as need be. David, please could you speak to Dr Harrison's driver; I don't think he should be driving back in this.

David hopped out into the portico and then out into the rain beyond.

— Please, Dr Harrison, let me take you directly to Madame Giroud. She is extremely eager to see you.

Stephen wandered through the gallery with Madame Giroud and tried to dispel his worry about whatever disruption Anna might be causing. Since learning of the gallery a year earlier, he had been fascinated by the very idea of the place and, truth to tell, he was more than a little fascinated by Greta Giroud herself. So he wandered along next to her, the essence of rapt attention, and allowed her to tell him of the paintings in spite of the barrage of other questions he was itching to ask.

For Dr Stephen Harrison saw the world differently from these other guests. Where they saw, he supposed, pictures, or possibly subjects, techniques, stylisation, he was troubled by the need for explanation and extrapolation. From causes and antecedents to destinations and consequents. They saw art. He saw the rationalising current of history as it carried such ephemera along on its wave crests. For him, the gallery itself was the puzzle, not Madame Giroud's collection. Gallery as fact and idea. The fact of the building and the idea of the enterprise.

And so, while his grasp of practicalities was weak as ever, he did notice the oddities as they went along. Electric lighting in the body of the rooms (a stable light for the pictures?) and gaslight by the windows (a relic?). An elegant, open portico built outward into the night, but opening straight into a wide atrium, with barely a hatstand or umbrella rack in between. He knew the building had been a residence for Greta Giroud before she had ever conceived of opening it up for visitors but it could not always have been intended as a house, could it? What future might it have here, crouched directly under the rock face? There must be rock falls, or avalanches even? Or perhaps the disposition of the mountain above was better understood than that? Maybe the paths of such things were reliable or mitigable? Dr Stephen Harrison was after all, merely a linguist.

— It was a warehouse, smiled Madam Giroud as she caught him staring into the ceiling. Or at least it was built on the plan of a warehouse. A deal of quarrying goes on further round the mountainside.

— Who built it?

— At the start, a M. Hector Allain, a financier who was involved in some of that business, but he died, even as his plans for the place were evolving. I made it habitable.

They moved on through the rooms, all carpeted in a dull, flecked maroon and decorated in different pale pastels. Around them Madame Giroud's other guests chattered and sipped champagne, nodding politely at her as they passed.

— How is she doing, do you think?

She was asking about Anna, of course.

— I don't know, he said. I don't know what I should be doing.

Though he kept the tears from his eyes, he knew his Adam's apple betrayed him.

— Stephen, you know whatever help you need…

He nodded and turned away, forcing them to walk onward, and away from the topic of his drowned sister and the nightmares she bequeathed her daughter.

Pyotr led Anna to a room of nineteenth century landscapes. He liked the storms and sunsets but Anna liked the faces better. She smiled as Madame Giroud and Stephen entered. Madame Giroud introduced Stephen to a Scandinavian couple and left him in conversation to return to other duties. Anna danced around the room looking at all the pictures, weaving carefully between the other guests and stopping at the biggest picture of all.

This was the odd one out. It wasn't a landscape at all. A brown and dusty cottage interior, dark cupboards, smoky black ceiling, candlelit. Revellers at a wake, rosy faced. Tankards frothing. On the right, three youths conspiring together, elbow on shoulder, sotto voce. On the filthy floor, two dogs and a girl. The characters at the table, similar at first glance, grow apart as eyes grow accustomed to the painting's simulated candle light. A swarthy face, scowling at its peers, a slender clerk, a pair of farm hands.

Anna froze, her tiny limbs locked tight and her small mouth gaping. A shock rippled out from her tummy to her ears and toes. She tugged at Pyotr's sleeve and looked around to see what anybody else had noticed but, as the quiet moments passed, her shock settled into a deep anxiety. She shook Pyotr hard but could not find her voice.

Stephen was deep in discussion when he became aware of her consternation. When she came to him, he first tried to calm her without breaking off, but as she fussed and tugged at him, other guests began to look on with interest, and he felt a flush rising to his cheeks. Finally Anna stamped and screamed and ran to the picture hanging on the wall pointing up into the scene it depicted.

Look!

Pyotr was the first to understand.

— Oh.

One by one everybody in the room fell silent.

Stephen's world was a world of words and letters, and the language of art was foreign to him. He took the longest to understand. He stared around in puzzlement and, following people's gaze with growing frustration, peered once more into the large canvas. First an uncomfortable chime of familiarity sounded in his mind when he looked upon the clerk, then an unsteadying gut-wrench when he looked again at the girl playing in the dirt with the dogs.

The ten people that Scottish opium addict, Peter Creed, had painted into his dark, rustic cottage in 1827 were the same ten people standing in front of his painting, right this second, over a century later.

— Pyotr, Stephen whispered, perhaps you could fetch Madame Giroud?

No-one moved. They watched one another with suspicion and wonder, and each compared themselves with their doppelgänger in Creed's mise en scène.

A dark moustachioed man moved first, approaching the canvas to inspect it more closely. He matched the swarthy scowler at the table, a man who appeared to be sweeping aside both cups and dice from the table, clearing a space for something as yet absent. Alongside the canvas, affixed to the wall was a small handwritten card, in Mme. Giroud's hand, and he read it aloud, in French-accented English.

The Wake - Peter Creed (1801-?) 1827 - oil on canvas. Frame 1902, Paris. Acquired 1932, Galerie des Témoins.

* * *

His voice died and a quiet murmur took hold in the room. They spoke in hushed voices in their little groups, no-one venturing anything to the group as a whole.

— It's another Anna! whispered Anna as her agitation lessened.

— *Ann-other...* compounded Stephen idly, hardly even paying attention.

— *Annoth*, simplified Pyotr, christening Anna's unruly counterpart in the picture.

For the three of them it was Annoth who drew the eye, even at the lower edge of the scene, caught suspended in a curious motion between the dogs on the floor. The other Stephen was unremarkable and though Pyotr was identifiable he was turned away from the viewer peering through a back door.

Madame Giroud entered the room, investigating the sudden quiet.

— Madame, said Stephen, managing to raise his voice just beyond a whisper, Greta, I think we need to know...

— Where did you get this painting? asked moustache man, brashly and with none of the deftness of approach that Stephen was still trying to muster.

— Monsieur Clindor, replied Greta Giroud, how lovely that you came. I hope your wife is well?

Anna noticed Clindor's face darken at something, maybe a reference to his wife, but maybe not.

Pyotr spoke up to try and draw Madame Giroud's attention to the painting:

— Madame, we have all just noticed something... difficult to explain.

Clindor interrupted again.

— Madam, is this some kind of joke? If so, please accord us a shred of respect and own up now. Have you commissioned this? Is this fake? He gestured at the Creed picture.

— Fake? exclaimed Madame Giroud, affronted. *Fake*? Why on Earth would you say that? It's a Creed. I've had it for donkey's years.

…her Swiss-French tongue curling oddly round the colloquialism in a way that only heightened Stephen's fascination.

— Yes. *1932* it says, but Madame, pressed Clindor, if this is not a joke, then you must be mistaken, you cannot have acquired this in 1932. It's not possible.

— Monsieur Clindor, we've known each other for three years now, have you ever had the slightest notion that I might be prone to such a blunder?

— But, that is just the thing Madame! Stephen murmured, cautiously and politely. If you first knew of this painting over five years ago and yet have only known Monsieur Clindor for three years, and Anna and myself for barely one, and perhaps others among us even less, then it becomes rather difficult to explain how every one of us appears in this picture.

— …and, added Pyotr parenthetically, if it is authentic and it is really over a hundred years old, then it is even harder to explain.

4. Laketown

Martoth, Timoth

The narrow Northward climb of Ekrasia was abustle — a type of busy unknown to Timoth, urgency to profit in Border being subdued by stuttering demand, a barter-based economy and a small and very pragmatic populace. Laketown by contrast drew outside trade from across Semele and, as the sole conduit of off-world merchandise, supported a prospering secondary market in information, culture and something that might have passed for tourism in a more mature economy. The commerce on the street was low price, low quality stuff, run by a second tier of operators who couldn't secure places in the market halls lining the street. In the halls, business was carried on with real currency. The town boasted several independent mints and rudimentary exchange and clearing house operations for trying to make sense of it all. On the street the situation was more varied and frequently goods could be had for barter, often safer for those used to Border-style living. The street was the main point of entry into the cash economy for visitors who arrived with valuables of a different sort, or with nothing but themselves.

The stalls were permanent structures with steep roofs and

crude wood guttering but traders were crammed into them more than one per stall, dividing the space in myriad ways up and down the street according to custom and long-established rules of precedence. Twice, Timoth saw a division defined by the surface of the stall's table, one vendor sitting cross legged amongst his wares on the table top while the other rested against the main struts beneath, sitting more comfortably but with a much inferior display.

The gloom of afternoon evolved into the gloom of evening as Timoth and Martoth picked their way up the hill searching for the hall they needed. Business continued and one by one the stallholders were lighting what seemed to be the common style of oil lamp in the town, a large, transparent and slightly iridescent glass sphere around the flame over a tiny gondola for the fuel, looking in the end something like an magical airship or a giant flower bud on the point of opening.

— Ever seen anything like this? asked Timoth.

Martoth shook her head. Laketown was only half the distance between Border and her life in Porton but it was the other way round the lake. There had been nothing to take her this way since early childhood.

— If I have, I don't remember.

They were both on edge. Each could sense the other's apprehension. Though everything around them was little more than an improvised copy of some aspect of Earth before the crises, or of The Leap since, it went far, far beyond their experience. They knew they lacked the instincts and intuitions to get by here without help.

— Gotta talk to someone I guess, muttered Timoth, without enthusiasm.

— Your turn.

— I know.

He halted at a stall selling knives whose scar-shaped blades appeared to be steel even if the larch hilts were poorer grade stuff. Ranks of them were arrayed, stabbed into some gently raking rice-plaster and glittering in the lamplight. Timoth was enchanted by the display, and not uninterested in the merchandise, so when the stall holder seemed unexpectedly intent on allowing her customer space and time to browse, he was a little perplexed about how to start a conversation. She leant against the wall, a step back into the stall's shadowy recess, sharpening a pale, narrow knife, looking up occasionally to take in both her customers and the throng moving about them.

— Um, hello, he said.

— How was the journey? she asked, stepping into the light. All clear on the Border Road?

Her smile was all sympathy but even if this was just reasonable guesswork, he had a sense she knew more about him than he felt comfortable with. He was struck by the unpleasant conviction that everybody had been watching each step they took from The Hole to here. He glanced nervously at the people around him but the street seemed as wrapped up in its own to-ing and fro-ing as ever.

— Easy, murmured Martoth at his shoulder.

— We are looking for…

— …Weakjohn.

It was a friendly interruption, made to assure and to encourage, but the knife seller couldn't disguise a little self-congratulation at her cleverness.

— I was going to ask for Havers Hall, Timoth protested.

— Of course, sweetheart. But Weakjohn is after you both. And if you'd cantered up the street at less of a clip she might even have caught you by now.

She pointed back downhill, over the heads of the milling crowd, towards an older lady who was approaching them, breathless and walking with the aid of a stick which she waved at them frantically the moment she had their attention.

She trailed them by perhaps twenty yards, but was moving slowly so she couldn't have been following for long. The people of Laketown were attentive enough to clear out of her path as she hobbled forward but did not offer any other assistance. Martoth gave Timoth a none too surreptitious shove with her elbow which he supposed was a cue to offer the woman some help, but the knife seller warned him off.

— No, no. She's a proud one. Let her come.

So they waited and Timoth turned back to the knives.

— Timoth! Martoth! Thank the manifold shades.

Weakjohn was shorter than either of them, with close-cropped grey hair, a narrow face and eyes of glassy blue. She took some breaths to calm herself and then, suddenly revived, was full of agitation. Her face came alive, patches reddening amidst the troughs and wells of age, and whatever disability lay behind her ungainly hobble up the hill seemed to fall from her. She bounced with excitement and grasped Timoth's arm with her free hand. Timoth was taken aback by the vigour of her grip but didn't flinch.

— Timoth. Tell me. Are you… *well*?

Timoth knew he couldn't read into the question exactly what was intended but he nodded and cast a nervous glance across to Martoth.

Weakjohn frowned.

— I mean, have you, have *either* of you had any… she paused, searching, struggling for the right word… *attacks*?

It was evident that Timoth and Martoth had fallen even further off the pace, though Martoth managed to knock a reply together.

— We are well and unharmed, Madam Weakjohn. We haven't been attacked and we haven't suffered any kind of attack.

The amused stall holder suggested her stall-front might be

more useful to her unblocked by such misfiring pleasantries, so Weakjohn swept the pair across the last few yards to Havers Hall.

They stood in a broad double doorway looking in on a bustling market hall. On the far wall, several feet above the heads of crowd hung an enormous wooden sculpture of the head of a Semele waterboar, many times the size of the real thing. Timoth had seen smaller sculptures of waterboar before but they had always been depicted with slavering, gaping jaws as if captured in a ferocious roar. This supersized head was not feral but majestic. It was set on the wall amidst some gaudy heraldic gestures in gold, scarlet and green.

— Through this way, said Weakjohn, we're going upstairs.

And they entered the hall. As they passed through the stalls, Weakjohn had a greeting or message for most of the stall holders and obviously knew many of the customers too.

— Jermine! Evening sir! Helbert! Joachim! Hey Joshua! Mekkle has something for you. Jermine, can I catch you for a minute after closing? Melijn, where's Nick?

Most of the traders in Havers were cobblers or woodworkers, and in here the trade was carried out with Semele coin, light and variable tinny pieces that seemed to come in several colours. As they passed across the floor, Timoth could see Martoth's mind working, trying to understand the mechanisms of the trade going on around her. Tables were asprawl with leatherwork and carvings, some arranged for display, many simply piled up high. When sold, items were just moved to one side rather than handed over. Where were they collected? When? How did the currency work? Were there denominations? Who minted it? Who trusted it? Were there any marks upon it? Martoth had read more widely than anyone else he knew and she had a head for these things in a way he didn't. Where he was instinctual, she could be methodical, penetrating. And, he also admitted: when he was wrong, she was right — when he was blind, she saw pretty much everything. He wasn't always totally sure he liked her but he'd trust her with his life and his mother's.

Even Timoth could tell that Weakjohn's upbeat mood was out of kilter with the rest of the townspeople. All the men and women in the market hall were armed, stall holders and customers alike. Many carried blades, ranging from a small daggers to machete-length weapons, sheathed and worn at the belt. Those without carried wooden cudgels, also hanging from the belt. Such a visible prevalence of weaponry was unusual in Semele society, at least as Timoth had known it from Border and the neighbouring settlements. And this was all despite the overt security the market itself provided: thickset guards at the entrance with quarterstaffs and uniformed staff circulating amongst the crowd. The hubbub seemed sombre to Timoth's ears — on edge perhaps but not aggressive. Were the shoppers according each other just a shade more personal space than was usual as they went about their business? It was hard to detect but he knew that something was up.

Weakjohn hadn't expected to feel like this when they finally sat down in front of her, these glorious youths. On the one hand it was quite something watching the way they behaved around each other, approaching one another with some high-tension mix of acknowledgement and denial, somehow in the rainbow of emotions picking out adoration foremost, as the only attitude so determinedly not expressed in their behaviour. She found it all so beautiful.

— Oh my dear things, she couldn't help sighing.

On the other hand, it was her own vanished youth that gazed back at her in the eyes of these two. The bubble-crush excitement of new sex drives taunted her from across a chasm. Whatever her mind did next, wherever she ended her days, there was no being that again. No second chances, no rerun to do it differently.

Okay then, Weakjohn. Look deeper. What's here? And here? First with your own eyes. And now, gently, and respectfully through their own…

Martoth. Marta's girl. Strong. Confused. Angry. Peevish. Suspicious. But, somehow…. noble, somehow. Yes, she is ready to stand up for something, god help her.

Timoth. Oh my word. Very *inward*. Oh! Smutty boy…

— What are you doing?

Weakjohn was shocked. Resentment rang out clear in his voice. He was not as unaware as she had assumed.

— I am sorry, Timoth, she fronted up. I let my curiosity get the better of me. It is a bad habit that people like me get into when they live in places like Semele where there is nobody to remind them of their manners.

— I don't get the impression of horribly bad habits going on here, remarked Timoth, indicating her clean, modest surroundings.

Martoth though, sharp girl, was way quicker on the uptake.

— People like you?

5. Education

Seronin

— Are you serious? he replied. I'm in the middle of the class!

The novice was five rows back, three desks in. Seronin had formed the suggestion directly in his mind. Smart kid didn't move a muscle.

Alert for anything in the flux, any flicker of awareness, any sudden imbalance, any welling of attention, Seronin regulated his own breathing. But for now at least, this room was blackboard theory only. The practicals were next door. And his camouflage would hold.

— How long have you got? he asked.

— Tomasz just went in. I'm like fifth or something.

…but this time there was a treacherous lapse, a pulse in his neck. Seronin's eyes flicked to the tutor. Her back was turned.

And so it all came to a point, didn't it? Spring the duplicitous pup or let them splay him to the corners of the flux. It wasn't a *serious* question —Seronin knew himself better than that— but being back here unsteadied him. It was in rooms like this, and through ordeals like this, he'd become the man he was today. He was never carrying a secret like this boy's into the scrutiny of a first cylinx-augmentation. But he'd had secrets of his own.

— Hold tight, he sighed, and, when I say, shift up with me. I'll hide you.

There was no need to specify *Happenstance*. A novice would not be capable of higher strata.

— Are you… nearby?

— I'm in the room with you.

The autumn sunlight streamed into the classroom and the tutor's chalk clacked sideways across the board. *Perspectivals*, noted Seronin, and hairy stuff. Must be a precocious year. He scanned the text, then let his mind flow around and into the particles of chalk dust and pitch, and, undetected, made a subtle and heretical modification. It was a childish irony that the very heresy that allowed him to stand in this hornet's nest unseen and unsuspected was now written in black and white for all to see. The Vigil could never conceive of a camouflage as complete as Seronin's because they could never free themselves from the shackles of the *tetrarchy*, their four strata of existence that governed and defined human experience through all history.

— *Now*! he said, and the classroom melted from view as Seronin and the novice shifted up into *Happenstance*.

— … really Seronin?

The cut-in was a formula, one of countless little expressions of the environment trying to reject him: the insects crawling at his feet, the electric itchiness in the air, his sudden left-handedness. In *Happenstance*, you always land in the middle of something, always catch the end of a conversation. Seronin was too experienced to let it disorient him. Nevertheless. There was a form to be observed. The shape of the world is the shape of the human mind.

— The very same, he postured.

But where to go next… *How the fuck did you get yourself into this mess? How have you kept it hidden?* Both pointless. Lethe and Candle would have covered all that. There was only one thing Seronin needed from the boy: consent.

They stood in The Forest, one of the *relics*, the archetypes that haunt the sleep of every human in the universe, natural or not. All the relics — drownings, drapes, forest and fortresses — recurred time and again in *Happenstance*. Vigil novices knew them well. They were encouraged to find them, inhabit them, explore them in dream and in *Happenstance*. The boy seemed more comfortable here than stranded amongst his classmates, despite the constant effort required.

— You know you could do all this yourself, said Seronin.

— No! I can't!

In the piano-wire tendons of the boy's throat Seronin could see the panic rise, the awful sense of a salvation that could so easily be withdrawn.

— You could just walk out of the door.

…but this was only half true. An escape needed distance, time, protection, misdirection.

The Forest was a placid sunless world of birch and towering pine that stretched so dense and deep that no line of sight could end in anything but tree trunk, be it near or impossibly far. It was a working out of Olber's paradox of starlight, realised in wood and bark and the quiet forest air. At times when the trees grew so tight together as to seem like the baleen of a gaping whale, dreaming of The Forest was like being at the world's centre of gravity, at some blessed point in space protected from annihilation only by the delicate balance of the mass of the world on every side.

At this centre point, Seronin and the youth faced each other.

— How attached are you to your body?

— I know what you're going to do.

— And you're okay with it?

— Please just get me out.

But something was wrong. There was a subtle alteration in the boy's eyes. They dried, lost their gloss. Seronin scrambled out and tumbled haphazardly back down into *Concreta*, battling suddenly to repair his camouflage.

The autumn light lay dead on the windows. All was dry and thin as if the breath had been drawn out of the world. A roar was growing, second by second, into a pummelling pressure on Seronin's eardrums. The kids were on their feet and the tutor was feeling outward with her mind.

Seronin croaked out a futile whisper:

— ...down!

Then: a moment that stayed with him forever, framed between the uncertainty of what preceded and the brutality of what followed. It was Seronin's hyperawareness burned into an image of fractal depth: a black cassock swaying over brown sandals as the tutor panicked; the algebraic chalk-dust that was the last lie they'd ever learn; wallcharts of the tetrarchy yellowing on the walls; samplers of the coldwake commandments; sprawling charts of the works of Diocletian; maps of the hubs and leys; other didactic trappings as crude as their subject was complex, the fashion being simplicity since the demise of *in silico* computation. This was a moment Seronin would voyage into many times, tracing the grain of the wood, the lines in their faces and the reflections in their eyes, but there was nothing to be learned from it.

A comet thing blistered across the classroom, tearing through furniture and flesh alike. Along a curve that ran from wall to wall, everything boiled or burst and fell to the ground. A chainsawing scar lit the tangle beneath, kids' bodies, limbs broken and altered by fusewounds, mashed-up brushstrokes of wood and stone and flesh. Some were screaming but they couldn't be heard over the spinroar.

At once, the flux was alive with minds. They were flooding in: other vigilants, tutors, Abbot Barnabas, Sounness. Containing the tear, staving off death and dispersal, patching wounds, working on the rip itself.

The lights were on. Eyes were everywhere. The kid was dead and Seronin could do nothing for the others. He had to escape. Only when he gathered himself for the hop to the way head did he realise he was hurt. And his route was fried.

He swore and crunched his burning back against the stone wall behind him. With a push, he fell through into the cloister behind, the East Cloister, he recalled, and he shivered off the old unhappinesses that somehow tore his attention from the pain in his back.

— Lethe, he called silently as he bled onto the flagstones. Lethe, goddammit!

The fusewound was a grinding agony. Lights sparked in his eyes as it melted its way to his spinal column. He was moving, somehow, though his limbs were spasming and hard to control. He bruised them against the stone floor as he flapped away like a tortured insect.

But lights in his eyes were nothing new. Nor were tics and spasms. Memories kept intruding on his suffering: the other kids being mean about his flickers; being laid up migrainous in his cell; and then, surely his earliest, learning to swim with his mother.

He was building up a backsnap debt that might finish him but he had no choice. Swimming along the cloister floor in a trail of gore was not winning prizes.

Then he remembered the room next door, and its cylinx. Could he...? Really? Right under their noses? If he augmented himself with the cylinx, he might escape. He stretched out with his mind, praying it had not occurred to the others to apply it to the rescue.

There! He felt it. It was clear.

He couldn't resist a vengeful smirk as he prepared for an act so impudent it stole his own fraying breath. As his mind touched the cylinx and he prepared to fuse, he had a vision of the room: a broad, low, milky-white cylinder glowing at the centre of its chapel. "Tomasz" was dead. His mentor too was a thin grey corpse that, with a twinge, Seronin recognised as Yorgen, his old perspectivals tutor.

Seronin concresced by his own desk, the wound in his back transmuted by monumental effort into a wound in his mind. He heaved in some giant gulps of the stale air, then howled in pain and frustration. In darkness he fumbled for something to smash but it was just papers, booktabs, charts. He thrashed his arms through the papers, swiping everything onto the floor and staggered over and glared at the unmade bed. A starlit whisky bottle peeked out from under the pillow.

— What the fuck just happened? he yelled at it.

There was no sign of Lethe or Candle.

There was something wrong here too, some residue of catastrophe. But his head was reeling with the onset of the backsnap and the nausea was coming. He wasn't going to solve anything for a few hours.

He smashed the neck of the whisky bottle against the wall, spraying the liquid up the wall in a flaring beam. He tipped back the broken bottle and poured its fire down his throat, making no effort to sieve out the glass-glitter, letting it scour his reflexing gullet.

He blacked out for half a second and came to, leaning on the wall, forehead and fists in the wet whisky smear. Half-consciously he dragged his fists across the rough paintwork, drawing a pair of monstrous bunny-ears on the wall. Seeing the effect, he added crosses for eyes and a lolling tongue, and used the last ounce of mental energy he possessed to ignite the whole thing, burning off the spirit and scorching the grotesque face into the wall. He stepped back with a proud smirk, then wrenched off his clothes and capsized onto the bed.

The backsnap hit. His heart palpated. His blood coursed fitfully. His muscles spasmed. His eyeballs jittered about. Hours later, two ghostly presences returned and sat to watch over him.

6. Coldwake

Seronin

This fear is not a new fear.

The child sought comfort in the words.

It is an old fear, even if it is new to me.

There was supposed to be comfort in the words.

But what was not shrouded in darkness was strange and scary and *grown up*. And he missed his mother.

He sensed tears on his cheeks and felt imprisoned by his own face.

Finally he recognised coldwake. Or found the courage to confront what he could no longer deny. He knew the coldwake commandments. He fought back the panic. (Do not lose yourself to panic, Yorgen would say. There are many enough ways to lose yourself without panic. That is the first coldwake commandment: do not lose yourself to panic.)

And this *was* coldwake, he knew it. The feeble euphemism from Abbot Demeter's syllabus, "perspectival disorientation", tasted like ash in his mouth.

Seconds ago, his first terror reigned. Am I *transient*? he cried. A *spark*, a shard that glitters only to shatter? (If you are a spark, you don't matter. Even if you think you do.)

But, though he might not actually be ten years old, he was at least one minute old. His circadia were working. He was stable. (The second commandment: *wait!*)

The next commandments he had learned by rote and always thought each should correspond to one more inch out of the horrible pit of despair. Am I this? Am I that? But now he understood why even the richest imagination is an affront to the truth of coldwake. For as he came to understand himself, he only plunged deeper into the pit. The starlit toe he wriggled, the thigh he pinched, the gross cock, that whole clammy landscape of flesh — they were all wrong. His body should not be like this. He was not this. His heart did not pound so. He had never *smelt* like this.

But... this body's flickers were his — they were in him now, tugging at his cheeks and fingers. Some of its scars were his too, like on his hand, where Belly said he could fly a brick but he couldn't really. This might be his future body. Or he its past mind.

Finally then: was he alone? He was a student of the Vigil. It was time to look with more than his eyes.

And when he opened his mind to the flux he almost spun out of control. He beheld his fellow mind, a shimmer in the flux of breathtaking intricacy and elegance. And he knew it for what it was: his older self. How much older he could not tell. If this other was the real Seronin, he, the child, could only be some kind of fossil.

Okay, come out, Yorgen, he wept. I pass your nasty test. It is not amnesia. It is not fission or dispersal. It is not transplant, puppetisation or reincarnation. It is overlap.

Fuckboom, is what Mean Janine would say. Belly would just flap his head up and down. Prick.

But it was not a test. How could it be?

He had had so little. Now he had lost everything.

* * *

The air sagged, pungent. Through the porthole a heavenful of stars twisted and staggered like plankton in an ocean of blackness.

— Seronin! It was Candle's voice, Candle's glorious voice. Seronin, wake up!

He shrugged himself awake and grunted at the darkness.

He hauled himself up in his bed, wincing as he touched its stains and dampnesses and tried to force his spinning head upright. There was no physical sign of Lethe or Candle. They wouldn't see the need for bodies just to find out how bad this all stank. At the foot of his bed an enormous black dead rabbit face leered down at him in the darkness and he couldn't avoid its gaze.

— Who was he?

— We still don't know, said Candle. I mean, the Vigil knew him as Merrick but he doesn't... he didn't remember anything.

— *Anything*?

— A name, but not his own. A "Meef Parton"?

It meant nothing to Seronin:

— How did he know what he was?

— He thinks he always knew, said Candle.

— Who tipped us off?

— Anonymous source, said Lethe.

Seronin padded off to spend some time in the shower. He turned it up a fraction too hot, then sat, curled up on the floor beneath for over an hour, letting the heat turn his skin red while he put his head back together.

Healing his back, fleeing the Abbey, navigating the leys. These were cruel demands on an overstretched psyche, even with cylinx augmentation. In raw power, Seronin was a match for the best minds in the Vigil and his vision went further and deeper than any of them. Perhaps deeper than any human since Diocletian. But you don't get a carte blanche for changing reality, that's a novice's wet dream. There was always a debt, however unpredictable, however fickle. Something somewhere had to give. You could shift it around like a bump in the carpet, take more of it physically or more of it mentally, defer it a bit, spread it thin or take it quick and brutal. That was backsnap and though Seronin was throwing every trick in the book at this one, he just could not get *normal*. He felt smeared out and sluggish.

After the commandments come the protocols, but the child didn't have the energy to go on. What did it matter what he knew, what he remembered? He was a relic and a shadow. His mother was dead, his friends aged or dead and the walls of the black pit stretched over him.

But then he heard his name and, glory of glories, it was Candle calling him! Candle! And Lethe was here too. A glimmer of hope lived still. How many times had they helped him in need? Protected him from the bullying and name-calling?

After the commandments, the protocols!

The first protocol. *Who are the Vigil?* Easy. The defence of humanity through mastery of perspective.

The second. *What were the crises?* Easy. Passing the threshold where complexity begets ruin.

Next: *Who was Diocletian?* Again easy, Dio- but wait, WAIT! Who *was* Diocletian? Who, actually, was Diocletian?

Without even knowing that he could, the child spoke:

— Who *was* he?

— We still don't know, said Candle. I mean, the Vigil knew him as Merrick but he doesn't... he didn't remember anything.

What? But how could we not know? He what?

— ...anything?

— A name, but not his own. A "Meef Parton"?

What?

...then the child understood his predicament.

The cabin was barely habitable so they talked in *Happenstance*, with the relic, Delphus, hanging its red drapes all about them. The drapes were the constant, the furniture changed. There was usually a mirror, often a fireplace, sometimes these velvet upholstered armchairs. On a low table to Seronin's side lay a fountain pen, an inkwell and an unfinished letter. He felt nothing of his normal fluency but he turned, picked up the pen and calmly signed the letter.

— Never again, insisted Seronin, rising from his armchair to jab a poker at the fire.

— Oh sure. Cancel the novice abduction programme, mocked Lethe. We haven't been that close in ten years!

Lethe and Candle had corporeal presentations here. They sat motionless in the high-backed chairs and watched Seronin take out his frustration at the fireplace. Lethe used the usual high-cheeked, curly-haired body that he sometimes used in *Concreta* and that Seronin had always assumed matched his birth body, though there was no real reason why it should. Candle, for reasons opaque to Seronin, was brunette when she manifested in *Concreta* but blonde in *Happenstance*. Everything else, her graceful face, her small stature and her youth did not change.

— *We*? Really? And why the fuck did "we" now?

But Seronin knew why they'd done it and he knew that Lethe and Candle saw parallels with his own story. He didn't see it that way.

— Extricating non-naturals who've got themselves into something they can't get out of is not the same as inspiring my rebellion.

— It's not a rebellion if you don't take anyone with you, pointed out Lethe.

— Others left too!

A response that even Seronin was embarrassed by. True, a few of his classmates took advantage of the chaos to walk away as well: Mean Janine, Andrew Bell, even timid little Kasper. But they walked, as a rule, in the first available direction where Seronin was not.

It would be arrogant to point out what Lethe and Candle already knew: they'd identified Seronin as the most original psychocephic genius to emerge since Diocletian and they desperately wanted him to develop away from the Vigil's poisonous orthodoxy. It would be arrogant and also foolish. It would take Candle precisely zero seconds to remark on his equally prodigious capacity for self-indulgence.

— Anyway, said Seronin, the kid was an idiot.

— A dead idiot, said Candle.

Seronin bit back a callous reply. Because it was a kneejerk. Because it wasn't what he meant.

— Yorgen's dead, he said.

Yorgen's face was in front of him when he closed his eyes, sharp, lucid, afire. Just like that first day that novice Seronin, shaking in his sandals, had first stood firm against his teaching:

— It's just..., he had quavered, ...I've... been *somewhere else.*

Had it not been so absurd, they might have cried heresy even then, for shifting at non-stratal targets was the sin of dilution. Later, when Seronin understood his ability to shift *down* to *Brainslang,* and accepted the mind-boggling doctrine of transversy it entailed, he knew better how to bide his time and keep his mouth shut.

Something deep had changed. Seronin felt it. And he was trying to understand it. It was like he had not come out of the backsnap the same as he went in. Was it something about the universe or something about himself? Not that the distinction was all that clear. He decided to keep it to himself. Lethe and Candle might be the only ones with any notion of the psychic world he inhabited but that's not to say they were receptive to all his half-arsed mystic intuitions.

— What happened anyway?

At first he'd thought it was something to do with the cylinx, a malfunction, or an abuse, but Yorgen would never allow that, not the Yorgen Seronin had known. Then as he'd got out of the shower he'd found the storm damage in his own cabin, detected the wispy traces of residue. And this was half a galaxy away from the Abbey.

— You sealed a tear here too?

— Candle did, said Lethe. I was in trouble, the mindstorm hit my substrate.

— Shit! You okay?

— He almost wasn't.

So long had Seronin lived with Lethe and Candle, it had become easy to forget their own vulnerability. Moments like this sent Seronin's mind trawling through the old memories, past the fights to earlier days, his first days at the Abbey when he was still getting to know Lethe and Candle and getting used to these mysterious, semivisible protectors who seemed to have adopted him.

He remembered sitting with Lethe and Candle up on the Abbey roof beneath a vast sky-dome of spray-paint neutrals, as ragged branches and tarpaulins jerked themselves around to their own inner madnesses. In the privacy of the open, their words screened by the rushing wind, Lethe and Candle had described their lives to the young Seronin.

And Seronin, untutored, unprivileged, unblessed prodigy, just weeks into his Vigil training became the first human to hear first-hand a tale of emergence, a tale of two human minds, one natural and one synthetic, born in the last death throes of the old world who survived the crises, outlived their physical bases and lived on into the uncertain reality beyond.

Seronin knew from that time that there were more things in heaven and earth than were categorised by the Vigil. How many more escapees were there? Refugees from humanity's burning past? Natural minds freed from their bodies? Copied, mutated, modified? Unnatural minds synthesised in the final flowering fusion of technology and psychocephy? Combinations? Filterings? Pattern minds duplicated out of complex systems, economies, ecologies? Processes become human? Humans minds splintered and merged? And how old were they all? The Vigil taught that Diocletian was the only emergence from before the crises. If he were not the *only*, was he even the *first*?

Seronin was struck suddenly with a curious thought. *Who was Diocletian?* It was an outrageous thought for a Vigil-trained mind. It was ironic because that very question was written into the coldwake protocols, right after the commandments, in the sense of: What do you know or remember of your heritage? Who, for instance, was Diocletian?

But *who actually was Diocletian?* The mystery of his natural origins was so eclipsed by his giant legacy that it was deemed improper to even speculate — not forbidden certainly, but the impulse to ask was quickly trained out of novice vigilants. Seronin had long since thrown the question aside. Why should it come unbidden to his mind right now?

— Do you think it could be an attack? she asked.

— An *attack*? said Seronin. What? On the whole world?

— On the Vigil?

— Who's got a problem with the Vigil? said Seronin. Apart from us, obviously. And a few other drop-outs and dissidents. And fusions and synthetics. Other non-naturals. And families of kidnapped novices. And most local authorities and enforcers. A few countercultures, cults... But apart from them?

— What about our anonymous source? she suggested.

— But why tip us off then slaughter the kid he wanted saved? said Lethe.

— Maybe rescue beats slaughter but slaughter beats exposure? said Candle.

There was a dig in that, but Seronin ignored it. He leaned back and stared upward following Delphus's drapes into a dark infinity above. It made no sense. The rip in his cabin could not be a coincidence. How many other rips had opened across the galaxy? Whatever this was, it wasn't the tantrum of a disaffected vigilant.

— But the *storm*... he said.

She had no answer for this. Storms happened — universal mentality begets its own weather systems. The Vigil measured just such disturbances from a thousand of points across the modern diaspora. The mindstorm that hit as the rip opened at the Abbey was notable not for its intensity but its reach.

— What do we know from the Tier Ones, he asked?

— Nothing concrete yet but there's damage to the leys.

Seronin nodded. He'd felt that as he fled. The ways he'd used to get to the Abbey were weaker and harder to follow on the return. For one desperate instant he'd thought he was gone. His self threatened to explode in a million trajectories across the allpsyche. He'd kept himself together but it was a hairier ride than he'd had for many years. To the few among the scattered remnants of humanity who were mindwoke, the leys and the ways were the plumbing of the flux. It was only these fibrous mental highways that made the Vigil's ideal of one humanity just the tiniest bit more than a bad joke. That the leys might be so vulnerable to bad weather appalled Seronin.

— So, said Lethe, you know that million ton concentration of hyperdense noumenal soup that you keep in your cabin that couldn't possibly be a risk because it's by definition inert, infinitely absorptive, and protected from perturbation by inch thick poly-recrescent shielding?

— I'll move the cylinx, said Seronin.

A cylinx could be a common factor, however irrational, between the carnage at the Abbey and the damage in his cabin, but by their very nature cylinxes were not easy to move. He knew a place on The Leap he could use, a rainy place of lakes and valleys, about the right distance from a city and its ley for the manoeuvres he had in mind, and where only a light camouflage would be necessary. But should he keep the thing anyway? In the years since he'd liberated it from under the Vigil's noses it had become as much of a liability as an asset. And what if now it held other hazards? But cylinxes were not easy to destroy either. Not safely at least.

— And this anonymous source, he said. Can we please just find out who they are?

He felt sick again. Backsnap, hangover, illness — he couldn't tell what it was and he didn't much care.

Very probably he needed a drink.

7. Weakjohn

Martoth, Timoth

Weakjohn's attic was not cramped. Haver's Hall was broad enough to support fifty to sixty traders over two storeys and the narrow stairs that led up to her room took nothing from her space but a square yard of missing floor. It was a single room without partition, its areas assigned their roles by habit, not design. The three of them sat on ricebags around a small table upon which Weakjohn was preparing a tea of some kind.

— I daresay we'll treat ourselves to some saki later, she said as she tinkered with the pot, but clear heads will serve best for starters.

Timoth and Martoth flicked surreptitious glances at each other as Weakjohn poured the tea. It seemed impossible that this little ceremony could have anything to do with the corpse by the paddy but they were astute enough to realise that much of Weakjohn's gentleness was artifice and by instinct they kept their patience. At length, she sat down and whistled to herself.

— So… this is a mad way to start. I feel like we've grown up on different planets, even though I've spent most of my life on Semele.

She paused.

— There is just so much. So much to try and explain. So much you don't know or don't know that you don't know. How can I possibly find a way into it all?

— How about starting with: why did a woman I don't know come looking for me and get… *torn up*… to death next to my paddy? asked Timoth. It came out more aggressive than he'd meant, but Weakjohn was unruffled.

— Oh my word, yes. Yes, that's a big one to get going with. You know who she was?

Timoth shifted uncomfortably and avoided catching Martoth's gaze. They had not discussed the body in anything but very safe, impersonal terms. He'd known as soon as he had seen the corpse's face. The chill that ran through him when he saw something in that face which was both Martoth and dead filled him with fear even now. But had Martoth recognised herself in that wet, white mask? She'd only seen the corpse for a matter of seconds but she'd been upset and talking to Ma and Mulkah and Jeppa constantly as they all tried to make sense of what had happened at the paddy.

— She was my mother, said Martoth, with no false show of strength and no hint of facade. Timoth looked at her clear, bright face, and the open tremble on her lips and he had to catch his breath.

— Yes, she was. For all her flaws, and poor Marta had a barrowful, she was your mother. She was also mindwoke, affiliated to the Vigil, and on her way to tell Timoth that he was in mortal danger. Weakjohn paused. There. Okay. Right. We've got somewhere. We're working our way slowly into this thicket now.

— What has my mother got to do with Timoth?

Martoth had drawn her knees up to her chest and was gazing sourly over the top. In the last week she'd gained a mother, lost a mother and now found Timoth somehow involved with her mother, and she didn't want that to grow into anything new.

— Nothing at all, Martoth, absolutely nothing. Apart from Timoth is a little bit special and it's been noticed. Marta and I have been the only people on Semele looking out for that sort of thing over the past few years.

— Special? spat Martoth, appalled. Oh. Just. Fuck. Off.

Timoth fidgeted uncomfortably.

— I'm afraid, said Weakjohn, I've always been bottom of the class when it comes to talking to people. Helping people through things or that sort of thing. I'm the only person around to tell you all this stuff now so I'm doing my best but I may occasionally just, you know, blurt something out. Please pretend that I'm doing this better? Okay. Martoth, dear. Back to Semele now. Back to Semele. Let's cut back some more of this thicket.

But Martoth was glaring at Timoth.

— The stones? The fucking stones. Why didn't you tell me?

Timoth didn't leave the protective crouch he'd assumed as Martoth had been getting more worked up. Instead he looked back to Weakjohn.

— Errr… mortal danger?

There was pity in Weakjohn's eyes as she regarded Timoth. She took a few seconds to compose her thoughts before going on.

— Marta, like me, was part of an organisation known as the Vigil. We were the Vigil's representatives on Semele. It's probably best to think of us as caretakers. We look after humanity in various ways. We're the good guys. Most of us, anyway. We are also a bit like an academy. Almost all mindworkers are trained by the Vigil at the Abbey. I hope you'll see it one day, but right now we have other concerns. Mindworkers everywhere are being attacked like Marta was and all sorts of hell is breaking loose. I've lost contact with everyone and I'm very worried, Timoth, that you are at risk as well.

Timoth looked blankly at her.

— Right, she said. More tea.

Weakjohn made them stand up, shake their arms, take some deep breaths. Then Timoth and Martoth sank back down in the ricebags while Weakjohn busied herself about the attic, opening and closing cupboards, shifting books, booktabs and papers around in bookcases, rooting through a family of crates and boxes. She seemed to be searching for something and as she searched she continued talking. Timoth realised that she didn't seem to use her walking stick around the attic.

— Okay Timoth, let's talk about you first. My guess is there are some things you've been keeping to yourself recently. It's going to be important to get honest with us pretty quick.

Timoth stared at her, unsure what to say, and feeling suddenly defensive.

— Of course, she said on her knees now, amongst some items she'd scattered from a shoe box, I get how you might not feel overjoyed, spilling this stuff to Martoth and an eccentric woman you've never met.

Indeed, Timoth found himself assessing the distance to the trapdoor and to the ladder leading back down to the market hall and wondering how quickly he could clear that distance. He was aware of Martoth's furious gaze burning deep into the side of his head and of the swampy grip of the ricebag that would impede his flight.

— …so we'll do what we can to make it more comfortable for you, dear. Won't we Martoth?

He knew Martoth wouldn't answer that and she didn't.

— …if you'd like me to disappear for an hour for a quick chat between just you two that's okay.

No!

— …or I can fix up someone to show Martoth around town while you and I do what has to be done.

— Stop! he gurgled finally, realising how deep he'd managed to burrow into his ricebag. There's really nothing much to tell!

— Of course not, dear. Now where is that… never mind, I'll find it later. Right, okay, let me come back to my tea and I can give you my full attention. Good. There.

Weakjohn sat and smoothed down her skirts, picked up her drink and began to ask questions. She spoke now more carefully and with only very rare eye contact. More often than not she was gazing into the steam that still rose from the cup of tea she cradled in both hands.

— Over the last few months, have you discovered you can do things you didn't expect to be possible?

— I guess. Yes.

Weakjohn nodded.

— We're going to talk about that in a minute. Over the last few months have you discovered that you know things you have no obvious way of knowing?

Timoth pondered this one.

— No, he admitted, I don't think so.

— Interesting, OK. Over the last few months, do you feel like you've been in a place that isn't where you are, or a place that shouldn't exist?

— No.

On top of everything else, Timoth now began to fear that he was a disappointment, that Weakjohn had a fairly clear set of expectations and he was falling short.

— And over the last few months, have you found you've been able to see things you shouldn't be able to see?

Timoth's heart accelerated but the life drained from the rest of his flesh. He heard a barely perceptible sound of rice shifting in a ricebag, the sound of Martoth moving a tiny fraction, carefully, trying not to be heard. And then he was imagining the shape of her in the ricebag, her legs, her hips. And suddenly he recalled her climbing the tree in his paddy. Life flowed back into his flesh, and flowed hard.

— What do you mean? he said.

— I mean, said Weakjohn watching him carefully now, seeing things that your actual eyes aren't actually looking at.

— No, I don't think so, he said. I mean… I mean, I think sometimes my imagination is quite, I don't know, visual?

There, that sound again, Martoth stretching, quietly, getting more comfortable, just an inch.

— Do you ever have difficulty distinguishing imagination from reality, Timoth?

— I don't think so.

— Ok. Ok, good. Now, then.

Timoth took a deep breath.

— What's all this "last few months" stuff? asked Martoth.

Timoth was glad to have Weakjohn's attention elsewhere for a moment. He reached for his own tea, and brought it to his mouth. He barely took a sip but allowed the scalding rim of the cup to sit against his lip for some seconds beyond where it became painful, let the tears form in his eyes, felt the reddening of his skin. It reminded him that he was his own self, not just the subject of an inquiry.

— It was about three months ago that Marta and I became aware of a change, said Weakjohn, a change which in retrospect I believe was Timoth's first accidental forays into… a new world.

Three months, thought Timoth, yes. Three months, that would be…

— My mother's been here for months?

Weakjohn winced but didn't answer.

— I know what you're talking about, you know, said Martoth. I know about psycocephy, I know about mindworkers, I've heard of the Vigil.

Weakjohn was stunned. Timoth shrugged:

— She reads *a lot*.

— Remarkable. But reads what, exactly? asked Weakjohn, suddenly intent upon Martoth.

— The stuff in the crates in the Border taproom mainly, said Martoth. I don't know where they came from. No-one else reads them.

— Ma says Mulkah brought them with him when he moved to Border.

— Did he now? said Weakjohn. Now that is interesting… Okay. Right.

Weakjohn stood now and paced around, tracing the edges of a large maroon rug, to allow the blood to flow freely in her torpid leg. She spoke as she walked.

— So we have this rather elegant situation don't we? Timoth knows what he's doing but doesn't know what it is he's doing. Martoth doesn't know what he's doing but does know what it is he's doing.

— I have no idea what it is he's doing! protested Martoth.

— Oh yes, right, so Timoth, what is it you are actually doing?

— You mean in the deep paddy?

— Well, I don't know if the paddy is all that important.

— Yes, in the fucking deep paddy!

— Okay, okay!

Weakjohn sat again. She'd picked up something and was fidgeting with it, turning it around in her fingers. They both looked at him and he flinched from their gaze. What to say? How to start? Memories flashed through his mind, moments, fragments defined more by their feeling than their detail, the stink of the water, the rush of the breeze, and then the awkwardness, the pestering sense of something spoiled, some offence caused. But what *did* he do? He knew he was changing things, but he wasn't ever sure how.

He thought back to three months ago — the first time, he supposed. He'd argued with Jessic; she'd got the wrong end of the stick. Not his fault. It stung.

The wind was up. Heavy low clouds tumbled across the sky and the paddy was choppy. Thigh deep, he'd found himself transfixed by the play of the gusts in the rushes all around him, not waves, not billows but a tugging, wrenching struggle, one way then the other, now up proud, now down flat. Days like this, the world wasn't just against you, it was in your face, spitting in your eyes. A rage had risen within him and spilled out somehow, flooding out onto the swirling paddy and the spasming rushes. And then, yes…

— I can make the reeds bend *into* the wind.

They stared at him.

— That's beautiful, said Weakjohn.

They continued to stare.

— I can make leeches swell up and die in the water?

— This is some sort of prodigy? said Martoth.

Weakjohn was expressionless.

— Remarkable, she said.

— It's not remarkable! It's stupid. Listen to it. Reeds blow around in the wind! Leeches swell and die! This is just what happens. This is my paddy, and Alban's and Teppen's and Jessic's. And every paddy on Semele. It's just what it's like.

Weakjohn continued to turn some small item round and round in her hands, her thoughts clearly straying far and wide.

— Yes, she said. Easy to write off. All these things. Very nearly a miracle that you'd even notice. Most people, after all, never do.

— I think I can move the air around me.

— Yeah, by opening your mouth, you idiot. Or your arse.

— I think…, Timoth ignored her. I think I could move something. Something small.

And Weakjohn stopped fidgeting, and held up what she'd been playing with: a small silver thimble. She tossed it from one hand to the other and then placed it down on the table between them.

— Splendid! Off you go.

Martoth wandered over to one of several small glass windows that had been built into miniature dormers in the attic roof. She found she could stand comfortably in the recess and look out into the night, across the tops of the market stalls lining the steep climb of Ekrasia, to the dark-tiled roof tops opposite. In the dark and the cooler air around the window, she felt calmer — calm enough to put this… *Timothism*… aside and reflect on her own problems.

Some point soon, he would emerge from this self-obsession and start to ask a few pointed questions of his own, start to wonder what she and Jessic had been up to, what she knew about Jessic's departure, hell, even why both of them were here. A razor-sharp glance shot in her own direction, had made it clear that Weakjohn, at least, wasn't fooled by her shallow tactic of deflecting everything she could onto Timoth. A different conversation was coming down the pipe —if not tonight, then tomorrow— and Martoth wanted to mull over how she felt about it, what she felt able to handle. Whether she wanted Timoth around at all right now.

The market below was emptying out and the bulb lights were being extinguished up and down the street. As the traders packed up and moved off, she wondered where their homes were. Were they all Laketowners, heading off back to homes inside the walls? Or did they travel in further, from Seaton or beyond? She noticed some of the traders were packing their stock into black wooden lock-ups along the streets. Some were setting off on *bicycles*, contraptions she'd seen once or twice when messengers came into Border, but was more familiar with from her reading. People could travel far on bikes but the countryside was rugged out of town and the Semele bike was usually more wood and iron than steel, the tyres were solid and the steering stiff; it was not well suited to the mountains. If they had something lighter from off-world then maybe they could come in from Seaton each day but not otherwise, and no further.

But now the off-world route was damaged, at least according to the guy at *The Hole*. She glanced at the polycast boots she wore. They'd been a gift a couple of years back, from Teresa through some friend of hers. They still fitted and she adored them — a bit worse for wear but she knew she would wear them till they fell right off her feet. Timoth must have sweated through three pairs in that time. That was worth a lot. That kind of thing had been flowing into Semele for three or four generations, ever since the first settlers, she guessed. Into Laketown too, not Cullen or Berren. She guessed Laketown was benefitting from the trade going out into Greater Semele, taxing it or something. What would happen if that dried up?

She was about to turn back to the others when she noticed something. As the market stalls had packed up, leaving fewer lights down on the street below, she'd begun to notice the lights from roof dormers twinkling across town, little niches just like her own, jutting proud of the roofs like glowing thumb tips. Most were dim, lit by candles or weak oil burners, but as she was turning away, at the dormer directly opposite her own, a bright sliver of light flared briefly and disappeared again as if someone had pulled aside a curtain. She stepped sideways into the shadier edge of her recess and watched. The other window was directly opposite; she and whoever stood behind it were separated by only twenty feet of thin air and the fading fumes of the oil lamps below. She had a peculiar sensation that whoever was there could not be looking at anyone but herself. As she trained her eyes on the window, she began to make out the dull shadow of a curtain and imagined she could even see it twitching, but it was not drawn back again.

— Weakjohn, that barman at the com house was talking about some—

— STOP! shrieked Weakjohn.

It took Martoth a moment to realise Weakjohn's shout was intended for Timoth. For his part, he was sitting by the low table, looking stung and confused.

— But I moved it! You said…

— Not like *that*!

Weakjohn seemed easily as disconcerted as Timoth.

— Okay, she said. I'm suddenly understanding something.

Her eyes seemed to Martoth like windows on an inner turbulence as if a whole new category of fear had now been thrown into the churn with her existing worries. As Martoth watched Weakjohn deciding how to proceed, she realised that their arrival was significant for Weakjohn too.

— Okay. Okay. Let's stop now and have a saki and I'll try and explain. Timoth, there are a few bottles on the side over there and cups in the cupboard. Could you do the honours? And Martoth, that vat over there by your feet is full of nuts, why don't you scoop a big bowl out and bring it over.

Weakjohn rose, closed curtains over all the windows then set some strange little globes around the room which fluoresced into a smooth glow at her touch, then she fetched a heavy-looking shisha pipe down off a shelf and filled it from a wooden water conduit that came down from the roof.

— You might not like this, she said, it's a little habit I

picked up somewhere along the way. And you never know, you might… Why don't you put out your sleeping stuff ready on the mats in the corner over there and then we'll sit. It's too late to fix anything for a meal tonight but we'll go out and get a big breakfast in the morning I promise.

So they sat, drank, nibbled and passed the pipe around.

— You moved the thimble then? said Martoth.

She didn't have to say *"with your mind"*. They all knew what they were talking about now. *Psychocephy* some of her books called it. It didn't really exist on Semele but people alluded to it sometimes and she believed the books.

Timoth humphed an assent.

— …did it wrong though, apparently.

Weakjohn fixed a stern stare upon him and chewed over her next words carefully.

— I'm sorry, Timoth. Usually it wouldn't be a problem. And it's my fault. There's always more than one way to do anything and the way you picked wasn't at all what I was expecting.

— But it was just like what I was doing in the deep paddy! I mean, a bit like it, but more…

— Yeah, I get that now. A few things have just become clear to me. The way you moved the thimble… it was by no means the easiest way to do it, you know. Actually, it was an extraordinarily difficult way to go about it. We'll come to why in a minute. But the point is, when you were changing things in the paddy last month, well, you were describing things that should have been quite easy, you know. The leeches, well, Martoth's right, that's the sort of thing that pretty much anyone can achieve without even realising they're doing it. Martoth might even have done it. There really isn't a dividing line you know between people who can do this and people who can't. Same with the reeds. Prettier image, maybe, but the same sort of thing. There's no way really that Marta or I should have noticed that sort of thing going on at all.

The shisha pipe filled the room with a sweet fruity smell that was difficult to pin down. A stone fruit perhaps, but Martoth wondered if it might be a flavour that came from off-world. She found it overpowering and it made her feel slightly claustrophobic so she passed on the pipe when Weakjohn offered it. Timoth seemed to be enjoying it though and took deep drags off the pipe as Weakjohn spoke.

— When you moved the thimble just now, and then I realised what you must have been doing to those reeds, well now I know why you were making so much noise. And, for other reasons, noise is what we'd really like to avoid at the moment. It's precisely noise of that type which seems to draw the *attacks*.

Martoth tossed a couple of nuts into her mouth and spoke again. Might as well tag along while she still could.

— So what's the easy way to move the thimble? she asked.

— The easiest way is to *use your hands*. And please god let us never forget it.

She was a peculiar character this Weakjohn, thought Martoth. She was prone to these emotional or aspirational asides but the tone of her voice barely wavered from the cold, calm, factual. If it were wit it would be dry wit, but it wasn't wit. More often than not it was genuine warmth, understanding or these throwaway appeals for divine intercession.

— And the next easiest… ?

— The harder ways all rest on the principles of psycocephy, and broadly speaking the process is the same whichever way you go about it. You expand your perspective to enfold a bigger mind, a fusion of yourself and the thimble, and then you use the fact that all being is thought: you think and that very thought is the changing of reality that you want.

— The difference…?

— The differences are in the way that you realise a fuse-mind and the thoughts that change the world. The easier way uses the ideas you have of the thimble, gravity, motion and so on, and builds the fuse-mind in such a way that those ideas are easily available to the fuse-mind and the thought that you need to have is a pretty direct analogue of the thought of the thimble moving.

— Oh! said Timoth, I think I might have done that too.

— Quite likely, said Weakjohn. The harder ways intercept reality at lower levels. In some layer of reality the physical nature of the thimble is made of molecules right? Or atoms, bosons, quarks, or whatnot. So with the right fuse-mind you might be able to have a thought which changes the world at that level, atom by atom. It's fiendishly difficult though. I wouldn't even attempt it and it seems a bit pointless anyway when our minds have evolved to take all that complexity off our hands. And there are other intermediate ways to do it as well. Levels in between stone and atoms.

— And it's one of these ways that Timoth did it?

Weakjohn was silent for a second.

— Not the *atom* way? asked Martoth with eyebrows raised.

— No, not the atom way. No, he did something much harder than that.

— *Harder?*

— Yes. And the complexity of what he did… well that kind of complexity is unfortunately a thing in and of itself. Something with its own mentality that might have its own consequences.

Only now did it occur to Martoth that Weakjohn was frightened. Not directly of Timoth, however astonishing his abilities turned out to be. It seemed more as if she feared the situation she was suddenly in. Martoth had a sudden vision of Weakjohn sitting amongst her glow-lights in a hall of a thousand mirrors where each mirror was a gateway to a predatory reality, and Weakjohn was simultaneously having to watch every portal for the first incursion.

— So the first principle... The first principle isn't even Psychocephy really. It's the first principle of Diocletian Orthodoxy, or "D.O." as the Vigil calls it, and it's the modern answer to questions that go back to Déscartes and beyond. Perhaps I can show you...

Then, without so much as a gesture, Weakjohn dimmed her glow-lights and set the air between them alight.

Timoth blinked as pale, three-dimensional shapes condensed out of thin air and hung before their eyes. Martoth opened her mouth to speak then closed it again.

— The world is not made of two substances, mental and physical as Déscartes supposed.

The colours before their eyes rotated into some diagrammatic representation but it was not a diagram Martoth could really interpret, like lines on a page or a map. The shape seemed to interconnect with itself in ways she couldn't follow and she wasn't entirely sure she was seeing it with her eyes at all. It seemed to be conveying something more than her eye should be able to accommodate. It hovered before her eyes, resplendent and spectral and swayed gently like a flower caught in the gentlest of breezes.

— The world is not, ultimately, physical.

Some of the colours fled from the floating hologram leaving an inferior, jaundiced representation of whatever it was that had been there before.

— Nor is the world ultimately mental.

The missing colours returned and the remainder vanished, leaving an similarly pallid half-view of the beautiful structure.

— In fact, the world is made entirely of one substance that

is neither mental nor physical, but via the connections and the interrelationships between this stuff and itself, it expresses physical and mental characteristics.

The hologram performed a swift, breathtaking motion that was at once a magnification and a rotation through hidden dimensions to reveal an impossibly complex textile of barely luminous filaments that together shimmered like the iridescence of oil on water. It swiftly zoomed out again to restore the original, multi-coloured hologram, appearing now even more glorious for the insight into its staggering intricacy.

— This is what we call the "rainbow expression", said Weakjohn. And that's "rainbow" because the breadth of expression that the neutral substance is capable of encompasses so much more than the two modes humans think of as physical and mental. The physical and the *perspectival*, to be more precise, are two opposite poles of expression and everything we normally see, feel or understand is a combination of phenomena at these two poles, but there are other possibilities, other ways that you could configure the instances of the one substance, the "noumena", that is.

Now the diagram became a cruder kind of mathematical allegory and Martoth realised just how metaphorical the visions she had been treated to were.

— All those things I mentioned before, the particles and so on, they belong to the physical expression of reality. So too do many aspects of our minds, most of the time: computation, memory… The part that is ultimately, irreconcilably part of the mental expression of reality, that's the perspective dynamics. In perspectivals we find the source of our awareness, our experience, what it's like to *feel* and to *be*. And there are other constructs in the more perspectival expression of reality — the *leys* by which we travel long distances, the *oracles* by which we embed our voices and knowledge for other minds and later generations…

Back now to the iridescent textile, and its impossibly complex weave… Weakjohn began to talk quickly, as if she'd abandoned any ambition to teach, but still needed to get the words out before they clogged up inside her.

— It's possible, you see, to intercept reality directly at the level of the noumena, to relate noumena to themselves and each other in new ways, insert, divert, pervert the prehensions between noumenal occasions. To interrupt right back in the phases of concrescence, right inside the very construction of their interconnections… and you have to understand "phase" in quite a loose way of course because time doesn't really exist at the level in the same way. The understanding of time and spacetime we got from physics are just constructions on or at least emergences from reality at the noumenal level.

Now by showing some reweaving of the textile and superimposing the original diagram with a twist and… No, it was a stretch too far. Weakjohn let the visuals dissipate and took a sip of saki.

— We're getting way beyond the boundaries of what we can hope to understand here. But understand it or not, I believe Timoth has been altering reality right at its noumenal foundations, making thoughts that intercept the phases of concrescence. And that is something I can't do myself and certainly can't teach. The only thing I can do, and I think it might be a good thing for all of us, is to teach him *not to do it*.

— You left something behind, said Timoth, pointing up to the space where Weakjohn had conjured the light show.

But Weakjohn was already throwing herself backward as fast as she could, floundering in the grip of the ricebag and in the end dragging it along with her.

— *Get away!* she cried. *Get away from it!*

They made for the walls, clambering over and around the low furniture. From three points at the attic's perimeter they turned and looked at what hung now above the low table. It was a ragged line of glitter, needle-thin, running about four feet vertically down from a point near the exposed rafters.

They watched it. Nothing moved but the coruscating play of colour along the line. Between the hammer blows of her racing pulse, Martoth thought she could hear a quiet crackle at the very edge of perception.

Weakjohn took a pace forward from her spot by kitchen cupboards.

— I didn't mean to illustrate our predicament quite so… concretely, she said softly.

— Is that… what killed…? asked Martoth.

— Something like it, nodded Weakjohn. A noumenal tear… A *rip*.

She walked forward more confidently and the glow-lights came back up.

— This one's healing itself.

…and sure enough, the rip was smaller than it had been. Weakjohn allowed them to approach to study it more closely, but it was gone before they saw anything that they hadn't already.

Timoth was pale as a sheet. He kept his arms tight by his side but Martoth could see them trembling.

— Was it my fault? he asked quietly, keeping his gaze steady on Weakjohn. At the paddy?

But she had no answer for him. Her face, though sympathetic, was pale as his. She hunched her shoulders and gave him a sorrowful look.

— Probably not? she hazarded.

8. The Cherished

Martoth, Timoth

They were shaken from their reflections by a disturbance in the street below. Weakjohn's eyes flicked to the windows and the glow-lights dimmed. She held a finger to her lips and motioned them each over to the curtained dormers in the streetward roof.

— Careful, she whispered.

Martoth squeezed back into the niche she'd used earlier and peeped out. The window across the street was now dark. There were people below her, moving in loose groups up the street, angry people carrying blazing torches and shouting. From the window she could see only the opposite side of the street, but there the people were hammering hard on the doors and gates with the butts of their torches sending sparks flying off onto the cobbles. Others hammered against the larchwood market stalls as they passed. A violent banging from two floors down warned them the market hall was receiving the same treatment.

— Do the guards stay overnight? she whispered.

— Yes. They won't open the doors to this.

Martoth tried to make out what the crowd were shouting

but couldn't hear anything that seemed significant. "Out", "Fight", "Burn"? There was no coherent chant, just the uncoordinated cries of lots of angry people.

In the centre of Laketown the air felt like a chemical reaction. A ferocity seemed to have permeated the very stonework like a barbed wire interlacing the cobbles. The townsfolk had deserted the streets, ceding them to tonight's mob of torch carriers, a mob bigger than that of two nights ago, which had been bigger than the one the night before.

Karim followed along, bouncing off the walls, pouncing forward then swivelling and hopping back down the street with his teeth bared in a roar of encouragement to those behind.

— Yeeeaaaargh! he bawled.

This was his cry, his very self stamped on the night. *Yes, in my name!* he might have said. But the growl worked too.

— Yeeeeaaaaargh!

He imagined the face he must have been pulling at the roisterers behind him, muscles stretched tight to form a fearsome grimace around his mouth, impossibly wide, a cavernous descent onto his thrashing tonsils. *Yes, I am with you.*

— Yeeeeaaaaaaargh!

The streets were theirs. The town was theirs. It was time to make the world theirs.

He didn't know where this fury inside came from —some bathtub sakis might have had something to do with it— but he felt superb now, unassailable, untouchable. And he'd never been so proud of Laketown. His town, the great town, and the one town which would now stand up and bravely win Semele back from the creamers and the cheaters. Oh gods it felt good. Good to fight back.

Look, he hammered, he yelled. This door, that door. He

hammered, hell, he hammered. Showered himself in sparks and growled as the hot flecks stung his face. *Out ya and tell raff if ya wanna! Stand and spill rot if ya got it. Anyone 'a say nay? Anyone a-raisin' doubt?* Ha. No. Course not. No-one would. How could they? What could they say? How could they look Truth in its face and deny it? Who could stare in *his* face, the image of his dead sisters and his trade-slave father and spit on their graves, call them by anything other than the sacred name they deserved? The Cherished! They all are cherished now and to not see that is to have lost your very wit and soul, to have mislaid the chit that borrows your right to draw breath. Time was ripe to right the wrong turn.

But rumours passed by now and then, beneath the night sky, and Karim's ears followed them as they went.

— They've strung someone up, went a whisper among them, back and forth, ripples reflecting in the street.

— Who?

— Don't know. Someone.

— Wow. I mean. Shit… who?

He growled again. Yes. Oh yes. Proof! Proof at last. Tears blurred his vision and he peered through them at the crowd that had grown around him. The sparse groups that had trotted out into the yawning streets had become a tight mass forcing its way through. Up to Daytime's Square. Was the whole town out here now? Everybody seemed to have multiplied. People he'd passed, he passed again. People who'd overtaken him kept cropping up. All of them, everywhere. All sharing this one thought and this one dream.

And he… Hey, that was odd… Was that a new type of…? He blinked the tears from his eyes and picked up his pace again, cantering forward through the crowd and knocking his torch butt against stalls as he passed.

There was a man who just slipped by him, he could have sworn,… Yes there he was in front, that man, fair hair bobbing a couple of metres ahead. Karim wove a path forward again and was within touching distance. Easy now, he just wanted to have a… He switched to the other side and climbed a little faster up the hill to snatch a quick glance back. It was difficult; faces, torches, raised arms kept getting in the way, but finally…

Karim stopped dead as a rock in the stream of bodies that washed past him. He steadied himself on his feet and lowered his gaze to his own hands.

His seeing that face — that was the start of a haunting, and he knew it. It was not so much the tar-black tears staining the fair man's cheeks but the dark voids that wept them. Karim's fury melted to a lonely numbness. He thought of all the vile things that he'd known happen to the human body: the ruptures and the tumours that Laketown healers could only distract from; torments inflicted and acquired; the bestial realisations of the extremes of hunger, of thirst for air or water; the bloated remains of his beautiful young sisters; the dry husk of his father. There had never been anything of illness or mutilation, never anything done to human by human hand, that looked like what he had just seen. He had witnessed the supernatural and it petrified him.

When had he fallen to his knees? What? Had his knees buckled? He crouched, one knee on the ground, one elbow on the other knee, and gathered himself. The cries around him now sounded foreign to his ears. A minute ago he had believed he was among friends, even seen some in the streets around him, but no longer.

He stood, again like the rock in the stream, and let the passing crowds buffet him. He scanned the bodies that came up the hill towards him and with a cold, silent horror he confirmed his suspicion. There were more of them. Two, three he could see, and those horrible black-hole eyes were fixed on him, he was sure of it.

He twisted and shrugged his way out of the crowd and ran off down the nearest alleyway.

Martoth stepped away from the window again.

— Who are they?

— They call themselves the "cherished", grumbled Weakjohn. I don't know who's organising them or where it all came from, but it was them or others like them, who torched the way head last week.

Martoth pricked her ears at this.

— Is that the route off world the barkeep at *The Hole* was talking about?

— Or some meaningless wooden ramparts around the edge. There's a huge anti-off-world sentiment behind them, and some vicious anti-mindwork invective doing the rounds too. That stuff goes over most people's heads but they all repeat it anyway. They're pro-Laketown, pro-Semele, anti-everything else. For now you're probably okay in those boots, Martoth, but I wouldn't shout about them. I have many friends here who are lying low right now, looking for a way out.

The crowd swelled and passed on up the street taking their hammering and screaming with them.

— They want to cut us off completely?

— We're already pretty cut off anyway, you know.

Martoth was coming to realise how precarious this balance must have been for the last few decades. Semele was a self-sufficient world and, like many others, it had deliberately turned away from the theoretical megaliths of the twenty-first century that most blamed for the crises. Semele was built in a humbler way, on the resources the land offered up, mixed with a rich vein of technical know-how that the settlers and later visitors brought with them. Like the bicycles: a collection of nineteenth century ideas realised crudely on Semele using mainly Iron Age materials. Like the plumbing, or the windmills, the techniques from weaving to smelting, everywhere it was twenty-first century smarts without the exotic materials and machinery.

But the simple ethic didn't stop this sporadic traffic of other technology flowing. Certainly most of the final flowering of human ingenuity was lost but clearly not everywhere humans lived did they live a life as basic, or as disciplined, as Semele. Her polycast boots did not predate the crises. They had been made afterward, somewhere out there with materials, facilities, techniques that went considerably beyond the aspirations and intentions of the towns of Semele. Was that dangerous? What sort of town or organisation made these things? Were they flirting with a new disaster?

Weakjohn turned the globe-lights up again and they went back to the saki.

— But no, she continued. They just burned some things at the way head. But that hardly encourages tourism. There are people who want to leave who won't go near the place at the moment and don't know how to find the help they need. But our real problem is what's happening to the ways themselves and that's got nothing to do with the fires. It's something to do with the attacks. And there is something else wrong at the way head too, I can feel it. Something that is not just the fire damage. I think we'll have to go down and have a look in a day or two when it's safe.

Martoth woke from first sleep with the drowning dream not yet fled from her eyes. She lay still and breathed the stuffy air of Weakjohn's attic until her airways felt normal then sat up and let her eyes acclimatise to the gloomy attic.

Timoth slept still against some ricebags just across from her and Weakjohn was asleep further away. There was time for thought. She rose and wandered over to her dormer again.

There was no light opposite. A far off murmur might have been a continuation of the earlier troubles but Martoth couldn't tell.

Where was Jessic? She could only have been a day ahead of them arriving into Laketown and so yesterday would have been her first night in the town. She might be in a com house. More likely with her contacts. Or she might even now be combing the streets for the mysterious Meef Parton, bearing Martoth's absurd commission. Had she put Jessic in danger? She'd known nothing of the combustible tension in the town when Jessic left. Jessic knew this town better than Martoth or Timoth but would she have the sense to keep clear?

And what an inert commission it was now… What had been, at worst, a barbed mischief, to engage the absent father to find the absent mother, on little more than promises, had now taken on a more sinister complexion. Martoth prayed that Jessic had not located Meef already. Even with the scant sympathy Martoth had for this character she believed was her father, she could see now an unintended cruelty in the charge that made her cringe.

In some ways Martoth was more a creature of Semele than Timoth and the Border folk. With only half a squint, she could see them as the Laketowners did: backward, rugged folk, clinging to their hills and paddies, and shunning contact with town. Whereas Martoth still spent half her life with Teresa in Porton, across the lake from Laketown. And while she was no Jessic Ang, she had a keener grasp of life away from the frontier than did Timoth.

Maybe that's why she felt more comfortable in Laketown. Timoth had clammed up since arriving. Even as they'd approached the town he'd been sluggish in chat and sunk in his own reflections. Now he was becoming even harder to drag out of his sulk. He'd resented Weakjohn's effort to teach him as much for the way her questions seemed to demand spoken responses as for any concentration she asked of him. He was clearly dealing quite badly with something and Martoth had an inclination that the problem was Laketown itself, not these mysterious capabilities that Weakjohn was trying to surface or contain.

But Martoth was so *nearly* native Border by now. She knew the people, the town, the ethic, as if she'd been born there, loved them for what they had given her and for what they never asked in return. When Rosie had reached the end of her long illness five years ago, some Border folk, Ma Mackelay included, feared they had lost not just a friend but also a daughter, for what reason had little Martoth to be forever making the three-day journey between Porton and Border now her Border-mother was dead? But even they, who'd known Martoth since she was toddling, underestimated her. They sent Rosie off Border-style in the grounds of Mulkah's taproom and, sure, the grief-ridden redhead hared off back to Porton with Teresa the next day. But, what-hell if that wasn't Martoth back in Border seven days later, seven days mind and there's six days travel in that too. Porton was home too she said, but she hadn't finished her season in Border yet, and by then the rhythm of the seasons was inviolable in Martoth's year: hard season Border, cold season Porton. She'd arrived in the taproom, barely in her teens and wandered shyly up to the women she knew. Ma Mackelay wasn't one to leave responsibilities like that hanging and she and the others saw to Martoth for what she needed. Pepped her up, bedded her down, instilled what little of the Border resilience Martoth hadn't already acquired. In a way, it made Timoth her brother, she supposed, but it had never been like that. So many kids were raised in communities rather than families now. And hell, her Porton life could have been another world as far as Timoth was concerned.

Yes, she must be the most native non-native Border could claim. Unless you counted Mulkah. Which nobody ever did. "Off-world", he said of his past and left it at that. Probably Ma Mackelay knew more.

And that was what filled her with rage: all these people she knew so well keeping secrets from her. It was all so needless. She didn't need protection. She didn't need to be put off. She had read more than any of them, from the books Mulkah kept, from Teresa's material, from other sources that came into Porton. She probably knew more about the last two centuries than any of them and yet the older folk, the folk who had lived part of it and known others before them who'd lived more, there were times when they just wouldn't let her in, wouldn't fill the gaps, wouldn't breathe any life into the text for her. Even when it came to her own birth, none of these questions she'd been asking all her life would ever have been answered if Jessic hadn't done her own digging. And if tugging on the thread of her father had eventually loosened a tidbit, it had taken the sudden actual death of her lost mother to turn up any information in that direction. She had been living with this growl of frustration inside that kept wanting to burst out. Just how delicate did they think she was?

The sense of shock she was feeling now was not just at Marta's death (what sense, when it came to it, calling her a mother?) but also this smashing head first into Weakjohn who was the total damn opposite of everyone else in the world. Everyone else was like Ma Mackelay, warmth, support, love but not ever a dribble of actual information. Now here was Weakjohn, warm words maybe but her manner as cool as ice, and, gods, the information was flooding out like a torrent. They had spoken for a long time before they retired and with the saki flowing, Weakjohn's reminiscences ranged far and wide. She would make some aside, or mull something over aloud, or illustrate something with a poorly chosen example and, suddenly, Martoth would be reeling in both exultation at the revelation and rage at the idiotic silence that had prevailed for sixteen years.

— I met you, she had said, back in the day.

— What? What do you mean?

— I mean you were only a foetus so, y'know, it wasn't really you as you are you now.

— When?

— When we packed Marta off to Porton. It was quite clear even then, I'm sorry to say, that she wasn't going to be a great mother.

— I don't believe this. Why?

— Oh she was just interested in other things, you know. She was Vigil, she was a mindworker and she had her preoccupations like all of us. Babies weren't her thing. Others before her have just stopped it happening, but, say what you will of Marta, she did care. I think she knew as soon as she arrived in Porton that there were others who would care better. You know don't you that Teresa was there at your birth?

— You know Teresa?

— Oh I did, I would say, a little bit. She was part of the same scene for a while.

— And no I didn't know. Teresa never, ever talks about my mother. Do you think just maybe, when we've got some time, you could give me this all *in order*?

9. Wanderpause

1938

Clindor snatched Stephen's notebook and threw it into the heart of the fire. Stephen's heart plummeted and he felt suddenly an overpowering sense of dizziness. The lamps and the fire took on strange and terrifying forms and the walls crowded in on him. He realised he was fighting for breath.

The other customers rose and made for the stairs. Stephen climbed unsteadily to his feet and took a pace towards the fire.

— Hey now! Look here! urged Harald, standing up too.

— Stupid, *stupid* man! growled Clindor at Stephen, pushing Harald back into his chair.

— Get it! Get it! Please! urged Stephen.

— Get it yourself!

— My notes, my… *everything*!

Anna jumped up and down on the bench behind Stephen. Lena reached forward instinctively as if to comfort her but they were too far apart. Pierre rose too and approached the fire nervously.

Clindor swore under his breath and planted both arms deep in the fire. After a couple of seconds he pulled out the notebook, dirtied and ashen. A few inserts were glowing at the edges, but it was near enough undamaged. He dropped it onto Stephen's table, hissing and shaking his hands violently in the air to cool them. Stephen dabbed at the book desperately with his gloves and a handkerchief.

— You *fiend*! he whispered. In anger and humiliation, he cast around for some further reproach. *Explain yourself!*

But Clindor's face was changed: exuberant now, elated.

Stephen and Anna had arrived first, armoured against the thick October drizzle in duffles and woollens, and eager to find a cosy berth in the *Bierkeller Wanderpause*. In silence, they climbed the stairs to the inn's second room and seated themselves by the fireplace.

Anna could not understand why they had to meet these people again if Pyotr wasn't coming. The gallery had upset her. Even when everyone had left and she was shuffled off to bed, her head spun in the darkness, and the storm's growl rang in her ears. She had an awful sense that somebody had done something very wrong, even if it wasn't very clear who, or what. She wanted to wash it all away and forget about it. And she wanted the growl to go away.

Since that night, Uncle Stephen had been distracted. The painting had got him very worked up. He was always off to distant universities to consult their libraries, leaving Anna alone with Mme. Durand at their lodgings. Even at five, Anna was wise enough to realise this was Uncle Stephen beginning to recover a life he'd interrupted for her sake. While she was happy his old fervour was restored, his world of books and theory was not a world she could share and she was desperate about losing him to it.

This meeting was all part of it. She'd said yes because she could tell Uncle Stephen wanted her to but she was scared of these people. And it even looked like Uncle Stephen was scared too, sitting forward and fidgeting with his fat black notebook.

Anna squeezed up tight to Stephen and wrapped her coat around her knees to feel snug. Wall lamps cast a warm yellow light over them while the fire was struggling to take hold. The rough plaster walls were decorated with antique kitchenware and primitive photographs of Alpine plants. Two windows looked out into the sodden grey world through unvarnished frames, their sills furnished with dried flowers.

There had been ten people in the gallery room and in the mysterious painting. In her head, Anna grouped them according to the pages of her old counting book: a one, a two, a three, and a four.

One was the old Polish soldier, Wojciech, with a mischievous smile beneath his grey bushy moustache. Uncle Stephen insisted on calling him Pan Groshek.

The *two* was the middle-aged couple from Norway, Harald and Lena. They had been friendly with Uncle Stephen in the gallery.

The *three* was the group of French climbers, Paul, Pierre and Bastien. They had young faces tanned by the sun and the three of them always seemed to be sharing private jokes even when they spoke English.

The *four*, though, sent shivers down Anna's spine. To keep to the pattern, you had to make it up from Anna, Uncle Stephen, Pyotr, and then the last, who scared her most, the dark-haired moustachioed man, Monsieur Clindor. (*French pronunciation,* Uncle Stephen taught her, *clan-door, clan, door, that's it, clan-door.*)

The fire grew taller. Uncle Stephen fiddled, restless. Anna waited. Who would come?

Stephen was a fluster of nerves. His eyes flicked about, from the fireplace to the pictures on the walls to the window and back. He placed his notebook on the table but could not resist tapping it with his forefinger, adjusting it to lie square to the edge of the table, picking it up, placing it back down again.

The events in the *Galerie des Témoins* had reawakened the metaphysical curiosity he'd discovered in Lucerne last Summer, in Professor Templeton's walking party, before news of his sister's death intervened and sent him hurtling across the continent to rescue her orphaned daughter. Suddenly his mental reservoirs of esoterica seemed relevant to *real life* and he was puffed up by a rare sense of significance. What he yearned for, in the seven strangers yet to climb the wooden stairs, was *students*. He was confident he'd find them willing —he could hardly conceive how the universe might fail to deliver them so— but such was his desire that he could not control his nerves. And these were nerves which failed him frequently when he ventured beyond the confines of academia.

Also, he was troubled by Anna's insistence on coming. It was wrong to consult her. He'd rationalised it as fostering a growing autonomy but really it was his own reluctance to take the right decision. At least the hour was respectable, the company unthreatening, the venue innocuous.

Even the time of year worried at him. *Remember me on All Souls, not All Saints*, Angela's note had said — a note for Stephen, left at the solicitors' with her will. Now as *Allerheiligen* and *Allerseelen* approached, Stephen felt a growing dread. Should he tell Anna about these festivals? Light candles? Memorialise the day that Angela claimed? Anna was too young. She was not ready. But in letting the day pass without mark, he would once again breach his sister's trust.

His thoughts drifted back to Professor Templeton's walking party. After the major libraries, Bern, Fribourg, Zurich, eventually Basel, he'd wanted to consult Templeton but found he dared not broach the subject of the Creed picture even in a letter. So he wrote instead to his old friend Hubert, one of the walkers familiar enough with their discussions to be useful but much less fierce than Templeton. This was an unmitigated failure. Stephen's letter was too elliptic, too hypothetical, and Hubert was more preoccupied with the recent publication of Templeton's fictionalised account of the walks, *The Lucerne Dialogues*. In the *Dialogues*, poor Hubert was rendered as a narrow-minded boffin who was a humiliatingly thin foil for the professor's conquering position, a position that had been shared freely and equitably among all the other characters, from *Professor Diocles*, Templeton's own alter ego, to *Harper*, a mercifully charitable take on Stephen. It was a cruel stroke of the professor's pen and Stephen felt for Hubert, who was taking it poorly.

— He was the son of a minister of course, said Lena.

Stephen nodded to himself. By now he could list every one of Peter Creed's works, recite his biography and sketch out a good part of his ancestry. The others though were listening intently. Obsession with opium amongst artists and children of churchmen was hardly noteworthy and Stephen was rather bored by it all.

Lena turned out to be an art historian. Mme. Giroud engaged her on occasion to verify the authenticity of her purchases or to track down works whose existence was implied by other material. Despite her lively response to the group's interest, Stephen detected in her narration a similar eye-rolling weariness to his own and he decided she was a kindred spirit though he had hardly breathed a word in her presence since the night in the gallery. Her husband, Harald, was a bushy-bearded, cable-knit Norwegian and Stephen would have guessed him a fisherman, had he not already known that Harald owned a successful manufacturing company in Oslo and regarded himself as semi-retired.

— Did he rely on the opium then? asked Pierre. For his inspiration?

Lena made a noncommittal gesture as she accepted a glass of wine.

— Not especially. We are not in wild artistic territory here. Everything you see is realistic. He painted from life. There are fantastic elements in The Wake but it's no delirium.

Stephen tutted at Pierre's question and indeed the whole direction of the inquiry so far. It was such a juvenile thrust at the problem. Pierre was only twenty but he was accounted smart by the other French boys and destined for the Sorbonne according to Greta. There was a primness in his appearance and a close attention to grooming that the other two did not share. The eldest, Bastien, was, to Stephen's eyes, a bundle of affectations: the beret, the beard, the delicately clutched hand-rolled cigarettes forever on the point of launch over his right shoulder. The youngest, Paul, was closest to how Stephen imagined a climber should be: compact, slim.

They were eight, gathered now. After Harald and Lena, the climbers had arrived with Pan Groshek. They had all enjoyed some drinks beforehand and the exuberance of the boys motivated a few good-natured interventions from Harald to remind them a child was present.

As the conversation went on, with Stephen taking no part, he began to lecture them instead inside his own head.

— What are the available explanations? he imagined himself saying. And, please, predestination is no explanation at all. It is merely a template, a narrative that even amplifies the questions we start with. No, no. The metaphysics are stark. There are two events: the painting of the picture and the viewing at the gallery. Either the two events have a common cause or one caused the other.

He paused for effect, and noted with satisfaction that

conversation had ceased. Not a rustle of paper or the scratch of a pen nib. *Rapt!* he noted, glowing.

— A common cause, he continued in the theatre of his own head, a predestination if you must, is the least economical hypothesis, so let us discard it pending corroboration from quarters unknown. We are left with two possibilities: Creed's painting caused the presence of ourselves, living manifestations, at the gallery that night, or our presence at the gallery caused the painting of the picture. Now, painting from reality is so mundane as to be commonplace, whereas the paintbrush controlling the birth and destiny of people would seem to be… appreciably rarer.

They were looking at him expectantly, as they should, of course. So he delivered his peroration, stripped of all subtlety.

— The rational conclusion is simply that Peter Creed painted us.

His triumph was short lived, of course. He delivered his imaginary conclusion to no effect. However, the expectant looks were real enough. Something had passed him by. A response was required.

Harald came to his rescue.

— We were wondering if you had any ideas, Doctor Harrison?

Stephen looked to his bulging notebook and then to the expectant faces. His heart hammered in his chest.

— N-n-no, he stammered, at least…

— Oh yes! cried Anna. Uncle Stephen's been searching in all the libraries!

Stephen took a slow steady breath and felt suddenly like he was letting go of the edge of the deep end of a swimming pool.

— I wonder, he said, I wonder, have you heard of Professor

—

…but he was interrupted by a shriek from Anna.

— Pyotr! squealed Anna. We told everyone you weren't coming!

He'd slipped through the door in the shadow of M. Clindor and leaned now against the doorframe watching the company react to Clindor's entry.

— *Zdrastvuiytye!* said Pyotr softly and bowed his head toward Anna.

As they talked, the group had grown accustomed to the noisy wooden staircase and come to associate a telltale crescendo of clunks and scuffs with new arrivals. The young waiter had tramped up and down several times and some other customers had arrived to take a table by the far wall to play jass together. Each time the group had looked up automatically as footsteps unmuffled and a figure appeared at the door. Somehow, M. Clindor and Pyotr had taken them all by surprise. No-one looked up until Anna's cry caught their attention.

Clindor was dressed in a checked cotton shirt and a grey waistcoat and he carried a thick coat over his arm. His thick black hair was waxed but less fastidiously than Anna remembered.

— Please, Doctor Harrison, he said softly. Please continue.

As Stephen struggled, the newcomers edged quietly round the tables, doing little to lighten the heavy silence. Clindor took up a space near the fire by Lena and Harald, while Pyotr squeezed into a spot with the French boys and sat forward, loose curls of his fair hair spilling down the side of his boyish face. Both turned their eyes toward Stephen.

— Well..., said Stephen but trailed immediately to a halt, his mind blank.

— Come, Doctor Harrison, said Clindor. I think it's clear you are the best qualified to solve our little puzzle.

— I'm not sure, really. At least, perhaps I should explain a little of my background...

— Doctor Stephen Edward Harrison, interrupted Clindor, famed Indoeuropeanist, renowned authority on Luvian and Lydian, cataloguer of the inscriptions at Ephesus, refiner of laryngeal theory, outspoken critic of Grimm's law, positor of the segundum hypothesis, first translator of the Zephyr transcriptions, editor of two collections of essays in the field and famously engaged, still, in the creation of a synoptic dictionary of the Indoeuropean noun. Alumnus of Balliol, St. Andrews, Göttingen and now Fribourg. And not yet forty.

Stephen's lips parted and would not close. A hot pins-and-needles spread in his cheeks and scalp.

— But Doctor Harrison, continued Clindor, we can all do homework.

Clindor turned then to the group and indicated Stephen as if bowing to an august personage.

— Doctor Harrison spends his life reconstructing a hidden truth from the most insubstantial of evidence. From mere echoes he pieces together a language that has not been spoken for thousands of years. I think we can be confident of a solution to our own little mystery.

Stephen was alert for any hint of mockery but persuaded himself Clindor could be taken at face value, for now at least, so tentatively, and with some encouragement, he began to explain his hypotheses on the picture. There was, he suggested, no predestination, no prophetic greatness. Peter Creed had painted them.

— It comes down to extraordinary vision on Peter Creed's part or extraordinary *visibility* on our own. Suppose that some kind of event occurred in the gallery which made us visible to Peter Creed, through the medium of the picture itself. The canvas connects both occasions after all. Suppose it felt right to Creed to place brush to canvas where he did because the very canvas showed him the way. I have heard some artists speak of such feelings.

— You mean the painting reflected us? said Lena.

— Quite possibly, said Stephen. The ancient Greeks had several—

— What *event*? cried Clindor. There was no event. There was nothing unusual at all apart from the foul weather.

Stephen was taken aback. He hadn't expected to be pressed so hard so quickly.

— There are… many things yet to be explained of course…

— Nothing's explained, shouted Clindor. I'm disappointed, Doctor Harrison. This is numskullery dressed up as intellect. You're a fraud! A plain fraud!

No-one breathed. Stephen felt Anna tense by his side and was aware of everyone's eyes avoiding him. He flushed red and felt sweat forming under his collar. He was mortified by the insult. He wanted to protest that his young ward ought not be treated to such an ugly display of manners, but to make Anna his shield betrayed more weakness than he wanted to expose. Anna wriggled closer.

— I don't find the alternatives very compelling, he replied.

Clindor launched himself towards Stephen's notebook.

— You felt it? asked Clindor, brushing streaks of ash from his hands.

His eyes shone now and his whole face was lifted by whatever euphoria had taken hold of him.

— Felt wh—

… but Stephen hesitated. His fury limped to a standstill. He *had* felt something, something quite incredible.

— My dear Stephen, said Clindor, now placid and amiable, stepping forward to clasp Stephen's shoulder. You must accept my apologies! I knew a demonstration would be needed. I really didn't know it would be so effective.

Pierre seemed grateful of the opportunity to retreat to his

seat. Harald let his broad chest deflate but stayed where he was. Stephen pulled himself free of Clindor's hold and turned to wrap Anna into a cuddle. He thought to settle her but she was already calm, as if the sensation that had struck Stephen had struck her too. Struck them all.

— What did you do? Harald asked Clindor.

Harald was still standing, not a yard from Clindor. Though there was nothing threatening in Harald's face or poise, his stature was every bit as imposing as Clindor's. While the two tall men stood, close and quiet in the centre, the company were on edge.

Clindor shot him a cool glance and then resumed his own seat. He began to talk, calmly, rationally.

— I threw Stephen's book in the fire, he replied. I caused a moment of stress. A moment of heightened possibility. Nothing else. What happened was not something I did. I believe it's something we all did.

The fire crackled. They blinked.

Stephen looked in upon himself and tried to recapture the strange sensation. It was fleeting — fled even before he'd recognised it. And now it was remote, like a dream too vivid to doubt but forever lost to the waking mind behind the grey wall of sleep.

What, across the slender bridge of memory, had he seen?

Some things he was sure of: He had seen his own unmirrored face from the higher eyes of Clindor and the seated eyes of the French boys. Also his own neck from a point opposite, a viewpoint that must be Anna's. He saw Clindor's face but also his back. He saw Anna's panic through many different eyes and Pyotr's pale cheeks through hers. He saw Harald's clenched fists through Lena's eyes, Pierre's uncertain advance through Wojciech's. The yellow lights on the walls were each a spectral smear of gold, a superposition of the subtly different modes of awareness implied by the visual apparatuses of all ten of them. The fire's burning had been beautiful, as if each persons' perspective filled a gap left by all the others, and when all were experienced together the fire became a glittering solid that was perpetually turning inwards, tucking exposed tendrils into pores within itself and then extruding new ones. Into this writhing creature, Clindor had thrust his arms to recover the notebook.

Other things he was less sure of. There had been something else that might have been cognition. Neither logical nor linguistic, but a sense of mind in motion. A sense of something that might be the seed of *purpose*.

— How did you know? asked Pierre.

— I have a military background, Pierre. Let us say, moments of stress are not unknown to me.

— Nor I, said Wojciech, but I have never felt anything like that.

— Oh no, agreed Clindor. I beg your pardon, no, nor have I. No. But I think I have had smaller events. Little confusions. I believe I have felt somebody else's pain, for instance. I wonder if you may have had similar small events that you haven't recognised. I urge you, in fact, to consider it.

Anna stopped crying once Uncle Stephen backed away from his row with Clindor, but she felt like she'd been shaken about. As Stephen hugged her, her mind was darting about between all the glittering memories of the moment they'd just lived through.

The grown-ups seemed lethargic, barely talking as they contemplated their discovery. She looked to each of them in turn and she watched their outsides with a new fascination, now she felt she'd seen something of their insides. Although it wasn't as if she really had. It was more as if they'd all shared thoughts for a second. And only such shallow thoughts. She knew much more about Pyotr from snippets of his poetry than from anything she could glean from the strangeness just now.

None of this scared her. In fact, it dissolved her early apprehension about these people. Harald felt already like an old friend. The climbers now seemed more daunted than threatening, Wojciech more impudent than imposing. The teeth had been pulled even from Clindor's ferocity. His angry words to Uncle Stephen rang in her memory more like the bluster of her playmate, Eric.

But something about M. Clindor did still frighten her. It was not his mockery, nor his cursing that bothered her but his sudden manners. When he bowed to Wojciech, she shivered. When he addressed Pierre by name, she squirmed. When he apologised to Uncle Stephen, she felt a chill she could not shake. As the adults began to make plans to tarry longer in Switzerland, she snuggled up close to Uncle Stephen and regarded Clindor with loathing.

10. The Fairy Castle

Seronin

There was a good-sized crowd in but the show hadn't grabbed anybody yet. They were sitting in their groups, drinking, chatting. Some played dice games. Two older gents were cramped up in a corner, their heads nearly touching over a chess set. At one or two tables, there were more exotic devices or plays of light that Joi didn't understand. Some of the girls were selling smokes, vapes, spines.

A sleety dirt had been trodden in through the main doors and, like always, the mood started cold as the sky. The punters were the usual mix: ten percent faces she knew and the rest in from elsewhere. She kept an elbow clamped firmly over her bag, lit a cigarillo, and slid between the tables, ready with a wink.

If she missed anyone's eye it was because hers were on the show. It was the normal crude puppetry. Bulbous papier maché figures covered in bright paint and sequins cavorted in front of black curtains, lofted about by Niall's boys who were covered in black body suits and climbing over each other to act out the bizarre show. The effect was imperfect and the entertainment all the better for it. Niall kept up a ridiculous narration and the boys screeched out character parts when the need arose. Most of the time there was music too but it came and went as the orchestra swelled and dwindled. Part-time musicians and enthusiastic patrons pitched in to help here and there. Right now all the instrumentalists had wandered off leaving Miranda at the piano, shuffling some sheet music and scribbling something down with a pencil.

Joi felt a hand on her arse as she passed and whipped round to glare at the suspect, a grimy-looking fellow, with kohl-rimmed, heavy-lidded eyes and his face made up into a permanent wince. In her dreams, she dealt with these moments better. In her bag, nestling in a dedicated sleeve near the top, rested *The Universal*, a glittering poniard, impossibly thin and sharpened to a devilish point. In dream there was no ungainly spinning around and searching out the miscreant. Instead, quick as thought, she was behind him with the point of The Universal at his jugular, a sharp but beguiling rejoinder on her tongue, and her other hand wandering suggestively down his chest... There was business to be done after all.

This man scowled and she dismissed him with a wave of the hand and moved off and turned her attention back to the ungainly "pageant of the planets" that Niall's boys were stomping out up on stage.

Was there anywhere else like this? Where an unwilling audience had so little in common? Sure, most of the punters ate, shat and shagged but it wasn't really the basis for sophisticated comedy. She felt sorry for Niall when shows got jeered, especially when he'd stuck his neck out and tried something a bit different. How could you write anything for this motley bunch? Probably two thirds of them came from the Tier Ones and each of those was a whole planet of variation, of cultures and conflicts. The other third would have drifted in from the rest of the modern diaspora. Could be twenty-odd worlds represented here, not counting the locals. Aiming low was Niall's best bet and he served that up happily even if half the punters thought it beneath them. But with Niall there was always a wild aspiration in the background. So yes his pageant was full of crude stereotypes. Here, for instance, was Humpoth, Niall's Semele "Rice Magnate", honking away happily on his weedhorn, getting rogered by Shirley Strapon the Schiller Shepherdess. But punters who were really paying attention would realise this was a history and a tragedy too. In less than an hour of pornographic farce and singalong-a-rumpus Niall and Miranda covered a sweeping history of the final years of the Earth, the migrations, the closing of the ways, and then a pretty solid grounding in the human geography of the known universe. Not many actually did pay that much attention.

She bumped into Sayds, one of the spine fairies she knew.

— Eyes up girl!

Yes, eyes up. She saw the shows every night. Punters didn't stay that long. She looked hopeful:

— Freebie?

Sayds smiled and tore off a spine for her. Joi jabbed it straight into her neck then crumpled the cartridge and flung it under the nearest table.

— The new one's on later, said Sayds, smiling at her. They all knew Joi liked the shows.

Joi frowned. Niall had sensed something else amongst the shifting population of the bar he thought he could tap into: There was never, not ever, any Vigil representation here. Everyone knew it. It made the place pretty attractive to a certain type — dissidents, rejects, whatever, they were certainly here. And in Niall's view that made the Vigil a target. Maybe there were enough of them to raise a giggle, she admitted, and as a rule they paid well. But they were a dangerous lot — they were the main reason she kept The

Universal. Drawing attention to that element was just a bad idea.

So, it was all go for later tonight, Niall and Miranda's new bonkers pisstake, almost guaranteed to bomb like a frozen cylinx: *Beware The Tetrawocky.*

There! That was an eye! A saucy, saucy glance without a doubt. Over in the busy area down to the left of the stage. Just in and not yet warm. Did he mean both of them? That was not how she liked to do things. Butterflies fluttered in her stomach. She grasped Sayds by the arm.

— Give me two, she said, fishing some cash out of her bag. And watch out for me will you?

— Hey, replied Sayds, passing her the spines, we're all busy here.

Joi adjusted her skirt and made her way across the room, keeping her bag pressed tight against her and dancing round another swipe.

— Evening boys, she said and slid the spines across the table. Free hit. Turns up the dazzle. You here for the show?

She knew something was wrong right away. The one she sat next to didn't even turn to look at her. She nudged him with her hip but he sat there still as ice. The other smiled, gathered the spines and pushed them back across the table to her.

— You could say that.

He was younger than she'd thought. Fair hair, grey-blue eyes and acne scarring. That hungry stare was still on his face but it was blank and blinkless. Not saucy at all.

She moved her bag to her lap and opened the clasp. There was a touch under the table, his leg against hers. She slid hers further in but kept her hand on her bag. A cold wariness filled her mind. These guys were unusual, therefore unpredictable.

— You looking for company? I could maybe sort out

something nice for you.

— Nice? he said and raised an unenthused eyebrow.

— Not nice boys?

There was a pause. Something passed between the two of them. A thought perhaps — their eyes didn't meet.

— See, said the man with the rough skin, I'm wondering just how nice you are.

And suddenly he was holding The Universal! Surreptitiously, just above the table, but he had it. He held her eyes while he tested the point against a thumb and hissed.

She tried to rise but found herself paralysed. She could not move a limb. She could not utter a sound. Even her breathing seemed to be running on a program that she wasn't in control of. She was as much a puppet as Niall's gross characters up on the stage. A crawling panic spread within her. *Mindworkers.* There was no worst thing that could happen to her now. Whatever could be imagined could be done to her. Whatever could be done to her they could imagine worse still.

For a brief moment the bar flashed out of existence and she found herself *somewhere else*, a wide dusty yard under the baking sun, and then she was back again at the table.

The fair haired man held the hilt of The Universal between finger and thumb and let the blade swing back and forth.

— So this is what you're *into* is it? This is what you like, isn't it?

His grey-blue eyes held her gaze as he slowly and deliberately moved the hand holding The Universal beneath the table.

She braced herself for pain, dreading where it might come. She couldn't turn, couldn't shout for help, couldn't even see whether anyone might notice her plight.

Again she was in the sunlit yard, for longer this time. She was bound to a wooden pole and she could hear the men somewhere behind her. Was this to be the scene of her ordeal then? A theatre of the mind, conceived for her torment? She looked down at herself. She was dressed as she expected and the bag was on her shoulder. She was not paralysed here, but she was bound tight and the sun beat down on her face and neck.

There was an enormous belching sound and a waft of sour beery breath as the sunlit world vanished again. The bar came back into focus and she found a gangly drunk sitting opposite. He swayed and squashed up next to the fair haired man, eyeing the spines that still lay in front of her. Under his breath, he was humming one of the pageant songs. That never happened. Nobody ever stuck around long enough to learn them and she was sure she didn't know this guy.

Her abusers scowled at the newcomer but he just smiled at her and semiburped:

— You going to do those or not?

Blessed fool, she thought. Has no idea the danger he's in. The prime arsehole's arms were still under the table and who knew where The Universal might be pointing. And still she could not move. She could do nothing but stare stupidly at the drunk as he addressed her, one cheek spasming furiously as he spoke.

— Hello! Wakey wakey cupcake. Hello!

He turned to his neighbour and stage-whispered:

— She dense or deaf?

— Take the spines, friend, and get on your way. We are not in a sociable mood.

— Ooo-oooh... said the drunk but pocketed the spines. Well I can tell *she* ain't. Must be you ain't bin treating her right.

— Friend, just walk ... away ... now.

The drunk was feeling the point of The Universal now. His face twisted in pain and he gasped aloud. Rough-skin's face hung so close, Joi could not but imagine his rank breath rolling across the drunk.

— I. Said. Walk.

A change came over the drunk. His eyes stopped wandering so much and his breathing changed. He sat straighter and turned face-to-face with her abuser. As a thin smile formed on his lips, she felt the brute to her right jerk suddenly in surprise.

She didn't know how it had happened, but though rough-skin and the drunk still faced each other eye to eye as before, The Universal was now floating *between* them, its tip a hair's breadth from rough-skin's eye. He didn't move. Couldn't, she guessed.

— It's time to rectify, enunciated the drunk, some misapprehensions…

Although now she wasn't so clear he was drunk at all.

— You thought you were the smartest guys in the room. You're not. You thought you were the most powerful guys in the room. Not even nearly. And you thought you were in a bar where people didn't care much about each other one way or the other. Sorry, not that either.

Still her abuser sat there, his breath rasping in his throat, the silver tip of The Universal hanging poised with only inches of buttery soft tissue between it and his cerebellum. There was terror in his eyes.

Somebody set down a stone tankard in front of the drunk and he turned from the deadly stare as casually as as if it weren't there.

— Release her, he said into his beer as he lifted it to his mouth.

— Why? She's just a fucking—

Something changed so quick she couldn't follow it. When her eyes caught up, the drunk had slid The Universal up inside one of rough-skin's nostrils, and had the heel of his hand braced underneath it, exerting the tiniest upward pressure.

— Go on, said the drunk.

A sudden wild fury shattered rough-skin's composure.

— She's a fucking synth! he growled.

This time it was not the yard. She found herself bodiless in an arena of dark space, the glitter of a trillion stars and galaxies turning slowly about her. At the centre of the rotation hung rough-skin, his feet upwards, back arched backwards, arms wrenched behind him and his face staring downward into the point of The Universal. Below The Universal, the stars were absent. In their place a wallow of thick blackness went down forever. Rough-skin howled and howled but the world kept turning and the dark pit yawned.

The drunk's voice sounded in her mind:

— Your choice, Joi.

The world revolved around them ten-twenty times before she answered.

— Am I? she whispered.

He appeared beside her and both of them had bodies again. He looked into her eyes.

— Are you what?

— You know what I'm asking, she said. Am I a synth?

He was looking at her with more than his eyes and she opened herself up in a way she never had before. In her head his touch was gentle. He withdrew. Did he pause then just a moment too long? A semiquaver rest that threw what followed into unintended syncopation?

— Of course not, he said. Synthetic minds are much, much rarer than everyone seems to think. It's a convenient slur in the mouths of the ugly-minded.

— But what if I am?

— Exactly. What if you were?

The bar came back into view and when she found she

could move she sobbed in relief. The two men lay prone against the table. Blood seeped from rough-skin's nose. She barely noticed as they were dragged off the benches and pushed outside into the snow. She sank her head down into her hands and let herself fly free in the exultation of her deliverance. Sayds and a few of the other fairies joined them at the table and gave her a hug.

— Night off tonight, whispered Sayds. Blitz out, Joi.

And when the hard drinking really got started, and the gangly drunk jammed both the spines into his neck simultaneously, Miranda carved a ludicrous double-handed glissando up the piano keyboard and Niall signalled lights down and everything got deliciously fucked up.

— Beware, giggled the drunk, the TETRAWOCKY!

And he dissolved into tears of mirth. His head kept slumping towards the table. He'd bruised his forehead on his own tankard and he would have a fearful black eye come the morning. He passed out for a minute then, all of a sudden, sprang up again, bolt upright wearing a blissful smile. He held out both hands as if appealing for silence, though no-one but she was noticing. A serious expression passed over him and a belch escaped.

— Sh, sh, sh! The, he beamed, ...the *Teratowookie*!

He'd done more spines than anyone she'd ever seen. She'd gone too far too. Every so often he'd move and she'd see these golden-green glistening threads in the air around him. They melted away when she looked at them, leaving her with a headache from the eyestrain. They were in her head. Just once she thought he might be aware of them too, as he started suddenly, and shot up off the bench, flapping his arms madly as if shooing a wasp. But he stumbled around flapping long after the threads vanished. No. He was shooing a spine-phantom of his own and, soon enough, he was back at the table, jamming more spines and downing ales as if he'd never moved.

— The *Tritticookie*! The *Trocheewochy*!

He was engaged in some mindbending puzzle of his own. Some of the fairies really were passed out but the carnage was continuing around them. Good Sir Teratowookie had been quite the reveller. They'd all been prancing around on the tables, all high kicks and squats and spins, but the drunk had somehow rigged up a slide from the bar and they'd all bustled and queue-jumped like kids to take turns sliding down it. A deal of clothing got ripped or lost along the way but the fun stayed clean. Ish. Now an obstacle course had been set up running across several of the tables, the bar, the slide and the stage and a ragged group of five or so were screeching and whooping as they wobbled their way around it.

Teratowookie had found Niall's show uproariously funny and as soon as the final bows were over, conjured some miniature light show variations on the table in front of him, chuckling to himself and shaking his head. She'd never seen him before but a few of the other regulars knew him and patted him on the back, or when his drunkenness progressed, ruffled his hair or spanked his arse.

The show had gone right over her head, but so had the pageant when she first saw it. It was clear Niall had done his research: he caricatured the Abbots in papier maché, invented colourful ballooning icons and idiotic personalities for the strata (*Concreta*, *Happenstance*, *Sanctum*, the *Apocryph*...), and they all bumbled around a gigantic dusty book they called the *Orthodoxy*, tapping their noses whenever they referred to it. Every so often a mysterious man in a rainbow superhero cape ran on, made a terrific farting noise and laid an egg-shaped turd on The Orthodoxy, which turd rolled off onto Miranda's piano, causing predictable hilarity. It referenced every conspiracy theory going: "Diocletian was the Vigil"; "the Vigil was the Vatican"; "the Vatican caused the crises", "the Vigil caused the crises", "Elvis was the first Abbot", "Diocletian was Elvis" and so on and so forth. It actually went down okay. She had a suspicion Niall might get into a lot of trouble if he put this show on anywhere else in the known universe, but right here, right now, everything seemed good.

— *Tatterwiccan! Totterwhacker! Tits-a-...*

He slipped off the bench and was knocked out cold. A couple of the revellers knelt in to look in on him but she waved them off:

— I'll sort him out.

She wanted to get away from the blitz-out in any case. It was on the turn now like milk turning sour. The fun was over. It was just a few determined masochists and late-starters keeping the old ideas going and something had turned dark in the mood. All by herself, she dragged the Teratowookie away from the dancing feet. Then she rustled around beneath The Universal for a needle and syringe that might be just the thing.

11. Puppetry

Seronin

Her skin was smooth to the touch, featureless, like plastic stretched taut. Somehow, out of the layers of intoxication, Seronin recovered a thin awareness of himself, born out of the muffled bass rhythms that seeped up through the floor. Out of the beat came his heartbeat; out of the deep dark couch, his bony knees.

She walked naked to the bedside table and picked up a pack of smokes. He watched her, eyes drawn to her elongated, almost alien, slimness flaring shallowly to the shape of her hips. Never before had he been so taken by the notion of skin as a container for flesh. She lit a cigarette and returned to the sofa. Kneeling astride him, she pushed the cigarette between his lips then brushed his hair from his forehead with a touch that was almost tender. She tilted her head and let her long straight hair spill forwards over the side of her face, then pulled herself off him to light another.

He didn't know or care where he was. He cared only that no-one else knew where he was. That was a kind of freedom, and, for Seronin, a pretty sacrosanct kind of freedom. He was still, after all these years, doing things he shouldn't, simply because he shouldn't, even though there was no-one to tell him he shouldn't anymore. Maybe Lethe and Candle ended up in that role from time to time but they didn't want to.

He refused to attempt any diagnosis of where his head was at. He couldn't even remember how he'd ended up in this room. Her impulse he presumed, but maybe, after all, there'd been some kind of transaction. He could believe it of himself. The agenda looked pretty nailed down from here on in and he wasn't going to fight his way out of it.

He stretched a leg and felt his toe touch something cold. He'd kicked over a bottle of beer. He sat up, swore, and the cigarette dropped from his mouth into his naked lap. He yelped, leapt off the sofa, and stepped right into the cold puddle of beer that was spreading across the carpet, then rising onto tiptoe, crushed the hot cigarette butt under the ball of his other foot.

— Agh—

He hopped around the damp patch, pitched forward onto the bed and raised his eyes shyly towards the girl. She wasn't even watching. She was crouched over the bedside table, vertebrae jutting inelegantly from her balled up back. Her frame shuddered as if she might be sobbing.

Seronin froze, feeling awkward and trapped by the situation. But her shuddering became more pronounced and then violent. She was fitting. The spines? He stumbled around the edge of the bed but, as he did, a deep roar eclipsed the bass from below and the colours of the room shifted.

She staggered back from the table as if blown away by an explosion, but she caught her footing just before she fell. She turned to face him and opened her eyes and…

— What the—

Seronin's gut coiled tight. Her eyeballs glistened black like orbs of wet obsidian, leaking a tarry mucus onto her cheeks.

Her breath was loud, scratchy, catching with a high whistle in her throat.

Darkness closed around Seronin. He thought first he'd slipped into *Brainslang*. The world fuzzed and jabbed at him and a screaming pain flared behind his eyes. Then a tightness in his throat and chest struck a nail of panic into his heart. He was choking.

He fought desperately to throw off the hijack but the void-eyed girl launched herself at him, driving elbows into his face and neck and a knee up into his ribs. He was suddenly helpless. His vision was failing. Colours were separating, opening up yawning grey crevices in front of his eyes. The world fragmented into tiny disconnected sensations. Cigarette-ash breath in his face. The sound of bone crunching against bone.

As his mind began to fade he experienced a mysterious release. A fog cleared and he began to see across some of the far horizons of humanity he'd touched in the past. If only… if only he could last, just a few more seconds, to penetrate these mysteries…

Then the terror and the pain dropped away. It was not the oblivion he expected but relief. Through shattered vision Seronin thought he saw the zombie girl thrown off him, against the wall, limbs still pumping, neck jerking around. There was someone concrescing in the room with them, someone not yet fully physical, but here enough to be flinging the furniture about, and letting fly in the allpsyche, burning off the blanket of fear that was smothering Seronin's mental functions.

— Are you some kind of fuckwit? shrieked Lethe, now in physical form.

He was hopping with fury over Seronin's prone body and prodding a cheek with his foot.

— I… I don't know what happened. Is she…? Seronin felt sick.

— This entire town is going to burn you alive in about ten minutes.

— Is she…?

— She's not dead, but she is very fucking far from okay and I don't think she's coming back.

— Oh God.

— I need Candle.

— No!

— Don't be stupid. We need her. I'm bringing her in. Get your clothes on, sit in a corner and get ready to fuse us whatever you can muster. Can you reach the cylinx from here?

— No.

— We're going to need you for the fix and to get out of this sty. There's fifty people downstairs who're going to be prying any minute, half of them mindwoke. At least see if you can get straightened up enough to hide us.

— *Now* Seronin, said Candle.

Lethe and Candle had the girl on the sofa. Seronin couldn't make out what they were doing but he knew how they worked. The manifold might be a rainbow expression of an underlying oneness but that didn't stop some people having a knack for the more physical expressions and others the psychic. Lethe would be closing up the cuts, making some kind of attempt at reconstructing the girl's eyes. Candle would be trying to stop her mind diffusing and keep it connected to the roots it needed to recover from this. And doing whatever she could to kill the pain. The girl was not conscious but she was moving and making occasional whimpering sounds.

But now they needed Seronin for a fusion so he opened up

and made himself available.

The fusion, *Lethe-Candle-Seronin*, woke, and was instantly aware of something else waking too, something not human, or something human in colour and origin but not in configuration. A darkspin, large and powerful and full of anger. It had not come from the girl. It had not been what possessed the girl. It was different and new and it was voiced and aware and it was somewhere nearby, thrashing and rampaging.

Sounds of crashing came from downstairs and a growing spinroar filled the air. Lethe-Candle-Seronin ignored the commotion and turned her attention to the girl's psyche and was surprised how well the girl's mind had healed. She wondered whether there were resources here she hadn't noticed, other processes that had been at work beneath her radar. Applying the full bandwidth of her fusemind, bolstered by Seronin's prodigious firepower, Lethe-Candle-Seronin smoothed the coronae of the remaining trauma and quickly stabilised the girl into a deep sleep before backing off. The crashing and commotion from the darkspin was getting louder in the corridor outside and perisprit impacts were starting to take hold in the room. Lights changed, balance teetered, doubt flowered.

— OK! came a Lethe-thought in the fusemind. OUT!

— If you'd called one second later, said Lethe, you'd be dead.
Seronin lifted his head.
— But I didn't call?
Lethe gave him a stern look.
— It was you. Sounding as disgusted with yourself as you do now. It's a tone that's getting tedious. But I haven't heard that fear in your voice for many years. It actually made me wonder if you'd suddenly started giving a shit.
Somewhere behind him Candle snorted mirthlessly.

12. The Othello

Martoth, Timoth

When daylight came, Timoth was ready waiting for it. While Martoth squirmed in her ricebag faking the sleep she still yearned for, he rose, stretched and pulled aside a curtain to check the street below. The stalls had escaped undamaged but there were many signs of the mob's passing, litter on the cobbles, scratches on the doors and a faint smell of smoke in the air.

— *Why are you here?* Weakjohn startled him, popping her head through the trapdoor.

He was smart enough to realise he'd run from Border not only for answers but also because he needed an escape but he hadn't intended to lay his emotions so bare. He began to mumble a response when he realised the question was meant for Martoth.

She rubbed her eyes.

— My mother…

— But, forgive me dear, yesterday you found your path to your Mother's memory and understood why she was tracing Timoth. But it seemed to me like Timoth's puzzle had been solved but yours hadn't. I think there's something else.

— Jessic…

Weakjohn humphed.

— A question as much for Timoth as for you. What else, Martoth? What are you looking for?

Martoth leaned forward on her knees, burying her hands deep in her hair.

— My father…

Weakjohn formed her lips into a silent whistle.

— Ooooh, she breathed. Oh my.

— You *knew* she was coming to Laketown?

— Only like hours before!

Weakjohn let them bicker while she gathered her thoughts. Timoth could bicker on autopilot. In another part of his brain, he was marvelling at Martoth's family tree: a mother who, if she was as like Weakjohn as he supposed, could set the air on fire, and a father, the mere mention of whom could stop Weakjohn dead in her tracks.

When they'd run out of steam, Timoth asked the questions he felt Martoth should have.

— Is he a mindworker too?

— No. Not that I know of, said Weakjohn

They both watched Martoth carefully. She'd simultaneously paled in the face and reddened in the cheeks and her mouth was pursed tight.

— He's some kind of investigator, she said as if daring Weakjohn to contradict her.

— Yes, said Weakjohn, yes indeed. I wonder what he's doing on Semele.

The two teenagers watched her expectantly.

— Oh dear, said Weakjohn. This could prove an expensive distraction.

— *Distraction!* cried Martoth, affronted.

Weakjohn winced.

— I'm sorry dear, but yes.

— Distraction from what? asked Timoth.

— From getting you to safety, Timoth.

This time it was Timoth who drew himself up in indignation.

— I don't need to run away!

— I'm not sure she meant *your* safety, said Martoth quietly.

Weakjohn closed her eyes and massaged her temples.

— I don't suppose we could start this whole thing again? she sighed.

Sun was streaming through the window where Timoth had pulled the curtain back.

— *Distraction!* cried Martoth.

Weakjohn winced theatrically.

— I'm sorry dear, but yes.

Timoth looked at them like they were mad. They were waiting for him.

— … from … what? he asked uncertainly.

Weakjohn fixed him with a serious stare and raised an index finger.

— From helping you meet your *destiny*, she intoned.

They were toying with him but he knew better than to rise to it.

— You mean the big breakfast you promised us?

…and Martoth actually squealed in delight.

As morning warmed the open spaces of Laketown and the streets filled with people the nighttime disturbances seemed ever more remote. Weakjohn took them to where one of the town's rivers broadened out to meet the lake and they crossed a long wooden bridge set with ornate lamps that would be picturesque by night, if any night were safe enough for sightseeing.

The streets were sparse, the buildings sporadic. There were

makeshift cafés with awnings and outdoor tables and Timoth's empty stomach growled at the smell of grilling meat. Martoth too: her eyes darted about following the plumes of aromatic smoke to the barbecues at their roots.

To their horror, Weakjohn led them past, into a tight cluster of housing and dirt-floored alleys, a gloomy neighbourhood of dark brick and weathered timber, and eventually to a building gutted by fire. The outer wood was scorched away, huge black stains grew out of every window, most of the roof was gone, and the brickwork was bowing and fractured. Above the doorway an iron strut jutted out that would once have held a swinging sign.

— This happened the night before last, said Weakjohn, the night your Jessic arrived.

Timoth took in the shell of the building. It seemed an unlikely destination for Jessic.

— You think she came *here*? asked Martoth.

— I really hope not. But if I was looking for someone like your father, it's where I'd come.

Weakjohn poked her head through a window and then closed her eyes and placed a hand on the brickwork.

— Ok, she said. There's nothing for us here. Let's eat.

...and to Timoth's relief she led them back towards the eateries by the river.

They found space at a long table with a view across the lake and Weakjohn ordered breakfasts as big as she had promised. In the spaces around the river mouth artificial rice paddies had been built and the ricers were at work already. The technique and the crop were so different from Timoth's they were barely comparable, men and women ankle deep and bent over, working the paddies in rows defined by slender wands of willow.

Between the paddies and the higher ground where they

sat, Timoth could see a cluster of workmen with carts and trollies that they seemed to be driving right into the river at a shallow point on the bend, filling buckets and vats.

— That bar was the *Othello,* said Weakjohn. It was an immigrant haunt, one of the places offworlders hung out. I used to know it well. As did your mother.

As they ate, a heavy-looking man came to sit on the corner of Weakjohn's bench. He sat facing away from them as if contemplating the mist on the lake, but while Weakjohn showed no acknowledgement of him, he spoke.

— How's the weaving business?

— Better than hospitality, answered Weakjohn without looking up.

The man gave a quiet moan and brought his hands to his temples.

— What will you do? she asked.

He hesitated.

— I've been here twenty-two years.

— I know.

— *Semele*-years.

He twisted his legs over the bench to sit properly at the table and stretched his arms out on the surface then laid his head down between them. He was clearly exhausted.

— Who got lynched? he murmured.

Weakjohn still did not look up but dabbed another morsel of grilled buckmeat into her sauce.

— No-one we know, she said. I went to check. Jack, my friends are looking for someone.

Jack raised his head, looking curiously at Timoth and Martoth.

— Black hair, tied back, small, mid-tone skin?

— That's her, confirmed Martoth. She was looking for a "Meef Parton".

— She found him.

Martoth and Timoth sat up suddenly, leaning in and dropping their voices.

— She was already feeling some heat when she arrived. Made useful friends pretty quick though. They got out just as the real trouble started.

— So she's ok? asked Timoth.

Jack ignored that. How could he know? Jessic had fled into the febrile Laketown night with Meef Parton and others. Anything could have happened.

— Did you get any help? asked Weakjohn.

— Putting the fire out. Once their own places looked in danger.

— *Timoth!*

It was Weakjohn — but she did not use her voice. Her lips did not move and her face gave no hint she was talking.

— Timoth! Don't *ever* do that again!

He gaped at her. She put her fork down

— Wha? he burbled.

— Sh! she whispered sharply. We must go.

Jack was slumped forwards on the table. Recounting the tale of arson had hurt. The torch-wielding gang, the scuffles at the door, the sparks, the blood, the burning oil, escapes through the back, groups rushing at the blockaded doorway, skulls cracked on the bar and doorposts... — each detail wrung out more of his spirit and by the end he was whispering into the slats of the table. There was nothing useful he could tell them about Meef.

— Jack, said Weakjohn wiping the last sauce off her plate with some rice bread, take what you can lay your hands on and get out of here. Get to Seaton or Border and make some friends.

And then she was up, stick in hand, and hurrying them away. She moved quicker than they'd seen her move, tapping ten to the dozen on the earth and loose cobbles. Martoth ran after her. Timoth, tore some last chunks of bread and popped a piece of sausage in his mouth, then jogged off to catch up.

— I don't know how you made it here alive, hissed Weakjohn as he reached her side. You're damn near incontinent. You *must* have been attacked!

— What did I do?

— *What did*…? You don't even know?

As they made their way back into the heart of the town, Martoth slowed suddenly.

— The crazy buck! she exclaimed.

Maybe they *had* been attacked.

On the way, Martoth told Weakjohn about the Semele Buck that bludgeoned itself to death on the croft door. Weakjohn's face darkened as she listened.

— Did you see its *eyes*? she asked.

But they hadn't. There were none left for them to see.

— Did you not even realise you were helping the firemen? asked Weakjohn, once they'd pulled themselves through the hatch to the attic.

He hadn't noticed anything particularly odd about the workmen struggling with buckets and vats in the river, though he'd certainly felt some empathy for them. Shifting heavy loads in cold water was kind of his thing.

— They weren't trying to shift it, you idiot. They were waiting for the pump!

— What's a pump?

— Timoth your mind was all over them, you were seeing things you couldn't see, you were changing currents, holding buckets upright. How could you not even know what you were doing?

He was at a loss.

— Laketown is burning, she said, with her cool even voice. Piece by piece. It has about five full-time firemen, and you're itching to get all the poor bastards killed in the only hours of the day they're not already roasting. And that's if you don't kill the rest of us.

A week ago Timoth would have been riled, but not now. Tears welled up. Jessic was lost and didn't want him anyway. Only Weakjohn knew anything at all and she and Martoth were ganging up on him. He'd run from Ma and Alban and all the others. And if he *was* just a little bit special —and he'd dreamed that he was— then it was only as some kind of walking lightning rod.

— You'll have to stay in the attic, said Weakjohn. Till we can toilet train you.

13. Cuckoo

1938

Stephen acquired the keys to an old lecture theatre in Bern and together they entered a dusty chamber whose history was etched into each wooden surface where student graffiti intersected with Jesuit iconography. To Anna the place was as mysterious and foreboding as a biblical tomb, and the air made her cough, but over the next month they levered open the windows, fired up the porcelain stove heater, cleaned the raked benches and then sat looking expectantly at each other. Quickly they came to know each other better, and shared a growing frustration at disrupted plans and concern for friends and relatives in every corner of a darkening Europe. Every attempt to reproduce the strange connection from the *Wanderpause* failed. Nerves frayed, tempers wobbled and resolve faltered. Stephen was full of oracular pronouncements, reminiscences of his mentor, Professor Templeton, but he seemed curiously unwilling to share any theories about the Creed picture or the *Wanderpause* event.

The French lads alone retained some good humour. They'd spent the summer camped out at Alpiglen, eyes set hard on the Eiger's North Wall, scrutinising the rock and the sky from dawn to dusk and gauging the bravery and commitment in one another's eyes. As other climbers approached the wall, the boys hesitated, tracing routes with their eyes, imaginary diagonals across the ice fields, paths and patterns on the "Spider". They knew the places where men had died and the spaces where they had vanished. Every morning as the sun rose the eldest, Bastien, stood outside with a roll-up cigarette in his mouth and his hungry gaze on the face. They finally packed up when news of the first ascent came in. Without ever understanding what had happened, they decamped and bagged some lesser Alps before family connections led them to the fateful soirée at the *Gallerie des Témoins*. This latest diversion was a release for them and they were quite content to spend the rest of the year in Switzerland at their parents' expense.

Harald grew used to acting as foil for Stephen's academic ruminations, delivered by Stephen in Harald's native Bokmål, peppered with bookish idioms and slips into sister languages.

— ...how sensitive to *the order we discovered these ancient texts.* What if we'd known Hittite before Tocharian? Tocharian before Greek? To get on at all you have to trust that once all the evidence is in, the end result will look the same but...

— Have you thought anymore about our own puzzle? interrupted Harald.

Stephen was instantly cautious.

— I have.

— ...and?

— I don't know how to make progress. There are explanations. But for us to espouse any of these wild ideas, for us, as rational creatures, to actually *believe* them... well I think they would have to be less outlandish than the notion that the picture and the gallery were just pure coincidence.

But coincidence was never going to satisfy the group, least of all Clindor, whose iron will brought them back to the dusty theatre day after day.

Then one day Wojciech burst in:

— I have something! he cried, and I don't mean the kettle.

…and indeed he was brandishing a kettle, a cheap chipped scarlet thing with a whistle end. He threw off his overcoat and hurried into the back room to set the kettle on a stove then emerged a minute later with a spider trapped in an upturned glass.

He set it free on the front desk and astonished the group with a third impossibility. As the spider shot away to the edge, Wojciech's eyes twinkled and his moustache bobbed but he leant heavily on his knuckles and beads of sweat formed at his temples. Suddenly the spider careened to a halt then after a pause, began, slowly and awkwardly to *reverse*, retracing every step back into its vitreous prison.

— What just happened, Stephen? whispered Clindor, a flush risen in his taught cheeks.

Stephen looked pallid and sickly and muttered something inaudible.

Anna had turned away as soon as the spider stopped and was hiding behind Pyotr and Lena.

Wojciech, tried to explain his trick. It wasn't instructing, or forcing or persuading, in fact it didn't even seem to Wojciech that it was something *he* was doing at all. Rather it was something that "we" did, he and the spider together. The trick, if there was a trick, was "becoming the we". And that didn't feel like anything he hadn't done a million times before. It was just *what being human was like*. And though he was the oldest of the group, with wisdom forged in the fire of war and the rank mud of battlefields, that was something he could not describe.

Clindor burned with rage, as if this was some kind of evasion. After Wojciech's demonstration he'd turned his back and walked up the aisle steps but now he came bounding down, two at a time, arms out like an angry bear. Somehow it was once again Stephen who had incurred Clindor's rage as Anna looked on in mute fear.

— Give him the words, Stephen! whispered Clindor, capillaries flaring across his face. We must know this!

Harald interposed himself between the two, remembering perhaps the ugly scene at the *Wanderpause.*

— Why not take Wojciech at his word? Stephen asked weakly. The *how* is something in what it's like to be him, which is just what he thought it was like to be human.

Avoiding Clindor's gaze, he turned quickly back to Wojciech.

— But my dear Pan Groshek, why should you think that is impossible to describe? There are very many people who have tried to do exactly what you claim is impossible. To describe what it is like to be human. Even what it is like… just to… *be.* Philosophers, Novelists, Scientists,…

— Poets! added Pyotr.

Quite how it was achieved, Stephen was not clear, but by the end of the session, he had set reading lists for the group and there, right at the top, was the *Lucerne Dialogues* of Professor Templeton. How else could he open their eyes to the world as he was finally convinced it was, if not through the words of *Professor Diocles* himself.

— Anna, calm down! begged Stephen as she shrieked and darted behind Madame Durand's sofa. You'll break something!

Anna decelerated momentarily but then leapt out, scrambling after the boy, Eric, who was mirroring her chaos on the other side of the room.

— Eric, appealed Stephen, Anna, children!

Even Wojciech's placid smile faded when the first projectile shot past his face. A ball, a stone? A sock?

— Anna Irma Wilkes! *Now*! There is glass in here!

The two adults launched themselves into the fray, Stephen clutching desperately at ankles or wrists, Wojciech more methodically, narrowing the angles, cornering Eric in a shrinking net. Anna would not stop giggling. She rolled under a sofa and then popped up behind it:

— CUCKOO! she yelled and darted sideways as Stephen swiped at her.

Wojciech's smile vanished in an instant. He froze and turned on Anna.

— Anna! he shouted. Anna! What did you say?

Her eyes passed from Wojciech to Stephen and back again.

— … cuckoo?

Stephen halted and even Eric skidded to a standstill to watch the old soldier turn fiery. Anna's eyes softened to tears. To have another adult addressing her like this was unusual. What had she done wrong? Except the running. And the climbing. And throwing. And shouting. Had she gone too far?

— Tell me, why did you say that?

— It's… it's a game, she protested.

Wojciech bit his lower lip and winced.

— So it is, he said. A certain type of game. But tell me: what is your understanding of the game of Cuckoo?

Anna's eyes welled up. Eric skulked quietly by the sofa.

— You're supposed to play in the dark, she said.

— Yes?

— And each player has… a gun…

Wojciech hissed.

— Enough. Where did you learn of the game of Cuckoo?

But somehow Stephen knew the answer before it came. Clindor. Wojciech cast a dark glance in Stephen's direction but his colour returned and his moustache relaxed back into its habitual charming droop.

— Okay child, thank you. I'm sorry for upsetting you. Now, Anna, I need to talk with your Uncle Stephen for a bit. Do you think you two can find somewhere a bit safer to play upstairs for a little while?

— Can we play Cuckoo? Without guns?

— If you must.

As the children went upstairs, Stephen prepared himself for the dressing down he assumed was coming, or at for some quiet words of advice, or a stern warning about some aspect of his nascent parenting style.

— This explains much, said Wojciech.

Oh, an ominous start, thought Stephen, waiting for Wojciech to draw some dire inferences for Anna and himself.

— It explains why my enquiries have led nowhere.

— I don't understand.

— No, I wouldn't expect you to. We soldiers, ex-soldiers I suppose, we tend to hear things others don't. Even in retirement, you know, I have friends, old colleagues, there's a grapevine of sorts. And you can imagine how dark are some of the things one hears. You may not have experienced the sweep of human brutality and desperation that emerges in the basest, foulest conditions that soldiers live through, but you're an imaginative man, Stephen, you can't be in much doubt, the things we are all capable of.

Stephen nodded.

— The game of *Cuckoo* is not so interesting in itself, it is one of the kind of freakish horrors that emerge amongst desperate military men who've exhausted all the entertainment they can from hard spirits, prostitutes, aimless brawling. It thrives where drunk violent men share a common death wish and that is more places than you may think. Two blindfolded men in a pitch black room shoot at the cuckoo calls of the other. It kills tens of soldiers a year and maims countless others. No matter. You might even think it beneficial — prunes an element of stupidity from the force you see.

He lowered his voice.

— The reason I find this so interesting, and let us for a second forget the ugliness of introducing the game to a five year old girl, the interesting thing is that I know where and amongst whom the game of cuckoo has most recently taken root.

Stephen abandoned his apprehension and engaged another part of his brain.

— … which would point, you think, to Monsieur Clindor's history?

— … which has till now been invisible, at least to my casual investigations. You see, Cuckoo has become popular over the last few decades amongst the malcontents of the Légion Étrangère.

— The French Foreign Legion?

Even Stephen was aware of the Legion.

— …this means that Clindor might not even be French?

— Oh he is almost certainly French *now*. Citizenship is a reward for service. But it's more significant than that. His real name is almost certainly not Clindor at all. The Legion will give you a new identity, a new life. They'll take you in, wherever you may be, whoever you are, so long as you have a certain sort of youthful malleability, they'll overlook minor indiscretions and they'll give you a new name, a new family. Twenty years later, you come out with French citizenship and the world at your feet, assuming you haven't had your brains shot out playing cuckoo in some pit in Algeria. "Clindor" is nothing but an alias he has chosen himself somewhere in his past.

Stephen wriggled in his chair and tried to make sense of this new information.

— I'm not sure it matters much, he said. After a couple of decades in the legion, it's who he is now that matters isn't it?

Wojciech shrugged.

— Maybe. And that, he said, is a man who shares soldier's pastimes with children.

— I'd better speak to her, said Stephen, rising from his chair and with a bow to Wojciech, making for the stairs.

— By the way, in case it's relevant... called Wojciech behind him, *cuckoo* came over from Russia. With the hordes of White Russians fleeing after the revolution. Half of them ended up in the Legion.

Wojciech was hardly intellectual —how General Giroud would have guffawed at that!— but he'd fought in the Ukraine, Lithuania, Belarus; he'd led raw youths past the corpses of their friends, though walls of bravery and cowardice, and he could still taste the bloody ice in his mouth. If he looked like a jovial walrus, he was nobody's fool. He knew people.

He had rumbled Pierre's painful secret: the heart condition he was concealing from his friends. The boy must have been sick with worry holding the ropes their lives depended on. Wojciech could imagine his loneliness, struggling for breath in the cold sky, counting every heartbeat, fearing any one might betray him. Did he blame himself for their failure at the Eiger?

Worse: when Wojciech had chanced upon the pill bottle it was nearly empty. He had left it well alone but soon found that *Clindor had not*. When a frantic clattering of tins came from the back room, it was only after Clindor slipped in that Wojciech belatedly recognised the racket as Pierre's desperate search for his missing medication. When he got there it was too late. Clindor breezed out with a mysterious smugness and Pierre was gazing into the walls, his face slackened by the transit of some deep emotion, surreptitiously pocketing something that Wojciech could not see.

— Are you alright, Pierre?

— Yes of course.

It was too easy to forget how young these boys were. He'd seen younger bayoneted in pits. He'd seen younger serve in firing squads.

— Pierre, you know don't you, if you need to share troubles, there are plenty of old heads here whom you can trust?

And one, he didn't add, *that you really mustn't.*

More had passed than the return of the last few pills. What further indebtedness had Clindor wrought in that brief time? What had he offered? A fragile promise of discretion? A doctor perhaps? Wojciech could imagine that. *Mention my name.* That would work.

It wasn't just Pierre. If Wojciech was right, Clindor had something on Harald, some ancient indiscretion that anyone but Harald would know Lena would forgive. And with Anna around, Doctor Stephen Harrison could be played like a fiddle. One hint that Anna was being bullied by that stray, Eric, the offered refuge of an empty furnished apartment, and Stephen was all at sea in straits he couldn't navigate.

The blackmail of Wojciech was more subtle and it took him some time to catch the insinuation. The context was the Jewish question, there was a nose-tap, a reference to his rank, and the Battle of Lida. The crux was this: There had been Jew-killings in Lida — not like Pinsk, and not what the Bolsheviks had been up to, but a stain on Poland's honour nonetheless, and on Wojciech's uniform.

Wojciech crumbled on demand, let his face fall and raised abject eyes to the fierce, conspiratorial wink of Clindor.

But *Wojciech had never been in Lida*; the hands soiled in Lida were those of some other Captain Groshek. Clindor had the wrong man.

Wojciech thought back once again to his old friend,

General Giroud, Greta's father-in-law, and remembered the private advice he offered when Wojciech's career began to show signs of life and a desperate need for more political astuteness.

— If they ever think they have something on you, he had told Wojciech, for God's sake allow them to think it. If you don't they'll never stop digging.

Wojciech came out and left a mug of tea on the desk behind Stephen who was standing transfixed by the blank blackboard. He carried another two up the steps between the benches. One he placed pointedly in front of Pierre who sat next to his friends near the front on the left. The other he kept for himself, and he went to sit in an empty bench off to the right behind Harald, Lena and Anna.

Clindor slouched at the back. Pyotr was missing again, though Anna turned frequently to the door as if his arrival was expected.

A cough from the back stirred Stephen into action and, putting chalk to the board, he began to speak his thoughts in short, clipped sentences. He spoke with his back to them and for each sentence, he inscribed a Roman numeral and a short mnemonic.

— The primary act of imagination is creation… All creation is imagination… Without creation there is no recreation… Recreation is creation out of creation… The secondary act of imagination is recreation… The secondary act forever eclipses the primary…

And so on. For those who had read Templeton's *Lucerne Dialogues*, and only Bastien, Wojciech and Lena had persisted far, the axioms were familiar if impenetrable. The others were united in their utter bafflement. Anna fidgeted. Harald scratched his beard.

— The first creation is *Concreta*, the concrete. According to

Professor Templeton, Concreta includes all physical things and maybe more, the raw ingredients of time, space and thought.

Stephen used the side of the chalk to shade a broad stripe across the bottom of the board to represent the concrete. Then with the tip he drew a soup of interlocking circles within the concrete and some arrows groping upward.

— From the concrete, through the act of imagination we have the Paraconcrete…

Anna produced a screechy parrot-like "crawk!" then ducked under the bench when the group turned their attention on her. It broke Stephen out of his concentration but he turned to give her a smile. When she popped back up he put his finger to his lips to shush her and Wojciech realised these two had already shared enough private exploration to develop some private jokes. Stephen turned the chalk sideways to draw another broad layer in his diagram, the target of the arrows that reached up from the concrete, a second *stratum*, the Paraconcrete.

— Every *thing*, every *happening* in the concrete is a component of an infinity of ideas in the Paraconcrete. Every interpretation of every pattern in the concrete becomes a happening in the Paraconcrete. And this is why it is also called *Happenstance*. It is a multiplication of the concrete, and our limited access to it constitutes everything that we think of as the meaning of what exists in the concrete.

Bastien had tobacco tin in front of him and was engaged in a delicate struggle to open it without making any noise. Paul and Pierre were more intent upon his progress than on Stephen's lecture and trying to suppress their mirth. When Stephen turned, Bastien's hands froze and he made a show of paying close attention to the board but as soon as Stephen turned back to the board, he resumed his task.

Stephen was again intent upon his diagram, intoning what

might have been the precepts of a long dead religion. He introduced two more strata above the Paraconcrete, the Divine and the Paradivine, realms of religious truth. Whenever the Paraconcrete was mentioned Anna squawked and giggled and as Stephen's opaque lecture droned on, Paul joined in with her.

Wojciech felt awkward for Stephen. Hoping to bring the excruciating experience to a face-saving end, he opened his mouth to speak but Stephen seemed to anticipate him and moved suddenly in a direction which really did catch everyone's attention.

— Airy nonsense you might think! he cried, turning to face them with a poorly disguised smirk of triumph growing across his face. Until you realise... first, this explains the spiders by providing a route for the transfer of perspective to combination minds... and second, it provides the means by which I am able to do what I have been doing *for the last five minutes.*

Wojciech's jaw dropped. Stephen was speaking, as always, in his light, precise voice. But *his lips weren't moving.* Stephen's voice was in their heads and had been from the very start.

Anna squawked again, once, twice, thrice. It was only Wojciech, sitting behind her, who realised that she too had been squawking in their heads.

When Stephen expounded the "stratal imaginationism" of his mentor, Professor Templeton, it seemed inconceivable that anyone would absorb the metaphysics, least of all the French boys. Paul and Pierre lacked the temperament and though Bastien kept one keen eye on the board, it was only because something struck him as beautiful in the language the Doctor used.

But days later, it was the three of them who turned Stephen's chalk smears into something they could all see.

While the rest of the group experimented with insects, the climbers persuaded Pyotr to join them in a game. Spiders were caught, miniature goals were set out, a halfway line was scratched, a rolled up scrap of paper became a football. The spiders were released and recaptured in invisible bonds by the minds of the young men. Slowly at first, but increasing in confidence, they moved around the pitch in the bodies of their spider hosts. After a few minutes, a goal was scored. Shortly after, the spiders were dribbling, feinting and fouling.

Anna watched them from her bench high up in the lecture theatre, drawing jagged squares and triangles on some pale yellow paper she'd found in the shelves below, colouring with the side of the pencil lead, allowing the cracks and crevices beneath to show through. The effect was like a brass rubbing but revealing instead of a glum monarch the innards of an ancient tree and some crude graffiti, all carefully constrained by geometric bounds she'd set. It took her mind off her annoyance at Pyotr.

And yet even as she looked away and busied herself with her artwork she knew what they were doing. She could feel everything they did with the spiders and the chalk. How, she could not tell, but every foray she predicted and not one feint deceived her. It was something like the raindrops and the growling presence in the storm.

When Paul let out a startled yell, Anna assumed they'd pushed too far. If all their game escaped them it'd serve them right. Paul and Bastien meanwhile, knew they were on the cusp of something. Together they'd glimpsed the same fleeting vision, as if just cresting a hill to find the weather closing in again and the view vanishing.

— There's a *place* there, whispered Paul. We saw it.

They let the spiders go and began to throw out fragmentary phrases, trying to describe what they'd seen. Stephen was with them quickly.

— A place… at the…

— …top?

— …apogee? tried Bastion.

Stephen, in some sort of divine transport, seemed ready to shake the words out of them. Stepping closer, their hands founds each other's shoulders and backs as they would at the start of an ascent. A wordless thought passed between them then the boys closed their eyes and groped with their minds.

— *Happenstance*, murmured Stephen.

When they climbed, Paul would lead the rope first, ranging ahead, testing the routes across traverse and driving pitons into the rock to secure the way for the others. Bastien would take the second turn, Pierre third. This is how they climbed now. Up and outward, struggling to relax their hold on this reality and regather somewhere higher, on the new plane of reality that they could feel waiting for them if they could only somehow hang suspended long enough to wedge in a piton of the mind. They worked together as they would on a rope, sensing each other's progress above and below, waiting at times to regroup and discuss the next attempt. Each push brought them more solidly into another mode of existence, a place where they could be aware of each other and interact without reference to their physical bodies.

Clindor watched from a bench towards the back of the lecture theatre, occupied with his own thoughts.

Stephen kept up a hushed commentary. If the means of expanding one's perspective to include the spider-mind involved transferring the perspective to *Happenstance* and then back into *Concreta* by a different construction, it should be possible to only do the first half, to somehow stay in *Happenstance*. All sorts of theoretical possibilities suggested themselves but Stephen simply couldn't imagine *what it would be like* and he stared at the French boys with undisguised jealousy.

— Red! Something is *red*! exclaimed Bastien as they tumbled down.

This didn't satisfy Stephen at a all.

— Again! insisted Pierre.

With each refinement, their new reality became more vivid. In the moments when they touched it, they began to see each other there too, and were able to wave at each other. But with what arms? What bodies? On each attempt they were able to further defer their fall back into the lecture theatre. Finally they were able prolong their stay indefinitely and come to a kind of rest.

The velvet drapes that surrounded them were the darkling red of a sunset's trailing edge folded over themselves a million times, disappearing overhead into the black vaults of the universe.

Bastien was in a plush velvet chair with a cotton antimacassar embroidered with peonies. His limbs felt fuzzy as if teetering on the edge of a violent cramp and a silent drumbeat of paranoia propelled his gaze around the room. Pierre and Paul, across the room, had said something, but Bastien hadn't caught it.

A shadow in the drapes emerged into the light of a standard lamp.

— M. Clindor! exclaimed Bastien. You were here before us!

Clindor shut a book that he was holding.

— You are too cautious you three.

— He used our ropes, said Paul. Did you not feel it?

Clindor moved around the room, tugging at the curtains and trying to push his arms through to whatever lay beyond.

— Do you recognise the chairs? he asked. Because the fireplace, the mantelpiece and the mirror over there, they are all very old memories of mine. As clear in front of us all now as they have been in the corners of my mind for over forty years. They come from me. But the chairs, the tables, the lamps, the drapes, the carpet, the rugs... they're from someone else.

Soon Wojciech, Harald and Lena were with them.

— You're all sitting down there with stupid looks on your faces, said Harald, gazing up into the gilt-framed mirror.

— The womb! cried Stephen, arriving a moment after Anna, who'd begun to feel left out. *Delphus!* The origin. A handful of us... we could have built any environment of our imagining, probably still can, and what is it we find that really unites us? A yearning to return to the womb.

Then paroxysmal, stuttering sniffs shattered the silence. Anna was crumpled in floods of tears on the sheepskin rug. In an instant, Stephen was down next to her and as she held him tight, head to his chest, she moaned loudly and let her crying free itself of all restraint, let the shaking, gasping cries crescendo to wailing pitch. He held her tight, whispered, shushed, comforted as the others winced at each other. She was such a young child. Of course this was all too much for her. How could they have been so insensitive? But as Anna calmed in Stephen's arms, as her spasms of gulping and sniffing became more sparse, Stephen shook his head.

— The armchairs, he whispered hoarsely, his own voice dying in the back of his throat. They were her mother's.

14. The Way Head

Martoth, Timoth

— You didn't really explain *anything* you know, said Timoth peevishly, watching Weakjohn thrust her bare arm into the mouth of the market hall's waterboar.

The waterboar was sculpted from mountain larch that had darkened with age and polish. It was many times larger than the real thing and, when Timoth wasn't looking directly at it, it gave the unsettling impression it was bursting *through* the back wall. The artist had spurned the hackneyed idioms of slavering and snapping, but a smouldering ferocity remained behind its narrow eyes, intended to warn off any who would cheat or steal or otherwise undermine the marketplace.

He set down his bags and pulled himself up to sit on the nearest table. It was a day of "quiet" and all the markets were closed. Weakjohn had allowed Martoth to wander off into town but seemed serious about confining Timoth to the attic so a few minutes in this grand empty hall was welcome.

— I botched the lesson, she sighed.

— By like tearing a hole in the world as I recall.

She stiffened with her back to Timoth. He wasn't sure whether he'd offended her or whether she'd found whatever she was looking for.

— It got better? he suggested, feeling the need to mollify her.

— That wasn't me, Timoth. It's the sort of thing people like me *could* do. Or people like *you*. But I didn't do it.

They were both silent for a bit. Timoth reckoned that the thing that kept him from pestering with questions, the sheer number to choose from, was the same thing that stumped Weakjohn. "How to start..." she'd said yesterday. She hadn't solved it yet.

With a cry of jubilation, Weakjohn extracted her arm, and before Timoth could even make out what she'd drawn out, she'd flung it to him, in a great looping arc, and he'd caught it instinctively.

— What is it? he asked, finding a wooden ball in his hands. It was the size of clenched fist, smooth and dark as the waterboar, but covered with a network of blackening curves and symbols that seemed to be burned into its surface.

— An antique, she said, motioning him to pick up the bags and follow her back up to the attic.

— OK. So what is it? he asked again.

— It is a pretty potent symbol of the situation we're in, she sighed.

— So what—

— Give me a chance! she snapped.

It took the ascent of both sets of stairs and the ladder, and for Weakjohn to empty the cotton bags and lay out all the food and to begin making sandwiches, for both of them to calm down. Eventually she spoke, again without turning or breaking off from her work.

— I am not a teacher Timoth but do I have a good idea of where I need to get to.

He mumbled an apology and went to look out of the window.

— We won't follow the Vigil curriculum, which, for your information, consists of the three pillars of Perspectivals, Tetrarchy, and Allpsyche. If you feel those categories are still a mystery to you after I have finished then please pester away.

He held his tongue.

— We call ourselves mindworkers, she said. Most of us are Vigil-trained, but occasionally others pop up. And, like I said, the dividing line is fuzzy. Without us, I don't know what the world would be like.

She finished chopping up the cured buckmeat and began to saw the rice bread into thick slices. She had an array of knives and boards to work with that Timoth had never seen outside the taproom's kitchens. Most Border folk made do with one knife for all their needs. Even those with a room of their own rarely accumulated more than a couple. Weakjohn had been here for a long time and acquired many things.

— I was born on Semele, Timoth, a first generation migrant. I hid that wooden ball in the boar's mouth when I was six Semele-years old. By the time I was seven, I was living a different life on a different world and I never saw my family again. At the Abbey, I learned what I know through a process of education that today I regard as a beautiful gift, even if it ranged from insensitive to brutal. One of the first things I learned is that the map that you are holding in your hands, which I'd once thought was the most beautiful and powerful object that could ever exist, was a worthless antique.

Timoth looked at it again. The wood was stained and smooth from handling that could never have occurred during fifty years hidden.

— This is much older than that…

— It is. It predates the crises. It may even predate the first migrations. I don't know how old it is. I've many, many times thought about checking to see if it was still there. It's not accident I chose to live here.

A life before the Vigil would be a life ended by the Vigil. Timoth didn't need to ask why she'd never tried to retrieve the ball.

— And now…?

— Now, said Weakjohn, it might not be worthless anymore.

— The way we travel between worlds is the same way mindworkers can travel on a world from place to place, instantaneously and without passing physically through the space in between. We call it "Travel In Concreta", or ticcing for short. Marta was the expert. I remember parties where she was always vanishing and reappearing all over the place, which was great fun at the time but not so much the next morning. Thing is: when you tic between worlds you need a pretty good idea of your route. You have to piggyback on landmarks in the universe, some natural, some artificial that are laid out in just such a way to allow you to pass through. The map in your hand is a very early map of these features, the leys and hubs. It has all the Tier Ones on it but few of the further worlds so I think it must have been used by pre-migration pioneers.

— But that sounds *really* useful!

— A map is only useful if you can't see the things it's mapping out directly. And for all the time I've been alive human mindworkers have had that ability, mostly because of the sheer amount of stuff we've built, not just hubs and leys, but oracles that broadcast thought, lines to communicate, cylinxes to augment and amplify and so on. All this architecture is part of what we call the Allpsyche.

She looked triumphant, having hit one of the pillars of the Vigil curriculum almost by accident.

— Problem is it's all melting before our eyes. I haven't been able to contact the Abbey for a fortnight now and I can't see far into the leys anymore.

She gave him a meaningful look and he raised the ball up to the window.

— This is connected to the rips?

Weakjohn wiped her hands and came over to the window to take the ball from Timoth. She held it carefully between finger and thumb and revolved it with her other hand, barely breathing, remembering perhaps how she found it and what it meant to her a lifetime ago.

— A couple of weeks ago there was… an event. We'd call it a *storm*, but not of thunder and lightning, a storm in the Allpsyche. Most people wouldn't have been aware of it, though they probably had a horrible, fearful day. You will have noticed something.

Timoth cast his mind back. There was a dark day he remembered, full of headaches and arguments, fights in the taproom. In his memory, the sky was like the dimness of evening all day long although he'd not noticed it at the time.

— On a day like that, I found this, she said, her voice dropping to a whisper. It was discarded by the way head. I wasn't meant to be there so I kept it secret.

— The Allpsyche is not simply a landscape, it is full of change, weather, echoes, ripples, subsapient minds like spins, chanters and of course us… The Vigil observe it all very carefully; it's what Marta and I did out here. But nobody saw this storm coming. When we tried to report it, we couldn't. It took the both of us two days to get a line and when we did it only lasted a minute. What we did get though was Abbot Barnabas himself. What he told us then about the attacks and the damage, is all I know now because that was our last contact.

Barnabas had told them of a spate of attacks that had

rained down upon the Vigil. He'd explained a link they'd quickly established that mindwork that seemed to trigger them. He'd told them the curious fact that long dormant sensors across the universe had begun to register the signature of Diocletian again, with readings that had not been seen since Diocletian was unquestionably alive.

— So the theory is, said Weakjohn, that he's back. And he's trying to destroy us.

She placed the starball back in his hand and gestured that he could keep it.

— A few minutes after we lost Barnabus, Weakjohn continued, Marta suddenly went *"shit! the kid out west making all that noise!"*

Weakjohn continued to bustle around, tidying and packing bags, while Timoth rolled the starball back and forth on the low table where they'd sat last night.

— Yesterday you mentioned "Diocletian Orthodoxy".

— I did. Pretty much everything we know was discovered or formulated by Diocletian. He started publishing his theories sometime in the middle of the twentieth century and continued through the first migrations up to about seventy years ago.

— Who was he?

— He was a genius who opened our minds to the fluidity of perspective and nature of the tetrarchy. Before him we were mindblind.

— Yeah but—

— We don't know! snapped Weakjohn. We don't know who he was, what he looked like, where he lived, what he ate for breakfast or very much about him at all. He published some early works in traditional forms — books, broadcasts — but nothing easily traceable and most of his output now is found in a form he created — *oracles*. They're built into the allpsyche itself, continually publishing thoughts right out into the world. Many more oracles have been built since which incorporate all his material and publish it out again. Once you know how to look you'll see we're swimming in all these works of Diocletian, even if there has been nothing new for seventy years.

While she was talking Timoth had done a little arithmetic.

— He was publishing for well over a hundred years.

Weakjohn frowned.

— That upset some people.

He waited expectantly.

— You don't realise yet how brittle this all is, Timoth. All these words mean the same thing — universe, manifold, flux, allpsyche, humanity… If I'm talking about noumena, I call it the *manifold*. If I'm talking about perspective, I call it the *flux*. If I'm talking about the weather, or infrastructure, I call it the *allpsyche*. Other times, I'll say *universe*. Sometimes I'll say *humanity*. It's all the same damn thing.

— Humanity?

— Same damn thing. All of these things are our human conception of what is. Outside of humanity everything is different in ways that we can't even conceptualise. It's not an understatement to say if humanity disappears, or dissolves, or becomes… muddied, all of everything else disappears or dissolves too. Protecting humanity, ensuring that humanity survives in a world where we're spread further apart than we can see in the night sky, means protecting our notion of humanity, which is the same as protecting the universe, everything that is. So there are boundaries that must not be tested.

— You mean things we were never meant to mess with.

— …one essential part of humanity being mortality.

— So now you're telling me immortality is enough of a thing there are people who have to be *anti-immortality*?

— And it's not just neglecting to die that's problematic:

there's also reincarnation, transmigration of the soul, the permanent departure from concrete body we call "emergence", duplications, permanent fusions and fissions… There are precepts prohibiting all these things for Vigilants.

— Wait, reincarnation is a thing too?

— And infinite variations upon it. The world is a terrifyingly fluid thing, Timoth. The Vigil looks after the stability we need to survive.

— But this stuff is forbidden only to Vigilants?

— We can hardly forbid anybody else from doing anything.

But she broke eye contact and Timoth guessed they weren't so shy of intervening as all that.

When Timoth confessed his feelings of guilt and revulsion, her first suggestion was *backsnap* but it didn't entirely fit. Backsnap was a price paid after mindwork, not a sensation accompanying every thought of it. *Backsnap and being a teenager* was her next attempt. Timoth gave her a venomous glare.

— Backsnap is the most obvious cost of mindwork, she said. Change the world in any way that involves perspectival shift and a balance needs reasserting. Usually you take it physically but you can work it out in other ways too. It's hard to predict and heavily dependent on the fickle nature of the manifold. It doesn't always correspond to your idea of the magnitude of what you're doing. Sometimes you get lucky, sometimes you're wiped out. The big mistake is thinking it's the only cost.

She was hinting darkly at something she didn't want to have to explain but Timoth was feeling raw and not inclined to let her off the hook.

— Always remember that the shape of the world is the shape of the human mind. The very notion of what we are gives rise to the tetrarchy we live in. Doing things outside the realm of our old-fashioned idea of what humans are capable of, it all changes our idea of humanity and our understanding of what we are and bit by bit it changes the world around us into something we don't understand. It all sounds very general and hard to trace back to individual actions and it is, but it's very real. It applies to individuals as well as the world. You may have seen elderly people for whom the world has changed so much from the world they learned to live in that they're a fraction of what they once were. The same thing can happen to mindworkers even when they're very young because they've accelerated it for themselves.

— It all sounds hopeless, said Timoth. We know we can do these things but we need to live in a world we can only have by pretending they are impossible.

— It's a delicate and very dynamic balancing act, she said, and that's what the Vigil is for: the defence of humanity. And since humanity became mindwoke it's had to be a very active defence.

While Timoth tried to gauge whether this was a sign of the Vigil's significance or the Vigil's arrogance, an abrupt change came over Weakjohn. She appeared distracted and concerned.

— I need to go and meet Martoth, she said. Stay here.

The mist was rising and turning to rain as Weakjohn and Martoth moved around the edge of the wreckage. They trod carefully amongst the charred flakes of larch and the growing puddles of rainwater. This was the spot where the first travellers to Semele had arrived, three or four generations back, and where the whole way of life Martoth knew had started from.

As the wide, broken circle of burnt wood walls unrolled upwards beneath the rising mist and as she stepped across into the sodden turf in the centre, she felt a sense of alienation she'd never felt before. As if the little of her life that did fit her was now threatening to unseat her too. She felt strangely detached from the enquiries Weakjohn had made on her behalf. No-one could be traced. No-one had been seen. She had travelled a long way from her life with no mother and father to find she had, after all, no mother and father, just somehow more irrevocably. The grand mystery of Semele had unfolded into a soggy quidditch pitch.

— Do you know what this is?

— Spaceship landing ground, she snarked idly.

— "Ark" might be more fitting than "ship". How many people do you think you could fit in here? Five, ten thousand?

— Probably more if they all stayed really still.

As well as the fire damage to the walls, the earth in the centre had been churned up over an area the size of Mulkah's taproom with chunks of earth rising to several feet in places. Even with the mist clearing, this wet mess of soil and grass had an unsettling mixed-upness about it. At the very centre, Martoth could see yet more wreckage. Strewn about in the middle, the dull metal and splinters of cracked timber all lay ravaged by competing discolourations of fire, rain and mud.

— They did, they had help with that. The best mindworkers of the time could move twenty thousand people at the same time. But there were billions on Earth. By the time humanity reached Semele, the closing of the ways was already complete and Earth was lost to us forever. The people who came here came via two worlds called The Leap and New Gobi.

— I've heard of The Leap.

— Good. New Gobi wasn't occupied for long but it was important in its day.

They edged further in from the ruined boundary.

— Semele's never been important?

Weakjohn gave a half-hearted laugh.

— Not like the ones we call the Tier Ones, the ones we migrated to from Earth.

— So what happened here?

— And to who?

Weakjohn followed Martoth's gaze to the churned up earth in the middle. The stains might be blood.

— Yes. We'd best have a look.

She rested her stick against her hip while she wiped her hands on her jacket and inspected her fingernails.

— Now Martoth, be cautious. These things can be hazardous and they can hurt you in ways you don't understand yet. Non-physical ways, emotional ways. Think of nightmares but also with the power to hurt you physically. I don't know whether this thing is malignant, I don't know if it is sentient though I doubt it. If you feel afraid, stand next to me and hold my shoulder. If it moves, stand behind me. Let's see what we can see.

— If it *moves*?

Weakjohn shrugged.

— At this point we don't know anything.

— Everything okay?

Timoth spun round guiltily but he knew that Weakjohn's voice was in his head. He was still alone in her attic surrounded by the jumble of odds and ends an elderly weaver-woman might need for a working life on Semele.

— Just talk aloud, she said, no-one downstairs pays any attention.

— Where are you? he asked out loud.

— We're at the way head. I think we might be about to find something unpleasant and I think it would be a very good idea if we were all together quite soon. Could you come to meet us?

— Errr… sure. Where? I mean I don't know anywhere?

— Ask George downstairs. Get him to direct you to The Tap and Spile. We'll be under the canopy.

Timoth's mind raced. Weakjohn's level of concern struck him as odd. He hadn't figured she would be quite so protective of Martoth. Surely there was nothing Martoth had done or said to suggest she was sensitive enough to tiptoe around. Was there something else on the cards here? What did Weakjohn think they were going to find?

The canopy at the Tap and Spile was a lightweight roof of wood and canvas which covered fifty or so square wooden tables, each with benches on four sides. As Timoth arrived and ducked under out of the rain it was heaving. It was standing room only, and precious little of that, as he slid into the crowd amid the steaming breath and bodies, searching for Martoth and Weakjohn. As well as serving the public house, it was a popular local venue for meetings and other events and, even in the thick bustle, Timoth could already discern a few areas under the canopy where a denser knit of bodies signalled gatherings intent on more than just drinking. Just as in the market hall, he noticed that everybody was armed, and the snippets of overheard voices and the living current of unseen shoves and unyielding bodies impressed a deep sense of tension on Timoth.

— Turn left, said Weakjohn in his mind. We're sitting against the pub wall. Don't get involved in anything. This was a mistake.

He obeyed, hastening his progress by diving through the rain-drenched spaces the crowds avoided where the canvas had torn overhead. Each time his scalp tingled as he came out of the rain and it evaporated off him. He found it remarkable at first that these gaps had been left at all, so dense was the crowd. Then he realised it wasn't available shelter that defined how the people were packed under the canopy. All around, people were pressing inwards towards speeches, arguments, angry disputes.

Fifteen yards into the crowd his way was blocked outright. A tight knot of young men was intent upon a speaker whom Timoth could hear but not see. His cautious attempts to insinuate himself forwards through the crowd were rebuffed with obvious irritation so he stopped for a time.

— ...because you, said the speaker, you are the *cherished*. It is you and the beast world. And it's time to stop letting the beast world rule you...

The voice was young, impassioned and attractive.

— ...how much do you know of our history? Our real history, before we came to Semele? Of the billions of innocents who died trying to reach worlds like ours? Died in the beast world they had created.

Weakjohn's voice came loud in his mind.

— Away from there Timoth. Back three paces and off towards the big chimney stove and there's a route around them there. Don't get involved. Find us and we're going to leave immediately.

He did as she commanded but listened carefully as he passed through the crowd.

— ...even now the beast world has its claws into us. The sins that angered the jealous god of reality, those sins we are committing again, and not just out there in the mysterious sprawl of humanity. I mean here, now in Laketown. Among us....

As he moved, these words, "the cherished", rose out of the crowd several times. There were others too: "coin", "fury", "murder", "truth", "pure", "toil", powerful, simple words, words that condemn injustice, that promise dissent. Timoth had no experience of the sort of thing that was at work here but he had some emerging intuition for the working of the human mind and he could feel the thoughts emerging and meshing here in a single common purpose, an animus crawling around in the tent, stalking something or someone.

— Quickly, Timoth!

He found them crammed tight together behind empty saki cups on a table near the pub wall, with Weakjohn engaged in some strained smalltalk with a few idle drinkers. It looked like Martoth had been crying —a rare thing in Timoth's experience— and recently too for her face was now set in a obstinate grimace. Without a seat, he squatted down between them and the creeper-clad wall and they turned inward, backward, toward him.

— The way head's abandoned, said Weakjohn, but still dangerous. There was an attack.

Martoth was silent. Timoth nodded.

— You said we had to leave.

— Yes, we have to go. But not back to the attic. Things are turning nasty here and you and I, Timoth, we need to be careful. I'm going to take us to a quiet place.

— In town?

— Just outside, she said. I'll go first, I need to get our packs out of the attic somehow. You sit here, Timoth, and in ten minutes or so you both get up to go.

They nodded solemnly.

— Which way? asked Martoth.

— I'll let Timoth know where to meet, whispered Weakjohn, leaning inwards. While I'm gone, you bring him up to speed. If there's any trouble at all, just go.

Weakjohn rose, assessed the crowd around her, pulled her walking stick out from under the table, climbed awkwardly over the bench, and then stopped to look down at the two of them as Timoth took her place.

— Oh, and, she added, with mischief in her eye. Stay *very* close to each other.

* * *

Timoth didn't want to ask. So he didn't.

— So then, was all he said.

She was close against him on the bench, her arm against his, her thigh against his, their ankles, no, their heels, touching, gently, accidentally.

— My father died at the way head.

— Oh shit fuck. I'm sorry.

They weren't looking at each other. They were too close. If they turned to face each other, they'd be… But there was something else. Something more than context, something that wasn't just local colour for the tragedy. Something more than Martoth's ever-growing loss. Something more she had to tell him but didn't want to.

They sat staring at their saki cups, ignoring the jostling about them, ignoring the ominous crescendo of the hubbub under the canopy.

— Timoth, he was with…

A second or two, suspended in nothingness and then Timoth froze; his blood drained to his feet and his head spun. Because he knew. He knew now what was coming.

— Timoth, Jessic was there too.

What was inexplicable to Timoth was not so to Martoth.

— It's my fault, she said, as she hauled him off the bench and pushed him towards the street.

It wasn't an apology. He didn't know why he imagined it should be. Or why he thought she thought it might be. His relationship with Jessic was a non-thing between them. Not spoken of. Nor even hinted at. And in the light of everything, now, it seemed curiously inert. Insignificant, irrelevant. Compare what Jessic's father would feel when Weakjohn's message found him.

I should be crying or screaming, he thought. And if they weren't running from whatever menace Weakjohn kept hinting darkly at, he'd probably gather himself and put together a little self-serving melodrama. But in truth he hadn't worked out yet what Jessic meant to him and now was not the time.

— I knew he was here, she said. I asked her to find him. It's my fault.

— Where were they going?

She shook her head. She didn't know. But his own words came back to his mind: *off-world tales, foreign gossip…*

— She took her chance, he said.

— *With my father*?

— We don't know anything.

15. Theremy

Seronin

— *Ellany?*

Ellany was a backwater, a tier-nothing world — a rock, some foul air and a Vigil outpost. The only reason for the outpost was its very remoteness. The Vigil simply hadn't found anywhere further out they could keep a station running. If the tip-off was from Ellany then their search was over. There was never more than a single soul on Ellany.

— Do we know who's posted there? asked Seronin.

Lethe shook his head. It would not be a sought-after posting, that one, and the entry requirements were probably stiff. The Vigil might award it for endeavour, but more likely for misconduct.

They were in *Happenstance* again, this time in a construction of Seronin's, a wood-panelled study with a broad, leather-top writing desk. An antique telephone stood on one side table, a decanter and a set of crystal glasses on another. There was a chair behind the desk but Seronin always avoided it. Lethe and Candle sat in front of the desk and Seronin slouched against a wall.

Despite the panelling, the room was airy because it was

bathed in natural light: the wall behind the desk was taken up by a large window that looked out over a wide, windswept wetland. In the marble sky, birds of many types flocked and swarmed. Here and there, others sheltered in island nests or waded in the shallows. Lethe knew each bird meant something. Each was a representation of something in *Concreta* but Seronin had never explained what. Lethe saw what he wanted to see in the window: a meditation on the lost Earth, its wildlife, its diversity. In reality it mapped the new reach and sparsity of humanity in the universe but the mapping was ineffable. Seronin had found the construction by intuition and he never felt he understood it.

— We've lost our normal comms, said Lethe. We don't know what's going on inside.

He paused, uncertain:

— Official channels are still available though, if you fancy a chat with Abbot Barnabas.

— I'm fed up obsessing about what the Vigil think, said Seronin.

There was a challenge behind his words. *We have the evidence, we saw the rips, the puppetised girl, we can map the allpsyche. Why should we need the Vigil?* But Seronin was never as sure as he sounded.

— Can we even get a line to Ellany anyway? said Seronin.

This question preoccupied Lethe for a minute or two.

There were networks and linkages crisscrossing the allpsyche even before humanity woke. Just living, breathing, treading the normal paths of human interaction shaped these structures. From resonances and entanglements to the ways and leys, they were all around us and human minds navigated them accidentally all the time. Humans explained, or explained away, in the habit of millennia but all mental life was lived amidst this fabric of connections.

Then, with the awakenings in the twenty-first century,

these meshes flourished and intertwined. The closing of the ways which left the dying Earth stranded was really the congealing of these mental highways around our mother planet.

But, away from the smothered Earth, this architecture of the allpsyche was the world that mindworkers lived in, the routes they followed, the oracles they tapped, the leys they'd built, the hubs they'd connected. And now it was all being laid waste. The allpsyche was disintegrating around their ears.

A month ago, talking to someone in Ellany would have been routine for Seronin, even though Ellany was at the frontier of the explored universe and establishing the necessary construction of simultaneity would have been fiendishly difficult. Now, with so much in ruins?

Lethe went limp in *Happenstance* as he shifted his perspective up into *Sanctum*.

— You have a theory? asked Candle.

Seronin frowned, unstoppered the decanter and raised it to his nose.

— Sure, he said. A very widespread coldwake context. And a trigger.

Candle's face soured and she straightened in her chair.

— *Computation*? You're saying a *program* is encoded somehow across the galaxy. And a million minds are spawning to execute it.

Her distate was evident but Seronin was too tired to tiptoe around Candle's sensitivities.

— It could be more sophisticated, he said, but it doesn't have to be. You wake, you understand, you act. Even if you're subsapient. Even if your one and only act is blazing a noumenal rip through the nearest mindworker.

— But how could any context be that widespread?

— I can think of at least two ways, he said. The cosmic

background and the platonics.

— Oh, don't be—

The telephone rang.

And all of a sudden, Lethe was alert and grinning at them.

— Your call, he said to Seronin.

Seronin put the decanter down and raised an impressed eyebrow at Lethe. He lifted the telephone's earpiece.

— Hello? came the scratchy low-fi rasp of a human voice, distorted by an immense and unimaginable medium.

The voice offered a new construction.

Seronin shifted.

Seronin jumped at a loud beep. A white arm was pushing an arched fencing foil into his chest.

— Yow! he complained and flicked it away with his own foil.

He backed up a few yards and tried to suppress his irritation. Through their gauze helmets Seronin could hear his adversary's snigger.

Seronin threw his foil to the ground and tore off his own mask.

— Bad day at the office? he asked.

The office would be a hangar on a bleak alien rock. There would be no company but a raucous menagerie of captive spins and there would be a frightening dependence on cylinx-augmentation to keep it habitable. All so that the Vigil could measure every fine-grained fluctuation in the soupy psychic evidence of humanity's past and present. Seronin reminded himself to be tolerant.

— It's been tough, came the muffled reply. The adversary did not remove his helmet but he did set his foil down. The mask annoyed Seronin. There was no guarantee a face in *Happenstance* would match the face in *Concreta* anyway. Why hide?

— I can find out who you are, said Seronin.

— Great. That's all I need you for.

He lifted the helmet off and shook loose a blond pony tail, then raised his eyes to Seronin. He was young, much younger than Seronin had expected, maybe only twenty, but it was his eyes that surprised. They were pale, glassy blue but with a depth that recalled the fading eyes of the elderly.

— You're a fusion! exclaimed Seronin.

The youngster nodded:

— My name is Theremy. And before you ask, I don't remember any more than Merrick did.

— Let us get you out!

— I don't want out! protested Theremy. I've worked hard to change things. I believe in the Vigil. Unlike some. And there are others. I won't desert them.

He turned away. Seronin considered the anonymous source who'd alerted them to Merrick's plight. That he'd be senior enough to run his own contribution had occurred to Seronin. That he could manage that as a non-natural human was mind-boggling.

— A fusion running obs in Ellany. How in the flux do you keep that hidden?

— We're not all as observant as the great Seronin, said Theremy, his face darkening. And now there are other distractions.

Seronin removed his gloves and opened the buttons at his neck.

— So what does the Vigil think is happening?

Theremy motioned him to follow and they stepped off the fencing piste, and approached a great oak door at the edge of the hall. Theremy pushed it open and they passed out onto a grassy hilltop. The slope looked towards the East where a liquid dawn was spreading across the sky. Below them a cedar forest thickened into a dense gloom as it marched into the distance. A bench rested against the wall of the hall. Above he could hear bats roosting in the eaves. They sat to watch the sky.

— What have you seen? asked Theremy.

— The storm hit when I was down with Merrick, with an enormous noumenal tear that killed most of his class. There was a rip too in my cabin, in empty space. Then a girl was puppetised and attacked me on Tiberia. And we can all see the ways and the leys are fraying.

— That's all?

— It's worse?

— Much worse. I'm only in contact sporadically, I don't have the latest. We've had forty or fifty fatalities, more casualties and the channels are failing. We've got all sorts of attacks, rips, puppetisations, darkspins, maybe even spearspins. Attacks in the Abbey and the stations, some in The Leap, Schiller, Tenistan, Chornymir... Mostly mindworkers or mindwoke, but not all... there is dangerous weather everywhere you look. Infrastructure damage is mainly the weather and the pressure but it looks weirdly selective. I've had rips on Ellany. I've had to destroy some of the equipment.

Seronin whistled.

Theremy stiffened suddenly and turned a face full of horror to Seronin.

— Ohmygod, he cried. Helpmeohmygod!

Seronin reached for him, rising from the bench, but Theremy had already vanished. He was in trouble on the other side of the galaxy, and Seronin knew if he got it right, he could get there in time. He loosened his perspective from the Happenstance construction and analysed it for the routes he needed, the thinnest of ways that Lethe had plotted and that Theremy had embedded in the construction. As Theremy vanished, Seronin downshifted to his cabin and prepared his psyche for the first of a thousand microsecond hops.

Seronin tumbled over Theremy into a dim grey chamber, taking something hard, a knee or elbow, to the face. He shot up some camouflage before rolling to a standstill. There were only two possibilities: another attack or a Vigil purge. Either way he didn't want to be seen.

The air was thin and he fought hard to get enough oxygen to start with. Almost without realising it, he made a few adjustments to his lungs and airways to compensate. The walls were stacked with warehouse shelving holding the arrays of captive spins and other sensors that Theremy was responsible for running. There would be a cylinx somewhere but Seronin couldn't sense it.

Three forms in black cassocks stepped out of the shadows on the other side of the chamber. *A purge then.* Their faces were hidden by hoods but their minds loomed large in the flux. One, Seronin recognised all too well. Sounness! The vicious right hand of Abbot Barnabas.

Had Theremy's cover failed at last? Seronin was struck by a sudden fear about the conversation they had just shared. It couldn't be a coincidence. Then, disgusted with himself, he remembered the bats under the eaves. Had they intercepted and poisoned the construction? What had they heard? Had he been recognised?

Theremy was shaking on the floor and his arms were jerking backwards as if someone was trying to truss them behind his back. His head smashing repeatedly against the floor and his legs kicked violently. Seronin assessed the attackers. Sounness was the danger — probably the best noumenist since Diocletian and aggressive as a pestered wasp. The other two, the two compelling Theremy in his tortures, were nothing. Seronin could stop their hearts and splay their minds before they even noticed him. If he was willing to show himself. He sensed their lack of will. They were not here by choice. This was forced upon them like a rite of passage. Seronin carried with him the shame of his own participations. He had no desire to kill them.

He made a quick decision. He fused with the air itself and unleashed a massive rip, scarring the fabric of reality from his finger tips to the space above the vigilants' heads. The noise was deafening and the chamber lit up in the scar's glittering corona. The juniors staggered back terrified. Sounness stayed forward and Seronin was aware of a gathering pressure in the flux.

Straining again, Seronin used another fusion to extend spurs out the rip and to twist its corona to make the edge look unstable. *Let them believe it's a ripspin.* It was a long shot, and it would never fool Sounness for long, but it might just give them pause.

Sounness looked confused but he barked some order at the others and in a second all three were gone, leaving Seronin kneeling over Theremy, and the Ellany observatory lit in the pulsating orange-green of the scar.

— Lethe, spoke Seronin down the merest hint of a link that his mind was still holding. Lethe, for flux sake please be listening, get him outta here.

Seronin watched the flux, zeroing in on every oscillation, every slight perturbation, quickly learning to discount the chaos of the captive spins on the shelves. If mindwork triggered the attacks, *anything* could happen now. The air was still in the chamber, but he could hear a quiet wavering howl as the fierce Ellany winds buffeted the outside and a constant rustle which must be disturbance from the instruments.

— There's something you don't know yet, said Theremy, clutching suddenly at Seronin's hand. In the storm, the sensors that tipped… They… *We didn't even know they were still working.*

He pointed up into the shelving. There were tears in his deep eyes but his voice was steady.

— It was the ones that haven't murmured for seventy years. They're museum pieces.

— Seventy years? You mean *Diocletian*?

— No-one knows how. But the same sensors tipped everywhere, from Pamyatnik to The Leap. Wherever we look, across the whole universe there has been an explosion of Dioclete mentality, a concentration a million times more intense than the cosmic background. And its all correlated to our simultaneity nets. It's a human phenom—

Theremy disappeared, translated along countless feathery leys to who knows where — wherever Lethe could stow him safely.

Pushing off the impending backsnap, Seronin, wiped cold sweat from his brow, and turned to face the rip, wondering if he dared stay to fix it.

Theremy woke to the sound of canvas flapping in the wind and the smell of wet undergrowth around him. A peg had come loose and the warm tent-light was yielding to the pale morning outside. He crawled out from under a pile of thick, fur blankets and forced the peg back into the earth with the heel of his hand.

— Where is my body? he asked.

— Right now, answered Lethe from somewhere outside, you have none. Don't panic. You're whole and safe. And out of the Vigil's reach. We are still working on the next step.

A thin rumbling rode in on the breeze, trailing a wave of moist air that caused Theremy to shiver. He rose onto his knees and rubbed some warmth back into his goose-pimpled arms.

— You might want to take a peep outside, said Lethe. It's spectacular.

Theremy groaned, chose a blanket to wrap around his shoulders, then drew back a door flap and hauled himself out onto his feet. The day was fresh and damp but the thin wisps of morning mist drew only the slenderest of veils over the view below them. From the far tip of an outcrop, Lethe surveyed the landscape beneath. Theremy picked a path through the thick bracken and windswept wildflowers, over the rocks, out onto the jutting platform to join him and what he saw stole his breath for many moments.

The breeze washing over their faces was hot with smoke and aromatic with strains of cookery and humanity, roasting meat, burning bay leaves, onions, then sweat and human bodies, the merest hint of sewage, and an organic earthen note that seemed to underlie it all. Below them flickered a million flames, camp fires each of them, stretching out to the horizon and beyond. In the dawn light, a glorious ideal of an army mustered and murmured. The rumbling in Theremy's ears was a sponge of voices, billowing fabric, squelching mud, and steel on stone.

The energy and inwardness that rose off the men seemed almost solid in the sky below, as if Theremy could stride out onto it. He imagined it: his one leading foot, toe to the void, trembling, hovering a deadly distance aloft, groping for the support of this invisible offering. Then, support granted, a wild, listing race out onto the roof of a world, the world of these men's fear and apprehension.

— Why are they gathering? asked Theremy.

— I don't know, said Lethe. But I doubt it's a coincidence. We're here because of her.

— Her?

Theremy looked again and this time let his mind withdraw to a vantage point more remote. He gasped.

— *Grace!*

Lethe smiled.

— Where better to tuck you away for a day or two while we get ready for the onward journey?

The Vigil's savagery festered at the fringes of their attention, where what they cared about petered out into the broader spectrum of what they knew about. In their blessed ideal of natural humanity there was no space for the near-human, the humanlike, anything they could see as poison in the veins of what it meant to be human. But more alien minds, minds further out in the spectrum of infinite variety, minds like Grace, the Vigil could not and did not proscribe. The world had always contained animals.

And yet minds they were, and more varied and more numerous than humanity, however you accounted. And some, like Grace, were large.

So the Vigil knew of Grace, watched her, measured her, even explored her without horror or disgust. They knew what she was; their minds met, briefly, warily, from time to time, across the stars, but in the main she didn't figure in their thinking.

But in her way, she was human too: one of the earliest epiphenomena of human systematisation to shear off her roots and replicate herself onto a new substrate. Her precise origin was long forgotten. She had been an economy once, each thought, each spark of emotion a grotesquely complex interaction of the desires and computations of consumers, traders, speculators, bankers. Which markets, which goods, which century, no-one knew. How long had she been self-aware? How long since she freed herself from these roots? Not even Grace knew that. But she was older than the Vigil, older than Lethe, older than Barnabas.

Theremy was dizzied by the sheer scale of the mind in

front of him. Such complexity. Such glory.

— Can I speak to her?

— You're a free human, Theremy.

— But is she…?

Lethe turned to Theremy with cautionary glance that conveyed both surprise and respect. *Rather you than me*, was that it? Lethe pointed out a narrow, natural stairway, some way off, that led down the face of the cliff.

— How are your circadia?

— Stable and locked in to Ellany-cycle I think.

— OK. We'll signal in two Ellany days from now. Prepare when you get the signal. Seronin will be taking you for the next leap. Till then, I'm going to leave you to it. And you can spend your time however you want.

Lethe looked once more upon the army beneath and then was gone.

Theremy made off through the wafting breeze to the narrow stairway.

16. Barn Attack

Martoth, Timoth

It was a disused rice warehouse, barn-sized, and set back some yards into the woodland by the road that led North to Greater Semele. From the way the undergrowth had returned anyone would have thought it abandoned, even though the structure was sound, the windows were unbroken, and the great door was sturdy.

The foxes knew better. They kept themselves to the rear and the sides of the building, in the thorn bushes and the fallen timber that lay composting under the looming eaves of the forest. So when evening fell and three soggy humans strode out of the dusk and forced their way into the building, neither the foxes nor their cubs spared one breath of concern. When strange clunks and scratches could be heard above the rain, coming out of the barn's dusty interior, the cubs rolled playfully together and the bitch scratched her back against the rotting timber.

But when the rain abated for a time and another, larger, figure stepped briefly out of the trees then vanished back into the shadows, *then* the foxes froze, ears pricked, hind legs poised and forelegs stretched low to the earth. Not a whisker, not an eyeball, moved. And then, as suddenly as they'd frozen, they raced off into the evening, each cub gripped in a parent's teeth.

Weakjohn dragged the door open with barely a grunt of effort though Martoth guessed it must have weighed more than the three of them put together. Inside, hundreds of chewed-up rice sacks had been left behind, dumped in piles amidst a debris of old tools, wheelbarrows, buckets. Dust lay thick on everything and even the thin light that came in through the tiny grubby windows seemed dirty.

— Hurry, said Weakjohn, somebody is trying to reach us…

She dropped her bags and her stick and paused to look carefully at Timoth.

— You're ready, she decided. Martoth, wait for us here. Timoth, follow me with your mind. I'm going to show you a way…

She motioned for Timoth to sit across from her on a low tumble of rice sacks and then, all of a sudden, she went vacant. Martoth and Timoth exchanged confused glances, then Timoth too appeared first distracted, as if listening to inner voices, and then gone, lost somewhere in his own head.

So it was that Martoth found herself alone in the thickening gloom with nobody for company but the corpselike statues of her friends.

Timoth closed his eyes, let the barn fall away, and accepted the touch of Weakjohn's mind against his. It was more than her voice this time. There were words but they were carried along by images and ideas that seemed to appear directly in his mind.

— Feel upwards, she said. That's it, you see, yes. Each time you push you can allow yourself to fall a little and catch on, yes, like that. Each motion, each of these little moves, each is rebuilding a tiny facet of your mind on a different foundation, a foundation that is made up of the patterns in *Concreta*. Does that make sense? Doesn't matter. You're doing well.

The technique came instantly but his courage nearly failed him. It was like an exposed ascent, a cliff face or an overhang, and the sense of vulnerability was enfeebling. He hadn't expected Weakjohn to lead him into such danger.

— Now, that's… uh, hold on, don't drift! Always make sure you're anchored. This should feel a bit familiar yes? OK. Calm now. Don't panic. Now. Sorry but you need to accelerate. Where we're going you need to rebuild your whole self like this and you've only just begun. That's how we get off this cliff face. And someone is waiting for us. So just a little, bit by bit, oh… oh wow, my word, OK good. And now, make it *visual*. Yes open your mind, wake up, yes, and…

He opened his eyes and shut them again, tight against the briny gusts that came at him off the roaring sea. He opened his mouth and tried to shout into the onrushing wind, eyes still closed against the spray.

— The *sea*! he wanted to shout — but no sound came.

This wasn't the relief he'd expected once he hauled himself over the brink into this new reality. The danger of disintegration had gone, yes, but the effort had not diminished.

— Come out, you idiot!

That voice was not Weakjohn's. It was male, youngish and, on the surface, more entertained than dismissive. Beneath the surface, Timoth fancied he heard somebody indulging a secret urge to lash out. His feet were cold and wet and each wave lifted brackish water further up his ankles. Seaweed tangled in the frothy shallows at his feet. He stared downwards.

— Come out, Timoth!

This time the voice was Weakjohn's. She was sitting on some driftwood some twenty yards up the grey sand beach. Beside her, a youth that Timoth did not recognise was wrestling with a small backpack.

Timoth kicked and stamped the seaweed off his feet and paddled out of the sea and up the beach to join them. At their backs the beach rose into grass-tufted dunes of drier sand that each gust of wind shaved into the air. A dark, indistinct horizon hemmed the sea beneath the deep blue sky. Only one or two lonely scuffs of cirrus wandered up from the sea over Timoth's head. Otherwise the landscape lay open to whatever universe spread out above and beyond.

— It's his first time you know, said Weakjohn.

— No shit!? the youth's eyebrows climbed in excitement. Come here, Timoth, let me have a look.

Timoth approached warily, and stood his ground as the stranger poked at his chest with his finger. Timoth felt something else too, an invisible contact like a brush against his mind.

— This is Theremy, said Weakjohn.

Timoth didn't think he could speak in this place. Somewhere beneath this new layer of consciousness, part of him was concentrating furiously on keeping him here, working to ensure that the him that was here was still the whole him and nothing but the him he knew. The effort of all this was draining. *Speaking* here — that would be a whole new challenge.

— Welcome to *Happenstance*, Timoth, said Theremy. I'm impressed.

— Yeah, on that, said Weakjohn. I've been trying to make contact…

Theremy turned his head away and raised a hand to ward

her off her the topic.

— I'm no longer part of the Vigil.

— What do you mean? cried Weakjohn, aghast. How?

Timoth tried and failed to shake the seawater off his ankles and found himself space on the sea-smoothed tree trunk alongside the other two.

Theremy paused, seeming suddenly to resent Timoth's presence.

— I wasn't really expecting so much of an audience, he said.

Timoth, licked salt off his lips and sat unperturbed. Weakjohn made no move to reassure Theremy.

— I guess I got myself into some trouble, he continued at last.

Together they watched the waves rolling in. Weakjohn waited. Timoth sat. Theremy chewed through his emotional gristle.

— I lied, he said.

— How?

— About my history.

— So what? What history?

When he'd finished explaining, Weakjohn felt hollowed out.

— Oh my god, she whispered beneath the wind. You utter fool. What have you done?

— Nothing, I've not done anything.

— Then what were you thinking of?

— Why not? Why shouldn't I?

— You know what a mess we're in. Now of all times? What in the flux were you trying to achieve?

— Of course I know. I know better than you, Weakjohn. Maybe I even care more than you. People have died since you were last in contact.

— Don't tell me what I care about, Theremy. Where are you anyway?

— Fennerstoil.

— Are they looking for you? Are we looking for you?

— I don't think so.

— Who's helping you?

— Seronin

— Sweet fuck.

The conversation had skewed off into a twilight zone that was pure entertainment for Timoth. With none of the background he needed to make any actual sense of it, he couldn't help enjoying it like a racquet sport of competitive indignation, punctuated with Weakjohn's shock, Theremy's touchiness, Weakjohn's disbelief, Theremy's shrugs.

At last he coaxed his reconstructed vocal cords into motion.

— HELLO! he bellowed.

Theremy and Weakjohn remembered his existence and dissolved in laughter.

— Why are we here? he asked.

Weakjohn ignored this and turned back to Theremy.

— What do you want? Why come to me?

— I want to trace someone. Someone's who's been on Semele.

— Fine. Maybe I can help you. But I want something too.

— What? he asked surprised.

— I want to get Timoth to safety.

— Where's safe?

Weakjohn shrugged as if to say *your problem*:

— You've been associating with some big hitters.

Theremy was momentarily speechless. He'd been depending on Weakjohn's goodwill and was recalculating.

— That's a big ask.

Her stillness acknowledged the point but offered no comfort. When he'd stewed in indecision for a few seconds, she asked:

— Who is it you're looking for, anyway?

— Just a name. The one name I still remember from before the Vigil.

— What name?

— Meef Parton.

Weakjohn somehow contrived to choke on her own breath.

— Oh my, she said.

— You know him?

Weakjohn seemed unsure at first how to respond.

— I'm sorry. He's dead.

She glanced briefly at Timoth and then back out to sea.

— ...but I have his daughter.

There was no question anymore. Theremy would move heaven to get them out. But something was bothering Weakjohn about this quest for his past.

— Theremy, she said, who was it who brought you to the Abbey all those years ago?

— You didn't know? he asked surprised. I checked the records. It was Marta. Same for Merrick.

Night was falling and already the back of the barn was shrouded in darkness. Martoth had no means of striking a light and no appetite for burrowing into Weakjohn's or Timoth's packs. Leaving her silent companions on their rice sacks, she set about exploring the barn before the light failed entirely.

She soon realised that it was not as neglected as it first appeared. The tools and barrows lying about the floor were rusty and worn but there was a tidy corner at the back where she found a cache of newer items and supplies that Weakjohn must have kept against just such an emergency as this. It was nestled in gloom behind another pile of rice sacks and beneath a rickety platform, hidden from casual inspection. Among the supplies she found a pair of oil lamps with flint, steel and char tin.

By the time she'd managed to light the first lamp, a viscous darkness had settled around her. She became the centre of a small globe of visible barn; the shadows thickened only yards beyond. This small orb of the world she could see began to feel like an extension of her body. Her beating heart, her prickling skin, the pounding in her ears, all felt like part of this island of light in the blackness. The bodies of her friends, halfway down the barn, might easily have been on another planet.

She could not leave them in the dark. Timoth might panic when he woke. So she lit the second lamp from the first and carried both across the thirty or so paces to where their bodies faced each other on the sack pile. Her body of light travelled with her matching each grating footstep as it echoed in the darkness beyond.

She dragged over a capsized wheelbarrow and set the second lamp on top. Materialising at the edge of her orb of lamplight, their figures sent a chill down her back. Pools of shadow lay in their faces: the channels of their frowns, the tucks of their chins and the blank orbits of their eyes. Veins of green and blue traced across their necks and temples. Their skin had a waxy pallor. They were like rigor mortis propped upright. As she straightened the lamp, giant shadows leapt across the sacks. She began to take some nervous steps towards Timoth, perhaps to check he was still breathing, but an irrational fear clogged her throat and instead she took her own lamp and retreated swiftly across the floor to her corner.

She placed her lamp on the floor and took a more careful look at the items in the cache. There were some slatted boards and trestles which slotted together to make a squat table. She set the thing up and placed the lamp on it. The lamp was fast becoming too hot to hold so there it would have to stay. Then she found two collapsible chairs, which she unfolded and set out, and a couple of canvas bags lying on top of a low wooden trunk. On the wall were three shelves full of tools and rivets, some jars and stiff cardboard boxes.

At the top of one of the canvas bags she found some woollen blankets so she removed her damp coat and wrapped one around her. She gave up on the idea of exploring the rest of the cache tonight; she would have to lift the lamp and it was now too hot to touch. She sat, and used the weak oil lamp for the meagre warmth it offered. How long would she be alone?

A human cry broke the silence. In her shock, Martoth jumped and knocked a trestle. The lamp teetered but righted itself without spilling. She caught her breath.

That cry, so like a human groan… She sat still and focussed every ounce of her attention on her ears but she could hear nothing now past the hammering of her own heartbeat. If it had been human it had been too quiet, surely, to have come from Timoth or Weakjohn. Or had it? She thought of the sort of noises you hear ten times a night if you lie awake in the taproom, the sound of dreamers lost in the theatres of their own heads. But she hadn't expected the silent figures of her friends to cry out, they'd seemed so energy-less, like living death. Perhaps it was only an animal, rooting or rutting in the night. Out here the night was theirs, and there were many whose barks could be mistaken for human voices. People had been tricked before. There were boar in these woods, and weald foxes, maybe even wolves. Putting an ear to the back wall she fancied she heard creatures snuffling and moving about in the undergrowth and then she thought she heard a thud from further down the barn as something knocked against the outside of a wall. She would hear more tonight if she lay awake between sleeps.

As her heart's thumping subsided, a tingling numbness spread in her face and fingers and she realised she had been hyperventilating. She calmed herself, concentrated on slow, measured breathing. Did she dare check on her friends again? She felt she had to, but she could no longer touch her lamp. She hesitated at the gloomy fringes of her globe of light and then plunged forward into the darkness.

Between the two lamps the darkness was thick but not absolute. She could make out the toes of her boots and her pale hands in front of her face. She counted her footsteps as they resounded in her ears. By twenty she was within the fringes of the second lamp, and by twenty two she saw round the sacks to where the bodies were.

Yes, Timoth *had* moved. She was sure. He was still facing Weakjohn, but something was different in the set of his arms. Perhaps he had slipped slightly in the sacks. She stepped toward him. She did not believe the groan she had heard was Timoth. She would have recognised it instantly. Should she, could she, touch him? What for? Lay a hand on his brow? Check the pulse in his wrist, his neck, his chest?

She took another step forward into the space between them. She heard a sighing breath. She span round to watch Weakjohn but Weakjohn had not moved an inch. Both of them were stock still. Martoth wasn't even sure she could see them breathing anymore.

A sudden spattering of rain rattled the roof above and then passed as suddenly as it had come. There would be more and it would be cold tonight. She came to her senses and abandoned whatever idea had taken her. She sped back through the gloom, watching the night through a far window as she paced out her steps to her own lamp.

Back in her corner, she found, or imagined, that her lamp's light had weakened. She retracted the wick to slow the burning. Semele nights were long and this one might stretch out into forever. She must not waste oil. Her luminous body shrank but its heart beat louder and its skin crawled. Between her table and the distant flame of the other lamp, all was now dark.

She wrestled with her dread of the darkness again. Should she go and dim the other lamp? Her head won and she set out once more. The night crowded in on her as she went back and forth and the thin, musty smell of the barn began to bother her. It was a faint, organic smell from the dust, the rice and the sack cloth that she imagined filling her lungs and settling deep so she couldn't breathe it back out. So weak now was her lamplight that, more than a few paces out onto the floor, only the two flames and the pale windows could be seen.

In the fumbling progress of her return journey, she became aware of drop in temperature, and paused. Her arms goose-pimpled, her sweat turned cold and she felt the kiss of a breeze on her neck. She spun around. There was nothing to see but the lamp and the windows, but she was certain that, out beyond the bending flame, the door had come open.

She was abroad in a no-mans land of gloom. He heart in her throat, she turned and followed the cold further out into the darkness. The trek across the barn seemed to stretch impossibly far but eventually the scrapes of her footsteps sounded drier, the breeze separated into fitful gusts and a dim line appeared where the barn was now open to the grim night beyond. As she went to the door, the sounds of the night swelled over the interior's muggy hush; she heard the wind rise, flurries of rain passing in the trees. The night crackled with calls of animals near and far.

She crept to the door where a glimmer of starlight touched the metal catch and she held on to the edge of the door and peered beyond. Only the barest sliver of moon lit the landscape and she could scarcely see further outside than in but her ears sang and her skin tingled. The wind soughed through the forest. Fitful sprays of raindrops blew into her face and spattered the barn wall. Just beyond the door the undergrowth was alive.

Something was flapping in the wind, a scrap of material caught on the broken machinery in front. She had not seen it earlier. She took a few hesitant steps out into the wind and drizzle to look closer. It might have been torn from their clothing as they arrived. She clambered over some metal struts into a patch of deep wet grass to get closer to it, nearly twisting her ankle on something solid lying on the floor. She could not see the colour of the fabric. The cold sank its teeth into her fingers and ears, and she felt suddenly exposed, alone in the dark and trapped amid these rusting trip hazards. Her curiosity gave way to fear and she turned tail and fled back into the building.

She wiped the rain from her face and then hauled the door closed against the wind. She tried her best to force the door's metal bar into its cavity so it would not come free again. Every clunk and scrape rang loud in the black space at her back and when she turned to face the darkness again her nerve nearly failed her. The flickering lamps seemed impossibly faint and remote.

She knew that waiting in the darkness was making her more tense. Her breath would only come in shallow gulps behind the monstrous pounding of her heart. She knew the shock she'd have if even Timoth or Weakjohn swayed unexpectedly into the lamplight. This was ridiculous. She counted out her breaths again. *In*, one, two, three... *out*, one, two, three... *in*, one, two, three.. *out*... *Own your fear*, she told herself, steal the initiative. But she found she had to close her eyes tight to get moving again.

As she approached the bodies, she suddenly heard the

fearful human groan again and *it was not Timoth or Weakjohn.* She screamed. Her legs surrendered and she felt herself hitting the dusty floor. With the first scrambling recovery of her legs, she found herself tearing, sliding, half-crawling her way across the floor toward her own lamp. Then skidding to a halt and spinning back towards the other lamp. Why flee her friends? But she faced the terror of their deathly torpor and quailed. Away, back to her corner. In her fright and indecision, she was thrashing her limbs but not making any ground at all.

Then she saw a human shape at one of the windows. She leapt and nearly passed out. Then the silhouette was gone. She was stranded between the two lamps. Her knees unsteady but her feet taken root. In the gaps in her pounding pulse, she heard a shuffling. Had the shadow been *in* the window or *against* the window? Was it outside or ...*inside*?

Something touched her. In madness she threw herself at the earth, the only solid in this liquid whirl of fear, but somehow she missed. She landed sprinting full tilt across the floor. She barely noticed her surroundings anymore, only fleeting sensations, a spilled lamp, burning oil spreading, flaring light and dark shadows at its edges, an appalling void where her friends had been, and amidst the pitchless roar of burning sackcloth, that groan again.

She bodyslammed the barn door and returned to her senses. Twisting her back against the door, she let the dizziness clear and tried to make sense of what her eyes were telling her. There were people in here, two or three, dark shades against the leaping flames. Timoth was there in front of the fire, crouching on his heels slightly, fists raised, dancing lightly on his feet as the shapes advanced. The shadow of Weakjohn stood further away, impossibly close to the flames, leaning on her stick and head bowed, but the flames seemed to eat away at the borders of her silhouette. How had this raging fire sprung up so quickly?

Martoth's fear had run itself out and a cool clarity came to her at last. She pulled at the metal door bar but it would not come away, so she cast around in the darkness for something she could swing. As the dark shapes closed in on Timoth and Weakjohn in the firelight, she crept into corners of discarded sacks, knocked her shins against some larger wheeled things and finally stubbed her toe on something that would do: a tool of some sort, a pole of old wood as tall as she was, tipped with a tantalising glitter that suggested metal.

She edged closer. There were three. One of them, a large man, lunged at Timoth, trying to grapple him. Martoth felt her muscles tense. But Timoth hopped back out of reach, so she held her nerve and pressed forward. Timoth tried to bounce back onto his front foot but the intruder did not flinch, so Timoth stopped himself. The attacker's motion was unnatural — human certainly, quick and determined, but somehow missing the expected reflexes. There was no hint of reaction to Timoth's feints. *Unarmed though*, thought Martoth, growing in confidence. She shifted the pole in her hands and felt the weight of it. Swing or thrust? Swing, she decided. She wasn't even sure what the odd-shaped metallic thing was at the end. If she came roaring out of the darkness to prod somebody with a blunt hook, she would only have found a novel way to lose her advantage of surprise. But whatever this tool was, it was reassuringly hefty. If she held her end just right, arms spread wide at first to get the pole moving and then slipping them both to the end to get maximum leverage on the swing, yes, she could do some damage.

Timoth backed away from something he'd seen but Martoth had not. He was right next to the fire where the air must be burning hot. Weakjohn had vanished right *through* the fire. Maybe she had got through to the other side, to the back of the barn. But what was there for her? No doors or windows, no escape. And if *she* could make it through then so could these strange attackers.

Three intruders advanced together on Timoth and with a deep breath Martoth launched forward and swung her weapon into the three of them at head height. She felt a meaty thump vibrate down the pole, catching the first with a blow that felled him instantly. The other two turned on her and as they did, Timoth sprang up and jumped onto one of them, a woman, dragging her to the ground and battering her with fists and elbows. As the last advanced towards Martoth, she retreated back into the darkness, sparks spitting from her weapon's tip as she dragged it across the stone floor. She tried to lift it again but her pursuer stamped on the end and wrenched it from her grip.

What had she left but her fists, her feet and her teeth? She bared them and crouched like an animal. Her hands became claws. She growled.

He came at her fast, no dancing around, no tiptoeing. She braced for an impact and raised her claws in front of her face. When the impact came it knocked her off her feet but it was a heavy thump of a hit, no teeth or edge about it. They both hit the ground at the same time but where she softened her fall with her hands, he fell like a dead weight. His head hit the stone floor next to her with a crack that would give her nightmares. And in the brief second before she rolled away from the dying man she saw in his face some disfiguring illness of the eyes which seemed to be melting out of their sockets, trailing a dark sludge across his cheeks.

— Martoth!

The voice from outside was intruding somehow in the night sky of her dream. She tried to shrug it away but it grew and spread, unfolding its wings across the heavens. Stars winked out one by one, then in two, fives, sevens, and finally her moon was eaten by the many-winged impostor. Then sunlight came, burning a hole through everything and as the edges of the hole smouldered into the back of her head, a face peered in through the aperture. A kindly face, warmth and concern: Weakjohn.

— Martoth. We have to get away from here.

— Is Timoth OK?

— I'm here, he said away off to her left somewhere. I'm fine.

Martoth's right side was aching and there were tender spots on her elbows and face which hurt like knifepoints when she touched them. The air smelled faintly of ash and oil but there was no heat in it.

— Am I hurt?

— Bruised quite badly, but I think you're solid. We were lucky. At least... Timoth and I were, to have you with us. I don't know what would have happened otherwise.

Martoth manoeuvred herself upright and looked around. They were out beside the barn, at the edge of the trees, some way off the road. The sun had only just hauled itself free of the horizon and the dawn chorus was settling down. Ordinarily this would be the sort of time she and Timoth would be arriving at the paddies, wending their ways into their own private working lives to break their backs for the supplies that had gone up in flames last night.

The barn surprised her. She had expected burning wreckage, a blackened frame cracking and popping in the heat of the embers. Or a fire still blazing — there was fuel aplenty. But no damage was visible from the outside. The glass windows were sound, the wood untouched.

— The fire was only partly real, said Weakjohn. You spilled the oil just as we were returning. About as clear an alarm signal as I could imagine! I used the idea of the fire and just magnified it a bit. I thought it might be helpful but looking more closely at our attackers this morning, I doubt it made any difference at all. So there you go. One of my two contributions to the struggle last night and it was basically an own goal.

— The other?

— Oh I tripped up the last guy as he was chasing you. That one was quite effective.

— Yeah, said Martoth. Yeah it really was. Thanks.

— Any time.

— What was wrong with them? came Timoth's voice.

— I've not seen it before so I'm not completely sure, but I think the bodies we were fighting were stolen.

— They were *possessed*? asked Timoth.

— "Puppetised" is the word the Vigil uses.

— Oh nice, he said.

— They were *innocent*? asked Martoth.

Weakjohn sighed.

— Doesn't mean you weren't right to bludgeon the big one to death with a single blow, dear.

— I think it does mean that, protested Martoth.

— First, Martoth, if you hadn't done that, we'd all be dead or worse. Second, the body's owner was not coming back anyway. He was already as good as dead. Don't waste your worry on him.

— When you say "dead or worse", said Timoth. Are you being… poetic?

— No dear. No, not at all, I'm afraid.

17. The Other Group

1939

More and more, Stephen regarded his life as a single zigzagging flight from eye contact. In Clindor he saw a stark and complete antithesis to himself: a diamond-bore stare, incarnate and locked in. But what Stephen could not see, and what Lena could, was the curious similarity between the two of them. Where Stephen was possessed by an awkwardness that infected those around him, Clindor inspired an equal awkwardness by his own utter lack of it. Clindor's unflinching gaze would deflect any trying to meet it. Stephen's shifting gaze would cause any more constant to deflect in embarrassment. Where Stephen was painfully self-conscious, every action of Clindor's appeared unfettered by any self-consideration at all. He was not altruistic: Clindor's hungers were open and obvious, unhidden, unreviewed. Stephen's drives were obvious but not overt, revealed instead in his artful attempts to conceal them.

Lena found herself recasting myth to explain these two: grown at the dawn of time from a single forbidding charisma, a single leaf on a bough of Yggdrasil, torn raggedly in two, the dawn and dusk as potent and malformed as each other.

She knew their lives would intertwine for years to come, whatever became of this strange common purpose that brought them all together in the here and now. How had they been made flesh in different places and different times?

But what now for Anna?

Lena watched Stephen watch Anna. His emotions could be read so easily as they played across his face. She could see the desperate love he had for the girl, the fear, the uncertainty, the determination so hopelessly misdirected by his instinct to self-punishment and she could see him ransacking his expanding mental kingdom for new resources to bring to bear. She feared both the power of his resolve and the waywardness of his judgement. What might he do? What foolishness might he be capable of in his desperation to ease Anna's grief, to shield her vulnerability? They had all moved on from spiders now. Their fleeting engagements with one another's minds had begun to open up terrifying landscapes of possibility. Leaving aside his genius for theorising and his gift for words, Stephen had not seemed to take naturally to any of the practical capabilities the group had been establishing. The spider-work appalled him. Meeting in the other place… well he could do it now but he was reluctant and strained, always last in and first out. But there had been times when Lena had felt a subtle, gossamer touch of his intellect direct upon her psyche, when she had begun to comprehend the power of his mind and the insinuating potential he might have. She feared for Anna. Too much love, too much grief… there were horrible risks she must confront. Stephen could be every bit as dangerous as Clindor.

She would talk to Harald. She must. But that was difficult at the moment because both were also aware of the uncomfortable fixation that Stephen was developing for Lena. There could be no resentment and no recrimination; it was as inevitable a consequence of their current circumstance as it was unfortunate. But, when Stephen was not watching Anna, as often as not he was sneaking furtive glances in Lena's direction.

There was a point when Clindor just seemed to take off. A point where, instead of taking the discoveries of the group and excelling at them, improving on them, he went beyond anything they could understand, beyond anything that could have come from them. Even Stephen, who Lena was convinced was the sharpest person she had ever met, and who seemed to be flying now right on Clindor's wings, fitting each new piece into the jigsaw puzzle they were assembling, even Stephen, who was normally so enflamed by new challenges, seemed to lapse into bafflement as the puzzles became absurdities, or as his careful theorising was scrambled by fright.

It was as if Clindor had found a new source of insight, a seam that all of them had missed despite their all their combined energies. Lena feared that the seam lay in Clindor's fascination with cruelty. It was becoming common now to find Clindor experimenting with physical pain — on the spiders or in a more limited way on the group. To Lena's distress, Stephen seemed to be supporting this development, practically as well as theoretically. Lena had witnessed them both driving compass points into each other's palms, and holding each other's knuckles against the hot kettle. She didn't dare consider what else might be happening that she hadn't seen.

Not for the first time she considered whether Anna should be spirited away and kept somewhere safe while this obsession played out. But this seemed hopeless too. Anna's emotional wellbeing was in so delicate a predicament already, having lost her parents and come to cling so tightly to Stephen. There was no question of separating the two. And if the two *were* separated, well, there were rumours of how orphans and poor children were relocated in these parts, stolen, even from their own parents, and transplanted by the authorities into other lives and other families, farms, factories. Maybe they were only rumours but with the world spiralling towards war, one could not trust authorities anywhere. Perhaps they had a powerful friend but, when it came down to it, they were a group of foreigners, living here on sufferance. She shuddered. No, Anna must be with Stephen, whatever else.

And then there was the troubling fact that Anna seemed to thrive on being part of this group. She rarely *did* anything but she certainly *could*. She could join them in *Happenstance*. She could do the spider tricks though she hated them, so when she did get involved with the spiders, she was normally trying to interfere with others. No-one had any expectations of her. She did not have to research, experiment, act as a foil or a dummy for anyone else's work. She could just sit and play, or draw her pictures.

When Pyotr was around it was different. Anna would be livelier and happier, monopolising Pyotr's attention, demanding Pyotr play with her. And he did have remarkable patience with her. Lena would not have marked him as someone who was good with children. He was precisely the wrong age for it, for a start, and his preoccupations were all older ones, romantic ones, literary ones.

Lena wondered whether Pyotr had had a sister back in Russia, and even a father like Stephen. She had never conjectured about what he left behind but the way he cared for Stephen and Anna, at least when he was around, was suggestive.

When he was around. Which was less and less and less. Lena felt he was drifting away from the group and she was sure that Anna feared it too. Again, he was exactly the wrong age. Since when had any fourteen year old cared for the company of adults or children? And there was no-one of the same age in the group. The closest were Anna and Paul, one a child, one a man. Then there was Pyotr's strange imperviousness to Clindor's influence. Ever since he had appeared with Clindor at the *Bierkeller Wanderpause*, he had seemed uncommonly prepared to disagree with Clindor or bait Clindor, or just walk away and not care.

And now Lena had worked her way round to what was really troubling her. She wasn't terrified by Clindor's ability to move objects with his mind. Stephen would explain it eventually and likely as not they would all get in on the act. It was Clindor's influence over the group that disturbed her and just how complete it had become over the past few months. In her mind it was like a net, like one of the ones that Uncle Per used to hold the fish that he'd just caught on the line. The fish stayed in the water, and in no immediate danger, they were just waiting while Per cast his line out again. But you could drag the whole lot of them this way or that if you tugged the net around.

Clindor's net was a peculiar one. If you cut a strand in your head, you would see how other strands remained, seeming to close the same gap. He was a charismatic man to start with. He must have led men in the army. He knew how to say what he wanted in a way that made it natural to obey. And he was not above using the spidery stuff on them too. But she knew he had individual holds over each of them.

Look at how close Stephen had become to him over the past month since Stephen had moved with Anna from their lodgings in Mme. Durand's into the new apartment. What role had Clindor played in that? She felt sure he had been involved in it somehow. More subtle than finance, of course. Stephen had independent means and Mme Giroud would not see Anna want for anything either. But there was something new between Stephen and Clindor. Maybe gratitude but more likely debt.

Or maybe even something as crude as the blackmail that Clindor had tried on Lena before he found the subtler pressure points he needed.

— I know Harald would understand, of course, he'd said, dangling in her eyes the ghost of ancient indiscretions.

The fool, not realising that Harald knew very well, had always known, right from the start, from the first time they had even breathed in each other's presence. Whether Harald "would understand" was so far away from being relevant it couldn't be measured. Had Clindor tried to use that lever he would only have enraged Harald against himself, woken the fury of the shaggy lion. And that lion could maul very well, very well indeed, though few enough ever saw it.

Unless… she froze. Unless of course Clindor had a chain around the lion's neck too.

She had a sudden strong intuition that he did. Poor Harald. Harald could easily have underestimated her, she thought. Underestimated her ability, not to understand, but simply to forgive. To grant whatever absolution to her big shaggy lion, though it had blood on its lips and a harem at its feet. Oh Harald, silly brute.

Lena wondered if Stephen could help.

The concierge checked his watch: one in the morning. He slid the slender green ribbon between his pages and closed his book. He tucked it away under the ledge of the desk and pulled a set of keys off a hook on the wall behind him. The young gentlemen from 22 would come in late again. 26 were on holiday. 1 through 10 were still empty.

He went off to lock the front door. He found an envelope on the floor for number 12 that he must have missed earlier, so he took it over to the post and popped it in their box.

As he turned back into the foyer, he stopped and his heart skipped a beat. It was the little girl from number 18. Just sitting there on the step, quiet as you like, in her nightdress, watching him lock up. There was no-one with her. Not that he could see. He had switched off the main lighting an hour before. It was only his desk-light and the two wall lamps set into the back wall that were lighting the place. He walked back into the foyer.

— You gave me a fright miss, he said.

She nodded.

— I'm sorry, she said. I miss Eric.

He'd had children of his own, of course, many, many years back. Two. Two in the beginning anyway, and both boys. He never really felt at ease with children but he found it easy enough to flood his heart with vague benevolence and trust that to see him through.

— Oh no, that's sad. Who is Eric?

— He was my friend.

He didn't want to ask what had happened to Eric. There were too many dangers in the world. It could lead to dark places and he was already out of his depth.

— You should be snug in bed, child.

— I was, she said. But I thought Eric might be coming.

He made a mental note to speak to her uncle, Harrison, wasn't it?, the academic.

— Is your uncle up?

She didn't answer.

Probably should be woken, he thought, but waking the residents usually got him into trouble. Harrison had a peevish temper on him too at times.

— Come on, child, I'll take you back upstairs. If I let you in, can you see yourself back to bed?

She nodded and he unhooked another set of keys from the wall. They climbed the stairs together and tiptoed across the thick carpet to door 18. He unlocked it, opened the door and was relieved to find a dim light coming from inside. She stepped in through the doorway and, turning, gave him a smile that was a perfect impression of the condescension he might have got from any of the residents, but somehow on her tiny face, it was charming enough to make his night.

— If Pyotr comes to see us, you will let him in won't you?

— Of course, child. Now back to bed with you! And sleep tight!

Many years ago, before he moved abroad and before Anna was born, Stephen attended a garden fête that Angela had organised. He'd recently published his first paper and, as if to celebrate, his good-natured sister introduced him as a local celebrity and invited him to spin the tombola drum. This drum came back into his mind now as he worked beneath the window of his apartment and the intruding street lighting fell in yellow trapezia across his scribblings. He remembered the satisfying resistance as he turned the handle and felt the drum begin to move and then the glorious rustle of the raffle tickets churning inside. He had imagined himself inside that drum, dancing like a madman amidst the ceaseless motion of the tickets.

His mind was the spinning drum. The raffle tickets were his theories. Everything was changing so quickly. Each week he had to revisit every discovery, challenge every assumption, question every premise, determine how much of his castle needed reconstruction. Was it even meaningful to talk of *matter* anymore? Was Templeton's tetrarchy still the right framework? Could he discard the Lucerne imaginationism and still maintain the stratal supervenience? And when and how would all of this have to engage with Einstein? Or Bohr?

The papers on his desk ranged more widely than they used

to. When he knocked his teacup over it was as likely to drench mathematical physics or evolutionary biology as a morphosyntactic analysis of Anatolian. But he was thriving on it, revelling in the sense of empowerment. He had finally become the dancing madman in the tombola drum.

But now he sat still, transfixed by the patterns of light on his desk, because his latest hypothesis filled him with dread. He had strayed too far. He had allowed his theorising to extend beyond the nature of the world they lived in (a flimsy, fluid thing, without doubt a proper subject of analysis) and explore the group itself (a fearfully personal thing and ferociously resistant to his methods). And in trying to resolve a critical tension, he had formed his latest conviction: there had to be *another group*.

It was an explanation as compelling as any Stephen had formulated. The first half of Clindor's capabilities were readily explained by the discoveries of Wojciech, the French boys, Stephen himself, each eagerly adopted by Clindor and subjected to his own peculiar talent for magnification. But there was at least half as much again that came from *somewhere else*. No-one in this group had opened Clindor's eyes to the possibilities that lay in the inanimate. If Clindor could do with chalk what Wojciech could do with spiders, could that truly be a leap that Clindor had made himself? It was a single leap that had laid waste to months of Stephen's thinking. More significantly, there was genius in that leap that Stephen did not believe Clindor possessed.

But, and here was the crucial move, if you add another group, there is no need for genius. Only the elegant simplicity of using the same explanation twice.

So there was another shadowy Dr Harrison somewhere, who had calmly explicated the spooky behaviour of chalk and then gaped dumbfounded when Clindor demonstrated a new trick with spiders. Other Wojciechs and Haralds who'd been led into *Happenstance,* other climbers who'd had Templeton's tetrarchy explained to them *by Clindor* and, in return, taught him the mental blows, the burning tricks, and the freedom that lies in pain.

Though maybe the pain thing was Clindor himself.

Stephen was instantly sure he was right. He even decided he had glimpsed members of the other group at times, disappearing round street corners or in the windows of passing trams. And Paul, too, had confided fears in Stephen and Wojciech just yesterday, when he returned from the funeral in Paris. He had been followed. Each and every day of his absence, he had been followed. By somebody who looked like him. Someone his age, his height.

If that were so, it suggested an asymmetry, and an asymmetry that was uncomfortable for practical reasons as well as theoretic: the other group *knew* about this group. Stephen and his friends were under observation.

Then, caught on a spike of doubt: since the Creed and the *Wanderpause* he'd had a sensation of being watched. It struck him at odd times, even where there was no possibility of it, like when they'd caught Anna playing cuckoo, or during Wojciech's demonstration with the spider. What if he had now just invented this whole theory to bolster his own paranoia? He sunk his head into his hands in frustration.

The door behind Stephen opened and a white ray of light telescoped across the floor. He froze and held his breath. Nothing moved except the ink that continued to seep from his pen nib onto the yellow paper. There were quiet words outside and the door closed. Tiny, bare feet crept through the gloom behind him and he heard another door shut, the door to Anna's bedroom. He let his breath out, put his pen down and rubbed at his forehead.

There was too much to be borne. The time was coming when he must stray beyond this theorising role that suited him so well. The madman must climb out of the tombola. Anna needed protection. Clindor needed neutralising. The other group must be exposed. Stephen was a seesaw that was beginning to tip. The dead weight of fear and inertia that had pinned one side to the ground was yielding at last. On the other side, a new gravity prevailed, the force of his knowledge, his power and his duty.

18. Escape from Semele

Martoth, Timoth

They came back to Laketown by a long circuit to arrive in the hills above the way head without meeting anyone. Their route ranged far up the mountainside but they took care to stay below the tree line. From time to time, they found themselves following faint animal trails but for much of the time they were just contouring on the endless soft beds of larch needles that heralded the onset of the cold season, layered over the floor rot of fungus and mosses. The air was cool and placid and enough sunlight broke through the remaining foliage to make the walk comfortable.

The trunks grew straight and were bare for some distance above their heads so they could see well into the forest on all sides and they strained their eyes into the distance as they walked. They knew the silent footfall on the forest floor was a danger. They would not hear an enemy. After her fright at the barn, Martoth found her eyes drawn to movements in the middle distance, or to shapes that seemed unnatural at first but were only, in the end, irregularities of the tree growth, fungi, cankers or broken boughs. There was a constant sense of watchfulness.

The way head sat on the North edge of Laketown as if under constant threat of eviction. By mid-morning, they came upon a break in the trees through which they could look down on it. It was a way off but they could make out the burnt perimeter walls and the tumble of wreckage. They dropped their bags and took the weight off their legs.

— We'll camp here, said Weakjohn. It might take a few days for Theremy to reach us. We have provisions for two of them. After that it's larch-smoked squirrel I'm afraid. If we can catch the buggers. The boar don't come up here.

— I can get 'em, said Timoth.

— Yeah, I've got a couple of tricks too.

— Is it really that dangerous to go down into the town? asked Martoth. Whatever's after us could find us here just like down in the barn, couldn't it?

She peered again into the larch forest.

— Definitely, said Weakjohn. But I'd like to avoid town. The Cherished stuff is turning nasty and I don't think it's unconnected. It might be just a subtler and bigger type of puppetisation. Till we see mobs with pitchforks coming up the hillside, I'd rather be here than there.

Underneath the needle beds the soil was rocky, a real bitch to get pegs into. It took Timoth and Martoth an hour of bickering to pitch the tent, during which Weakjohn rested on a boulder looking down toward the town. Martoth was feeling sour about the new plan and angry with Timoth that he wasn't. Ma Mackelay and the others would already be expecting at least news, maybe even hoping for their return. The idea that Timoth would vanish off the face of Semele without a shred of concern for his own mother enraged her. That he should have been so blown off course as to desert his family was a new unpardonable zenith of self-obsession. She wanted to shake his stupid little arse out of it. She indulged in a little vengeful fantasy as she hammered another peg in and snarked out her side of their ongoing bitch tennis. Mentally, she prepared herself a comfy seat up on the moral high ground: whatever the fuck Timoth was going to do, she was going to return to *his* family in Border.

When they'd finished, Weakjohn drew their attention back to the town. Five columns of smoke were rising into the sky, growing up from dense black trunks into a thinner murk that diffused and caught the wind, bending off to the east. At the base of the nearer columns, they could make out the tiny red-orange furnaces that spewed them forth, burning through rooftops, out of upper windows, and through the wood and plaster between.

— That was quick, said Timoth. What's burning?

— Can't tell all of them, said Weakjohn. But that one there, I'd say that looks like it's on Ekrasia…

— The attic? asked Martoth.

Weakjohn nodded, a sheen of moisture on her eyes.

— But how? Why?

She sighed.

— My background is supposed to be secret. In theory I'm just a weaver and no-one knows anything different. But the secrecy hasn't ever really been important. Not for my sake anyway. It was never dangerous here. The Vigil just doesn't want to disturb a place which isn't really mindwoke. So I haven't been especially careful. My weaving output has been pretty limited.

— You think they know you're from the Vigil?

She shrugged.

— I've associated with a certain scene in Laketown, the Othello, other bars where the off-worlders tend to end up. If you're going to attack the way head, you're going to attack the people who use it. One or two of those fires have got folk from the same circle in 'em I'd guess. *They're* not mindworkers. They're just from out of town.

— I don't get it. This stuff should happen in times of hardship right? Blame the foreigners when the crops don't grow… but everything seems okay doesn't it? Border seems okay anyway.

— 's'what makes me think it's unnatural. It's not blame. It's more like purification.

Laketown had many stone and brick buildings, at least in the centre. But there were timber frames, wooden outhouses, dry thatch, and the gaps were narrow. The town's fire service was a small force of volunteers. Despite Timoth's interventions, they were well-drilled with numerous reservists to call upon, but they would be spread too thin by this. As Martoth watched, the five columns thickened and filled the sky and even from up on the hillside they could now smell the smoke. Were they watching the town burn down? Would they soon begin to see columns, not just of smoke, but of people, streaming from the town gates? And where would they go? To Border? Seaton? Camp out on the lake shore?

Weakjohn was nervous. She walked away from the view to look into the forest. She looked up the hillside through the larches to the evening sky and kicked away the needles at her feet.

— Can you sleep yet? she asked them.

Timoth turned away from the view:

— I'm not sure I'm going to be able to sleep tonight. We can't all sleep anyway.

— It's best if I keep watch, said Weakjohn. I can control the sleep impulse properly and I can watch in ways you can't.

He seemed to accept this. Martoth, at least, felt that sleep might be possible if she could shake this feeling of being watched. After last night she was feeling stretched thin, and she knew she was jumping at shadows.

— Any idea when we might need to move on? she asked.

— No, said Weakjohn. But if I need to wake you it will be abrupt. If you can catch up what you need sooner rather than later it'll be better.

Martoth nodded and took a final look at the burning town. As the evening wore on the columns had turned a dirty blue against the rose sky. The flicker of flames could now be seen at the base of each of them, either because the daylight was fading or the fires were growing. Two of the columns had acquired spiralling grey offshoots from the town's attempts to fight the fires.

She picked up her rucksack, pulled back the flap of the tent, crouched down and crawled in.

— You coming? she asked Timoth without turning her head.

— In a minute.

She was asleep when he crawled in next to her. He had no light to see clearly but he could see the pile of blankets she was wrapped in and a pale arm outside the covers. A bare shoulder. At her head lay the rucksack, and some indistinct folds of material. Her clothes?

He sat and removed his boots at the entrance then kneeled and ferreted some blankets out of his own bag as quietly as he could. He took his jacket and trousers off and paused, then his jumper, shirt too. He stopped there, wrapped himself up and lay down. He wriggled some soft material between him and the lumpy ground and some insulation between him and the cold. But he didn't feel cold. He felt warm.

She was full of vitriol as ever. She had shamed him, called him a coward — an ungrateful, uncaring shit. She hit her mark. He didn't show it. So she hit it again, and again, and again. Maybe she was right, maybe he should walk away from this, back home to Ma. Help fight the fight if bands of void-eyed monsters fell upon them. Or if Border folk got puppetised too. What if it happened to his friends? Alban? Or Mulkah? Or *Ma*? Maybe it was happening already.

For all the warnings, he didn't feel like a target. He didn't think he was going to end up like Martoth's ma. But what could he do to help anyway? Yes, he was scared, but it wasn't escape that was driving him now, it was a thirst. A strange new world was opening up for him and he wanted all of it. No matter that each time he so much as paddled in the murky waters he had these overpowering sensations of guilt and the smell-memory of decay. He wanted the power he had glimpsed. And he knew he was a shit for wanting it. And that was why Martoth hit her mark.

When it came down to it though, it wasn't just shame she was serving up. There was a secret exhilaration in the fact that she kept coming at him, kept caring enough to want to rub his nose in it, seemed angry enough to strangle him. He imagined her finally losing it and throwing herself at him, on top of him, punching, slapping, throttling.

He breathed deeply.

He was close enough to smell her. A smell that could never be split into its strains, its flavours, hints of memories and analogies. A smell made only from the effects it had on him as he breathed it in.

He was liberated from his cursed shyness by the simple fact of her sleeping. He could be here silent, still in the darkness. Just breathing. Just knowing. Just imagining. For an hour if he wanted, all night maybe.

By the deep paddy, he slept naked. It was a hard habit to shake. Did she?

He groaned out loud. He didn't hold out even the remotest hope of sleep. Not like this.

A cold dawn broke and Martoth shivered awake. Timoth was asleep, sprawled against the opposite wall of the tent, snoring through a mouth squashed open against the groundsheet. There were voices outside: Weakjohn and one other. She pulled her clothes on and emerged.

The two of them turned — Weakjohn, calm but inscrutable as ever, and a young man, perhaps only a few years older than she and Timoth. His eyes were lively but there was a depth in them that reminded her of the elderly, some ledger of shocks absorbed and lessons learned that persisted in the fading iris. His stare was tactful but it disconcerted her.

— Morning, she said. Hi.

— Hi, said Theremy.

Below them the wind had dropped and the five columns had merged into a single cushion of smoke suspended over the town with parts tinged brown or glowing red according to the spread of the fire. Martoth fancied she could feel the heat, even at this distance and she could smell the smoke on the air. Finally, people had begun to muster outside the gates.

Theremy recounted how he had arrived at the way head some hours before. Even at night, he could see clearly by the firelight. The underside of the lowering smog was tarnished copper by the turmoil below, reflecting the flares and flashes of the fires as they spread. Out in the field, the noise of the fire was a thin rumble in the middleground, out of which human voices surfaced from time to time against an uneven crackle of collisions and crashes. He crouched amongst the debris in the centre to let the backsnap hit, hiding from the shadows that patrolled the perimeters. When he recovered, the first rays of dawn were burnishing the copper smog and the patrols had vanished so he took his chances and ran like the clappers for the yellowing larch skirts of the mountain.

Timoth poked his head out and raised a hand in greeting. He'd put on fresh clothes, Martoth noticed.

— You didn't go into the town then? she asked.

Theremy shook his head.

— No, there were too many buildings alight. You can see more down under the smoke. I could sense the fear, some people still trying to douse the fires. I don't think there are any rips, but there's an evil weather under there. It's a ruin.

— There have been puppetisations, said Weakjohn. We were attacked last night after we spoke.

He nodded but didn't look surprised.

— At the Abbey too. Have you been in touch? It was a living nightmare when I left. The place is torn apart.

Weakjohn shook her head. It had been two weeks since she'd been in contact. Since then all the things she needed seemed to have gone.

— How did you get here, Theremy? Were the leys okay?

— From Riverrun. And barely. Lethe said it was like the old days. Merest thread of a route. He helped me through. We need to be back there tonight.

— Tonight? Daylight would be better.

Theremy shrugged.

— You want to delay till tomorrow?

They had a small, dry breakfast from their provisions of rice bread and cured buck meat then threw the crumbs to the birds and set about packing the tent away. Theremy made them split their belongings in two: a smaller set of essentials they could take with them and the remainder, including the tent, which they would discard as they descended to the way head. For now they kept everything with them.

They had nowhere to be till sunset. But now there were four of them, Weakjohn was comfortable allowing them to split up so throughout the day they went off in pairs to stretch their legs and explore the area around them. In the early afternoon, Martoth and Weakjohn found themselves together on one of these forays while the others kept watch over the burning town.

— When are you intending to leave us? asked Weakjohn as she hobbled carefully over some tree roots.

Martoth wasn't surprised. She'd made her feelings clear to Timoth and Weakjohn had just made the obvious inference. Martoth didn't need anybody's help to hike back to Border. Laketown had been a dead end. Where else would she think she should be?

They were poking their way towards some thicker forest below where the larch trunks were hanging with ivy and the spaces between filled out by ferns, brambles and a congregation of wiggin trees. Tiny songbirds fled from the clusters of red berries as they approached and then darted to and fro between patches of shade in the trees.

— It would be a mistake, dear.

— Because everything's going to shit here?

Martoth had thought she had Weakjohn figured out and she was disappointed that the whole escape idea had come from Weakjohn.

— No. Because there's so much more for you elsewhere.

— But everything and everyone I care about is on Semele! said Martoth. You've been here so long. I don't get how you can just drift off with Laketown burning behind you. Some people will be *dead* in that mess.

Weakjohn stopped and looked away.

— Some of my friends are already dead, she said and Martoth knew that her own mother was front and foremost in Weakjohn's mind. A very great number of those below us might be dead soon. I can't stop that. If it weren't for you and Timoth, I would stay with them.

— But everything I want is here, between Border and Porton. What could I want anywhere else?

She glared furiously at Weakjohn, daring her to say *Timoth.* Go on. Say it. But she didn't.

— Maybe what your parents wanted?

— My parents are dead.

And what did her parents want? Did they even want the same thing? They barely knew each other as far as she could tell. She only really knew what they *hadn't* wanted: baby Martoth.

— Do you know how many worlds humanity has spread across now, Martoth? I don't. The Vigil keeps a close eye on thirty or so, but there must be hundreds more. The universe that once looked so cold and alien has turned out to be anything but. Until a few weeks ago, someone who knew how could travel in a few days from Semele to Riverrun to Fennerstoil to The Leap to Schiller and back again, seeing a million wonders, natural and otherwise. And do you know how many people actually did? How many even thought of leaving the world they were born on? Basically none. A handful from each generation on each world. Near as damnit none.

— After the crises we had this giant momentum. It carried us through migration after migration in just a few years. It seemed each time some people stopped to settle on a planet another fragment would carry the momentum onward, rolling though world after world, fresh worlds, friendly worlds that suddenly appeared almost everywhere we looked. The migrations got smaller and eventually the momentum died. Maybe we all got tired. Maybe if all the mindworkers capable of travel wanted to turn aside then that was it for the rest of the group. Maybe some are still wandering out there finding new worlds. If they are, we have lost track of them.

Weakjohn's mask always slipped slightly when regret dominated her thoughts and Martoth could see it now. Weakjohn became inward, her edges less sharp.

— I've not travelled much, you know. I've seen a handful of worlds but most of my life has been here or the Abbey. But your parents. My. They were both among the very, very few who truly did stride out across the universe. Your mother for the Vigil. Your father for his own reasons. And you are very much their daughter, Martoth, whether you like it or not. If you ask me, it wasn't the Vigil that caused Marta to travel, nor the business that caused Meef to. There was something inside them that drove them on. They were restless. And I think you have the same thing.

Weakjohn was looking away again, keeping her eyes from Martoth. Martoth mulled the words over.

— I don't, she said.

She knew she was testing Weakjohn's patience but she was determined. If Weakjohn was frustrated she didn't let it show.

— Do you know why Theremy is here?

— For Timoth.

— No. For you.

— Me?

— In a way. Theremy's been through a lot lately and now he's investigating his own past, just like you were. The odd thing is that the only thread he has to pull on right now happens to be the same one you've been tugging away at... Meef Parton.

— What? But I don't know anything!

— And you never will if you stay here. Martoth, most of the trees around you have lived longer on Semele than humanity has. Here, we are just a thin crust that has formed at at the edges of humanity in the universe. Behind us there is this sprawling, diverse mass of love, hope, hatred, despair... How long till you've read every book from Mulkah's crates? How long till you've read every book on Semele? And what then will you know? How much more than now? You are not like these people, dear. Whether you like it or not, you are more like Meef and Marta than Teresa, Rosie, Ma Mackelay, even Timoth.

— We are not a crust. We are people.

Weakjohn relaxed some of the tension in her face and seemed to slump slightly. She fixed her gaze quite steadily and firmly upon Martoth - a gaze without force or flattery - and said simply:

— Martoth, my darling, there may never be another chance.

— There are people gathering on this side of the way head, said Timoth.

Weakjohn squinted down over the forest. There were twenty or thirty people in the grassy space between the way head and the eaves of the larch forest. She risked a quick, gentle probe outwards. They didn't seem like puppets.

— It's flat and sheltered there. Are they just camping?

…but there were no tents amongst them and she couldn't see much baggage even. They were too far off to make out clothing or weaponry. But everyone in Laketown had been armed recently.

— Refugees would try to get further from the town wouldn't they? Or to other settlements, or even up to the forest?

— Maybe they're just not ready to abandon their homes yet.

— I'm not sure we can take that risk can we? said Theremy. We are due at the way head in just a couple of hours. And we can't take the direct route now. Unless we are prepared for a fight.

— Oh arse, she sighed. Right then. Ditch your ballast, kids, we're suddenly in a hurry.

They emptied their packs of the non-essentials, swung them up onto their backs and set off down through the forest. They were moving fast, Timoth and Martoth at a swift walk, breaking occasionally into a jog, Weakjohn somehow managing to skip along leading the way even with her stick.

— We'll go around to the east and head for the Winter Gate, shouted Weakjohn, just above the Lake. There are too many people at the main gates. I'll be seen.

They spread wide over twenty yards or so as they descended, giving each other space to leap over the tree roots and hollows without fear of collision. After a few minutes they reached the wiggin tree copse that Martoth and Weakjohn had visited earlier and swerved left to skirt around it on the East. Just beyond it Weakjohn skidded to a halt suddenly enough to raise a small wave of larch needles.

— Here! she screamed. Get tight to me! Now!

When they reached her she was down on one knee, both hands planting her stick firmly into the ground. Theremy knelt down too, facing the other way. Martoth and Timoth squatted down beside them. They were silent for a few moments, staring out through the forest, ears pricked. No longer could they hear the twittering of songbirds or the croaks of the crows higher overhead. The forest around them seemed poised, attentive.

— I don't feel anything, whispered Theremy.

— No, me neither, said Weakjohn. But turn and look over this way.

She motioned upwards towards the wiggin copse. Lying beneath the lowest of the trees, only thirty yards away was a corpse. It lay on its back, two booted feet down the hill, and its face hidden beneath damp, tangled dark hair.

— Puppet? asked Theremy.

— I can't tell. He's long dead.

Theremy crept over to the body and pushed the hair aside with a twig. He dropped it, stood tall and scanned the ground all around him before returning to the group.

— Puppetised, he nodded. Dead more than a week.

— That's before we were attacked, said Timoth.

Perhaps even before they'd reached Laketown, while he and Martoth were hiking over from Border. Martoth wondered how she and Weakjohn had missed it earlier. They must have passed then closer than they were now. Weakjohn's frown suggested she was just as perplexed.

— What was it doing here? asked Martoth.

— The attack on the way head... said Weakjohn, I wonder —

— We don't have time to work it out, said Theremy. Come on.

A refugee camp was developing in the fields outside the Eastern Gate and, despite the late hour, some pockets of people were starting up the lake valley toward Seaton and the road Greater Semele. If Weakjohn had wanted to avoid meeting people she must have been disheartened as soon as they broke from the skirts of the forest and the town came into view. While they kept wide of the main campground, in crossing the broad fields that fringed the east road, they came upon several groups of people keen to put more distance between them and the dirty hot clouds that hung over the town.

Weakjohn knew some of the travellers and was able to glean news from inside the town. All efforts to control the fires were now abandoned and all over town people were packing up and moving out. Amongst them some of the cherished were still waving their torches around but they were being attacked by the fleeing townsfolk and, often as not, left for the flames. Just as disturbing to Timoth and Martoth were reports of looters picking through the mess. Some areas north and west of Daytime's Square had become superheated furnaces and there were some gruesome rumours circulating about peoples' eyeballs melting.

— The Winter Gate does look quiet, said Timoth, but I

don't see why we wouldn't just go in the main gate. We have to get back through all the people anyway. Whether we do it outside the town or skirting the inner wall doesn't make any difference. We're not going to get any further into town than that anyway — we'd choke to death if we didn't burn.

— Martoth and I are going further in, said Weakjohn.

The other three stared at her. Timoth was too shocked to protest but he didn't miss the look of surprise on Martoth's face. Whatever Weakjohn was planning was not a plan they had hatched together. But Martoth was bold and he knew she trusted Weakjohn. He didn't expect to see fear in her eyes and he didn't. Theremy recovered quickly too. His momentary confusion gave way to what looked like calculation. His brow was furrowed as he stared deep into the burning town. Had something else passed between Weakjohn and Theremy? He had been the jumpiest of all of them about the passing time and about getting to the way head for their rendezvous.

— There's something we need to do, said Weakjohn, aloud.

— OK. We'll go together, said Theremy, I can help in the fires.

— No, you get to the way head with Timoth and start preparing.

— I was counting on your help for that!

— Use Timoth.

Theremy had no inhibitions about showing his dissatisfaction with that idea and he pouted quite openly. Once more, though, his changing expression suggested to Timoth that more was passing between Theremy and Weakjohn than they were bothering to say out loud.

— Fine, he said, fine. He's right though. There's no need for us to follow you in through the Winter Gate. We'll go the other way, and we'll take your packs.

— Makes sense, said Weakjohn. See you in… about an hour. I hope.

* * *

Like all Laketown's gates, the Winter Gate was more of a gap than a gate. Unlike the others it was narrow, no wider than a house doorway, and there was no watchtower. It might have been left as an oversight, or a means of shipping waste away from these buildings. It certainly didn't provide easy access to anywhere of note. On entering the gate, a traveller would come right up against the rear walls of the neighbouring buildings and be forced to turn immediately left or right along the passageway to find other ways through to the streets of the town.

Though the alleyway was smokeless, it was dark beneath a brick red sky and Martoth could feel the heat in the air. Weakjohn turned north along the inner wall, shuffling along with her stick. Each time they passed gaps between the buildings on the left, they caught sight of flames, not too far off.

— Weakjohn, what are we doing?

— There's something I want you to see. Something about your parents.

— Really, it's not important.

All Martoth's instincts were telling her that getting any closer to the inferno further in was madness. There were few people still emerging from the town as the evening came down and inside she imagined the scenes must be volcanic. She was anxious not to die, especially at the hand of an old psychic's sentimental streak.

— You'll be safe with me, said Weakjohn. Most likely.

— All the same…

Weakjohn hushed her and slowed to match her pace to Martoth's, so she could talk. There were warm gusts of air passing down the alleyway carrying thin black cinders along with them. Martoth brought her hands up to cover her nose and mouth.

— Listen, Martoth. I want you to go with us when we leave tonight but I'm not going to force you. I think this is more important. Please, please listen to me when I say regret is a horrible thing and time is all any of us have. I am *begging* you, dear, as I may not have time to persuade you: do not write your parents off so easily. Yes, of course you are right — they have nothing to do with who you are, but they have so much to do with who you might become. You are not betraying Rosie by having the same dreams Marta had. You are not sinning against Teresa's morals by understanding Meef Parton's better. For fuck's sake, stop worrying about whether your parents deserve your attention and start wondering whether you can be enriched by what they've left you.

— They didn't leave me *anything*! Except genetics.

— That's what I thought till a couple of nights ago. And that is a petulant way of describing something quite profound. But now I'm not so sure…

— What do you mean?

— I think there might be something else. Something small and maybe nothing. But enough of a possibility to risk a bit of a singeing. I'm asking you to trust me. If there is something, we'll fetch it now and you can either take it home to Border or Porton if that's what you want, or you bring it along with us and I'll help you figure it out.

— Weakjohn, we could both be killed in there.

They came to a gap on their left and Weakjohn halted. Here, a narrow gap between buildings led out of the Winter Gate's passageway into a street beyond.

— I hope not, she said. Now listen to me carefully. I'm not that great at some of the things I'm going to have to do in there. Theremy would be better for this but he's got to worry about the way out. I guess I'm saying I am a bit out of my depth. I'm going to need to concentrate pretty hard and I need you to help as much as possible. Stay directly behind me, as close as you can. I may not be able to speak so I want you to watch me carefully ok?

Martoth nodded.

— Assuming we make it to the way head, I'm going to be exhausted and probably quite sick for a bit. You may need to help me.

Martoth agreed. They stepped out into the gap.

The next hour of her life felt like a dream, both as it unfolded and in the years afterwards. As she remembered it, the very air seemed to be alight and all around them demons of molten gold were crawling over the black skeleton of the town. In the open spaces —and often they could not tell street from razed building— sparks and cinders cavorted in the churning air. They passed the roasting corpses of people and animals. They saw rock that glowed and metal that flowed. Through it all, Weakjohn seemed to glide forward unnaturally, propelled by an unseen motor, and Martoth stumbled along behind her, grasping onto Weakjohn's clothes when she could. She was aware of the heat but it did not burn her or her clothes. A purer vision of hell she could not imagine.

What was Weakjohn risking with whatever magic she was working? Martoth thought of the rip in the attic. Lurking in the flickery dazzle of the fires there might be thousands such. They might be under attack even now, every second they travelled through the inferno. It was too late to turn Weakjohn away from this insane escapade. They were already in the heart of the blazing town.

Finally they emerged into a flat space that had been scorched away entirely. Here and there across the baked earth were glowing embers which might once have been trees. Weakjohn led them out into the middle of the space and stopped, looking around her to its four edges. Martoth realised they were standing in a quadrangle, and each side was a ruined cloister rising up from the fallen remains of its roof. Weakjohn caught Martoth's eye and narrowed her eyes slightly to indicate they had reached their destination then she picked up some charred wood and held it out in front of her. She took a few hesitant steps as if dowsing with it, then dropped it and motioned Martoth to follow.

They stepped into one of the cloisters and Weakjohn kicked aside some smoking rubble so they could stand then she pointed up at the walls. Only yesterday this would have been a tranquil place, thought Martoth, cool in the sun, sheltered from the rain. Now the cloister was wide open to the fierce copper sky and its rain of ash and sparks. At least it afforded enough light to make out what Weakjohn was pointing at.

The surface of the cloister wall was not the grey stone that was found all over town but a mishmash of mismatching ceramics, broken pieces of tiles or potsherds, some glazed in white or blue or other colours, some unglazed terracotta. They had been inlaid in the wall like the tessera of a mosaic, each going only halfway toward filling the gaps around it, but there was no big picture or grand scheme and patches of blank space remained. The pottery pieces had clearly been accumulating here over some time, probably for as long as Laketown had existed, Martoth surmised, each embedded by different hands for different reasons, driven by a common compulsion.

As her eyes adjusted, Martoth saw that there was writing on the pottery. Every piece in the wall was inscribed, either by rough carving, or painted in glaze. There must be thousands of them, she thought, across all four cloisters. Then she saw that the floors were decorated in the same way. Beneath the smears of ash where Weakjohn had cleared a space there were more fragments, bigger, flatter, but inscribed just the same.

Weakjohn picked up a charred piece of wood from nearby,

held it up to the wall and blew on the tip. As she blew, it glowed and lit the wall just brightly enough to make out the lettering. She passed the wood to Martoth and indicated that she should read.

Martoth held the wood aloft and blew on it several times to explore the wall. There were names on the fragments, many, many names. Most of the pieces contained two names, some more. "David and Daniel". "Fricka, Menydd". "Mel, Alban, Antony". Others carried dedications or cryptic snippets of text. "Zoe and Max - a month to last a lifetime". "Mary - I will never, never forget, Bohuslav". "Flora - that I might have known you. Susan". "One hour to miss what we never had. Zho and June".

She understood now why Weakjohn had brought her here. The stories she began to glimpse through these stones were bringing tears to her eyes even before she found the one she knew now must be here, the one that Weakjohn had guessed might be here, the one that went some way towards healing the rift in her heart. But when she found it, when her eye caught the ruby glaze just as the glow from one breath faded and she gasped out another desperate illuminating breath, when she saw the names she sought and more, so much more, when she read the words her parents had put there once so long ago, and then again later, and again and again and again, she wept and wept and wept.

— Marta and Meef, said the ruby glaze.

— And Martoth, added the emerald, my beautiful daughter.

— Martoth, said the ruby, our beautiful daughter.

— I want the world for you, said the emerald.

— I want the world for you both, said the ruby.

She should have been choking from the smoke and the fumes but it was grief that got her. Grief she could never have felt for a bloated corpse or some tangled wreckage, ugly signs that meant only the death of an idea, the end of a vain hope. Grief that now folded its black wings around her so tightly she thought she would lay down and die in the fire.

She did not notice as Weakjohn prised the precious tile away from the wall. Nor did she notice as Weakjohn extracted a long tube that had been embedded in the mortar behind it.

She did notice though as Weakjohn dragged her to her feet and pressed these objects into her hands. She noticed as Weakjohn gave her a firm slap on the back and pushed her back out of the cloister. And she was just about alert enough to chase Weakjohn closely when she strode our into the quad and set off motoring through the blazing town again.

As Timoth and Theremy jogged out onto the black field of the way head, their frantic race was burnt into Timoth's vision as a tangle of glows and streaks. The darkness came as a blessed relief. Whatever terrors it might hide, breathing came easier in the relative cool of the field. They made their way towards the centre but Theremy halted them a few yards away from the wreckage. They lay all the packs down in a circle and sat down in the centre.

— OK, said Theremy. What we're going to do is difficult and I don't want to involve you if I can help it, but I need to know I can use you if I need to. What I want to try with you is a very limited type of fusion. It's a way for you to make some capacity available for me.

— Capacity for what?

— This sort of travel… it's like shifting to *Happenstance*, it's a matter of reconstructing people on a different substrate. But it's harder than that because you can't do it incrementally like when you ascend to Happenstance. So you need to internalise the whole pattern, right down to the noumenal layer. Remember how changes work. I am going to create a fuse mind that contains the pattern and have a thought which is the realisation of the pattern in reality. There are shortcuts and tricks but I'm not an expert at this and I am going to need to do it hundreds of times. Each time, I need to capture all the essential detail to apply it on the next step. Lethe is going to help with the route but I need to carry us all.

— What do I do?

— I'm going to show you if you'll allow me.

Timoth felt the touch of Theremy's mind on his own, gentle at first but then more probing, as if Theremy was foraging around looking for something.

— Here, he said in Timoth's mind, you recognise this?

It was familiar to Timoth but not as a thing in itself. He recognised it as an accompaniment to his strongest memories: chasing birds with Alban in the school yard at Bereston, hiking with his father out to Boston Fields, Rosie's funeral, his first night by the deep paddy, the corpse by the paddy, being in the tent with Martoth last night... memories that felt deeper than a nexus of the visual and emotional, memories he could smell, even touch.

— Yes, you've got it. That's what I need to use. Don't worry, I'm not prying.

— Are you going to erase anything?

— No. It's not storage I need. The world is full of storage. It's that capacity you have there, for capture and assimilation.

— Let's do it, then.

Timoth saw them first as a wart on the black horizon, wriggling upward into the glow of the town behind. As the lump wriggled closer, he realised it was two people moving together as one, leaning against each other as they staggered forward. He dismissed the familiar sense of shame that nagged at him after the exercises with Theremy. He leapt over the packs and ran towards them, leaving Theremy alone in bag-henge, focussed on his preparations.

It was Weakjohn who was sick or injured and was struggling to walk. She seemed to be perpetually coming alive to push off with a leg and thrust herself forward and then lapsing into dead weight again. Martoth was trying to half-lift, half-drag her along but she was carrying something else too and Weakjohn kept slipping off her shoulder.

Timoth reached them and unceremoniously hefted Weakjohn into a fireman's lift and hurried them back to the packs. He let Weakjohn down next to Theremy. The darkness was deep but from the fire-tinted glitter in her eyes, Timoth could tell that Martoth was crying.

— Is she okay? she asked, trying in vain to prop Weakjohn up as she jerked around.

Theremy felt Weakjohn's forehead and checked a pulse but showed no other sign of concern.

— Backsnap. I think she's coming out of it already. I hope so anyway, we've got about five minutes.

Martoth went over to her pack and put away whatever she was carrying.

— Thanks, she said to Timoth.

It offended him, seeming to increase the distance between them, the suggestion that thanks were necessary. He brushed off the annoyance.

— You found something?

— Yeah, she sighed. Yeah, we found a memento, I guess.

Theremy looked up at her but didn't pursue it. Timoth knew better too.

— I, I can't see properly, said Martoth.

— Come over here, said Theremy. Show me your eyes. Sorry, closer, it's dark…

And there they were, Martoth and Theremy, an inch apart in the darkness, gazing into each other's eyes. Timoth didn't bother hiding his jealousy from himself. Rather he cursed his own failure to reach for such shallow tactics. Check your eyes... Nice one, Theremy.

— I think they're fine, said Theremy, just the brightness of the flames.

Did their faces linger just a microsecond too long? Was there even a hair's breadth of movement towards each other? On her side or his? Timoth found himself rustling his bag, making a noise, standing up ostentatiously to check on Weakjohn.

Weakjohn did seem to be improving. Her breathing had slowed back to normal and Timoth thought he could see her eyes open, cold and staring into the sky. They sat in silence for a few minutes, listening to the hiss and crackle of the smouldering town, and then Theremy motioned them to get up.

— Packs on. Help Weakjohn. And all get close together.

— How will we know? said Timoth.

— You won't, said Theremy.

And then the world dissolved.

PART TWO

19. Into The Leap

Martoth, Timoth, Seronin

It was night when Martoth became aware of herself in a darkness deep enough she couldn't be sure her sight had returned. She blinked till the fluid darkness clotted into stable shapes, but the ghosts of Laketown's fires lingered on, stepping in and out of the shadows.

She strained to see. There were signs she couldn't yet read and patterns of tiny weak lights she couldn't yet make sense of. The four of them were outdoors, by the feel of the air. They were in a kind of large cage but with bars set wide enough to walk through. She sensed high walls or tall buildings towering over them on every side. Lights flickered, attached at head height to invisible surfaces, but none were closer than twenty yards. The lights themselves were like nothing she'd seen before. Glassy, grotty, industrial.

She was standing on a surface that gave slightly under her feet, like old wooden boarding, and a sound she couldn't describe —buzzing? humming?— came and went in the distance. This place was as alien to her experience as anything she'd dreamed or read. She peered at her hands through the gloom, flexed her fingers and breathed the fumes of whatever world this was.

Theremy was squatting down attending to Timoth who was curled up in a foetal position. Weakjohn was climbing to her feet.

— *Quick*! urged Theremy. It's not safe here.

Timoth groaned.

— ...sick...

— Where are the attendants? asked Weakjohn in concern.

— There was one, said Theremy. I sent him away. These places are targets now.

The place *was* dangerous. Even Martoth could feel it. The grubby lights picked out five alleyways leading away from them like the spokes of a wheel, each receding through a couple of hundred yards of darkness to an inconstant blur of light beyond. Those *could* be streets. But the alleyways themselves... in places they were black as pitch and the pinpricks of wall lighting barely punctured the gloom.

— Which way? asked Martoth.

— It doesn't *matter*! said Weakjohn impatiently.

Martoth stepped out of the cage onto a floor of gritty stone, then, uncertainly, into the mouth of the nearest alley.

— Where are we?

— The Leap, said Theremy, drawing alongside, supporting Timoth on his right shoulder. One of the bigger towns. Hitspeke, I think. Come on.

— Hitspeke! cried Weakjohn. For flux... how do we not know?

— Lethe was surfacing the ways for me, said Theremy, firming them up... some of the traces were so weak, it was like he just imagined them into existence... He was throwing them at me, new options every step of the way. I had to make some... quick choices.

Theremy's uncertainty cast a pall of fear over Martoth. On Semele he'd been assured but now he'd adopted a tone of command and it seemed overdone — paper thin.

Martoth's mind was racing. She chased her tired eyes around the gloom, devouring the complete otherness of this world. The material of the walls, that must be *concrete*, concrete blocks, she'd read about those... the lighting *electric*? She could make out dirt-crusted cords, *cables* pinned along the walls. If there was electricity, what else? Those sounds, transport? *Cars*? These things she had read about.

She was certain Timoth had precious little idea of these things, of the breathtaking intricacy of humanity's heritage. She squinted at him through the darkness. He was recovering quickly now, matching Theremy step for step, leaning less upon Theremy's shoulder and walking taller. Still, he moved cautiously, right arm extended in front as if feeling for obstacles. She was suddenly aware how fragile he might prove in the face of this dislocation. She'd accused him of selfishness but he was also running scared of an invisible threat which might kill him just for thinking the wrong way. He was holding tight to Weakjohn and Theremy because he needed protection.

She explored every aspect of her experience. The ground was strewn with a fine grit but it was not dusty. This was not a dry world. There must be rain from time to time. Rain meant pitched roofs... she looked up but the looming walls dissolved somewhere into a crystal field of stars. *Stars*! What stars? What constellations? Would there be *anything* she could recognise?

— Quick! Now! Quick! urged Theremy. There is something behind us!

Timoth shot forward into the gloom ahead. Theremy skidded after him.

— Okay, it's okay! called Weakjohn. It's not following.

Martoth looked back towards the cage but saw nothing. Their journey through the alleyway seemed endless and, as it stretched on, Martoth felt a deep anxiety lurking at the edges of her consciousness. Theremy was jumpy and continually looking over to Weakjohn but she was preoccupied, marching solemnly with her head down. There was a rhythm to the lighting and the shallow recesses in the alley walls — two then a gap, three then a gap, two then a gap, three… Martoth let the rhythm numb her mind.

Near the end of the alleyway, Martoth's heart surged. Lights sparkled around them and the background hum, now unfiltered, differentiated into a thousand components, rushing, sweeping, honking, yelling. It was a world she could have described but never pictured, a cast-off, an outpost, a faithful, frozen, snapshot-microcosm of its precursor, Earth. Cars, pavements, streetlights, shop fronts, gleaming pictures, posters, screens, panels, litter, people…

But she could tell the people were frightened. They were all moving in the same direction, left, along the street, and those not already running were pushing along in a hurry, on the verge of breaking into a run. The cars passed in the same direction but slower, trapped in a kind of stop-start queue, making a mechanical cacophony unlike anything she'd heard in her life.

Theremy urged them forwards right into the path of the creeping traffic.

— Into the car! he said. Get round, get in!

Martoth watched, stunned, as Theremy leapt over the jutting front of a vehicle round to a door that must house the controls. The door opened and a glassy-eyed woman emerged, clearly lost in her own thoughts. Theremy pushed her gently aside and climbed in, casting a dark challenging look at Weakjohn.

— Don't judge me! he hissed.

— You just carry on young man! beamed Weakjohn, opening the opposite door. You're doing fine.

* * *

— Search it!

Weakjohn's hands were already busy, opening compartments, feeling behind flaps. Theremy had two hands on a wheel and was operating something with his feet. He was in control of the vehicle now, making it go forward when the car in front moved, and stop when the queue in front crunched up again. The windows were a carnival of glowing smears and reflections. She saw faces of pedestrians mingling with her own face, the faces of her fellow passengers and then other faces she saw in the gaps between, imagined or illusory.

— We have money, said Weakjohn, and a gun.

— A *gun*? Theremy was shocked. Fuck… if I'd known… Who is she?

— Nothing to say, said Weakjohn. Don't really want to look properly.

They edged forward.

This was difficult for them, Martoth realised. They were both used to living very differently, using their skills freely. Now suddenly they were scared of it. They were like birds with wings clipped.

— What's going on? asked Timoth.

Weakjohn and Theremy looked at each other, each willing the other to respond.

— OK… proper chat later, said Weakjohn. But you can feel what Theremy and I can feel, Timoth. Can't you?

— *Careful*! warned Theremy.

— Yes, careful! Don't go looking. Just say what you feel.

Martoth watched Timoth. He frowned and looked at his reflection in his window.

— It feels like the rips, he said, and like the body.

— Right, said Weakjohn. But it's bigger and further away, over a mile behind us. Something that big will have caused casualties.

She glanced at Theremy and he nodded as if to confirm.

Martoth spoke.

— Weakjohn, you told us these things need to be dealt with. Contained, you said.

— Yes.

— So why are we going in the wrong direction?

Unspoken thoughts were passing between the mindworkers in the front seats.

— Lots of reasons, Martoth. Hitspeke is not like Border. The Leap is not like Semele. The Leap is mindwoke. People here know what rips are. They know the dangers. Some of them know how to deal with them, though I doubt they've seen anything this big. You see every so often a car passes us in the other direction?

— Yes, said Martoth, they're going to deal with it? So it's not our problem, you're saying.

Theremy laughed bitterly.

— It might be our problem, said Weakjohn. We don't know yet, but we are worried by the size of this.

— Because more people have been hurt? asked Timoth.

— No, said Theremy as he brought the car to a halt again in the traffic. Because we are asking *why*?

— The rip by the lake, Timoth. That was about the same size as… its target… wasn't it?

— Oh, said Martoth. You mean: bigger attack, bigger target?

— Yup, said Theremy, drumming fingers on his steering wheel nervously. And, if we *have* managed to land in the right town, it just happens that the three wackjobs we're trying to connect with are probably the biggest target in town. Or on the whole damn planet, for that matter.

— So you think it got this Seronin? asked Timoth.

— Or Lethe. Or Candle. Any of them could warrant an

attack of this size.

Martoth watched Timoth again as his features hardened against some inner fear. In his eyes, prickling with orange-lit almost-tears, she saw a ghost of loneliness.

— …or cause it, said Weakjohn.

— In any case we are not in a fit state. We need to get safe. So I don't care if that rip took out the entire bloody Vigil, it's not time for heroics.

Weakjohn was regarding Theremy with some concern. Something had spooked him badly. The nervousness, the uncharacteristic decisiveness, the edge of aggression.

The perpetual inching forward was grinding away at their nerves. The darkness evolved in fits and starts; each momentary surge forward cast a new pattern of broad-mottled chemical colours around the car's interior.

— Wherever we are going, we could walk faster than this, said Timoth.

And again Martoth was aware of other discussion going on that she at least could not hear. Theremy's jaw had tensed in irritation. Weakjohn kept the surface conversation alive:

— It might be frustrating, Timoth, but until we know where we are going there really isn't anywhere safer than right where we are. At least we are not conspicuous here. And Theremy and I can begin to understand our surroundings a bit better.

— But what are you actually *doing*?

— Timoth, *please*, snapped Theremy.

There were fewer pedestrians now, but occasionally one would hurry past, or wait by an unknown door on unknown business. But as the streets cleared of people the column of traffic remained, creeping forward yard by yard.

Then, unexpectedly, Theremy cried out in relief.

— Oh thank flux! he laughed. Oh jeez.

His relaxed in his seat, gulping down laughter and deep

breaths of relief. Without warning, Martoth's door yawned open and a man climbed in.

— Budge up! he cried.

She shuffled along into the centre of the back seats, allowing the newcomer to take her place and pull the door shut.

— Thanks, he said, giving her an easy smile.

He was young, medium height, slim build. He had a fresh-faced, easy expression created by short curly brown hair, bright eyes, and a naturally upturned mouth in a clean-shaven jawline beneath high but narrow cheek bones. There was an energy about him. But while Theremy's tension had melted, Weakjohn was frozen motionless in her seat, watching through the mirrors. The new arrival was all activity and ease.

— Weakjohn, he nodded. Nice to put a name to a face.

— Lethe, Weakjohn acknowledged curtly. Something passed between them, some chord of mistrust and acceptance, a makeshift pact of non-aggression.

Lethe greeted Timoth and Martoth with a friendly salute and reached forward to pat Theremy on the back.

— Keep it together driver! It's all looking good!

— Good?

— Yeah, it's good, relax, said Lethe.

— The others?

— They're fine. They'll meet us later. They're... helping out.

— You mean with the rip? asked Martoth.

— Or the shitshow aftermath, Candle's patching some people up and Seronin's... well, let's say he's working hard beneath the radar. Hard as he ever does, anyhow.

What this was supposed to mean, Martoth had no idea and did not ask.

— You can talk straight, said Weakjohn, I'm not as touchy

as you seem to think.

— Okay, accepted Lethe, same goes for all of us. So let's keep the chat audible too?

The two in the front seemed uncomfortable, but assented.

— Blinding! Let's go then…

— But where?

— Crowbeck! announced Lethe like it was a million dollar punchline at everyone else's expense.

— Where?

— You're gonna love it. Out of town, Northbound, fifty K up shitty dirt track number five.

— *Where?*

— Let's get out of this queue, turn around and take that right we just passed. And get moving too, we've got an hour's drive and we have to check in before midnight.

…and to Timoth's vast relief, Theremy pulled some kind of star-shaped manoeuvre to extract the car and they shot off back the way they'd come, past the toiling traffic and off into the streetlit unknown.

— Aren't we going to stick out a bit in Crowbeck? asked Weakjohn.

— Not if our ever-unreliable friend has done his job, said Lethe.

Weakjohn had asked politely enough but Martoth could tell she had deep reservations. Lethe went on:

— *Should we be worried?* you might ask, and the answer is "probably not". *Should we be vigilant?*, you might ask, and the answer is…

— …is always, sighed Weakjohn.

— Always.

The streetlights streaked away to pinpoints in their wake, as did the city —a city without outskirts or suburbs, a city rimmed with nothing but sudden, clifflike, nothing— and before they knew it, they were in the countryside, their way ahead lit only by headlights and the stars. There was no moon. Was it unrisen or had The Leap no moon?

Their road was no dirt track but the surface was rougher and narrower than those in the town. Wild hedgerows grew on either side and crinkled boughs of trees snaked far into the road causing Theremy to swerve from time to time.

— Crowbeck is a kind of in-between place, explained Lethe to Martoth. In between towns, in between jurisdictions, in between farms, factories. There are loads of them on The Leap, stop-over towns, motel clusters. Some are early frontier posts that didn't make it or fell into the shadow of faster growing towns nearby, some just grew at natural breaks along the roads, by rivers, or in sheltered spots. Weakjohn's right, minds of our calibre are more exposed outside the big settlements. There are fewer mindworkers, less activity, less weather, less landscape. But if we can pull off the necessary camouflage, it's a much better place to *watch* from. And unless anyone wants to announce any visionary insights, watching is all we've got right now.

— On Semele, mused Timoth, a "beck" is a stream…

— Same here, Timoth. And the one that Crowbeck is named after runs through the hills above the village. Though I doubt anyone in the town realises. So much history gets forgotten so quickly. It can hurt that, if you're someone who knew the Earth. The Earth is still the source from which all these things ultimately spring. Even The Leap which preserves so much, forgets way more.

— There's no-one left now though, said Timoth.

— Ha! laughed Weakjohn. How old are you Lethe? What? A hundred?

— Ninety seven, thank you kindly, answered Lethe, depending how you measure. And there are a few older than I am, Timoth. Yes, there are a few of us who still remember

Earth and remember how we escaped, how we got here and all the things we lost on the way. But I'll take you up to that beck tomorrow. It might help you two feel at home and it's important to keep hold of things like that.

They all fell silent and Theremy drove onward through the night. Martoth drifted into a shallow sleep and the passing countryside flowed through her faltering dreams. She imagined she was a shivering, naked giant with legs taller than the oaks. She strode across the landscape groping for a missing moon. As she travelled, the ground grew hillier then craggier under her colossal feet and soon she was clambering over fells and screes in her search, all the while, growing taller and taller. Eventually her face touched damp layers of cloud, unlit barriers beneath the far canopy of stars. Off to the horizon she saw the towns of The Leap as lonely lights on the earthen floor with only a sparse twinkling of smaller settlements scattered in between. The missing moon frightened her and began to take on deeper meanings in her sleep. The moon that she missed became both her father, once fled, now dead, and her mother, a seeress, turned carcass.

When she woke, they were driving into a small settlement. She saw clusters of buildings crowding around the road ahead of them. The first building, coming up on the left, was broad and low, and wrapped round with strange-coloured tubes of light. It stood in front of the settlement proper like a gatekeeper. Theremy slowed and Martoth realised that this was their intended stop — an outthrust perch on the edge of an in-between town. There were other cars standing dark and unattended on a black, tarry surface beyond the main building. Theremy drew up next to them, let the engine die, and breathed a long sigh.

— Nice job, said Lethe, opening his door.

— What is this? asked Martoth.

— Just a motel, he answered, a place we can stay and wait

for the others.

As they all got out of the car and stepped out onto the neon-lit surface, a sudden change came over Lethe.

— *Wait!*

They froze, straining their eyes and ears, but there was nothing to see or hear. Only silence from the road and the motel. No movement, not a flicker from the lights. A delicate breeze passed. Lethe was stock still.

— Something's changed, he said.

They watched him, snapshotted in an expression of confusion, brow furrowed, his eyes watching something elsewhere, somewhere they couldn't see. Martoth looked at Timoth; he was as confused as she. And then Lethe came back to life.

— It's okay, he said. Seronin's dealing with it.

B. Xxz. Fffflr. FFflr. Seronin. Fzz. Affiant. Fwero Jiqua. Xxz.

He came up to *Concreta* for air and to gather himself before going back under. But *Concreta* was nearly as chaotic: sirens wailed, lights flashed and Hitspeke's competing authorities climbed over each other to respond. Seronin hung back from the action, using a broken streetlamp for support as he dipped in and out of *Brainslang*. He was fifty yards from the rip but he could see it clearly over the wrecked vehicles. It was the size of a building but moving in all sorts of disquieting ways — drifting, oscillating and twisting unpredictably through hidden dimensions. So unstable was the boiling corona that the tear was barely transparent. Across its surface, colours saturated and desaturated in bubbles and patterns that cheated the eye and seemed to drag Seronin inwards.

Down.

Xsquill. Bb. Of the. Fflr. Terratetramagnamaramürrer. Xx. W.

Maintaining a perspective in Brainslang was like walking

through a burning sponge. Without preparation, Seronin couldn't stay down for more than a few seconds at a time. And it was difficult to make sense of anything in there until afterwards. The effort required to form a coherent thought in *Brainslang* was insane. But, seeing as it shouldn't even be possible, Seronin cut himself some slack. Mainly he shifted to *Brainslang* when possessed by the occasional masochistic impulse, or as an exercise to stay limber. But every so often, it had real uses. Every so often a perspective in *Brainslang* enabled you to see to the very roots of concrete reality.

B. Gxxz. To. By. Haematode. Winky. Xrr.

Times like now.

His eyeballs ached.

Down again.

B. 'Pp. Up. Herrick. Esio. Xr. G. Meery Pins. Xxz. Rp.

Out again. Process. Analyse. Rearrange. Dive. Down again.

Zff. Agarg. Rememoratorer. Awer. Awor. Bbp.

Times like now. Because there was something in there, something like a cause or a catalyst. If not a *why*, at least a *whence*.

The Hitspeke City Watch were first on the scene after Seronin and Candle, just two vans, a handful of men and women in pale overalls and body armour and only one or two mindworkers amongst them. They did little more than tally the few casualties that hadn't been swallowed or torn beyond individuation, and they allowed Candle to tend to the handful of survivors. Seronin melted into the shadows as soon as the watch arrived but Candle stayed around. None of the watch were too eager to indulge their curiosity and they were glad of the help and an unpanicked presence amongst them.

Then the Vigil landed, complicating things somewhat. Two novices first, concrescing near Seronin and reeling from what must have been a pretty nasty journey. Candle fled immediately. In the nick of time, as Sounness himself arrived a second later. If Seronin could risk an ugly confrontation with the Vigil, Candle could not. Seronin was operating now under heavy camouflage and he was constantly aware of the Vigil minds working at the rip. He was having to dance around them or plunge into *Brainslang* to evade their notice. They'd started well. They assumed command from the watch, cleared the survivors, marked and measured bounds, checked for growth or proliferation, propelled test spins into the rip, discovering what Seronin had already established: it was not sentient. It was a simple noumenal tear — vast yes, unstable yes, and with a fearsome retained momentum, but it was not sentient. They'd assessed it in *Concreta* and *Happenstance*, and Sounness had even shifted through *Sanctum*, tracing a path that Seronin had taken twenty minutes earlier.

Then a motley trickle of doctors and medics began to show up in their own vehicles. They were freelancers responding to desperate summons from the council. Any need for medical expertise had passed —the only casualties were dead or gone — but these were calm heads by and large, and, being honest heads too, and on the payroll for tonight, they set about cleaning up what they could, with one or two even lending power to the Vigil's containment.

If Seronin was in danger of being impressed by the smooth response, a flurry of other vehicles then turned up to disrupt things: the city's Battalion to quell a crowd which simply wasn't there, Federated Guild Security Services (FGSS) at who knows whose behest, some outfit who claimed responsibility for the roads and two antagonistic vigilante groups with opposing political sympathies that Seronin didn't take the time to understand. The operation descended into chaos at roughly the same time the Vigil determined that the rip was growing.

Ui ui gkacarrow. 'mk fleche.

Seronin retched. He'd found something —something that couldn't be seen up here— a trajectory, a history and a future. And deep, so deep that Seronin could hardly tell whether it was in *Brainslang*'s fiery swamp or in some reflected morass of his own psyche, he'd found a place where, with superhuman effort, the rip might be drained and sutured.

A watchman screamed. The rip had jerked around and expanded outside the safe zone. Under the sodium orange of the street lighting and the bilious green phosphorescence of the rip, Seronin could see him pounding his fists against the road. A roiling fusewound was carved through his legs and still growing, eating up flesh and road as it spread. His blood was spilling freely onto the tarmac. The man's colleagues rushed to help him while the Vigil moved everyone back and extended the safe zone.

Seronin braced himself. To stay down long enough he was going to have to make some changes. Gripping his lamppost, he stealth-shifted up to *Happenstance* to do some quick reconfiguration and prepared to dive right through *Concreta* all the way down…

Xxz. Feruhqwakur. Xzzz. 'Fpp. Iruhoiph.

In *Concreta* the rip mutated swiftly, as if someone had leant against a dimmer switch. It became pinched in complexion, its sprawl across the visible spectrum narrowed and it seemed to jellify inside.

Sounness started and his head jerked this way and that as he scanned the scene — the road junction, the vehicles, the windows of the buildings.

— On your guard! he yelled into the flux.

Seronin emerged into *Concreta* to find quake damage in the mental landscape. His camouflage, bent out of shape, no longer touched the sides. There were holes.

The spinroar had lessened and the pulsing pressure of the rip had relented but there were Vigil minds out there marauding, hammering, searching, turning over stones. And it was no longer just Sounness and the novices, there were other minds joining them, or probing from afar.

— SHOW YOURSELF! burned a voice in Seronin's mind.

He stayed still beneath his lamppost and smoothed out his camouflage. There was some desperation in this swarming of Vigil minds. They had not identified him. They had not located the unseen presence. What might they be fearing? What did they think was coming next? He began to prepare himself for some kind of confrontation but events outpaced him.

The area was reaching a saturation point. The chaos in the physical expression of reality, the lights, the bodies, the rip, was being outrun by an emerging chaos in the mental expression of reality. The world was beginning to *tip over*. This was now less a rubble-strewn road junction than it was a communal soup of thought and dream.

Seronin felt the onset of panic. He had seen the threshold breached before but never in such mayhem with so many unpredictable influences skewing one another's orbits. He didn't know what would happen. He couldn't tell whether physical reality would survive in this region. What would happen at the fringes, at the edges where roads travelled into what had been this junction?

He realised he was exposed. There was no way to fix a camouflage in this dream world. He could sense the others, the novices, Sounness, Yorgen, Barnabas… they were all in this, some ensnared, others just riding. They knew he was here but they had no time or attention for him. He began to understand that he was sheltering them somehow. It was if everyone was now holding tight to Seronin's lamppost while a gale blew them off their feet.

And then, suddenly, a coherent fixed vision, a momentary island of stability in the chaos, hung for a second in front of all their minds: a man with a burning stare and blood on his hands and on his face. A waxed moustache, tightly cropped black hair threaded with silver, an old-fashioned grey jacket, waistcoat, shirt and trousers, torn and battered... The bloodied hands reached forwards in menace and his vicious eyes narrowed.

The Vigil's terror was a flinching animal, stark and tangible in the dream soup. Seronin cast his mind at the apparition, touching, tracing, but it hung inert like a notice of intent, a warning of what was to come, etched with anger and blood.

And a name.

Clindor.

Seronin was bound deep into the dream soup but slowly and laboriously he drew each filament of his mental fabric out from the morass. In the heart of the mess the closing rip was shedding energy, the Vigil minds were extracting themselves, and once more the physical expression of reality began to dominate. The road junction that reasserted itself was a reprocessed version of the original, rounded and simplified by the conflagration. Rough edges had melted, leaving a bold geometric approximation.

Crude forms of people were suspended around him, solidifying out of a smoky shade in the air. The Vigil.

— We're here, said Lethe and Candle, behind his shoulder on the fringe where Hitspeke joined this melt-world.

— Flee, he said. I've got this.

— Seronin.

A gust of wind from the town passed into the melt-world. The two of them stood facing each other: one, in the open now, standing tall, every facial muscle under conscious control; the other with an explosion of grey hair framing an ageless face and eyes of steel, his black cassock ruffling in the breeze. Two minds grown bitter using each others' betrayals to excuse the measureless sins of their own. Minds that would never meet by choice.

— Barnabas.

As they crossed the tarry surface to the lit-up building, Martoth fell into stride with Weakjohn. She sensed friction between the three senior members of the party and was shy of asking questions but she and Timoth had been dropped into this moonless world without the most basic vocabulary to understand what they were seeing and hearing. Nobody had specifically asked for silence, so she stuck close and asked about the more obvious puzzles: the motel; neon lights; car parks; power lines. Timoth stepped up his pace to listen in.

Weakjohn kept up a commentary for them as they followed Lethe and Theremy into a bright reception room. A brass bell rang and a thin-haired, slack-faced man came out to serve them. Lethe negotiated a suite of rooms for them and then led them back outside to find it.

— What did he say? asked Weakjohn as they left.

— Vigil were sniffing around last week, replied Lethe, know anything about it?

Weakjohn shook her head.

— My last contact was before Theremy's. I don't know what our interest here would be.

— You realise we have certain expectations of you from now on, right?

— I know what boat I'm sailing in.

Lethe looked carefully at Weakjohn.

— Why do I have this nagging feeling you're so much friendlier than you're letting on?

Her face was firm and expressionless. The neon light painted her with cloudy yellow eyes in a crystal blue skull and Martoth realised for the first time that Weakjohn's inscrutability was not only intentional but well practiced.

— Not everyone has always been fair to everyone else while they've been trying to be fair to everyone else, she said.

Lethe snorted.

— OK. Let's get inside and start figuring this stuff out. The others are going to be later than we hoped.

In the end they were too tired to figure anything out. They found themselves berths spread around the suite with a nod to notions of propriety that none of them truly shared but they all ascribed to each other. Theremy and Timoth took one room and Weakjohn and Martoth another, but the doors were ajar and partitions rolled back. They might even have been arrayed around the floor of the Border taproom, if it weren't for the peculiar comfort of the bedding and the background buzz from the lighting that kept Maroth awake, fretting about the missing moon. Lethe had disappeared entirely. Neither Weakjohn nor Theremy seemed surprised.

20. Hunted

Martoth, Timoth, Seronin

Lethe was very much present the next morning, blustering about, ratcheting open blinds and clattering anything that could be clattered. Martoth endured her first experience of television, which Lethe introduced to two rooms at full volume. Content was local, like everything these days, but Crowbeck received channels from Hitspeke and it didn't take Timoth much tinkering to start getting some coverage of last night's rip.

The channel had some amateurish footage from soon after the rip and one long segment of the ruins captured in the early hours of daylight. They were cycling all of it as text crawled around the margins of the screen and bodiless voices reiterated the established facts. Timoth and Martoth moulded their duvets into reasonable imitations of ricebags at the foot of the bed and sat down to take it all in.

Latest:, ran the text, *30 passed. 22 blessed.*

— *Blessed*, said Weakjohn, sitting up against the headboard, is *Leapspeak* for wounded. *Passed* is dead.

A newsreader voice, female and serious, circled back to the top.

The rip occurred two whits into seventh as Hopworth junction filled with rush hour traffic — the fifth major rip in Hitspeke in the last two weeks and by far the largest, stretching the full width of Hopworth junction... the junction which, by the way, is now ruined following the events of last night. Several cars were completely destroyed. The Watch have traced all owners and occupants. Witnesses report that the rip grew significantly in the first few minutes, hampering aid efforts, although all casualties were removed from the scene within the hour.

Jerky footage showed the rip from several angles, through clusters of silhouetted heads. They could see it oscillating, iridescent above the wreckage, but none of the TV shots conveyed the disconcerting sense of scrambled up reality that Martoth recalled from the way head.

What happened next is still mysterious although facts are emerging slowly from sources at the Watch's office. It seems authorities' attempts to contain the tear were unexpectedly bolstered by volunteers and even, by some reports, off-world intervention. The junction was inaccessible for most of the night. When reporters finally got near the scene this morning, this is what they found.

— *Lethe*, called Weakjohn, what the flux is that?

Lethe and Theremy came through from the other room. Lethe frowned at the screen.

— That, he said, is a right royal rats' arse of a fuck-up from your buddies. And less than a barrel of laughs for Seronin.

— ...and not so technically? prompted Martoth.

Lethe wandered over to a desk, slid onto it, and sat cross-legged on the surface. He flicked the TV's sound off but left the imagery rolling.

— OK, this is hairy stuff. I'm giving you a crude simplification of something that pretty much no-one properly understands. I don't even think there's a word for what happened last night, unless Seronin's invented one, and he says he's only seen this happen once or twice.

— So, he said, the world is made of this *stuff*…

He looked to Weakjohn, unsure what they already knew, but Martoth pushed him on.

— Noumena? she said.

— Exactly, he agreed. *Stuff*. What sort of stuff is stuff?

— Things and thoughts, recited Timoth.

Lethe nodded.

— …and the crucial point here is things and thoughts are both made of the same stuff, just expressing itself in different ways. At its root the world is made of neutral stuff. *Physical* and *perspectival* are just modes of expression arising from interactions of noumena. And wherever we look we see this complex mixture of both. Nothing is truly inanimate. This is why you can fuse with stones, Timoth. They can be mental in their own way. This is all known and understood by the Vigil and by other mindworkers. It's the basis of a lot of the things we can do.

Lethe twisted his head left and right as if to stretch out a crick in his neck.

— Also well-known is the initially unsurprising fact that physical expression generally *dominates*. If you look around, you see a world in which most noumena are expressing physical characteristics way more than they are expressing mental characteristics. It is a world of things, even if some of them are thinking things.

— I say *initially* unsurprising, because you can persuade yourself to doubt it. And when you do it becomes all the more mysterious and surprising that it is true.

— Anyway, when there is lots more mental activity in an area, it's possible to reach a threshold, a point where the perspectival begins to dominate in that locality. Not many of us know what that is like, but according to Seronin it's pretty weird. And that is what happened last night.

— The Vigil got involved. Not one or two, but *hundreds*.

Add in some firepower from Seronin, Candle, a handful of Leap mindworkers, spins from the rip, the residue of the casualties, a whole stuffy fug of Dioclete weather and at some point it all just tipped over.

— So, you've got an area of Hitspeke which used to be a road junction which suddenly isn't a road junction anymore. Or at least, if it *is* a road junction, it is actually *more something else*. And that something else doesn't behave or evolve in any way like physical reality should. Frankly it's a miracle that we've got something back out of it that is shaped a bit like the road junction. It might even be possible to drive on it.

— ...and "Dioclete"? asked Martoth.

— Hmmm. Yes. Indeed. It's about time for our Council of Elrond isn't it?

Martoth looked at him blankly. Timoth was lost in his own contemplation.

— I need some air, said Theremy. Can I take an hour to wander into the village?

Lethe looked at a clock.

— Take a couple. I want to show the others the beck anyway. Seronin is involved with the Vigil, I don't expect him for a while yet. Be careful.

— The Vigil? said Weakjohn uncertainly. I... should be there.

— Oh yes! taunted Lethe in a parody of realisation. Yes you should, shouldn't you?

They all knew she wouldn't.

By daylight, without the garish motel light, Crowbeck looked very different. The clusters of houses were built from a mixture of grey stone and red bricks suggesting two waves of settlement. The fells rose steeply to the north and south, while the road ran broadly east-west, with the village extending to the east and Hitspeke back out west.

Martoth felt at home. Semele had landscape like this, even if the vegetation was different. She breathed in the fresh air and gazed up at the peaks.

— It's four miles up to the beck, said Lethe. You two look in good shape?

— Just let me at it, said Timoth.

Weakjohn chose to take the air nearer by, staying at the foot of the hills while the others went up. Theremy had slunk off into town.

As they climbed they spoke. Again it was Martoth who pushed for answers and this morning, she felt bolder than before.

— Weakjohn warned us against you, you know.

— Me?

— Well Seronin mostly. But you and Candle too.

— Ah well, that's not surprising. She's right in her way.

— …to warn us?

— Maybe. She's certainly right in what I think she was getting at last night, that there are good people in the Vigil. There are, and I believe she and Theremy are or were two of them. She's also right that we don't always get everything right. Seronin, in particular, can be quite… unpredictable.

— …but?

Lethe turned to check how far they'd ascended. The motel stood a few hundred yards below. Beyond the road a similar landscape climbed and spread to fill their view. Timoth trailed some way behind and called up to them.

— Hey, there's a cave over here!

Lethe's face went blank for a moment.

— It looks safe, he called back, why don't you go take a look? The beck is just the other side of that summit.

Martoth stopped, stunned, and touched her ears. She was certain Lethe had not spoken aloud. He'd used his mind and *she had heard.*

Lethe grinned:

— You thought only Timoth could hear?

— I know Weakjohn's been talking directly into his head.

— There are different ways of doing it. But it's perfectly possible to be inclusive without talking out loud. It just takes a little more effort.

Behind them, Timoth diverted left round a boggy patch and took a new route upward.

Lethe turned uphill and reverted to his vocal chords.

— Weakjohn is Vigil through and through. She has a Vigil mindset and Vigil prejudices even when she tries to overcome them. And we offend those prejudices. That was the start of it anyhow. I think maybe we've done a few hurtful things along the way. It can get quite heated. Most of the people inside the Vigil don't realise how controlling the regime is, or how little freedom they have.

— So Theremy's escape... I get it. But what prejudices?

— They treat non-naturals as subhuman. Worse than animals. Each non-natural is a threat to the very idea of humanity. Theremy's case is especially difficult. He's a stable fusion — a composite of pre-existing minds. Somehow he managed to go undetected within the Vigil and reach a position of some seniority. He wanted to change them from the inside... show them that non-naturals are people too. But they see it a bit differently. They'll have something nasty in store if they catch up with him. Weakjohn must be pretty conflicted right now. If it hadn't been for you two... well... She seems to be quite... flexible but she's having a harder time coping with us.

— Why is that?

He laughed.

— In Abbot Barnabas's eyes, Seronin is a heretic, I am a deviant, Candle is an aberration. What's she supposed to think?

They climbed silently for a minute before Martoth asked:

— Do I even want to know?

— Most people do, he smiled. Candle's synthetic. There was never a baby born that grew into Candle, so, in the Vigil's eyes, she's not human. I know she's synthetic because I made her. I made her when I was twenty-two years old, as the Earth spiralled into crisis. Well, in the Vigil's eyes, a twenty-two year old male, synthesising a female mind… you can get where they're coming from.

— And Seronin?

— Seronin was a very perceptive novice who saw things the Vigil couldn't and could do things the Vigil didn't want to believe in. It just happens he took our side and got into a big fight about it, making a lot of unpleasant noise before disappearing off to live his own feckless, reckless life, that no-one really approves of at all.

— I'm not sure what to think.

— Of course. Candle will be upset I've told you so soon.

— I won't tell her.

— She already knows.

The sky was a weave of ash grey and limpid blue and, when the sun shone, the day was bright and brisk. Martoth savoured the wind buffeting her face. She slogged upwards without a break, tying her hair back as she went, relishing even the aches in her thighs and calves. The alien textiles that lined her off-world boots were finally wearing through but somehow her blistering heels only anchored her more firmly to the life she'd left in Border.

Lethe clearly loved this landscape too. When she wasn't pestering, he was content to climb in silence, breathing the fresh air and taking in the views. They climbed up to a broad saddle that connected a lower summit to a steep shoulder of the upper summit. Timoth had disappeared from sight below them.

— You can see the beck now, said Lethe, running down the ridge there and down into that valley.

— No crows though, she mused.

— No. The summit above is called "The Crow". I'm not sure why. Could be the name of the first person to settle here. Might be some story behind it. We could skirt round this side and look down from there. It's a nice view over the beck as it gathers pace.

Martoth breathed the mountain air and let it fill her up, wriggling it out to the very tips of her fingers. She looked up to the Crow and other peaks beyond. This was a day to be alive.

— Or we could just nip up to the top quickly, she said. If we have time?

Lethe's face lit up. He stood tall and stretched his back.

— You won't regret it, he said.

Some cave. Close to, it was nothing but an overhang and a cloak of ivy bending in the breeze. There were better on Timoth's paddy trail. Only a small dark recess hidden behind brambles to one side persuaded him to scramble up to the ledge to look closer.

He plucked gingerly at the thorn bush and knew immediately there was something in the hollow. There were glimpses of light in the branches and evidence the plant had been dragged across to cover the gap. He paused, suddenly wary, and considered fetching the others. He doubted he could summon Lethe using psychocephy; it didn't feel beyond him but it would take time and the sort of experimentation that Weakjohn had expressly forbidden. Whatever else, he had to avoid mindwork. Also, Lethe and Martoth —everybody in fact— felt strangely absent here. Even the birds had gone silent.

Could this light be something of Seronin's? They were here

because Seronin used the area as a base from time to time and there'd been scant evidence of that while they waited for him at the motel.

He dragged back enough of the bramble to find the niche ended abruptly at a blank rock face with only an inch-high horizontal cleft at floor height, far too tight to enter. The cleft was deep though and something giving off a milky white glow was lodged deep inside.

He sank down and sat leaning back against the wet rock, intending to give up and ask Lethe about it later. Weakjohn or Theremy might have peered in with their minds but even if he hadn't been warned against solo experimentation, all Timoth had shown himself capable of so far was the shift in the barn and fusing with stones and thimbles. And there was not even anything here to fuse with except the bushes, the rock, the earth and the...

Then so many revelations tumbled over one another he was thankful he was already sitting down. He could not have seen the milky light with his eyes — it was at floor level and he'd been standing on his feet as he pulled aside the brambles. And *what evidence* the plant had been moved? There was no dust or debris on the cave floor, no damage to the bush.

He'd been looking with his mind again without even realising it. How else could he have enumerated amongst his fusion candidates this... *thing* — the thing so like the rock of the mountain but so fluid, so open, so flat? It had been there all along, eclipsing everything else. It was the reason he couldn't feel Lethe and Martoth further up the hill. His mind's eye was stretched wide enough just trying to encompass this enormous *thing*. He felt as if his face was pressed up hard against it. Not only could he fuse with it, he could hardly see how he could not fuse with it. It opened up to him, more like a yawning entrance than the cave itself, and he was standing in its mouth.

But the *fluidity* of the thing. It was not like stones or reeds that had their shapes and systems and ways they wanted to be. It was blank, inviting, formless. He could take whatever he wanted into the fusion. Without intending to, he expanded his perspective into tiny exploratory fusions at the edge of it and began to feel its power. In dwelling on fragments of his recent experience he found every detail exploding like fireworks into glowing trails and meshes. The ley from Semele to The Leap leapt into sight as a crinkled thread in an impossibly delicate network that was wilting before his eyes. There seemed to be no limits. He felt he could trace these routes, see what was happening, watch from some impossible vantage point the crumpling of the world he'd just begun to discover.

He fused deeper, became a new *cylinx-Timoth*, let his magnified perspective crawl deep into the crevices of the world around him. He saw the waves of attacks, the rips, the puppetry, pulsing across the world, but he could not see a source. The ripples crossed and interfered as if emanating from many places at one. But no, he was *seeing* from many places at the same time. His perspective was somehow strewn across the universe and he was as yet unable to piece together the overlapping data that poured in.

He tried to focus to avoid drowning in the immensity of what he was becoming. The places and people he knew were easy to find. Even here he felt echoes in the world of Alban, Mulkah, Ma. He could see their present and their potential futures, lines grown from the traces of their past he'd carried with him from Semele. He saw the routes the puppets might take to Border, saw the flames that could engulf the taproom, saw charred timber floating in the deep paddy. And he saw back to Marta's death, extrapolated from the tiniest imperceptible marks that her arrival had left on him as he worked in the paddy that day, saw that it was not his transgression that had caused the rip that killed her but her own, a foolish impatience, a leap across a hundred yards to the shore.

As *cylinx-Timoth*'s confidence grew he found himself looking for a change he could make, a fix, a fight-back. He burned suddenly with a sense of justice he must have caught from Martoth, and he believed he could make a difference at last. He became as impatient as Marta. If he could *see* the attacks, how could he not still them? He reached further into the universe, chasing thread after thread, oblivious until far too late to the noise he was making.

It took nearly an hour of scrambling up the steep shoulder crag to reach the small platform summit and look down over the landscape. The could still see below the lower mountainside where Timoth had turned off but the trees and rocks down there were tiny now.

— I guess this is like it was before humans came, suggested Martoth.

He nodded.

— It's easy for me to forget how alien it all is. Everything, the grass, the trees and the birds, it's all so like a place I remember from my childhood. But when you look deeper it is frighteningly alien, right down to the DNA. The *really* odd thing though…The place I remember was as much a product of thousands of years of cultivation as it was natural. Whereas this place, it's near pristine and yet it's eerily like the end product of both the natural and human processes on Earth. Like it's skipped straight past a few stages and inexplicably targeted a human ideal. That or we somehow shaped this world too, and further back than the hundred years we've actually been here.

— Is that possible?

Lethe shrugged.

— I don't know. The Vigil call it serendipity. One of the great mysteries. We've found the same everywhere.

— There's no moon.

— So no tides, agreed Lethe. That has a few other unexpected effects. But it is unusual — most of the other worlds we've populated have a single moon like Earth and Semele.

— You miss the Earth?

— Martoth, even you miss the Earth, though you don't realise it.

— There are plenty of mysteries still then. You and Seronin don't have it all sewn up.

Lethe laughed.

— Seronin doesn't—

...but suddenly he froze, his jaw clenched, and colour drained from his face.

Martoth followed his gaze. Three streaks of fire raced out of the distant sky, leaving trails like claw marks scratched across the world. As the meteors fell towards their mountain a deep roar filled the air and Martoth felt her teeth throb.

— Timoth! cried Lethe, and ran a few yards down from the summit.

The flaming meteorites, or whatever they were, hit the ground half a mile down the mountainside in a vaporous explosion. The trails cooled from glowing white into an oscillating near-transparency and Martoth realised they were noumenal rips, miles long, emerging out of distant clouds and terminating where three room-sized balls of light were now beginning to roam across the hillside in a twisting, tumbling motion.

— Ripspins! shouted Lethe as she tried to follow him down the crag.

Timoth had appeared below and though he was hardly

more than a pinprick in her sight she could see his terror in the way he held himself, almost in the air, hopping lightly on his feet as if trying to disappear into some space behind his head, trying to will his body into a sprint but not having the command he needed.

— *NO!* Lethe commanded her, get back to the top and *stay there!*

She retreated, keeping her eyes on Timoth, frightened of losing him in a way she hadn't been back in the barn. Lethe hopped down the crags at a perilous pace but way too slow to get to Timoth.

— Back to the cave Timoth, barked Lethe in their minds.

And then he vanished before her very eyes.

Then, there he was, down below with Timoth as the ripspins converged. Timoth fell back and Lethe stood in front. He was doing something — she couldn't tell what. It was invisible and she couldn't think straight with the roar. But when the floating masses got too close to Lethe they dulled, quivered and tumbled back. After some fruitless sallies against Lethe's invisible barrier, they tumbled down the hill instead, leaving Lethe and Timoth to flee back to the cave behind the lower summit.

Weakjohn! thought Martoth suddenly. Where is she? Still at the foot of the hills?

She set off down the crag. It was senseless — she was nearly two hours away from Weakjohn, but she couldn't just sit up here in the clouds while her friends died down below. Using hands and feet, she hurried down the mountain, ignoring the noise and the streaks in the sky, all her concentration focussed on getting down quickly, and, if she could, safely.

Weakjohn sat on a rock with her stick beside her and contemplated her death as it tumbled down the slopes above.

No sense running. They moved faster. No sense fighting. She hadn't the strength. It wasn't a pretty feeling. Her mind turned to regrets, missed chances, humiliations, griefs and jealousies. The effect of the spins? Or her own worth? In her mind the spinroar dissolved as the demons approached, or as her silence recalibrated to accommodate them. White light spilled across across her sight and she found herself blind for the last few moments. No matter, she thought, just let me die as myself, let me not disperse into these things, and then across the world. The end must be the end. I deserve that, surely.

But in her last moments came a sudden throb of concern for the safety of others behind her in the motel. A quick calculation, a reconfiguration... Might her death not be entirely in vain? As she felt her grip loosening, felt her body fall away and her mind fragment, she made some changes, began to shape the dispersal of her perspective, turn it outwards, while simultaneously shifting into *Happenstance* and—

But. Wait.

The whiteout imploded and her broken eyes recaptured a blurry sensation of the scene in *Concreta*. The roar was waning and the spins were draining, drawing back the tentacles of anxiety they had wormed into her mind.

There was something new here, a power greater than the ripspins, thrashing about, attacking them with a mad abandon, with scant regard for the world around them. It flicked the sunlight on and off, churned the earth up, buried, excavated, buried again. Beyond fear, she felt her body shaken around and thrown backwards.

As the world briefly came into focus, she could already feel that focus departing again. But something was nagging, something keeping her, something unresolved. Must. Speak.

— Seronin?

— Hush.

A female voice.

— Seronin, please, said Weakjohn, clinging onto consciousness. There were *three* of them.

Timoth stood at the lip, watching helplessly as the light show by the motel died down. Lethe squatted next to him, pallid and retching, forcing his eyes open to watch. Sweat bathed his hair and ran off his face. He tensed as cramps seized him.

— Timoth, he gasped, am I seeing right?

— What?

— The *residues*, he said. Solidifying out of the air. *How many*?

Timoth, watched carefully and began to see the residues he meant, wispy things like netting or gauze that seemed to crystallise out of the air and catch the wind. They were delicate but large, larger than the ripspins. Timoth watched them drift with a sinking feeling in his gut

— Two, he cried in horror.

Three tears hung in the grey sky, mocking him.

— Oh god, said Lethe, clutching his stomach and trying to stagger to his feet. *Martoth*! I can't…

Timoth was already off the ledge and racing up the hillside.

— Help me! she wailed with blood on her lips. Hold on to me!

Timoth was on his knees.

— Careful! warned a voice. Away from the wounds!

Martoth screamed and clutched Timoth.

— The blood! she cried. Oh god, the blood.

He looked down. There was a lot of blood. And flesh. And seething, creeping otherness.

— Hold tight, he said. Help's here.

Who was here? There were others he was sure. There was activity around him. Lethe was here. Lethe must have transported them somehow. But there were others. Weakjohn? Seronin? Candle?

Martoth was convulsing, coughing blood and gagging on it. Her arms and chest jerked in Timoth's embrace, her legs, pelvis, stomach, they were a mangled mess of fuse-matter and reconstituted flesh.

— Oh God! Oh God! Oh God! she whispered.

Then… a presence… *Candle?*… was in their embrace. Not physically but every bit as wrapped around them both as he was around Martoth. Whatever she was doing was helping them both, soothing, supporting.

Timoth heard her voice in his mind, a voice of clarity and allure, of such presence that he had to remember to listen to the words and not just bathe in the sound.

— Timoth, she said, I need your help. Give yourself to me. Loosen your perspective.

A blueprint appeared in his mind, a picture of a method. He understood but he could not do it. There was a part, a surrender, that he could not do. It was surely death to try. Could he, would he sacrifice himself for Maroth to live?

Yes, he could.

No, not now.

Yes, now.

— Yes, yes. I'll do it. I can't. How do I let go? Help me.

— Trust, Timoth. I need your mind. I can't force you.

— Force me! he yelled, Please! Take it. Take whatever you want. I can't. I don't know how.

— Give it, she commanded. Quickly. She's dying, Timoth.

— I don't know how!

— Yes *you do*! Do it!

That image again, the blueprint, was pushed deeper into him, lain gently over the matching parts of his psyche. He began to follow but it was no good. He reached the final yielding and he could not let go.

— Force me! he wept.

Then a change. The uniting embrace became suddenly, overpoweringly sensual. Candle was all over him, visions flashed, sinuous and fleshy, he felt rubbed, caressed, touched. As he felt his body surge up an unspeakable peak, he saw a vertiginous fall beyond, a drop into terror and darkness.

— Give it to me. Now!

And he surrendered.

21. Power

1939

— Can you feel it, Wojciech? asked Clindor.

Together they hopped across the tramways of central Bern as all around them sombre front pages blended the pope's death with grim news from Spain. Desperate statecraft was the order of the day in London, a flu epidemic raged in Belgium. The Swiss had even crumbled to Canada in the ice hockey.

— I know little of where you served, under whom... but there are times in the military, I'm sure you've felt it, when everything is turned on its head and normal laws just don't apply anymore, ... there's nothing left for them to get a grip on. Everything is transformed into a chaos of power and pain.

The air was crisp and the sounds of the town rang in their ears. Wojciech chose his words carefully:

— My experience of the army was entirely the opposite of that, Monsieur. An epitome of order. Tedious, repetitious. Drills, drills, drills.

He laughed, as at a memory, trying to distract Clindor from his *idée fixe*. But Clindor was undistractable as ever.

— …but there were times. I know there were times. You know what I mean. When the very soil is on fire and horses swarm across it. The brakes are off, commanding officers are gone or pouring oil on the fires, and you're faced with reality totally… unfiltered, undiluted. And you have to catch your breath for fear of combusting on the spot, then you realise your own place in the power spectrum, how much you can push and be pushed against. And in a way you are more alive than anyone else in the world.

— I know what you're talking about, murmured Wojciech.

— Well is this not the destiny that Europe is converging on right now? Every government suspending the normal rules, changing laws, reacting to the actions of everyone else. So these desperate ideas are just rippling around the continent and everything from constitutions to customs are wobbling like jelly. No-one can rely on safe treatment anymore. Things we took for granted are becoming cherished ideals. Illusions are dying, one by one, and all the time we get closer to that raw reality of the battlefield. In the molten core of this vortex, Berlin maybe, or Munich, it is the only reality there is. I can feel it spreading.

It was so like Clindor, thought Wojciech, to mix undeniable fact with his own perverted view of the world in just such a way that objection seemed impossible.

— It doesn't matter who actually *wins* this war, continued Clindor. It's what emerges which is important. When the battlefield reality recedes it leaves a suppleness — an ambiguity. I'm talking about opportunities, Wojciech. Possibilities.

Wojciech's discomfort grew.

— I'm an old man, Clindor. Opportunity is for the young. And we are not at war yet, not in Switzerland, not in France, and not in Poland.

They turned along Bundes Gasse, heading for the Dalmazi

Bridge.

— Listen, my friend, have you not considered the implications of what we can do? What it means for Switzerland or Poland or Germany or the Soviets?

— No, said Wojciech. For science, yes, for physics maybe, psychology certainly, psychoanalysis perhaps. Not for politics.

— But you discovered it yourself, Wojciech. There is a mind that is you and the spider. There is a mind that is all of us. There are larger minds out there, rampaging around Europe, the East, Africa. There is a mind that is every human being, maybe animal too, species minds, genus minds. The world is awash with minds. And so far as we know, we are unique in the history of the world: the only people able to make thoughts happen in minds that aren't ours. Just think how powerful that capability is.

Something of the sort had occurred to Wojciech of course. He even believed he had touched the surface of some of these larger minds, but he would never admit it to Clindor. As they strode onto the bridge and his teeth froze in the gusting wind, his thoughts were dark. Clindor's sympathy for elements of the German regime was evident. His interest in the mechanisms of power and the sentiment of the masses was beginning to show. He followed the newspapers avidly, regardless of political polarity, and he always picked up pamphlets and flyers.

— Look, said Wojciech. I don't want to make this a weapon. I don't want to get any of us embroiled in the horrors in the papers. None of us do. Soon I'll make my decision, whether I stay here or head home, just like everyone else. Then the best thing we can do is keep our heads down and help our friends the best we can.

— "The best we can", repeated Clindor.

* * *

— Ah, Dr Harper! exclaimed Clindor as he hopped down the steps of the aisle.

Harper was Stephen's alter ego in the *Lucerne Dialogues*. Clindor had been assiduous with his reading over the Christmas break and now knew the text better than Stephen. He delighted in Templeton's crueller observations and seemed to have swallowed whole some of his self-aggrandising fictions which Stephen found demeaning.

— Where is Anna? asked Clindor.

Stephen's head shot up.

— She…

Conversation stopped. Lena rose and turned her head:

— She was just…

Then they were all on their feet, turning this way and that, taking a pace or two up the steps, into the rows, poking heads behind the blackboards, into the back room. Anna was nowhere to be found.

Stephen flew up the steps and through the door that Wojciech had left swinging. He halted at the doorway and looked both ways up the corridor, uncertain where to fly to next. He came back to the room looking defeated, eyes swollen and cheeks flush. Lena went to comfort him. If it weren't bad enough Anna vanishing, that it had been Clindor of all people to have noticed…

But Stephen could not stay still. He ran out again, off this time as far as each end of the corridor. He could not bear to leave in case Anna appeared.

— Harper! cried Clindor. Control yourself!

Stephen shot him a poisonous glare.

— *You..!* he cried, but no concrete accusation came to his lips and in a matter of moments he was calm, as if Clindor had brought him to his senses, or some other idea had occurred to him.

He lowered himself onto the end of a bench and sat with

his elbows on the ledge in front, his hands at his temples and his eyes closed. They felt his mind moving, though how and where they could not tell. It seemed like several shifts up to Happenstance, perhaps repeated attempts, or refinements of the construction he needed. At length there was a stillness to him that they did not know how to interpret. They waited, nerves stretched.

— She is safe, he said without opening his eyes.

A smile of relief flickered across his face but anger followed swift behind. His eyes opened and fixed on Clindor with such distilled malevolence that Harald felt the need to step between them.

— She has the paper *you* sent her for, said Stephen and launched to his feet, scrambling over the benches towards Clindor.

Clindor skipped back and chuckled.

— What an intriguing new capability you seem to have discovered Dr Harrison. I'm a little upset you didn't share it with us.

Stephen was too outraged to respond. Harald grabbed hold of him as he seemed set to throw himself at Clindor again. Meanwhile, Anna appeared at the top of the steps carrying a ream of paper in her small arms and carefully stepping down the steps, peering over the package, leading each time with her better foot.

She delivered the paper to Clindor and then ran straight to Stephen, hugging his leg.

— We don't keep secrets, Stephen. Why is it you need reminding?

Stephen stroked Anna's shoulder and rested his hand on her tiny neck, ready to cry with relief, but he was suddenly aware of a smell, or the thinnest hint of a smell. Of burning, he thought, but so faint it might be the smell of his own nose or moustache.

Looking down, he saw some microscopic spots of red-orange glow consuming individual flyaway strands of Anna's hair. So tiny, so near invisible, none would see but him. She would feel nothing. Her hair might end up neater than ever he and she could manage themselves. He placed a hand down firmly upon her head, quenching the tiny sprites.

— *Do* you need reminding, Stephen?

— He's a bastard, said Paul, digging into his schnitzel.

Bastien didn't respond. Pierre was more measured:

— He's driven. I do not think we should know so much without him.

— What we know is from Dr Harrison!

— But how much would Stephen have established without Clindor?

With the thumb of his cigarette hand, Bastien brushed some foam from the gilded rim of his beer glass and chose to side with Paul.

— You're endorsing his methods of motivation?

— No. I… It's just…

— Just…?

Pierre flushed.

— I just think we should recognise the world isn't as nice a place as we thought.

— What the hell does that mean? asked Bastien.

— Well, did you try the pain thing?

Bastien turned away and grimaced. Pierre swapped a knowing glance with Paul then grabbed Bastien's right arm.

Bastien transferred his cigarette to his left hand and allowed Pierre to unbutton the sleeve and roll it up past the elbow. Then he waited as Pierre did the same with his own arm. Bastien knew the idea. Clindor had been explicit.

They placed their elbows on the checked tablecloth as if preparing to arm wrestle, but they did not clear their beer or food away. Instead of grasping each other's hands, they gripped the flesh just above the elbow locking their arms together.

— Loosen, said Pierre, like you're going to shift.

Bastien obeyed.

— Okay. *You*, whispered Pierre.

Hesitantly, Bastien dug his nails into Pierre's flesh. Pierre hissed but suppressed a cry.

— *Me*, whispered Pierre, and dug his nails hard into Bastien. You… me… you… me…

Like the beat of a slave drum he carried this gruesome thing forward, faster and faster until blood gummed up beneath their nails and he could no longer speak. Still they continued.

Bastien gaped. He realised how free his perspective had become, how easy any shift from here would be. Instinctively he kept the cycle going while he shifted to Happenstance and back, fused with Pierre, with Paul, with the beer glass, with every blessed thing in sight.

Finally, he let go and stared at the marks on his arm.

— It's like a bloody laxative, he said, but, as he said it, he was already beginning to feel sick. A minute later he was vomiting in the toilets.

— That's the other thing, said Paul, stubbing out the cigarette Bastien left burning in the ashtray. It gets quite easy to take it too far…

Bastien mopped the blood with a handkerchief. On his way back to the table, he looked out of the window. Below, the River Aare flowed round the wide bend it carved through Bern and a raucous population of birdlife was interfering with the small traffic along the riverside.

None of them knew why they were here, nor, really, why they stayed, though each could admit privately it was more than the excitement of their growing power. What held the group together was Clindor.

— *The woman at the table by the door.*

It was Clindor's voice in their heads, like Dr Harrison had been teaching them, but from what distance? They looked urgently around the restaurant. Clindor was nowhere to be seen. It had not occurred to any of them that such a thing was possible. Meeting in Happenstance, talking in each others heads, touching each others minds — for all these things they had needed line of sight, or at least proximity. All depended on fusing or sharing a construction. How could you…? Then they remembered Dr Harrison's search for Anna. Clindor must *already* have taken this seed and grown something else from it. A common fear hung between them: was all privacy gone? They'd spoken freely just now, carelessly, in frustration, but it could easily look like sedition to Clindor. None of them relished the fallout from that.

— *Follow her!* came Clindor's voice again.

Their eyes flipped to the woman by the door. They had not paid her any attention till now and she was rising to leave. A member of staff brought her grey coat and helped her on with it. She seemed harried. With some haste she tied a floral scarf around her head, picked up a brown bag and left.

Bastien and Pierre worked through the implications of Clindor's new ability, with an awful sense of foreboding, but Paul was fresher and angrier. He had already made his own great stride forward:

— Follow her yourself! rang his voice *in their heads.*

Bastien gaped with disbelief:

— *Paul!*

Pierre swore and rose, sliding his chair back with a screech.

— You pay! he said to Bastien, pulling on his coat and heading after the woman.

When Paul and Bastien emerged into the sunlight, Pierre

and the woman had vanished. Locals passed on bicycles and the pavements were busy with tourists and the lunchtime crowd. But there was no sign of their friend or any indication where he might have gone.

Bastien raised his eyebrows at Paul as if to ask whether Stephen's new search capability was within his grasp. Paul nodded and his gaze lost focus.

— Down to the bridge, said Paul. Hurry!

When they got there it was too late. Her body hung by a thin cord from one of the bridge's iron girders, swinging in a stiff breeze that blew across the river. Pierre stood a few yards off, white as a sheet and swaying, balancing on the rocks at the edge of the water. In his hand he held the woman's brown bag.

— I... he said, staring at the bag as if surprised to be holding it. I found her.

As Bastien and Paul picked their way down toward him, shouts went up and a crowd began gathering above. Pierre dropped the bag and looked to his friends for help. For the first time in months he thought of his place at the Sorbonne and the aspirations of his father. He blinked in the sunlight, breathed steadily, alert for the slightest deviation of his treacherous heart.

The police investigation was short and curiously unmeticulous. Once fibres from the cord were found in the woman's bag, and testimony on her state of mind was taken from her grieving widower, little effort was spent investigating the foreign climbers who discovered her or tracing any connections that they had to the deceased, one Denise Clindor.

— But *why*? asked Pierre, days later.

— He's warning us, said Bastien. It's a lesson. Like Anna's disappearance.

22. The Face of Diocletian

Martoth, Timoth, Seronin

— Where am I?

...but his window framed three pale streaks in the late evening sky and he answered himself:

— The motel.

— Yes, still. We can't move you yet. Though we'll have to soon.

The voice was new.

— Seronin?

— We meet at last.

Timoth squirmed, trying to get comfortable in the sweat-drenched sheets.

— Martoth?

— Martoth's okay, we think.

He raised himself to a sitting position. Seronin sat in a corner between the wall and a slatted wardrobe door, his legs crossed and arms resting upon them. He was tall but not imposing and remained disconcertingly still as they spoke.

— Think?

— She's sleeping, we can't be sure yet.

— Her legs...?

— …we reconstructed with the help of your uncannily precise memory. She's whole and sound. Lethe and Candle are with her.

— The others…

— There's nothing wrong with Lethe. Weakjohn… Weakjohn has changed, but she's still with us. Theremy, not so good.

— *Theremy*? exclaimed Timoth. Theremy wasn't with us. He went into town.

— …and got himself beaten black and blue by the locals. He's next door spitting his teeth into a glass and feeling sorry for himself. I'll deal with him shortly.

— What the hell is happening?

Seronin barked a humourless laugh and walked out.

— You can touch her, said Candle.

But he was too awkward and he didn't know how, what to touch. So he just sat there, close, watching the rise and fall of her bedsheets. Martoth's hair was still pulled back into the ponytail she'd worn on the mountain but it was wet and knotted and sticking to her. Stray straggles splayed out on her pillow. Her neck, exposed shoulders, … he found himself seeing her in a new light. He saw now with shame a naked vulnerability in her that stood lofty in accusation passing over his idiocy with the cylinx and calling out his desire, the stolen glances, the places he allowed his gaze to linger.

Daylight had faded and lights were on by her bedside, on the ceiling, on the walls. Her window faced away from the claw marks but Timoth found he was aware of them anyway, constant reminders of the terror that had almost taken Martoth from him.

— Has she woken at all?

— Not yet, but it won't be long. It's not a coma. She's just exhausted.

In her sleep, she turned her face towards him. It was not the serene face of untroubled sleep. Her eyelids and cheek muscles were moving only slightly, at the very limits of his ability to discern, but her lips moved ceaselessly, reflecting an internal monologue that would not stop. He sat back, disturbed.

— She's dreaming. We have to let it play out.

Timoth wanted to ask questions but he couldn't bear to turn to face Candle. There had been something dreadfully intimate in that final union. How had they saved Martoth? What had they done?

— Have you spoken to Seronin? She asked.

— A bit. He didn't seem to want to hang around.

Candle snorted.

— He's sitting out by the road. Why don't you take some beers out and sit with him? I'll let you know if she wakes.

There was a glass-fronted cabinet by the wall containing a variety of bottles. In approaching them, Timoth found he was forced to turn his face towards Candle and meet her eyes. He had expected a siren, a bee-stung pout or an eruption of blonde hair, dark rimmed eyes, hips, boobs, something to unsteady him. But Candle was not like that at all. She was smallish, unthreatening, dark-eyed and straight-haired, sitting calmly, with a blue padded anorak draped around her shoulders and a booktab on her lap. She pointed to a bottle-opener lying on a shelf then she turned her eyes back to Martoth.

Seronin was sitting on the stone wall gazing across the road into the shadowy landscape beyond, facing away from the claw marks in the sky. His hair was short and a little unkempt. He wore a shirt that seemed too large, its shape defined by tent-pole shoulders rather than anything more substantial.

— Shit, said Seronin as Timoth stood in the darkness behind him. You're going to ask difficult questions aren't you?

— I've brought… "beer"?

— Then you can ask whatever you like.

He passed the two bottles to Seronin while he pulled himself up onto the wall.

— Is it like saki? asked Timoth, studying the bottle that Seronin passed back.

— Never had Semele saki. Let's hope we can visit one day and compare.

Timoth didn't want to think of Semele or the chaos in Laketown. He didn't fear so much for his mother or the other Border folk he felt so much pride in. They were hardy souls, they'd live off whatever the world served up. They wouldn't be caught up in conflicts. If the world tore itself to pieces, they'd go down singing and dancing and blame none but fate. But Martoth wasn't all Border. There were vulnerable people who'd cared for her in Porton, and friends in Seaton. He knew the dread she'd felt leaving Laketown in flames. Maybe she even cared more shrewdly than he did for his own family and friends. He assumed too much, lived too much in his own troubles. She would think to worry whether Alban would wander off a cliff edge after too much saki. Timoth just assumed he wouldn't. And since Rosie died, Ma Mackelay had been as much Martoth's mother as his, when she was in Border at least.

— Martoth asks the right questions, he said. She's started piecing the puzzle together better than me.

— What puzzle's that?

— The one you don't even notice when you live your entire life in Border. But as soon as you're shown something different, something like this place, and you have to believe in both of them, it just becomes obvious, and you go, well, …

how the fuck did we get here?

— Oh that.

— What else is there?

— There are a million puzzles, Timoth, from the trivial to the ineffable. And ninety nine percent of them can be formulated as "how the fuck did we get here?".

Timoth grunted and took a swig of beer. Seronin pointed into the darkness across the road with the hand that held his own beer. After a second, Timoth saw what he was pointing at: pinpricks of pale green light floating lazily between the trees, every so often darting off their paths like sparks.

— In ten minutes that whole space will be full of them. They're just little insects, but I like watching the patterns when they all come out.

— Yeah? said Timoth. You wanna see rainflies.

They watched in silence. The road was dead at their feet. The arrival of a car like theirs was a once-a-night occurrence here. Amongst the trees opposite, one by one more lights joined the dance.

— Martoth doesn't know about the cylinx, said Seronin quietly.

He left the rest unsaid but Timoth caught his drift: *you may want to think carefully about telling her…*

— Candle said I should come and chat to you, said Timoth. Seronin grinned.

— I know. Candle is, I think, eighty years old or something? Lethe's basically a hundred. I think she's just thinking we are more a similar age.

— Weakjohn says you're some kind of mystic superhero.

— "Hero"? Not "villain"?

— My words, not hers, I guess.

— Mystic might be right. I certainly see more than I can explain.

— What's it like?

— Too hard a question.

The beer was growing on Timoth, bitter but sweet, and sweet along a different axis than Semele's saki. He could feel a gentle, reassuring drunkenness in his future and began to wonder how many bottles they had in the motel.

— Why is no-one here? he asked. The marks must be visible from Hitspeke. I thought we'd be hiding somewhere. Not sitting in the open.

Seronin hesitated.

— Weakjohn's bought us a little time, he said. In any case, Hitspeke has its own problems. They have groups rioting on the streets as we speak.

Timoth grimaced. The cherished had turned Laketown into a smouldering wreck in a couple of days. Maybe Hitspeke was better equipped to deal with trouble but was this going to happen everywhere they went?

— What happened to Theremy?

Seronin shrugged.

— Just cos The Leap is mindwoke, doesn't mean they're all that open-minded. We sprung Theremy from the Vigil because they found out he was a fusion. That sort of thing doesn't make you popular. I guess he was indiscreet.

Seronin looked carefully at him, then smiled and turned back to the fireflies.

— Twice now, Timoth, you've contributed your mind to enterprises which are considerably beyond your ability to comprehend. More or less willingly.

— Yeah, about that…

Might as well confront it. He took another swig, held the bottle there by his lips.

— That thing. With me and Candle.

— Don't worry about it.

— But I…

— Candle needed something. She took it. You weren't

giving it up. You're like a, what, sixteen year old male? It's really horribly easy to push your buttons. She used it. She used you.

— I can't shake it off.

— You've got to. Together you saved Martoth's life. Lethe was working on the fusematter and I was chasing down the last ripspin.

Seronin's jaw tightened and he lowered his beer bottle.

— Look Timoth. You've got a shitload to learn. You won't get a lifetime of formal training like you would with the Vigil. You're going to have to work your arse off. And there are a few things you're going to have to let go of on the way. One of them is a certain kind of naive sense of...

— ...dignity? suggested Timoth.

Seronin grinned.

— Candle said you were good.

— Wha-?

Seronin was sniggering in the darkness.

— At the healing I mean! She said you've got a very big...

— Oh stop already.

— And you don't need to worry about Lethe. He and Candle have been engrossed in their own passion for eighty years without let-up, they're almost one person. You needn't feel you've shared anything with Candle that even registers on their scale. In any case. She's used that technique before...

They caught each other's eyes. Timoth hadn't expected this. Here he was, maybe whole galaxies away from his roots, his things, and suddenly he was having the sort of relaxed knockabout chat he could have had with Alban in the taproom.

— Another beer? asked Timoth, draining the rest of his.

The fireflies were out in numbers now. Several patches of dancing lights hung like ghosts in the space between the road and the mountains, each its own intricate system of curves and perturbations.

— Why don't you ask Candle to bring some out?

— What? I can't!

— Look Timoth, I don't know if you've realised but it's Candle who's going to take over your training now. Weakjohn's given you some basics, a bit of theory but if you're going to be any use, you need to accelerate pretty fucking fast Candle's the one to do it. If you can't even ask her to pass a beer, we're going to get stuck pretty soon.

— No! I mean, yeah it's a bit rude but, the main thing is, I can't do the talking in people's heads. I can hear Weakjohn and you guys when you talk to me but I don't know how to speak.

— Sure you do.

— How?

— I'm not going to tell you, Timoth. You are *so* able to work it out on your own.

— How?

But Seronin remained stubbornly silent.

They talked for a while about Semele, about Timoth's childhood, rice harvesting. Timoth made a couple of attempts to shift the conversation toward the topics that interested him —to psycocephy, the Abbey, the Vigil— but he quickly realised the depth of Seronin's fascination and guessed he hadn't had much of a childhood of his own.

— Yow! said Seronin, as Candle sneaked up behind the wall and smacked him round the back of the head. What now?

An arm thrust between Timoth and Seronin and clinked two open beer bottles together as it set them on the wall. An arm that Timoth knew well.

— Martoth! he spun round.

— Yo, fuckhead.

— How are you feeling?

— Filthy, she said, pushing some hair back behind her neck. Candle said fresh air was more important than a shower.

— Come see the fireflies!

So they sat along the wall in the neon-stained gloom. A few minutes later Lethe and Theremy joined them. Lethe carried out a bag over his shoulder full of beers and snacks. Theremy hobbled uncomfortably up to the wall and leant against it, seeming to weigh up the pain involved in hauling himself up.

— One sec, said Lethe, I've got an idea.

He went off to get the car and reversed it into the gap in the wall and clicked open the boot. He emerged, threw his bag into the boot and sat on the rear bumper, slapping the space next to him.

— Better?

Theremy smiled and sat awkwardly next to him.

— Weakjohn? asked Martoth.

— Weakjohn needs a bit more time, said Candle.

Lethe passed the snacks around — nuts and some kind of fluffy corn-derived things. Then he opened a beer for himself. Theremy drank from a bottle of water.

— If you can rebuild my whole body, arse down, pointed out Martoth, could you not fix up Theremy a little?

Theremy had a black eye that merged into purple-blue bruising covering the whole left side of his face and he seemed unable to move his left arm.

— He's a bit proud, said Lethe.

— I'm fine, insisted Theremy.

— In any case, said Seronin, he can bloody well do it himself.

They dropped the subject.

— Okay, said Lethe. You gonna tell us what went down in Hitspeke?

— Well I thought I should cover a bit a context first, said Seronin, uncertainly.

— God… How much?

Martoth was rubbing her legs, ostensibly to massage a bit of warmth into them but really to confront the madness of destruction and recreation she'd just lived through. Her mind was trying to insist that they were not her legs, that they were a kind of construction, something partly conceived inside the heads of the men around her. And not just her legs and thighs… How much of this was Timoth's sweaty imaginings? But it wasn't, couldn't be so. She felt like herself. She looked like herself. She felt normal. Or no more unusual than she might wake up feeling on a bad day. There'd always been times she woke up feeling like her body wasn't the same as the night before. And Candle had explained some of it — they'd used a sort of forensic time-reversal technique, a speciality of Lethe's, that worked off the residual evidence to reconstruct the past that caused it. She knew her body was built to her own plan, not Timoth's, and if it was hard to shrug off that sense of intrusion it could at least be eclipsed by the other enormities she was now grappling with. She thought she was dying earlier today. She couldn't remember the pain but she remembered the fear.

— Can we start, she said, when my mother appeared out of nowhere and wound up dead by Timoth's paddy.

It didn't hurt so much to speak this way now. Or at least her expanding horizons put things in perspective. The way she used to see things, through a lens of abandonment, just didn't fit the bigger world that had impinged on all sides now. On Semele she'd been as self-obsessed as Timoth. Solving the riddle of her birth had once seemed like solving the riddle of the universe. Now she could take that failure as a small part of something much bigger. She wasn't lost because part of her history was lost. Yes, she was still curious about this ridiculous woman who'd been her mother but more dispassionately. In the last forty-eight hours she had grieved and grown. Yes, it still stung —her resentment had not entirely spilled away— but she was now able to keep it in its place, amongst a whole jostling bedlam of other concerns.

And now there were these visions, the dreams from which she'd just woken and the images that hovered still in her mind's eye. She'd been shown something at the point when the spin had begun to devour her. There was a fury that drove the spin on, and a dreadful memory that dwarfed her own problems. She'd caught a hint of it. She had to tell the others.

Seronin opened another bottle and flicked the bottle top into the car boot over Lethe's shoulder.

— 'Kay. Two months ago. Big picture: Humanity dispersed across the universe. A few generations since the crises, the migrations, the loss of Earth. The dear old Vigil, self-styled guardians of the flame of scholarship, recognise thirty or so human worlds that they keep tabs on but they must be aware we are spread much more widely than that. Humanity has changed in a hundred years though many people are living their lives in old-fashioned ways that allow them to ignore it. Each of our worlds is an enigma, not perfect but serendipitous. Each seemed somehow to be waiting for us. Number of humans alive today: impossible to say. Number of natural-minded humans alive today: a tiny fraction of the eight billion at the time of the crises. Probably a few hundred million escaped.

— Are we more or less now? asked Martoth.

— Less, said Seronin. All of that stuff is still true because I've ignored half of reality. When we consider the allpsyche, everything has changed.

Martoth was sitting between Timoth and Candle. To her right, a foot or so of space allowed the night's breeze to brush between her shoulder and Timoth's. Candle sat closer on her left, radiating reassurance and support. Did she want Timoth closer?

She felt a chill catch her and she zipped up her outer coat, stretched her legs out forward, pointing her toes into the night. As she did, the flesh of her thighs spread wider against the wall and the edge of her trousers inched imperceptibly closer to Timoth. What childish game was she playing? She remembered sitting next to him under the canopy at the Tap and Spile, pressed against him from shoulder to side to hip to ankle, neither of them acknowledging it but each aware, and not moving, keeping whatever it was going. She wanted that again, and more, but not right now. Now she needed these few inches of space and the delicate breeze.

Seronin went quiet as if stuck for words and she realised his struggles were for her benefit. Timoth could be shown, the others all knew anyway. She felt awkward until she realised she was able to continue herself.

— The allpsyche, she offered, is everything there is, when you include the landscape of the world's mentality, the things we built that *aren't* physical. And that's what's now crumbling around us.

— Yes, right! said Seronin. The leys are withering away faster than we can hold on to them, the oracles are too hot to touch, even the relics are changing. In a few days, wherever we are, we'll be stranded and blind.

— And everyone else'll be puppetised or burning alive, said Timoth.

— We don't know that! challenged Martoth. Take away your psycocephy, take away your leys and shit and maybe the rest of us will be just fine.

She was surprised by the aggression in her voice. And yes, maybe some of what the cherished had been pushing in Laketown was starting to make a lot more sense. But she was entitled to a little grumpiness after what she'd been through and it wasn't like she was torching buildings. Everything had been fine hadn't it? Till Timoth and Weakjohn and Seronin, all of them. She'd been exhilarated by the miracle of her recovery but a growing impulse to *blame* was taking over. All these others had been blessed with something she hadn't and she was the one getting hurt. She turned a steely gaze on Timoth —an easy target— but his face was all blank naivety.

Seronin just threw his hands up and sighed.

— You might be right, Martoth. Really. You might be right. But it's not clear cut. Everybody has a mind. Everyone is part of the allpsyche. Don't you ever dream of drowning? Do you ever dream of a deep forest? Of red curtains, flying fortresses?

Lethe, aged beyond Martoth's ability to imagine, was a more natural historian than Seronin.

— We don't know who first discovered psycocephy, he told her, but some pioneers were active as far back as the twentieth century. Some of the evidence… some features of the allpsyche are quite archaic. And they left their marks everywhere. Think of the relics. It's a reasonable bet that a good part of what we all share today comes from memories of a few people.

— The most important, added Candle, being Diocletian…

— According to the Vigil anyhow, said Seronin, who teach his work like a religious text.

— Itsh not a relijshon, protested Theremy, through his beaten-up mouth.

— So why am I a heretic, then? challenged Seronin.

— So they can burn you at the stake, grinned Lethe.

— Hey! I actually had a cosy chat with them yesterday.

— And we're *still* waiting to hear about it! said Candle.

It had been a bizarre exchange from the start. First there was the abstract setting, the odd lack of detail in their surroundings, like the whole road junction had been carved into a boiled sweet and then sucked for an hour. It made Seronin feel like they were a chess position, the Vigil personages condensing in black out of the thin air around their king and Seronin himself a lone white piece, unsupported in enemy territory but still dangerous. Then there was the peculiar way Barnabas had greeted him, "young man", exactly as he had in the days when he would pop his head into Yorgen's perspectivals class to extract Seronin on one or another transparent pretext.

If Barnabas did now regard Seronin in the same light as when he'd first burst into his teens, devouring everything the Vigil could offer and, often as not, spitting it out upside down and inside out, then Seronin was at a loss to explain where Barnabas had filed away the intervening years. They had met, fought, cursed each other a hundred times since then and this attitude, this "young man" voice had been gone for decades. Possibly it was a deliberate strategy, Barnabas's attempt to restore a long extinct structure of authority. The disturbing thing was that it almost worked. Seronin could feel something inside him drifting in the Vigil's current. After all that had passed between them, to find some cheap rhetorical trick pulling his levers… Then there was that recurring hunch that there was something important he was missing, something that he should have spotted days ago. It's foolish to brush off hunches like that but he didn't really know what to do with this one. If he was smart, maybe he could pull the answer out of Barnabas. That man did not miss much.

But the conversation that developed wasn't quite what Seronin had expected. The opening sallies were tame — some light sparring to limber up. Seronin chose his words carefully as always, matched Barnabas's each remark, but he couldn't help feeling there was *another conversation going on*. Nothing that he wasn't privy to. More like there was another conversation going on using exactly the same words uttered by exactly the same people. Some kind of overlay, an extra dimension of meaning that eluded him.

Barnabas asked how he had coped. "Coped", really? Who did he think he was talking to? Seronin assured him of his continuing survival and thanked him for his concern. Then there was that pompous "well done" from Barnabas, dusted in the bone-dry, near-undetectable sarcasm that Barnabas honed.

After that it should have been all-out war. Seronin was so sure of the way things *should* have gone, he could have prepared a script. Barnabas would throw out a few jeering but exploratory remarks about the company Seronin kept. Seronin would make a point about the narrowness of insight of Barnabas's own blessed apostles, playing up the religious overtones to needle him further. Barnabas would wonder how Seronin's "research" was going, possibly making reference to some of the less savoury venues where Seronin had been sighted. Seronin would wonder whether the Vigil's orthodoxy had sprouted enough epicycles to explain reality even half as well as the wisdom that Seronin found in a pint of beer. Barnabas would enquire as to whether the world he saw through his pint of beer looked quite so romantic as it once had. Neither would mention Theremy.

But none of this happened, none of it at all. If Barnabas had once burned with the flame of his own self-righteousness, that flame was now burning dim. What had happened at the Abbey? wondered Seronin. What really has been the cost to the Vigil, these past few weeks?

— If you have any insight, Seronin, said Barnabas, I know you'll share it.

— You seem pretty confident about that.

— You are Vigil in the eyes of everyone but yourself. If we can't stop him, you won't escape any more than I will.

And there it was again, that unwanted sense of belonging. This sort of thing hadn't bothered him for years. The Vigil was a dead end and a dead part of his life. He'd made his peace with that. Taken the learning and rejected the ethos. Why now should the words of Barnabas, of all people, affect him like this?

— "Him"? You're still running with this Diocletian-resurrected theory?

Barnabas nodded and, without taking his grey-steel eyes off Seronin, motioned a few of his disciples forwards.

— I'd love to hear an alternative that can explain this, he said.

…and they showed him the once-great Abbey.

— It's all in ruins, said Seronin. It even brought a lump to my throat. The buildings, the cells, the classrooms, the halls, all gone. Old Demeter's wishing well, the morning stairs, the new Xeras theatre. The walls of the tablets of the abbots. The survivors have dispersed into the countryside and are keeping isolated as far as they can. Barnabas and Sounness have a kind of council-in-exile going but there are other scattered groups keeping clear, wandering about, doing their own thing. I'm sorry Theremy, there have been so many casualties…

— What are they going to do? asked Timoth.

— Don't know. They believe Diocletian is back and he's executing a personal vendetta against the Vigil. Which is a sucker punch and a half, seeing as they're the ones who've been polishing his portrait for the past century. Maybe that explains why there's so little wind in Barnabas's sails right now. But they can't explain how Diocletian could be back, or why he would be so pissed off with them. And if it is truly all about the Vigil, why is the whole bloody allpsyche unravelling, and not just the stuff they built?

— Do we have an alternative explanation for all this? asked Timoth, tilting his head back towards the scars in the sky.

— Maybe, said Seronin. I shared some thoughts with Barnabas and his people. They didn't rule it out but I don't think they were impressed. The big news is the face of Diocletian.

— The what?

— The actual face of the real man. The face. And a name, even. And maybe there's more.

— What are you talking about? asked Lethe.

Seronin explained the bloodied apparition that had appeared to them all at the sublimation at the junction. They listened in silence.

— I've seen him too.

The voice was Martoth's.

— When the… I think it was then. When everything disappeared in the white light, I realised I was looking through eyes that weren't mine, like I was there, like I was someone else. And this "Clandor", the man with the moustache and the… those eyes… he was there. I'm sure. But it wasn't just him. There were other people with him.

— Others?

— Men, youths, a girl… They were looking at a painting.

Candle whistled.

— Diocletian and a proto-Vigil… said Lethe.

— I don't think it was an organisation, she said. And… I dreamed about him too, just now. I'm sure it was him.

— *Candle*! said Lethe urgently.

— Already on it.

Candle had tugged a confused Martoth off the wall and was guiding her across the car park back into the building. Lethe followed. After a few paces he turned back, his white face bathed in every shade of the pulsing neon. He didn't bother whispering, or mind-talking.

— Seronin, he urged. Get Timoth away from here.

23. Torment

1939

Stephen's frail and naked white body was clamped to the chair with iron bands. Dark body hair was plastered to his legs and chest. There was blood in the sweat-drenched curls of hair.

— Take her away, he whispered, away. Not in front of her. Please.

A few of the group glanced awkwardly at Anna, shaking, hiding down in the footwell between the benches, arms wrapped around her head. Others could not tear their sickened eyes away from Clindor and Stephen.

She stays. Clindor's mind was a tightening noose. Necks snapped back to watch.

The pain enhances us, Stephen. Your pain teaches us.

— Please, take her away. Please. Pyotr?

But Pyotr had left weeks ago. Maybe he'd seen where this was going. Maybe he'd been round this circle before with Clindor. Maybe he only cared about himself.

Clindor knelt by the chair. His eyes were closed, hands clasping Stephen's wrist.

— This is release, Stephen. I release you from your terrors.

We are going to take all those things you are scared to lose. This is *freedom*. Do you realise what we're creating?

— Don't. Please. Don't.

Then they saw for the first time the darkest implications of Clindor's power. He bowed his head in concentration and long cuts opened along Stephen's legs. Stephen's scream was something outside sound. The group felt their minds join together in concert, united by a hidden flaw that held them all in check. In this hamstrung fusion, Stephen's scream passed like a searing fireball and it scalded them.

Anna was up and frantic, jumping up and down and then back on the floor then back up again. She whispered but did not scream.

Someone had been sick.

Clindor spoke now with all their minds. *Your body is under our control now. And we will wreck it for you. Every crushing thing, every mutilation will be something you can't bear to lose, something irrevocable, something you can never get back. We are destroying you for you Stephen. You are too… tethered.*

Somewhere in the blood and the terror, a door opened.

She walked out of the door, out of the hallway, down the steps, through the quad, past the gate, across the bridge and into the town. She walked along streets, round corners, through parks, past statues, through subways. She walked onward, sideways, back on herself. She put one foot after the other, each step fouling the ambition of the last. She walked into the night, through the terrors of the adult mind. She walked into the dawn dew, her death crisp on her tongue.

— Annochka! Annochka!

She walked through dreams into a forest whose sounds she knew. She walked through shipyards and factories, past smelting and transmutation. She walked in the open and in the shadows, through the starlight and canyons. She walked through doors that had never been, through curtains newly drawn, along paths worn by her own feet. She walked over and over and she walked beneath.

— Annochka! Annochka!

She walked on the waters of her growing capacity for love. She walked through the heavens of her child's imagination. She walked into an abyss of Stephen and a cliff face of Clindor. She walked through the painting and onto the palette of Peter Creed. She walked through the orchestral storm and the bursting rivers. She walked through universities and hospitals, churches and prisons. She walked from birth to blood, from spark to fire.

— Annochka! Annochka!

She walked.

She walked into Pyotr's arms.

— I saw it. I saw what they did. Anna.

Anna. Mute. Staring. Mind wheeling. Fizzing.

— I saw it. It was like I was in there. I saw everything. He… Anna, I'm sorry. I should never have left. I'm so sorry.

Anna. Mute.

— Annochka.

Madame Giroud stared in shock at the telegram that Robin had passed her an hour ago.

— Not here, she whispered, for heaven's sake — it cannot be here. Can you imagine what she'd feel, how she'd react driving up here again, seeing the portico, the glacier. Oh good God, not here.

How could she bear it? Parents, suddenly, unexpectedly. Stephen devoted and besotted and gone, mysteriously. How much could a young mind take? Christ, even she, Greta Giroud, once merciless scourge of the Swiss art world, wasn't sure she could go on with this dreadful existence. Her chest felt tight and her breathing came hard. But providence had at least left her the shred she needed, a reason to survive, a young, vulnerable, grief-damaged reason to survive. She needed to think and she needed to act. She couldn't just sit here, staring all night.

— Get a telegram back to Pyotr. Send them to the house in Lucerne. Lukas should be there. Warn him please. I'll be there tomorrow. Have some writing paper and materials sent to my room. I need to write some letters tonight.

What to do? Whatever to do?

— Comb our guest lists for the past five years. Ignore the Nazis. Find me anyone professionally involved with children. In education or medicine, boy's or girl's I don't care. And anyone who deals with mental trauma, in psychiatry or religion. I want names and addresses to me by tomorrow morning.

— Oh, and Robin. Get word to my solicitors and the bank, I need appointments with all of them. And, Robin, dear Robin. Could you have a word with your family and the other help? We're selling up. We're going to England.

24. Lives Apart

Martoth, Timoth, Seronin

They brushed the dust off their backsides and looked at each other. Theremy slammed the boot and indicated the car with a questioning look. Seronin shook his head.

— What's the time? he asked.

— Im Leap tchime? asked Theremy. I ngever get ushed choo it.

— In are-the-bars-still-open time.

— You're joking right? said Timoth, who was four beers down and feeling pretty tired.

— I want to meet these friends Theremy made last night.

— Jush leave ikh will you? said Theremy.

But Seronin set off up the road and Timoth chased after him.

— Guysh! The bottlesh? The car?

— Lethe'll sort it, called back Seronin.

Somewhere on the Leap they made a lot of bricks, thought Timoth, and wondered whether the beers were affecting him much, directing his attention away from the important stuff to trivialities like this. He knew Martoth would notice these things. She'd file them away and slot them into the big picture later on when she could see where they'd go. He hadn't even noticed the moon thing till she'd pointed it out to him.

Martoth — what was Lethe so worried about?

The roofs were made of clay tiles, not so different from those you sometimes saw on Semele, but like the bricks they were uniform and countless. Mass-produced. Driven here in cars, he guessed, or bigger things.

— There, said Theremy as they entered. Tkhable on our lefkh.

Seronin didn't bother looking but Timoth did, swaying his head around like a mammoth's trunk. There were three. One was massive and bald with a thick neck, sitting unnaturally upright against the cushioned bench on the wall. He saw them instantly and signaled to his friends who turned in their chairs to stare. The other two were smaller but still imposing — tight, compact frames with tendons taut in their necks and hands that Timoth could easily imagine as fists.

A young lad behind the bar disappeared to fetch his manager, who came out just as they reached the bar.

— I'm not having any trouble, she said.

Her eyes flicked between Seronin and Timoth and she squeezed her lips into a tight frown. Timoth saw suddenly how he might appear to others, not as the unsure teenager he was, but as an intimidating young man, lean and firm. He returned the gazes of the three men at the table without fear. Theremy was trying to burrow into the woodwork.

— Oh… said Seronin, all surprise. Err, two pints of mild and a beaker of water please?

He smiled innocently and fished some cash out of a pocket. He inspected it in his palm.

— Will the big coin cover it or will it have to be the note?

The boy reappeared but skulked at the back, gripping the counter behind him with both hands.

— The note, replied the bar lady, assuming you're buying for Rich Wright's table.

— Oh what a kind thought, said Seronin. May I have a tray then please?

The boy pulled a tray off the shelf and passed it to the manager.

— Remind me, said Seronin, why am I buying for Rich Wright again?

— It's his birthday.

— Sherronin, mumbled Theremy. I, uh, might have left wivhout paying befhor.

Seronin straightened and regarded him sternly.

— Oh for fuck's sake, Theremy. You're telling me when Lethe came and found you unconscious and bleeding into a stinking drain, what you were *actually* doing was bleeding into a stinking drain *while not paying*.

He turned back to the manager who was pouring their beers from the large hand-pull taps.

— Can you believe this?

She looked warily at Seronin as she poured, assessing this escalation.

— ...changes *everything*... purred Timoth, wanting in on the act.

— So it does, agreed Seronin, transferring the drinks to his tray. Let's join the birthday party.

— What's happening? asked Martoth.

They were back at her bed. Someone had changed the sheets and turned down the room. There were new drinks in the fridge and all the lights were on. Candle motioned her to lie down and wandered into the bathroom with a glass.

— Maybe nothing, called Candle over the sound of a tap running. She came out with the glass filled and passed it to Martoth. But we're a bit worried about after-effects from your ordeal today. And we'd also like to know a bit more about the vision you had at the point of contact.

— After-effects?

— Well there was a lot going on. Timoth and I were holding your mind together, to stop you fragmenting or dispersing or similar, all fancy forms of dying when it comes down to it. At the same time there was also an important and very dangerous mind that was quite active in there with us, a mind that was made of both you and the ripspin and it was thinking away, thinking frantically in fact. That mind had very deep access to everything you are and it was quite malicious, not very much like you, I'm afraid. It might have stolen thoughts, it might have planted thoughts, it might have rummaged around and rearranged things. I was trying to block it by anaesthetising you.

— It might have read my mind?

— Oh it definitely did. But that's not what you should be worrying about. It's dead and it wasn't likely it had any opportunity to share what it found. Any secrets you are keeping are safe.

Martoth's mouth hung open.

— Well that's just hugely reassuring.

— I'm much more worried about what it might have left behind.

— *Left behind*?

— Oh dear. You've had a rough day haven't you?

The floor was undressed, unvarnished wood and Timoth heard every footstep Seronin paced out on his way to Rich Wright's little gathering. No-one else made a sound. Seronin affected a complete lack of concern. He made an exaggerated show of balancing the loaded drinks tray and they allowed him to come right up to the table and place the tray down and start passing out the drinks without objection or interference. They neither thanked him nor moved an inch to accommodate him. Timoth, who had some fixed notions of personal space, found himself flinching at the mutual trespass.

Seronin sat down close to the large man. Too close, as if nudging him to share a private joke. Theremy and Timoth lifted their drinks from the tray and took stools at the adjacent table. Despite the airy confidence he was honest enough to credit to the beer Timoth was nervous. His faith in Seronin had barely outgrown his suspicion. He was disturbed by Seronin's unblinking acceptance of the beating Theremy had taken, as if these things happened day-in day-out in Seronin's world. He had a strong sense that Seronin had faced a few of these in his time and he couldn't square this with the seemingly godlike powers that Seronin was reputed to possess. Theremy looked glumly at his drink and tried to ignore whatever Seronin was up to.

Seronin cocked his head sideways to speak conspiratorially into the enormous man's ear:

— Rich Wright I presume?

The men exchanged glances that Timoth couldn't read. Maybe trying to decide something. The Leap was mindwoke, he recalled. They could be adept. They could have been speaking to each other the whole time, planning an attack.

— No, said one of the smaller two. I'm Rich.

Theremy hissed a laugh, yelped as pain wracked his delicate mouth, then seemed to struggle to stifle the resulting garbled swallowing sound. Seronin's expression passed through momentary confusion and settled in relaxed amusement. He allowed a second to pass.

Had the men uncoiled slightly in that second? Was the heavy air just an ounce lighter? Timoth still couldn't read the situation. He kept his hands on the table but did not touch his drink.

— My apologies, said Seronin.

His wrong-footing was genuine but short-lived. He seemed to decide at last how to play this encounter.

— Look. Are we going to do one of those stupid things where you guys say how you don't want Theremy's kind round here and I spend a few minutes trying to educate you before realising the whole thing's futile and getting frustrated and just hurting you like you hurt him? You know I can do that, don't you? Cos if that's what we're going to do we can shortcut the bit where I give a fuck about what you think. Timoth and I have some drinking to do and time matters to me.

So their caution was partly because they realised something about Seronin, noted Timoth. Or could sense something.

— *Any of your kind*, said Rich.

— Any?

Seronin looked at Theremy questioningly.

— So this wasn't about…

Theremy shook his head.

— Funny how you leap to assumptions isn't it? mused Seronin.

— Something you want to tell us about your friend? asked the big man.

— What's our kind? asked Timoth, feeling braver now.

— *Vigil*, said Rich.

And Seronin spat his drink down his front.

— What I'm asking for here, Martoth, is your consent to a range of quite invasive procedures. You need to trust me and you need to trust Lethe and Weakjohn who are going to help me.

— Weakjohn!?

— Yes I'm here sweetheart.

But Martoth couldn't see her. From the bed, her view was the ceiling and Candle's gentle expression, a face so unassuming for the glory of her voice. Somewhere in here was Weakjohn, somewhere too, Lethe, but she could see neither. For all Candle's benevolence, she was white as a sheet.

— I'm not trying to play down what we're intending. This is a kind of surgery, do you understand? While it's happening you will be, in many ways, dead. We will inspect every piece of your mental architecture.

— You're going to read my mind?

— No. Or not intentionally. We might be exposed to things. You need to trust us. If we find a way to experience the vision you had, we might, with your permission, take the opportunity.

— Will it hurt?

— No. But it is risky.

— Risky how?

Candle paused.

— The main worry is your own mind working against us in unexpected ways. The risk is, I guess, that you *don't come back*. If that's going to happen, we have a responsibility to you to make it clean.

Martoth gaped. She was grateful to be lying down. The prospect of her own death shone a harsh light around a room in her mind, casting thoughts like shadow puppets on a wall. What would Timoth do? Would Ma Mackelay ever know? Would anybody solve the mystery of her parents? What did she need to tell people before she went? How… how would her friends get going from this motel if it happened? She found that she was crying.

— How likely? she sobbed.

— Pretty unlikely. One in fifty. You've already survived a one in a million today.

— No! she decided. No. I'm fine as I am thank you. I think I'll have another beer.

— Martoth, said Weakjohn's voice solemnly. Whatever is in there, it is deadly.

— Deadly?

— Much worse than what Candle's proposing. We can't look very deep without you helping us. The sort of encounter you had today is extremely rare and the little experience we have is not encouraging. Martoth, I have a very bad feeling about this. I think you should allow us to help you.

— We'll start at the surface, said Candle. We'll only go as deep as we need to.

Candle's face floated there above her. At a time like this, her voice was truly a thing to fall in love with. Martoth *did* trust her, completely. And Weakjohn too wherever she was.

— I don't trust Lethe.

Awkward but true. Lethe expressed no surprise or offence and she felt right for having said it, but Candle's face darkened with irritation.

— I don't blame you dear, chuckled Weakjohn. I don't blame you at all.

Candle's face soured further.

— Weakjohn—

— There's an alternative, interrupted Weakjohn.

— ...I'm listening.

— Sure. I chaperone him from a totally different perspective.

— What? How?

— Lethe and I fuse for the procedure.

Lethe swore. Candle raised her eyebrows in horror. Neither said anything immediately.

— Of course, Weakjohn continued, the kind of thing I'm proposing would need Lethe to trust *me* quite a lot.

Some time passed before Candle spoke again.

— OK, she said. Time out. Weakjohn, stay with Martoth.

Theremy was alert now, noticed Timoth. There was something about today's incident that he had missed too and now his eyes narrowed slightly as he started connecting up the dots.

— We're *so* not Vigil! said Seronin.

— Bullshit.

— And errwhat on the Vigil anyhow? They're pasted onto their own backsides right now without any of your help.

— Bullshit, said Rich again. We saw him. You shits never stop lying.

Theremy groaned and gently pressed his forehead to the table. Seronin looked quizzically.

— I gotkh my beer, said Theremy, raising his head and talking to Timoth, went to shtand outshide in zhe fesh air. Shun wash bight. Sho. Arrhm out. Khover my eyesh. Ripsh in the shky… bang on my headgh.

Seronin was baffled but Timoth cottoned on. He turned to the men in incredulity:

— You're not serious? he said. You think Theremy broke the sky?

They had begun to doubt it now. They'd seen the mess Theremy was in. Still, they had rage aplenty between them and they weren't going to let it drain quickly. If he hadn't torn the sky, Theremy was surely to blame for something.

When Timoth could fix his attention on the issue, he realised they weren't far wrong. The ripspins had come for *him*. He had brought them, whether he had meant to or not, to a tiny village of a hundred such men their families. The men should have come after him, not Theremy.

He drank deep from the dark beer Seronin had bought him and watched Seronin begin to untangle the mess. For all the beer, Seronin trod now with an invisible tact round the men's prejudices and he drew them into a conversation that provided the background that would make their mistakes obvious.

They all lived in Crowbeck. Rich's work took him away a lot, travelling between three or four of the bigger towns, passing goods and data this way and that. Royston and Rock were general builders working mostly in the village. They'd seen the footage from Hitspeke, plus a later reel that showed Abbot Barnabas by the wreckage. Seronin raised his eyebrows at the name recognition here. Mindwoke or not, Vigil Abbots were hardly counted famous outside pretty rarefied circles. But it turned out there had been a bit of attention recently. Rich's inclination to blame the Vigil was already becoming a common reflex, enabled by, even pushed by, the Hitspeke media. The disturbances in town had an all too familiar anti-mindwork sentiment, but unlike in Laketown, the rioters could name their enemy.

— Not often I feel sorry for the Vigil, said Seronin to no-one in particular, but this is tough from their point of view isn't it? First they're decimated by the mind they've hero-worshipped for centuries. Then they're battered by everyone else who thinks they are the ones to blame. You got out just in time, Theremy.

Theremy nodded.

— You're *ex*-Vigil? asked Royston.

— And a fushion, said Theremy, issuing a challenge with his pale, deep eyes.

…but Royston either didn't understand or didn't care.

An hour later, they were all sitting round three tables pulled together: Rich and friends, Seronin and friends, the bar staff, and the other patrons, a priest, Father Roderick and blonde twins Kim and Hel Burton. Two hours later, Timoth was teaching Rock an old Semele drinking song while Father Roderick did press-ups on the tables, to the delight of the

Burton twins. Seronin, Theremy and Royston were playing some idiotic game with their elbows and beermats. Three hours later, the twins had Timoth on the floor with them to help determine how many beer glasses needed to be placed next to each other to run around the perimeter of the room. Sometime after that, Timoth found a window of relative sobriety to ask Theremy about Martoth.

— She will be okay, won't she?

— Gon't shkhink aboutkh her! he admonished, shocked. Ghrink more beerh!

It finally dawned on Timoth that this whole escapade was never meant to avenge Theremy's beating. Seronin just wanted to get Timoth so drunk he couldn't cause any further damage. It wasn't till the next morning that the realisation began to bother him.

Candle was weeping. Lethe was beside her, an arm round her shoulders.

— Did it work? asked Martoth.

Lethe came to sit next to her.

The silence was too long.

— Not like we hoped.

His voice was even and though she searched it for a tell, good or bad, she came back empty-handed.

— There is something I must tell you quickly, Martoth, he said. Your thoughts are not private. We... we had to make a change... to *help*.

He was upset. His face was stretched and his cheeks withdrew into the shadow of his cheekbones.

— We did it to help, he stressed.

— What? she asked, her fear growing.

— Weakjohn is *in there* with you.

She was startled.

— Weakjohn can explain. Please stay calm and keep your

mind as blank as you can.

She froze and gazed into the featureless ceiling. But minds aren't blank. Even Martoth knew that. Minds are rippling sunbursts of intricacy masquerading as the mute pointing finger of attention. Minds are not blank.

— Calm! whispered Weakjohn with Martoth's own mouth. Calm! Lethe, Candle, leave us.

— What have you done? Martoth wailed.

Lethe and Candle fled towards the door, Lethe casting a fretful glance back.

— What have you done? she moaned. I was okay. What have you *done*?

25. Mutiny

1939

The days that followed were bleak days, days that mixed and parted like fluid moving along strange channels, transecting the normal boundaries of light and dark. The trauma that bound them was like a living thing. A thing with thorny tendrils that slipped deep inside each of them and yoked them by their throats. And, inside them, it weighed like lead, pinning them down while the irregular procession of light and shade passed over them, as history went forth around them. Each was prone to tears. Each suffered nightmares in the dark and in the daylight, each discovered a dwindling of their powers of concentration, a failing appetite, a vanished libido. For a time there was little to distinguish them from their own shadows. Each felt like their shadow was their true substance, casting an unsteady image into the strangely desiccated three-dimensional world.

In the end the trauma bound them tighter even than the steel of Clindor's will, the will that had trapped them in the theatre of Stephen's murder, the will upon which they had written the warrants to silence the telltale concrete: Bloodstain, fade; Corpse, sink; Child, flee…

Stephen became a missing person, Anna a double, triple, orphan, fled abroad with Greta Giroud, though none knew where. Pyotr knew but Pyotr had no part in their trauma and they dreaded his gaze. They knew he knew.

Though the will held them still, they found at last that they could use their trauma. It allowed them to share their thoughts as once they had in the *Wanderpause*. They could use it at any distance at all, to talk privately, to rendezvous in *Happenstance*, to establish some independence from the force that had engendered it.

— He truly can't hear us?

— He's not here.

Here they were again amongst the red drapes — Stephen's "womb", *Delphus*.

— The mirror was his though?

Wojciech waved it away. It disappeared, all of it, the mirror, mantelpiece and the fireplace. Only the heavy red drapes remained. Wojciech reminded them:

— Our memory of his memory built from our old confusions underneath. Remember how we are here. How these things are *our* construction.

Harald nodded.

— Let's move, he said and he seemed to be offering something.

They took his offer. Then they were outside, aloft in the alpine sky then landing in a broad moraine beneath remote icy peaks. The new openness reflected their hearts' wish to release one another. The empty heavens, lit through by the cold-blazing sun, were their privacy.

— Where is he taking us? asked Harald. What is he trying to do? What is he using us for?

— Power? asked Bastien.

— Revenge? suggested Lena.

— For what?

Lena shrugged. Half of Clindor, they knew intimately. They could read his mood by the twitch of an eyelid. The could predict his rages and his fascinations. But there was, there must be, another half a man there too, a half that was the key to their trajectory, the maniac, or the damaged ego that sought redress. This half a man they did not know at all.

— I don't buy the story anymore. The reason for secrecy.

— Our silence protects all of us now, said Wojciech, not just him. Maybe that was his plan from the start.

— One by one, we're losing our ways out, said Paul.

— I'm not, said Lena. There are still things I would save even if it ruined every one of us.

— You mean Anna?

— Anna and others.

— Telling the world isn't without its complications, said Bastien.

— You sound like Stephen, she said.

— If we all want it, we can escape, said Harald.

— If we understand the means by which we are bound.

— You were the first to bind a living creature, Wojciech. Is it not the same?

Wojciech was silent, inspecting the shape of his own mind, half-attempting some reflexive mental somersault, making himself the spider, and merging with... No, it was not only impossible, it didn't make sense. What then? How best to understand?

— It is not so simple, he said. I might, if someone will let me try something..., he looked around him cautiously.

— Anything.

Wojciech chose Bastien. He knew it would be intimate. He feared stumbling through secret doors and private spaces. Lena or Harald he could never have touched. There was a sanctuary there that all of them valued, and a vault of the feminine that a rough old soldier should only tiptoe around. Paul and even Pierre he avoided as too close to the tempests of early adulthood. Bastien was different: calmer, quieter, more content with the world as he found it. Wojciech fancied he had few secrets to keep and, if he did stumble, Bastien would trust him with what he found.

— Should we meet in *Concreta*? asked Bastien.

— It would be easier, said Wojciech.

— Before you go, said Harald, what's our plan? What do we do when we meet him?

Clindor's silence had bothered them all. He had not released them. Perhaps he was still dealing with loose ends. Perhaps he was finding another room. But they knew he'd summon them soon.

— Do nothing but what we would do if we weren't planning anything, said Paul. Be angry, be upset, be sullen, be obstructive. But only so much.

— *Are* we planning something? asked Pierre.

— Hell yes, said Harald. Something.

Over a week Wojciech lived deep inside the mind of Bastien. Together they worked in Wojciech's apartment from dawn till dusk while Lena and Harald brought the provisions they needed and cooked simple meals to sustain them. While their bodies slept and while Bastien rested with titanic patience, Wojciech inspected every twist and reflex of Bastien's mind. Where he found fibres he tugged gently at them. Where there were surfaces he shone himself upon them and watched the reflections, or dropped lightly upon them and watched the ripples. He watched the rotations where the perspectival met the physical, where sensation met subject. At last he found what he was looking for: a thread that did not end where it should, that trailed off impossibly far into the distance, a thread that could only be...

He turned his attention on his own mind and found the same thread, a thread that had once been taut, stretched impossibly thin and dragged far off into the world, but like Bastien's, it had gone slack. He looked then to each of his friends and found the same.

— I think, said Wojciech at last as he let Bastien recover. I think he has left us behind.

But none of them trusted this reprieve and each found that sleep came harder, not easier. They all knew that the calm that falls too suddenly is the eye, not the storm's passing. Whatever Clindor's real designs were, they were not finished.

So used did they become to meeting in Happenstance, that for many days they missed the other marks the trauma had dealt them: tics, headaches, flinching from noises and lights. Bastien and Wojciech were among the first to notice the darkest emblem of all, working close together as they did, but it affected all of them, in each stratum, and they could not overcome it: from this time onwards, not one was capable of meeting another's eye.

It became inevitable that the group should split. None could see a way forward. Whatever purpose it might have served it served no longer. Lives that they had forgotten or hidden away began to resurface. They found commitments long overdue, opportunities fast expiring and they itched to be away. As their old lives began to reassert themselves, small surprises arose that strained their unity further. Bastien destined for the *priesthood*? Wojciech *divorced*?

But they weren't yet ready to split.

— We have to find him, said Harald, or we'll never be free of him.

But wily Wojciech had already called in some favours. A hanged wife was all the start he'd needed. He found a house deserted, bank accounts drained and clutch of very interested creditors. And the trail was not yet cold.

— He crossed into Germany a fortnight ago, said Wojciech. I'm going after him.

It was madness of course but in the vacuum of Clindor's absence they also began to feel a growing sense of the extraordinary power they had at their fingertips. Wojciech with a full life behind him and precious little to lose, felt like a comet blistering through the firmament. He was ready to tear the continent apart in his search for Clindor.

As the summer of 1939 lit fires across a combustible Europe, Wojciech left Switzerland and headed north through the furnace.

26. Electrical Storm

Martoth, Timoth, Seronin

A hand was shaking Timoth's shoulder. His cheek was pressed against something dark, smelling of varnished wood and stale beer. He could taste a sour mucus in his mouth.

The hand shook him harder, grinding his cheek into the surface. But he was desperate to return to his half-remembered dream: a memory of Jessic so real he could taste the salt tang of her skin, and a memory of Martoth he wanted to inhale. He shut his eyelids tight and pushed his face hard into the table as if the dream was in there somewhere. It jerked underneath him. Somebody was kicking it. He groaned and a hint of phlegm rose in his throat.

— Timoth, we're going.

He tried to focus but everything was reeling. He was dragged off his seat and slipped straight to the ground, smashing an elbow into the floor. Somewhere he heard a glass shatter.

— *Timoth!*

It was night. In the pub. Candles were lit, reflecting everywhere in bottles and glasses, prickling his tender sight, poking at the dry constricted feeling in his head.

— TIMOTH!

Theremy's voice. The arm on his shoulder. Then two, hauling him up. He fought the dizziness and loped to the nearest wall and sagged against it, kicking over some empty glasses on the floor.

The air felt strange. It should have been beery, motionless, musty. Instead it was electric. All over his body hairs stood on end and his scalp itched. But it was not still. There was a door open somewhere and a tiny unpredictable breeze touched his face.

— Where's Seronin? he mumbled.

— Gone already. Trouble's coming.

Timoth rubbed his eyes and explored the candlelight. Father Roderick was lying face down on a bench. Rich and Rock were snoring at a table, heads resting on crossed arms.

The front door was open wide. Theremy pushed Timoth out onto the pavement and the feel of the air did not change. What had felt oddly mobile in the pub was uncannily still in the darkness outside. He saw trees in lamplight, their leaves still as stone. There was no sign of the claw marks; the darkness overhead was a thick mass of ferocious cloud.

Theremy wouldn't let him rest. Timoth was dragged along the road, held so tight he only noticed the plummeting temperature on one side, where his fingers stiffened and his skin tightened.

As his legs stumbled and tripped beneath him, Timoth re-entered the world of his dream. He'd slept with Jessic then, kneeling over her flawless naked body, argued with her about the way she'd got herself killed, blaming her for what she'd denied them both. But he'd stopped — cut himself short. She lay there, same as ever, wittering on, like she hadn't even listened. And he didn't care enough to go on. He looked at her with pity and frustration and groped for the words to say over her when she paled into a corpse before his eyes, still jabbering on, and now, in a strange triumph, without having to pause for breath. Then he'd felt tender fingertips at the back of his neck and when he realised it was Martoth he was electrified. His heart raced and he swelled up and lit the sky with lightning. He'd turned and felt such deep longing...

Lightning fractured the sky. A peel of thunder vibrated in Timoth's skull. The patter of rain on leaves started somewhere but the air on his face was still dry and cold. Theremy dragged him faster as more lighting ripped across the heavens, illuminating giant stacks of cloud. He began to hear wind in the trees and saw a banner fluttering by the motel entrance.

The car was still in the entrance to the car park. As they reached it, the heavens opened. The wind howled bringing torrents of icy rain that battered them and the car. Theremy opened the rear passenger-side door and pushed Timoth onto the seat, tucked his legs into the footwell and slammed the door on him.

Once more Timoth found his face squashed against something but this time it was the comfort of the leathery interior and what he soon realised was Martoth's thigh.

— Timoth! she whispered.

— My love...! he warbled, yearning turning his voice to a whinny.

There was a pause filled with the roar of rain on the car roof.

— You're drunk.

Her disappointment was palpable. He pulled himself up and sagged into the corner by the car door. Rain ran down the windows in torrents, rippling the neon motel-light on her skin. She was the world-changing Martoth of his dream — the one thing, the only thing that mattered.

He crawled slightly out of his corner across the seat

towards her and extended an arm. She pushed it away.

— Timoth, sober up quick, the others are out there.

He'd forgotten the others. He could see nothing through the sheets of rain so he rolled the window open and peered out.

— The roof! she whispered.

Sure enough, above the neon fringe of the motel and its halo of glittering rain he could see figures up on the roof, four of them stationed around the edge of the roof — Seronin, Lethe, Candle, Theremy. His first instinct was to join them but Martoth pulled him back.

— Timoth, I need to say something.

He closed the window and felt a surge of warmth as he returned into a precious atmosphere that was theirs alone — his and Martoth's. Something was smouldering deep inside him now. He wanted Martoth, wanted to explain how he felt, how he needed her. He wanted to apologise for everything, wanted to tell her even about the cylinx, even about the weird nearly-sex-stuff that Candle had used on him to save her. He was so full of things he wanted to explain and yet here was Martoth wanting to talk first.

He realised his drunkenness was hazardous now and strained hard to act sober. He tried to imagine how he'd behave if he *was* sober and began to overthink every breath. No melodrama, he told himself. Be calm. Funny. Have a laugh. Be a mate.

— O... kay, he said carefully and precisely.

— It's about me.

— You're pregnant! he clowned and regretted it before he'd finished saying it. *Moron*, he thought. Wrong for every fucking reason.

— Don't be an arsehole, she replied and her eyes showed him the contempt he deserved.

Normal service resumed, he thought, kicking himself.

— Sorry, he said looking into the dark footwell. Look, I wanted to say something too, just…

— No! she stopped him, putting a firm hand over his mouth.

— Shush Timoth! It was Weakjohn's voice but it came of out of Martoth's mouth.

What the fuck? Timoth started in shock.

— *No!* howled Martoth. No! Quiet! Quiet! It's not fair!

Timoth could tell she wasn't talking to *him* anymore. Her fists were clenched and she was punching her own thighs.

— You *said* you wouldn't interfere! she cried.

Timoth flinched back and pushed his door open to escape into the storm.

Timoth scrabbled at the drainpipe, shivering in the wet and the cold. His palms and fingernails slipped right off the slick pipe. His feet wouldn't get off the ground. They just splashed in the gushing outflow.

Theremy's voice came from above and raising his face to the falling rain Timoth saw a head poking out.

— There are steps, Timoth.

As he traced the edge of the building, a loud *zpfft!* broke through the roar of the rain and the neon died. For an instant the world was pitch black but by now the forking lightning was frequent enough to light Timoth's way. He found the wet metal stairs, blundered up them and tripped over a gutter, grazing his knees as he fell onto rough surface of the roof.

— Your wheelhouse, Seronin.

It was Candle's voice, tight with aggression.

— He's safer drunk, replied Seronin.

Timoth climbed to his feet and was buffeted by wind and rain. The air, even washed through by the downpour, remained electric and his hot skin tingled beneath his soaking clothes. Something was afoot up here on the roof.

— He's not safe either way. I want his help, insisted Candle.

Somewhere Seronin's voice swore. A tall shadow strobed through the darkness and grasped Timoth's head with both hands, fingers digging into his scalp. He yelled out.

— Quiet, shouted Seronin. Pretend you're eating chocolate.

— What's choc—?

His mind exploded into a rainbow. Just as it started clearing, coloured crystals of awareness melting into the thick reality of the storm, he felt a hammering in his eardrums and Seronin threw him back to the ground. A yard-long rip hung where his head had been, its sparkling green-orange corona intense in the gaps between lightning strikes. All the rain that fell on it disappeared or boiled or transmuted into something that fell like molten lead onto the roof beneath.

— Fuck—

— Can you seal it? asked Lethe.

— Back off! screamed Seronin. Use it. Stick with the plan.

Seronin dragged Timoth a couple of yards along the puddled surface and Timoth kicked his legs to get some leverage and staggered to his feet. His head was clear. Whatever Seronin had done had burned off the drunkenness.

— Did you get a look? Seronin asked Candle.

He was marching back to a corner of the roof. The other three were stationed on the other corners of the building but they weren't facing outwards as Timoth assumed but *inwards*.

— You did that on purpose? she gasped.

— Of course I didn't. Lethe, how long do we have?

— Ten minutes. But we can handle a few of them.

Seronin growled.

— We're wasting time, said Theremy.

Timoth began to understand. Trouble was coming. Puppets perhaps. But the storm was part of it too. He could sense it wasn't all physical. This enormous thing playing out around them was *perspectival* too, an event in the Allpsyche going way beyond the wind and rain. And instead of fleeing they'd seen some opportunity.

— Let's go, argued Theremy, this is stupid.

— No. Again! You know what's at stake. Fuse with Timoth. Candle can use you both.

— No—

— *Do it!*

In a second it was done. Theremy offered something — presented the picture. Timoth loosened his perspective and they became a fuse-mind. *Theremy-Timoth* joined a looser communion with the other three and watched the raging mindstorm. As the physical elements of the storm blasted across the sky, *Theremy-Timoth* could see the chaos at the perspectival pole. He saw bursts of liquid fury crashing across the roof, pools of despair cascading from the heavens. And the four of them were deliberately *intensifying* it in the area over the flat roof, each forcing reality hard in a different direction, stretching it, creating some kind of gradient. All the while Candle...

What was *Candle* doing? He couldn't follow. It was part violent, like she was cutting or scything the air in between them, trying cause disturbances just as Timoth spun whirlpools when the paddy got rough. But partly it was like she was *fishing*, like she was trying to catch the whirlpools and keep them.

Then Lethe got involved. And he was trying to help her push these eddies further. Candle was *creating minds*, and then they were both trying to develop them somehow make them more *human*. Nothing lasted more than a microsecond before dispersing and returning to the storm. They risked one more but Seronin was already letting the tension go. *Theremy-Timoth* saw him shift out of *Concreta* and shifting... *down...*

Timoth came out of the fusion taking a lot with him, not

only the memory but an understanding that must have been informed by Theremy. They were testing Seronin's theory that there was no Diocletian, just the hostile world he'd left behind, a world so poisoned that it would spawn spins and puppet minds or twist itself into tears whenever it was poked or prodded in the wrong way. He also knew Theremy was blind with rage.

The rip was healing in response to whatever Seronin was doing. Its corona dimmed and the void at its core narrowed as reality smeared itself back together. But Timoth could feel that somewhere in the stuttering world below hundreds of puppets were crawling through the landscape towards them. Some quite close.

— It's no good, said Lethe, we need more distance.

Seronin caught them at the steps and they skidded down together.

— How much distance? asked Candle.

— Astronomical bloody distance, said Seronin pushing them forward impatiently.

Timoth's foot slipped on the wet metal and slid off a step. He caught himself just in time on the cold handrail.

— You mean, coincidentally, said Candle, exactly how far away you wanted to stash Timoth?

She saw the instant when he grasped what had happened. It was like someone flicked on an electric lightswitch. His face flickered then revealed an unvarnished distaste. She needed no mindwork. He was always transparent, even in the painted gloom of the car's interior. His cheeks tensed, eyes narrowed, forehead crumpled, lips parted. He might have been pulling a leech off his flesh. He controlled it quickly. Half a second... maybe only a tenth. It was accidentally brutal.

She wailed at Weakjohn. He mumbled something, fumbled

open the door and escaped. She closed her eyes and fell back into her seat, and as she did she felt another vision coming. The torrents on the windscreen began to take on shapes, human figures gathering and separating into groups. She saw a man's face reflecting in the windows and mirrors. Pallid, dark hair, maybe Clindor, maybe someone else? Maybe *Diocletian*? The floor beneath was moving like the deck of a boat in rough water and she felt an urge to be sick.

— Weakjohn! she gasped in panic.

Then she felt herself stabilise. The world flushed briefly and softened somehow. Weakjohn whispered some reassurance. The windscreen was just a sheet of water and glass. The mirrors were empty. She forced her breathing to settle.

— Something's out there, said Weakjohn.

— Well I fucking hope you've packed what you need, said Martoth sourly, hugging her knees, 'cos I'm not going back out there.

Lightning flashed, thunder rolled, and everything went pitch black. No more neon. No light from windows or lamps. No moonlight. As Martoth patted around in the car interior, more flashes lit the sky, and the car seats and her pack stuttered in and out of existence.

— What could I need? sighed Weakjohn in her head. But the tile and tube from Rubato Park... you have them?

Martoth had forgotten these. Her pack was in the front seat. She felt for it and pulled it over into the space where Timoth had been and slipped her hand into the top pocket. Inside she felt the ceramic cold against her hand and the smooth narrow cylinder like an extra finger between her own. Another flash of lightning, and Martoth cast a fearful gaze through the windows, looking for movement in the dark, for any evidence of Weakjohn's fear. She pulled out the tube and felt all around it in the darkness.

— What is it?

— Some kind of canister. It was embedded behind the tile.

— Can we open it?

— *Not now!* cried Weakjohn, her voice climbing with sudden alarm.

A weight hit the side of the car and the car rocked. Martoth shrieked, remembering the feral buck that bludgeoned itself to death on their door. A dark shape scuffed along the side of the car and she flinched away, clambering into the centre of the car.

They rounded the corner of the building and Timoth's heart skipped. The strobing sky flashlit a dark figure by the car moving with the forced clumsiness he recalled from the rice barn — a puppet. He cried out and launched forward, sprinting through merging puddles in a direct line to the ambling thing.

He caught it in seconds and threw himself on it, slamming hard into the side of the car, taking the force of the collision in his ribs. He felt it go limp and let it slide to the ground, keeping his knee forward to direct its fall. More lightning lit the trail of red and black sludge it left on the window and the car door. As it slumped to the ground, Timoth planted his knee hard into its gut and raised his fist, but the body was still.

— It's okay, I already had it, Timoth, said Seronin's voice in his head.

It was Father Roderick, or used to be. His once-white dog collar was stained with rain and the black mucus that leaked from his dead eyes. Timoth shivered and rose to his feet, peering through the falling rain towards the town. He had been the death of them after all. He felt sick.

His friends reached the car and surrounded it. They waited and watched but whatever was lurking just out of view did not come closer. Lethe and Candle vanished in to the tormented air. The others got into the car with the litres of rain water in their clothes and wrinkled flesh and slammed the doors. Theremy hit the ignition, switched on the headlights and a minute later they were through the sodden village of Crowbeck and out on the roads beyond.

27. Haunting

1939

Wojciech ducked through the doorway into the mortuary. The white walls were recently tiled but the floor was damp concrete. Old bulbs hung from the ceiling, giving off a wavery uncertain light that cast grotesque shadows in the furrows of the pale body. Despite the cool, the corpse seemed to sweat beneath the bulbs.

It was Clindor alright. His dark hair was unkempt and matted, his moustache untrimmed, his jaw covered by a few days' beard growth, his eyes closed and face blank. It was hard to imagine Clindor alive, now, looking at this body. It looked so fake, so uncharacteristic, so dead, so unlike anything that might have held the fuming rage that was Clindor.

They were in a type of concrete building that's only ever called a "facility" or referenced by number. It was hidden in thick forest, half a mile from the Russian border. Several armoured cars and motorcycles were parked outside and sentries were posted where the dirt road met the perimeter.

That Clindor's trail should lead him back to Poland never surprised Wojciech, for Poland was still the heart of his world: a vantage on the Bolshevik bear, a toe in the icy Baltic, a gun trained on the Nazi sabre rattlers. One day it would crown the third Europe. That the trail should lead past the jewels of Krakow, Warsaw, Bialystok without a hint of deviation merely confirmed his assessment of Clindor. That it should take him so far East *was* baffling. He raised it in long-distance discussions with the group back in Switzerland. *What could he want with the Soviets? Why pass through Germany first?*

The mystery deepened when Wojciech stumbled blinking out of the trees onto a grassy airstrip and face-to-propeller with a Czapla reconnaissance plane. Within a minute, four honest Polish gun-barrels were trained on Wojciech's cardinal points and, not for the first time, he thanked heaven for past comrades and the names he knew he could drop.

A day later, he was showered, well-fed and being ushered into the facility, some miles further East, and the eyes that were on him were full of deference and curiosity.

— You *know* this man? We thought he was *Byelorusskiy*.

The sergeant was half Wojciech's age, anxious for social interaction, and happy to overlook the small detail of Wojciech's retirement. The doctor was older, and government not military, but despite a suspicious glance now and again, he followed the sergeant's lead.

— I've been tracking him across Europe, said Wojciech sombrely. He killed my friend.

Wojciech closed his eyes to disguise his distraction as his remaining friends in Switzerland assembled. A barrage of smells assaulted him: high notes of alcohols and solvents, and a damp, organic base that hung about where the corpse lay.

— *Is he dead?* It was Harald's voice.

Wojciech realised he'd stiffened up, trying to keep this second conversation from showing in his face. He opened his eyes.

— *I should say so*, he replied. *But, … if you could only see what I see…*

He bent over the corpse to look closely. All around Clindor's head, passing through his eyebrows and just above his ears, was a thin russet line where an incision had been made. In some places the cut was fringed by further ragged cuts. Wojciech raised an eyebrow at the doctor who shook his head.

— This is how he was found.

— Cut clean through! confirmed the sergeant. You can see too… it was sewn back together afterwards.

— But not in any sort of way that makes surgical sense, the doctor hastened to add. It is crude, like the work of a child or a drunkard. It was hanging off when he got to me…

— But why on Earth…?

— …and his brain is absent.

— *Was* absent! emphasised the sergeant, when we found him!

Wojciech allowed his confusion to show.

— I thought you said he was killed by a Russian sniper.

— You have reason to doubt it?

Wojciech was nervous about where the sergeant's curiosity might lead. He was already calculating how little information he could provide in return for this visit.

— Well no. Only that this … post-mortem surgery seems eccentric, doesn't it?

— The red army have their lost boys and experimentalists just like the Nazis. You have an alternative theory maybe?

— No. No I don't.

Wojciech considered the head wound then turned his attention back to the doctor.

— I presume this *was* post-mortem?

— Of course, it would be impossible any other way.

The sergeant was looking expectantly at Wojciech. His

silence encouraged the doctor to share a further detail.

— There is… one puzzle that I cannot yet explain.

His embarrassment was clear in his face and the lightness of his footing. He avoided Wojciech's eyes as he went on.

— The skull appears to have been cut *from the inside.*

Twenty minutes later Wojciech was on his way, bouncing along the forest tracks back to the hidden airfield. An army driver took the wheel and Wojciech, sitting alone in the back, finally found enough space to address the presences in his head.

— Okay. I can verify that *most* of Clindor is here and *most* of Clindor is dead. But there is one critical thing unaccounted for, namely, his brain.

— !?

— He was shot. No doubt about that. I saw three bullet holes, two in the chest, one in the thigh. Enough to kill him. Would have been quick but not instant. He might have lasted a few minutes. Then some time after death, maybe an hour or two, it looks like his brain got up, carved its way out of his skull and bounded off into the night. Meanwhile some forest goblin happened upon the scene carrying a needle and surgical thread and made a crude attempt to sew the top back on his head.

— Shheeeesh. So…

— So.

— So, *is he dead*?

A pause. Then Pyotr's voice entered softly:

— Well I think we have to assume he's not, don't we?

They'd alerted Pyotr, invited him too, but no-one was keen to hear his voice.

Harald agreed:

— We don't know what he's capable of. This might not *be* a

shooting, this might be an *escape*. Suppose he planned this…
he could be anywhere. He could be *everywhere*.

— We must scatter.

— We must stay together!

— Both, said Harald.

He began to unfold a new future for the group: Never in
the same room again. Never in the same country. Change
names, lead new lives.

— We talk like this. Meet in Happenstance. We continue
the hunt. We defend ourselves and each other. After
everything that's happened and all we've done, I'm damned
if we're going to allow that bastard any sort of future.

At some level, separation was what they all craved —it had
become excruciating to face each other— but maybe a
mission was what they needed.

— No.

— Pyotr?

— No. I'm not part of this. I never was.

Wojciech was not surprised. Harald was aghast:

— Pyotr, don't be an idiot. None of us can defend
ourselves alone. You need us. We need you.

— Alone? Have you already forgotten, Harald? Anna's
alone. She's surviving. Putting every last ounce of herself into
just surviving. Forgetting everything. Turning the living
nightmares back into sleeping nightmares. Trying to be
normal again for the second time since she lost her parents
and then Stephen.

— He wouldn't come for Anna, would he? Lena was
alarmed. I hadn't even…

— I hope not. She was only ever a tool to torment Stephen.

— But for us, said Harald, he'll come for us. All of us.

— Maybe, said Pyotr, but I'm walking away right now. If
he wants me, he won't find it difficult to find me. And Anna
doesn't want your help and she doesn't want you interfering.

Leave her alone.

Once Pyotr left the silence was hard to break, but Wojciech's jolting ride somehow transferred the impulse he needed.

— Harald, we must meet once more, he said, before we scatter. I can't reach you but the rest of you can meet. This evening in Stephen's apartment. It's still empty. Clindor was paying the rent, keeping the landlords out. I don't think Madame Giroud has reclaimed anything.

— There's something he hoped to find there? asked Harald.

— Oh I'm sure something's there. There was a package delivered once while I was visiting. Stephen begged me to keep the secret because he didn't want Clindor to know. I didn't see what was inside but the package was, oh, about six feet by four feet and very flat...

— *He had the Creed!* exclaimed Bastien. What did he want with the picture?

— We may never know, said Wojciech, but I don't think we should walk away without checking that place carefully. And in case you still need such things, I have a key.

Fifteen hundred miles away and they could hear the twinkle in his eyes.

And where should that key be hidden but in the lecture theatre itself? None of them had been there since *that* day. None wanted to go there now, at least not individually. But they steeled themselves and went together.

They met in the corridor outside where once Stephen had frantically looked for Anna. Harald pushed open the door and they waited silently on the threshold for whatever demons might emerge. As the seconds passed, nothing crept out of the darkness except a familiar mustiness of damp, mice, chalk dust and the memory of paper.

Each sensed something different. Lena trembled under an appalling conviction that Stephen was with them again. She caught herself looking down to check on Anna. She blanched from the doorway and Harald reached an arm out to steady her.

Bastien felt a groping from above, like walking through hanging creepers but these creepers were suspended from a higher plane.

Paul's eyes were wide with dread.

— The spiders! he whispered. They're angry.

Pierre nodded. The colour had drained from his face and his breathing had become laboured. He reached an arm out to lean on the wall by the door and said:

— It's not right in there. I don't think we should go in.

— Should we contact Wojciech? whispered Bastien.

Harald shook his head.

— He can't help. Do you think we could get in *without* the key?

— Yes, said Bastien. It might take a while but we've started to be able to move precise things like that. And we can climb.

Harald frowned and looked back into the darkness.

— I think we have to go in here.

He snaked his left arm round the doorframe into the darkness and patted around on the wall searching for the light switches.

He flicked the switches and the buzz of the electrics invaded the eerie silence. One by one the overhead lights clunked and stuttered to life.

From the doorway, it seemed much as they'd left it, although the cobwebs had returned. Down at the front, the blackboards were covered in a chalky smear with only hints of the many diagrams that they had scrawled over the months. Each had seemed like a huge advance in knowledge, new detail in the blank spaces of the map. Now they seemed like nails in a coffin Stephen never had.

Harald stepped into the room and waited. He cringed at the smell of the place. It was hard to shake Pierre's words. Something was not right.

He climbed down the first few steps of the aisle into the heart of the benched area and looked around him. It was cold, musty and damp. The burner had not been lit since that day and there was moisture visible on the cracked windows. One of the overhead lights flickered and failed. He felt a presence by his shoulder and turned, expecting to see the group filing in behind him, but they were still waiting by the door.

— Well *come on then*, he urged. His voice sounded horribly loud and it grated on his nerves as he spoke.

Bastien strode in down the steps and stopped next to Harald. He drew his tobacco tin from a breast pocket and began to roll a cigarette.

— This, said Bastien, this whatever-it-is. It's all Stephen. There's nothing of Clindor here.

He was right, thought Harald.

— I haven't… he paused, searching for the right word, … explored.

— Should we?

Bastien struck a match. As he lit his roll-up another of the ceiling lights died and the room sank further towards darkness. Bastien and Harald flinched toward each other, sharing their fear without meeting each other's gaze. The light from the remaining two was yellowish and dim and came from behind so their double-shadows interfered on the steps at their feet.

— They haven't been on for a while, said Harald. They might all die.

— Had to be at the bloody back didn't it?

They heard Lena's careful footsteps coming down the aisle above, to halt just above them. Paul and Pierre followed.

Harald urged them on and led them down away from the benches into the teaching area at the front. *To the very spot*, thought Lena, and searched the wooden floor for a mark, a patch of discolouration or evidence of scrubbing. But there was nothing but dust and their footprints. The buzzing was softer now half the lights were out.

Pierre looked pale and sick. Paul was watching him closely.

— I'll go, said Bastien.

— Wait, said Harald. There *is* something here. I'm sure of it. We need to be ready to defend ourselves.

— *How*? asked Lena.

— Pierre, Paul. Happenstance might give us a view down on whatever this is if we come up with the right construction. Can you try it together, see what you can get? We can follow you if we need to. Lena, you and I, we'll—

Lena screamed and tripped backward against the front bench. She raised her hands to her face as if to ward off something flying at her face.

— I saw him, *I saw him*, she gasped. He's here!

— Who? whispered Harald. *Clindor?*

Up above, another light flickered ominously but stayed lit.

— *Stephen*! she wailed. By the blackboard!

She sank onto the bench and then for a second, Harald saw him too, on the bench right behind her. He swore and lurched towards her but Stephen had gone.

Bastien sprinted off into the back room as the penultimate light, the one that had flickered, fell dark. One final light shone now above the benches by the doorway and it seemed to be swinging gently though none of them could feel a breeze. The shadows that thickened around the desk and blackboards stretched one way then another in the swinging light. Sounds of shouting and crashing came from the back room.

The final light stuttered and for a seeming eternity would

not resolve either way, to temporary light or inevitable darkness.

Lena wailed and covered her eyes.

The last thing they saw before the light went completely was Stephen. Stephen standing against the wall at the end of one bench, and then another, and then all off them. Tens of Stephens like pillars of flesh, vaulting the chamber walls, that ran slick with blood.

Lena heard Harald cry out in the dark and felt something crash past them up the stairs and then they were all scrabbling, on hands and knees, bumping into one another, climbing over each other, clutching at anything they could to pull them closer to the light of the doorway.

Somebody slammed the door and Lena opened her eyes. Harald was standing with his back against it, looking in concern down at the boys. Bastien and Paul were crouched over Pierre who was out cold. Harald was distraught.

— I'm sorry, he said. That was stupid. *Stupid*. I'm sorry.

He growled and slammed his fists backward against the door.

Bastien had his ear down by Pierre's mouth and said:

— He's breathing.

They pulled back his eyelids, checked his pulse.

— He's fainted? asked Lena.

Bastien frowned:

— Maybe he's in Happenstance. If so, I can't see how to follow. Should we take him to a hospital?

Wojciech's kettle lay on the floor beside Bastien.

— You got it! she cried.

She knelt up, reached for it and turned it over in her hands. A cheap red whistle-kettle. A few drops of water spilled out as she upended it. She pulled the lid off and looked inside and then underneath and then finally on the underside of the lid — where she found the key. It was welded on with a slender piece of solder. She turned the lid and showed it to the others.

— Well at least Pierre won't have to climb up any drainpipes, she said.

...and at the sound of his name Pierre stirred. Paul relaxed. Bastien stood up and looked past Harald at the door. His face tightened and he gripped his lower lip with his teeth.

— Problem? asked Harald.

Bastien didn't answer immediately but bit his lip and winced.

— My cigarette. It was *lit*...

— Oh God, Harald breathed. You think...?

Paul dragged Pierre up into a seated position against the wall.

— Should I go back in? asked Bastien.

— No. We're going. Quickly.

After some discussion, Lena walked straight in, past the concierge. She was still shaken but determined as ever and she accepted she had a better chance than the others. She was ready with a lie but it was easier than that. She had him look the other way.

She let the others in through a back door. They walked quietly up the stairs and along the carpeted corridor to number 18. They moved together as group, as quietly as they could but making every effort to look natural. At the door, Lena passed the key to Harald and stepped away.

In they went. Again it was Harald who turned the lights on. This time they sprang to life smartly, shining a crisp light on a modern and well kept apartment: a rich blue carpet and a suite of white armchairs, side tables, a bureau, standard lamps. It was tidy and clean apart from the desk beneath the window and the doors left open leading to other rooms.

There was none of the sense of foreboding that hung around the lecture theatre. Lena felt confident enough to pass from room to room switching the lights on, although she halted at the threshold of Anna's with her fist at her mouth. The bed had been left unmade. There were books, toys.

Peter Creed's *Wake* filled the main wall by the door, in the same heavy frame as at the gallery. None of the group had seen it since that first time and they gathered together to witness the miracle for a second time.

— It hasn't changed, said Bastien. I had wondered maybe...

If Stephen was right, the picture had never *changed*, not since Peter Creed had painted it in the last century. It would not respond to human tragedy any more than any other event. If there was more to be found in the painting, it could only be something they had missed earlier.

And as they looked they began to see things. There was detail that had not caught their attention last year in the shock of their first acquaintance, detail rich as, and interpretable as, dreams.

— Anna! whispered Lena, the dogs!

Where last year they'd seen Anna's character as a wild ragamuffin rolling around in play with the two scruffy dogs, this time they could not be so sure it was play at all. Although she was certainly laughing, her child's cheeks flush with a generous daub of red ochre, she had a hand in the mouth of one of them, and, even harder to interpret, the other's mouth was at her neck. And chillingly, Bastien noticed some snaking smears that might be leashes, tied to the leg of Clindor's chair.

Clindor was stern and fiery as ever, frozen in the act of sweeping some trinkets from the table top, clearing a space for something new, something that was still not evident.

Pyotr, whom they'd barely noticed last year, stood with his

back turned peering through a door at the rear, which led to where the coffin rested, a black coffin whose gold-edging was another detail they had neglected. The French trio and Wojciech revelled around a large barrel that was leaking onto the floor at their feet.

— Look at the *reflections*! said Harald.

What reflections? There was no mirror. But one by one they found them. Bottles on the table, the grubby window, a dish of water for the dogs, a broken vase, a puddle of spilt beer. They were all over the room, in every colour, facing in every direction, and many barely larger than the strokes of paint that comprised them. So how had Peter Creed contrived to have Stephen's face staring out from each and every one? Stephen, who sat next to Clindor, looked in all respects subordinate, smaller, less colourful, but they finally began to realise that a small trick of the eye had been played upon them. While the eye was drawn to Clindor, it was Stephen who was at the centre of the painting.

— He had photographs taken! said Pierre, who had wandered over to check the desk and was pushing papers and books around.

After a minute of searching, he brought over the photographs he'd found.

— He's circled the coffin, said Pierre, as he handed them out.

— Who's in the coffin? asked Bastien.

— Who are *the dogs*? asked Lena.

Harald was fed up and very conscious that their last foray had not ended well:

— Just take the photos and let's get out of here, he grumbled.

They met next under the clear alpine skies in *Happenstance* and they told Wojciech of Stephen's ghost and the Creed. He told them of traces he had found, from mutilated farm animals and spirit photographs, to mysterious radio broadcasts and spontaneous human combustion.

— It could be any of them or all of them or nothing, he said. I can't follow it all on my own and I don't know how far afield to chase.

— We cannot waver, said Bastien, there is too much at stake. If we are to save ourselves…

Wojciech nodded:

— I don't believe he is dead. Everything here feels like him. I think his power is growing. I've seen the look in people's eyes that I used to see in Stephen's. And there's something else — *the thread is pulling tight again.*

They knew he was right — they could feel it even now, the beginnings of a dark compulsion taking them again. It seemed to grow more acute as they talked as if it was fuelled by their very togetherness.

— Is it him? asked Lena, looking up to the snow-capped summits that surrounded them. What is he doing to us? I thought he couldn't get us here?

— It's not about here, said Wojciech. Till we can get rid of it, it's—

A silent fire blazed across their moraine like a melting frame of cinefilm. As their heads filled with intolerable pain, they dropped out of *Happenstance*, each grasping the first support they found as they re-entered the concrete: tables, armchairs, passers-by. None was ever sure whether their privacy had been breached or whether their own shame had finally turned to fire.

They met for the last time in a hotel foyer, without Wojciech. A waiter brought tea and went about other business nearby, folding serviettes and arranging newspapers on wooden holders. Still their eyes would not meet. Pierre took Le Figaro. Harald enquired if the herring were available in the foyer.

— This is where you've been staying? asked Paul, impressed.

The group that had once been ten was finally five. Even the five was really a couple and a trio. They had fragmented at last. Each group was making its own decisions and each had come today to broach them with the others. Harald and Lena ate at one table, Paul, Pierre and Bastien sat at the next.

— We can't stop, said Harald as he poured the tea through a little ornate strainer, even if our time together is over, even if we are fleeing the only way we see how. We must still look to fight, and trust to our independent efforts to save us all. One day we may meet again. Ooh, macarons!

— But we cannot be entirely uncoordinated! protested Pierre. We will be constantly discovering and investigating each other. We will be forever stepping on each other's toes.

— Whatever coordination we need, we establish now, said Harald.

And this is what they had all seen already. There were only two purposes to be allotted: to hunt and to protect. The vengeance and the vigil. One group to range north with Wojciech to chase Clindor's trail. One group to go west, to England, to guard the one thing they could not bear Clindor to find.

Each group had seen this and each had decided their role. Neither had predicted the other group would agree.

— You know you can trust us, Lena, said Bastien.

— It's not that, it's... I mean I always assumed...

There were tears in her eyes but Lena had reached the same conclusion. Even if homeward had not already meant north and west. The boys had futures in the real world. They could be transplanted but they needed to be allowed to take root somewhere. If it were never to be the Sorbonne for Pierre, at least it might be Cambridge. And if Bastien's vocation was genuine, there were opportunities in England. Paul may be at a loose end right now but his path would become clear in time. Let their elders chase shadows around the continent, elsewhere people still had real lives to make.

— You do know what *fens* are don't you? she asked the climbers.

28. Parting

Martoth, Timoth, Seronin

When Timoth woke it was a white-grey morning and the rain was a faint, quiet drizzle that stippled the windscreen. Theremy activated some automatic wipers that squeaked to and fro, clearing away the water. The mountainous landscape had given way to flatter farmland and periodically they passed milestones that marked their progress towards a place called *Beechbark*.

After waking he did not speak for a long time. He stared morosely into the wet landscape and pondered what was going on with Martoth and Weakjohn. He listened to the others and pieced together what he could from the conversation.

There *was* something left inside Martoth's head, some change, some link to elsewhere that they couldn't remove. They hadn't known what to do. Weakjohn volunteered to go inside Martoth's mind, to watch it, study it and protect her as best she could. Weakjohn's body was gone anyway and she wasn't yet capable of instancing herself directly on the noumenal layer like Lethe and Candle. She'd been surviving on the cylinx in the cave. This plan killed two birds with one stone. Everyone felt pretty bad about it but what were they meant to do? Without Weakjohn in there guarding Martoth against this cancer in her own mind she might drop dead at any time. And Weakjohn could help understand the visions coming from this mysterious source.

It was properly fucked up though. He knew he'd screwed up with his reaction but he'd been surprised. He'd felt threatened by a sudden exposure, an intrusion into something shared with Martoth that he'd so wanted to grow. And there was a sense of disgust that he found harder to explain, something deep inside him that recoiled from the unnaturalness of the human arrangement that was sitting beside him. He wondered if it was something like the prejudice that people like Theremy and Candle suffered. He'd never had such a feeling before and it troubled him. He couldn't find a root for it, it seemed to come from nowhere.

Martoth was silent as Timoth. When he dared to look across, she looked as sick as he felt. She stared out of the window, lost in her own unhappy thoughts.

Seronin wanted to avoid Hitspeke so they were heading on to Beechbark, the next nearest town where a way head would have operated. Lethe thought the ley would be strong enough for a few days yet though it was not clear to Timoth where they were hoping to get *to*.

— Your theory gives us less to work with than the Vigil's, complained Lethe.

— What do you mean? asked Seronin.

— Well if it *is* Diocletian returned, at least the threat's *coming from somewhere*. We could find him and deal with him.

— Deal with *Diocletian*! exclaimed Theremy, unable to believe what he was hearing.

— Otherwise the threat is universal. We have to stamp it out everywhere, or do whatever Diocletian did to propagate it over the last hundred years, but in a few days and and backwards.

— If I'm right, said Seronin, the threat is dumber. It's barely more than computation. We can subvert it.

— That's pretty abstract, Seronin, said Candle.

— Do you want to fix this or not?

— So where are we going? asked Timoth at last.

— We can't risk getting trapped here, said Seronin.

— If you're right, it's as good a place as any, protested Theremy without lifting his eyes off the road.

— Not true.

— You think we should be at The Abbey? challenged Theremy.

— I don't know where we should be, Seronin admitted. So for now, somewhere where we can get to everywhere else.

— A *hub*? said Lethe. You want to take Timoth to the *Polyclasm*?

They saw him as a liability. Since whatever he'd done with the cylinx. Gone was any ambition of harnessing his innate talent in a fight against the Dioclete threat. Now it was just "let's keep him where we can see him."

— Maybe, said Seronin. Do we have any idea what the situation is there?

No-one did, but at least Lethe was still ready to explain to Timoth. The hubs were another great mystery. Or part of the same great mystery as the serendipity of worlds. When humankind reached out across the universe, growing in desperation and arrogance, they found not only the new worlds but also the leys, paths of lesser resistance, ways that were already worn as if smoothed by the passing of unknown feet. As we travelled and explored we built our own ways, sometimes on the foundations we found, sometimes driving them through the unyielding flesh of space by brute effort of the will. But even from our first explorations, there were places, the hubs, where large numbers of leys came together, nexuses too exceptional to be chance, but whose origin was lost in time.

A handful were found. A handful more were added in imitation of these. Each a planet or a moon. They were important as we moved migrants off the earth and ferried them on to deeper tiers. They simplified travel and they were a platform for more remote exploration. But as the migrations faltered many became less important. Most of the habitable ones were abandoned and became like their inhabitable peers, nothing but transport techniques, tricks shared amongst travel-in-Concreta specialists and forgotten by everybody else.

But one still thrived in its own spectacular way: *The Polyclasm*. Most of the time it was the biggest concentration of human mind power outside the Abbey. The rest of the time it was bigger. Unlike the Abbey where power was tempered by discipline and expressed in moderation, the Polyclasm was brash and volatile. A tiny world, it would not be habitable at all without the interference of the minds jostling on its surface, altering the local fabric of the planet, filtering rays, transforming the atmosphere. So mindwork was ubiquitous and extravagant. Most matter was synthetic, life support was erratic, and what society there was was loose and lawless. It was as much an experiment as a settlement. Seronin recognised the sublimation in Hitspeke because of his experience of the Polyclasm.

Timoth stole a glance at Martoth. Instinct told him she was talking with Weakjohn and jealousy gnawed at him. Weakjohn had been the first person to teach him anything about what he could do but it always seemed Martoth got more from the lessons than he did. Now she was getting her own tuition every second of every minute and who knows what other help she could expect? Who knew what Weakjohn was sharing?

The rain stayed light and intermittent but in places it pooled in the worsening road, causing Theremy to drive with more caution. There was livestock in the fields, cows, Timoth supposed — they'd never made it to Border. Domestication of the native wildlife of the Tier Ones had been a long story of failure and mishap, so these beasts would be Earth species, brought across during the migrations.

The cows huddled together in the rain, clumped up against fences and trees and staring blankly into the road at the passing vehicles. Without intending to he found himself exploring their mentality. He could feel it as they passed: a crude stoney thing, undifferentiated and indistinct. The animals seemed less separate than humans were.

The shape of the world is the shape of the human mind, someone had said. Lethe or Weakjohn? It started to raise more questions in Timoth's mind. What of the animals? Did they not live in *our* world too? Had they not shaped it as much as we had shaped them over the millennia? Was it accident that the world was shaped like us? Or was it victory in an evolutionary struggle? Or predestined? Or did these animals really live in another world — *cow world*? How did *we* look in cow world?

— I have something to say, said Martoth.

Timoth felt the car decelerate and he caught Theremy looking up in the rear view mirror.

— Speaking for me and Weakjohn, she said, we are going to go to the Abbey.

— No you're not, replied Seronin without turning round.

— We are.

It was still Martoth's voice, but Timoth heard something of Weakjohn's inflection too and the rootless disgust rose in him.

— We've been studying the visions. There's more to them

than we thought. It has a bearing on Diocletian and the Vigil. We need to work with Vigil historians to decipher it all.

— Lethe can help you, said Seronin. Let *me* see them.

— I will. I'll show all of you. Nothing against Lethe but the Vigil could have dozens working on this and they know more than Lethe does.

— If they're still alive.

— Weakjohn even thinks they might be *coming from the Abbey*.

— They're not.

— Anyway, there's something else…

— You're not going to the Abbey.

— The Abbey is the front line. People are dying there. And we actually *care* about those people.

— Or one of you does, anyway.

— Fuck off! …and that was pure Martoth. We *all* care! And so do you. Maybe you have the right idea… stay fleet, stay mobile, burrow deep, poison the poison. Fine, keep Timoth, deploy an antidote, whatever. But we need to be on the front line. And we need to get the visions to the Vigil.

Timoth's excitement drained when he realised Martoth was proposing she went one way and he another. There was scant appeal in sticking with Seronin's team of superpowers when he was such a useless part of the team. He was at best an apprentice and by his contributions so far he might as well have been a battery pack… And deep inside he'd begun to blame Seronin, Lethe and Candle for the horror done to Martoth. Never mind the ugly Weakjohn arrangement; Timoth would rather be with her.

— How do think the Vigil will react to your new configuration? asked Lethe quietly.

It incensed Timoth. Martoth reacted badly too. As she opened her mouth to respond, Lethe continued:

— Yes. I know. We're sorry. Genuine question though, to

you Weakjohn. You're bringing them an experimental subject. And one very like others they've treated as animals in the past.

Martoth turned pale and paused before replying.

— The Vigil is going to change after this.

— Then I'm coming too, said Theremy.

Seronin swore and slammed his fists against the dashboard.

— You can't stop us, Seronin.

It was then that Timoth understood how much of this decision was Martoth's own. While she'd argued with such assurance, he'd heard her voice mixed with hints of Weakjohn's and assumed that Weakjohn was driving — with Martoth's consent of course, but to a plan of Weakjohn's. Now he realised how wrong he was. It was not Weakjohn's nature to drive people like that. She would happily tell Seronin what she thought of him but she wouldn't push Martoth down a path she didn't want to go down. Hers was the knowledge but Martoth was making the decisions. The lodging arrangement was changing Martoth faster than he could have predicted. How much would he even know Martoth by the time Weakjohn moved on? If she ever did. He had an uncomfortable hunch the arrangement might work out very nicely for Weakjohn.

Seronin stared bitterly out of his window.

— You're wrong, he said. There is no front line.

— Possibly. You keep working on your theory, Seronin. Two lines of attack is better than one.

— Show me the visions.

She ignored him.

— I might need you to go somewhere else, Theremy.

Martoth was ordering Theremy around now? On what planet was that a thing? Timoth knew this was Martoth, not

Weakjohn, and he had an unbearable vision of that moment of closeness between Martoth and Theremy in the dark of the Laketown way head.

Theremy looked up into the rear view mirror.

Martoth reached into her pack and pulled out a white tube. She inspected both ends and shook it a few times, then passed it to Timoth.

— Can you open this? she asked.

It had neither seal nor seam. He tried some exploratory twists but nothing gave.

— You need to break it, said Seronin. And please use your hands.

— Careful! cried Martoth but she made no move to take it back.

Timoth bridled with frustration. He snapped the end of the tube off without any delicacy and handed it all back to Martoth. She stared at him for a few seconds, maybe hurt, maybe angry.

— Thanks, she said.

She tipped out the tube and a few things landed in her lap. There was a small device that she and Weakjohn identified as a key. There was an uncomfortable-looking ring cut entirely out of a transparent blue stone, a number of small sea shells, and there was an address, printed carefully on a small piece of paper: *Parton Investigations, 35 Helicon St, Merriweather, Marston, Schiller*.

— Schiller! said Theremy.

— Wait, said Timoth unable to contain his hurt. You're trusting *Theremy* to go and look through your family's personal stuff for you? Why not me?

Martoth ignored him.

— Oh for fuck's sake, *not now*! pleaded Seronin. It's got nothing to do with *anything else* has it?

Timoth saw a moment of uncertainty then she backed

down. But the car was travelling faster again, and Theremy seemed possessed by a fresh and powerful resolve.

By the time they rolled into Beechbark, Timoth was deep in a slump of self-doubt. He saw everyone else making decisions while he seemed to be cursed to trail around like a pup with no will of his own. In only days he'd dropped like a stone from a heady sense of empowerment to this inert torpor, while Martoth seemed to have travelled in the opposite direction.

Somehow Seronin found them an empty house near the centre and they dumped their bags. Timoth and Martoth explored while Seronin and Theremy went off for supplies.

Timoth found a room upstairs and threw himself down on the bed, burying his head in the pillows. It wasn't made. He had no idea when it had last been slept in or by whom. He didn't care. He wanted darkness and comfort and silence.

He thought he had it until a whisper surprised him, right by his ear:

— Timoth.

He groaned.

— Timoth, look at me.

He twisted his head and opened an eye. She was kneeling by the bed, her face inches from his. She? They? He watched her lips as she talked.

— Timoth, I'm leaving. Now, before the others get back.

He closed his eyes and screwed up his face. He regretted ever leaving Semele. She'd been right all along.

— Timoth, listen. You need to see the visions before we go. The others… we can maybe talk later but we're not sure. So you need to take this.

He turned over and glared at the ceiling.

— Hit me, he croaked.

Then he was in another world, a world of men, women

and children unlike any he'd known, of mountains and lakes that were giants compared with Semele's, of blackboards and chalk, of strange cars, newsprint, waistcoats, hats, banks and pillared buildings. He knew their names: Clindor, Stephen, Bastien, Harald, Lena... He heard their words, saw their experiments, guessed at their theories. He followed them through rooms and spaces, through events that must have been separate visions as Martoth experienced them, collected now for his benefit. But it was fragmentary, episodic — there were gaps. And something was hidden, something important that lay behind it all. Something going on between them. He couldn't read their emotions, couldn't map the web of trust and suspicion that seemed to unite them. It ended with a gruesome image of Clindor, bloodied and mutilated and bound to a tree, with every feature alive and saturated with menace: ferocious scowl, groping arms. This, then, was the man who became Diocletian. A pretty ghastly figure to build a philosophy on.

— Got it?

He nodded.

She was on her feet and moving, her pack already on her back.

— Wait! he cried and pulled himself up.

She stopped at the door and for a brief moment looked uncertain. Her eyes met his. She launched herself back toward him, pushed him down to the bed and kissed him, first soft, then hard. Their teeth clashed. The iron tang of blood was her most mortal goodbye.

Before she fled she left something on the bedside table. Through bleary eyes he saw the broken white tube, its contents spilled out around it, and a small white tile.

29. Vigilance

1939

A smear of moonlight lit the charcoal night over Lucerne's medieval rooftops. Harald and Lena walked quickly out of the Chapel Bridge, crossed tram-lines arm in arm, and hurried away from the departing concertgoers into the quieter streets of the town. Their heels clicked on the cobbles. Harald hummed the Idyll to himself and could be heard up and down the street. Otherwise the streets were silent.

They stopped outside an unlit shop and Harald rapped gently at the door. A small light flared inside, approached the glass, and some words were exchanged. The door opened and Harald and Lena were ushered inside the showroom of a radio shop. All around, the lamplight picked out dials, speakers, wiring and Lena was reminded of the ancient pipe organ in the Hofkirche that filled the walls with controls, console, pipes. They were led through a back room, up a narrow staircase and into a windowless attic lit by three electric table lamps.

Finally they could see the man who'd admitted them, the overweight and sweating proprietor, bald and flushed from climbing the stairs. He sank into a chair by a desk where the largest of the lamps illuminated a number of notebooks, papers and a large wireless set. He invited Harald and Lena to sit in an old settee by the door. There were two small tables set in front of the settee. Each bore its own smaller lamp and a pen and some paper, clearly intended to serve as a writing desk if necessary.

— I can't offer you any refreshment, announced the man, indicating his surroundings. I am *Eloise* — a code name, obviously.

Harald nodded.

— Of course. You may call us… *Harald and Lena.*

Eloise chuckled and relaxed.

— We have heard, Eloise, that you've been disturbed by something unusual recently.

Eloise stretched back in his chair and sighed deeply.

— Disturbing goes with the territory. Unusual is pretty much a daily thing as well. This, well… this is unworldly.

He tapped his fingernails against the chair arms and looked carefully and Harald and Lena in turn.

— I don't entirely trust the means by which you were made available to me.

— I'm not surprised, said Harald, but that might be a problem. We need to know what you know.

Lena looked at Harald. He had grown in authority over the weeks since Clindor had disappeared. The group had always respected him and depended on his ability to unite them, but now the group had moved apart and all grown in power themselves, now he seemed to walk through the world with an assurance he'd never had before. Wojciech was desperate for Harald's arrival. But maybe Harald was losing something too, something more than his appealing veneer of vulnerability.

— Perhaps just a little demonstration might help establish our credentials, offered Lena.

Harald looked curiously at Lena. Eloise was genuinely baffled.

— If you don't truly believe we can help you, why would you even want to trust us?

— No, I mean, I don't think... began Eloise but stopped sharply. *Mein Gott.*

Harald smiled. Lena had grown too and it seemed to him for the first time she was the one pushing back the boundaries. Freed from the relentless browbeating of Clindor and the impossible superiority of Stephen, she was able to follow some ideas of her own and she was developing a new subtlety that went beyond his. The illusion she had worked here was spectacular.

The two table lamps in front of Harald and Lena continued to shine as before but the tables on which they had been standing had disappeared. The lamps hung perfectly in mid-air with not a thread or strut to support them. Lena kicked her feet out underneath her table.

And then they were back again. Neither Eloise nor Harald had noticed them vanish, and neither saw them reappear even though their whole attention was on the lamps.

— I think it's safe to say, said Lena, that while strange goes with your territory, *even stranger* goes with ours.

Eloise nodded, looked at his watch and seemed to resolve on something. He turned to the wireless apparatus on his desk. He flicked a switch and as the valves warmed up a hiss of white noise filled the room. He pushed a jack into a socket and the noise died.

— That, said Eloise, is what Europe used to sound like.

He placed a headset on and riffled through the pages of a notebook till he found what he needed. He tapped his fingernails against his seat while reading and mentally deciphering his notes, then he sprang to life. He twisted a dial, quickly at first, but then fine-tuning in response to something he was hearing. When he was happy with what he had found, he tugged the jack out of wireless and flicked a switch. Over a mid-range crackle, a thin, scratchy voice came through the wireless speaker, talking carefully and mechanically in German.

— This, said Eloise, is the "music" of a "pianist", as the Germans call them. Troop movements, logistics, armament. This man is somewhere in Switzerland, perhaps quite close. He has been broadcasting for a couple of months now. He is not alone.

He flipped the switch back and plugged the cable back in, then he was off flying through the frequencies again, just as before, wild turns of the dials then slower more careful adjustments. Then the switch, the cable tug, and the speaker crackled to life again. Another voice, deeper, cut through by bursts of static.

— This pianist is further afield, he said. I believe it's coming from the Reich.

Again he recalibrated, finding this time a voice so marginally differentiated from the background noise that Eloise felt the need to hold up a finger to draw their attention to the accents.

— This one is speaking French. But there are more every week. You see, the world is arming, not just with munitions but with radios. Soon these isolated pianos will be orchestras and the war will be waged along the whole width of the spectrum. My customers… I am starting to keep tabs…

He flicked the switch again and embarked on one final recalibration. This time as he turned the dial, he explained to them:

— What you are about to hear, I call the *ballet*. Its frequency hops around but I discovered that the pattern is predictable. Sometimes it dances with the pianists across Europe, echoing their information, sometimes translated into English. Most of the time though, it's just this impenetrable jargon. Ah. Here we are.

Again he popped the cable and flipped the switch and the speaker flared to life. The voice was unearthly, high and screechy but it spoke slowly and carefully as if reciting from a text.

— *...through pain, to the paraconcrete, the stratum imagined on the concrete, a construction...*

Lena and Harald's head snapped round to face each other, though Eloise noticed they didn't look in each other's eyes.

— *Got him!* exclaimed Harald and raised a fist in triumph. Do we have any means of tracing this?

Eloise stuck out his bottom lip and shrugged his shoulders.

— I can sell you a wireless?

In the first week Bastien had caught Greta Giroud's eye and he knew instantly they must never be seen again, by Greta, by Anna, by the servants, the congregation, or any or the people in their lives. Greta would have no mercy. Her eyes were like gravestones and the hell she had in store did not lie far beneath the surface.

So they began to live separately, meeting only in London or away in the lakes. They each found ways to watch and they shared their techniques in *Happenstance*. They designed rotas and shifts and began to codify their vigil.

On one visit to London, Paul dragged them to a shop and gathered them around a wireless while he fiddled with the controls. He managed to tune in to a station broadcasting a warbling voice delivering some kind of lecture. He shushed them.

— ... *incorporate perspectival dynamics into a coherent noumenon ...*

— It's Stephen! cried Bastien.

— His *ghost*, corrected Paul. Should we tell her?

— Don't be insane! said Bastien. She must never know!

— But he's basically her father!

— Not anymore.

They let it play for a few moments and then Paul scrambled the dial.

— Well that's it, said Pierre. Soon everyone will know.

— Maybe not, said Paul. It's not as easy to find as all that. And it's not always there. And who would actually listen to that drivel?

A fond memory of Stephen passed between them. Then their minds went to Anna again and the deep love she'd had for him.

Pierre said:

— Write it down for her. All of it. Maybe, one day…

30. Growing and Travelling

Timoth, Seronin

— HOLD IT! Too fast! Candle's urgent cries seemed to come from his own insides. *Keep. Yourself. Together!*

Timoth could feel himself falling apart. He was at once having thoughts that weren't his own and at the same time seeing his dispersing self through other eyes as an intrusion, a permeating threat to some a greater mind. Every element of his self was *becoming* in new ways growing toward alien suns, rooting in strange soils. He was drowning in something that was already partly himself.

— Focus, Timoth! Focus or you'll lose everything! Keep. It. Together!

She sounded desperate but Timoth sensed a salvation in his dispersal, an abnegation, an absolution, a release. He let himself drift.

Then she was screaming with Timoth's own mouth. Clamping jaws, pinching, percussing, probing, penetrating, pulling hair, sinking teeth into Timoth's side, the nape of his neck, his buttocks. Blistery visions came at him: Martoth clothed in vapour, lit by chainsawing lights; Jessic trailing ice cold fingertips across his chest; Border rising from the earth into a scarlet sky. Finding in them a kernel of truth, he began at last to resist.

It was a struggle but he grew into the fight. Each ounce of effort seem to strengthen his determination and he knew that Candle was inside him now, fashioning her own willpower into the struts and tethers he needed to keep the fight going.

Once he had control, Candle slowly pulled out.

— Eurgh. Oh God. That was rank, Timoth breathed weakly. What in fuck's name did you do to me? Is this…?

— *Sanctum*, Candle confirmed. X-3. You're stable now. Look around. And don't fuse or shift without me. You've already lost some quite important things.

— ?

— !

— .

— As for what I did to you, it's nothing compared to what I did to Seronin when he first shifted here. He still hasn't forgiven me.

Timoth let his mind's gaze wander, looking outward and inward at his sanctum-body. Imagery was less robust here than in *Happenstance,* or at least more plural. Where was he? A suboceanic cathedral? A salt mine? It was a shifting dreamscape. Candle and he were the most stable things in this world, except from something else he couldn't quite define but seemed to be a quality of the light. Parts here and there were always glowing, or always glimmering, while the underlying imagery rippled and cross-faded. Flying buttresses of laser light and luminescent shorelines persisted though they transmuted between coral and rock.

— You see why it is so hard to maintain a perspective here? Candle's presentation was male, thickset, broad-browed and greying, but her voice in Timoth's head remained feminine. She extended her arms and the fluctuation decelerated.

— With effort we can control it, and through it, the lower

strata, but it's hit and miss. The Vigil thinks of it as religious but really it's more capricious.

Together they travelled, or part-travelled and part let their surroundings travel around them. Timoth began to understand the relationship between *Sanctum* and *Happenstance.*

— You see the shoreline? asked Candle.

— Uh yeah.

The shoreline was constant, superimposed upon or constructed out of the other imagery.

— The tide is always going out. Always leaving us. Always has been. Maybe always will be. Do you know what lies beyond?

Yes.

The *Apocryph.*

The fourth stratum. He could feel its power, its potential, as if the weight of the world were poised at an absurd altitude. And as he looked, a crawling terror encircled him, a sense of balance lost on a cliff edge, or a hardness of breath at the brink of strangulation. The eternal recession of the tide bothered him. Had it always been like this? Since humans first looked? Had there been a high tide? *Where had it started from?* What were we all losing as that tide went out?

— There are other idioms that you'll start to notice. It's not like *Happenstance* where one scene is distinct from another. Many things are always there on the edge of your awareness. Seronin sees more than anyone. Our link back to *Concreta* is tenuous here. To change things in *Concreta* requires genius. In the history of the universe, maybe a few thousand humans have shifted here. Less than a hundred have managed anything beyond tourism. Since the Vigil was founded, humanity has kept up a constant watch on *Sanctum* but it is not ours in the way that *Happenstance* has become ours. *That* —Candle indicated the shoreline— has been crossed by one mind and one mind only.

Timoth paused, uncertain of how far he dared bend this lesson into more personal territory. Darker shapes swam around them, shadows of reef sharks and rubber smoke.

— You say *ours*…

Candle's presentation solidified into a marble Plato.

— Just because I'm not natural, does not make me inhuman, Timoth. You can see that everything I say, I do, every way I appear, everything I am made of is human. We couldn't have this conversation if I was not every bit as human as you.

— I don't really understand.

He'd been torn from a naivety close to mind-blindness all the way into X-3 in a matter of weeks. Notions as nebulous as humanity were never going to be securely pinned down while everything else was rebuilt.

— I have other questions.

— About Lethe?

— And Seronin.

— Ask Seronin.

What must the hawk know of the dead city on the horizon?

It sailed in the sky wherever it chose, surely far and wide if it sought food in this dry landscape. Timoth followed it down from the rocky peaks behind and out over the dusty salt flats ahead. He lost it in the sun then found it again, a lonely, diminishing dot in the endless blue.

Three days they'd been here now, he and Candle. Three days and this was the first time she'd allowed him time to sleep. That was the first thing she'd shown him: how to control his circadia. A neat trick, he'd thought, before he realised her brutal intention. Was he even the same person he'd been when they made it here? He felt like his mind had repeatedly grown turgid and then been wrung out. It had been pumped full of facts, theory, technique then squashed tight in the vice of drills and exercises. Was he finally starting to understand the talent he'd discovered months ago in the deep paddy? Or was he drifting further and further from the shore? Candle seemed to have an curiously exact sense for his limits. She always pushed a little beyond where he felt safe. She had no compunction letting him struggle in deep waters but he never felt abandoned. Now after three days with only occasional forays out into the sunlight, he guessed he'd reached another kind of limit and she'd left him to himself for a while.

When it came to it, he couldn't actually sleep. He might have attempted some adjustments and brought it on artificially but he was enjoying sitting in the sunlight and contemplating the ruins on the horizon.

This was New Gobi: a Tier One, but only if you knew your history. And Timoth was beginning to.

Was it entirely abandoned? he'd asked. The city, yes, probably. The planet no. There were still human minds here somewhere. Candle could feel them at times but they seemed scarce and lonely. For decades the city had been regarded as a Babel, a lesson in humility for a briefly hubristic humankind. Buoyed by their migrations, their spread across the galaxy, their control of reality and their grasp of the roots of catastrophe, they forgot the sheer weight of nature and the toll it would take to keep it suspended. For a number of years the city had been like the Polyclasm, a bouncy castle inflated by the pump of continual mindwork. But unlike the Polyclasm, the city was large and ambitious, and maybe, in the end, too complex. Maybe the paradoxes of organisation played their part in its demise, just as they did the Earth. Candle thought not. It was just a case of pushing too hard at forces that were always going to push back harder. A city in a desert. It had been done before, of course, but never exclusively by the power of the mind.

What remained? From Timoth's viewpoint, it was a grey stump on the horizon. If he wanted to look closer then maybe he had something of the necessary skill now but he was too exhausted.

Away to the left there was a speck moving on the flats, too far away to see in detail. Some kind of native animal probably — Earth imports had not fared well here. He watched it as it meandered towards the hills to his left and his thoughts returned to Martoth. He was in a much better frame of mind now than he had been back in Beechbark. The therapeutic effect of hard work and his many successes had given him something of a lift. Also he was well aware Candle had indulged in a little informal psychiatry, talking him back from a few edges. Mostly though it was the electrifying memory of that kiss that was keeping him up.

In his lap lay the tile Martoth had left with him. It had become the most important thing in the world. When he looked at it everything else seemed to fade. He could feel it tingling against his thighs. Again and again he had read the glazed messages in red and green. Again and again he probed the material with his mind. He revelled in the trust that Martoth had shown him and yearned to be where she was.

The tube he'd offered to Theremy. If it was from Meef Parton, it had some personal meaning to him, and Martoth had clearly meant him to take it. But Theremy refused, reasoning that her leaving it with Timoth superseded anything before. In any case, it was irrelevant to the Diocletian problem. It could wait. Timoth had assumed then that Theremy would head on to the Abbey, but he was still with Seronin when Timoth and Candle had slipped right through The Polyclasm all the way to here.

For weeks as winter set in and one by one the great gates

closed, Quartz-in-Tiberia reeked. Warm wet summers brought pestilence and rot. The human dead were buried in the sky, but vermin clogged the pipes and the narrow gaps. As the winter night descended, their bloated bodies froze and expanded. They could be found and poked out with stiff brooms. In the streets, rancid pools frosted over and could be chipped away and thrown into the gorge. By the time the deepest winter-dark was reached, Quartz-in-Tiberia smelled of food, drink and freedom.

Though living was crude, Quartz was mindwoke, and Seronin was known here, if not for what he truly was, then at least as the fallen priest he sometimes was, and certainly as a man, no better or worse than the rest. Travellers passed through throughout the year but mostly in the winter night — you could dress against the cold but not the heat. To the townspeople, the travellers were sorcerers, bringing danger and riches in equal measure. Their perception of mindworkers was skewed further by the complete absence of Vigil representation amongst them, a fact which did much to enhance the town's reputation among the more dissident or anarchic of the minds capable of travel-in-Concreta. It was a refuge for some, a showboat for others. Most travellers were not averse to the more earthly pleasures which Quartz-in-Tiberia served in abundance. Despite the play of such power amongst them the township remained in authority. They set the rhythm of the winter-day and the boundaries of the winter-night.

Lethe, Seronin and Theremy trudged over trampled snow to the rear of the crowd. Cold air nipped at their ears and cheeks and sputtering torches burned flares in their vision. It was the closing of the last gate, Quartz's oldest ritual. People were busy on the slender ramparts and men below were clearing the last of the snow and mud to free the enormous gates from the earthen beds they'd settled into during the warmer months. What they were closing the gates *against* was as vague as the dark. There was no-one else out there. But for the next few months, none would venture out to beat back the wild and it would grow close against the walls. One narrow tunnel remained open on the east of the town but the townsfolk took no responsibility for that: the tunnel to the way head.

— Recognise anyone? Seronin asked.

He meant mindwoke.

— Zipmind, replied Lethe, and, I think, Cadux. And *Candle's* been here...? What the...?

Seronin looked sharply at his friend and began to explore carefully himself. Getting a line to Candle was no longer safe or easy. He knew Lethe was worried about getting them out. If there were traces of Candle here it wasn't because she'd been. He had a hunch...

— Not in *Concreta*...

— No, you're right... she's taken Timoth into *Sanctum*.

Seronin turned an eye towards Theremy who'd been silent for the last hour.

— Ever shifted to X-3?

Theremy shook his head. Sanctum would hold extra terrors for a fusion. The immense pressure... If you were even slightly worried about your *seams*... but Seronin never saw any seams in Theremy's mind. He did understand how Theremy was able to hide it from the Vigil. In fact he'd began to wonder how he had seen Theremy's nature on that first meeting. It was an intuition he couldn't trace. Maybe the novice, Merrick, was fresh in his memory. Or maybe he'd seen something like a regularity, a structure...

— You're a hexagon, aren't you?

Theremy scowled and looked away. It was impertinent but Seronin suspected Theremy's discomfort was more to do with Quartz-in-Tiberia. Quartz was no-go for vigilants and

Theremy was still working through his identity crisis on the Vigil thing.

— Come on, said Seronin, I'll buy you a drink.

As the great wheel turned and the massive gates creaked into motion, a murmur grew amongst the crowd. They packed the narrow street that led to the gate and hung from windows on either side, holding torches aloft. Lethe continued his trawl.

— So Zipmind, Cadux definitely, both here. Traces of Candle and Timoth. Then we have Janine, Hoarder-Hugh, Sago, Bax, and maybe Andrew Bell. A real party that.

Seronin groaned.

An enormous thud echoed out into the gorge — the final closing of the gate. Some muted fireworks spat off the top of it and a cheer went up. From the foot of the gate, the crowd dragged a large wooden carving. Eight men and women took ropes to haul it through the snow. It might have been a horse or a rhinoceros or some other hefty, hoofed thing, rendered amateurishly according to the standards of the town. It was a symbol that resonated with Seronin. The wild beyond the gates no longer existed. The only wild now was the wild that men dragged in with them. The crowd moved off towards the heart of the town, leaving only a few to pack the loose earth back around the base of the gate.

These days, when anyone thought *hub* they thought *Polyclasm*, so long had it been pre-eminent. All but a few forgot Quartz-in-Tiberia. It was a very different type of place: well-connected even when first discovered —shortly after the Tier Ones— and its leys had only been supplemented once or twice by human intervention. Despite the planet's giddy tilt, it was habitable, although Quartz-in-Tiberia was the only real settlement. When Lethe and Seronin found the Polyclasm's leys degenerating fast into what its denizens were calling the *pudding-psyche,* they made the obvious choice, and passed quickly on to the older, smaller hub, while Timoth and Candle made instead for the safest solitude they could find at a distance that might help test Seronin's theory. They were convinced now that the allspsyche was being unravelled in reverse order of construction. The older leys of Quartz-in-Tiberia might survive for longer. But how long? And what then?

— You're right at home here aren't you? said Lethe.

Seronin was aware of a tic flickering above his eye, pulling his eyelid around. He had let his mask slip. For any of them a life without mindwork, confined to Quartz-in-Tiberia, was not liveable. But Seronin would go out with a bang. Lethe would be dreading eternal separation from Candle.

— In some ways it's very like where I came from. Provincial, mindwoke in a half-arsed kind of way, full of its own quaint, warped customs. And without Vigil influence. I could live here if it wasn't so busy.

Theremy would be full of dread too. He stopped as they turned onto the snowy square that lay in front of The Fairy Castle, then hung back in the shadows as the others stepped out into the lamplight. Lethe turned to coax him on.

— You'll be fine, Theremy. No-one's going to think—

— No, he said firmly. I… I have to be somewhere else.

— Oh jeez-fuck, sighed Lethe in frustration. What is this? A you-do-your-thing-I've-got-to-go-off-and-do-mine contest?

Seronin put a pacifying hand on his arm. They stayed as they were for a minute, snow falling silently through the lamplight onto Seronin and Lethe, Theremy shrinking further into the shadows.

— You know where I'm going, came his voice from the darkness.

…but Seronin must have looked as baffled as he felt.

— We spoke last night! exclaimed Theremy.

— What? No we didn't!

— Oh for fuck's sake, Seronin. Look. There's a mind behind these attacks, however degenerate. And it is not a natural mind, not anymore. Allow me the same intuition you trust in yourself. It is something *like me*.

— Theremy, pleaded Lethe, you're not a monster.

— We *haven't* talked about this, Theremy! protested Seronin, Come inside and—

He trailed off and stepped back in surprise, crunching haphazardly through the snow, scanning the space around them. Theremy was gone. It was neatly done, he realised, soft, and gentle as the falling snow. Neither Seronin nor Lethe had noticed, and nor had whatever unnatural intelligence that lurked in the substance of the world.

A second speck out on the flats.

Out to the right at about the same distance as the first.

It moved slowly, stopping frequently and straying off its path as if foraging in the dead salt plain. Timoth's eyes sought out the first again. It was closer than he'd expected but still too far out to see what kind of animal it was. He wondered as Martoth might what predators hunted in these barren plains. Whatever these things were, they were too far away to cause trouble but he decided to mention it to Candle.

Then: a hot coal of doubt. Should he probe? Could he, at this distance? What should he expect? He remembered the dull herd mentality of the cows on the Leap. These would be different. They must be solitary, scavenger minds, sharper, more competitive. In imagining, he found he had already begun to reach out across the plain, his mental whiskers tumbling across the scratchy surface out towards the first speck. As he approached he began to recognise what he had feared, deep down.

— Stop Timoth, said Candle in his head, you know what it is.

He let his exploratory probe explode in a puff and disperse into the flux. He pocketed the tile, stood up and shielded his eyes from the sun to scan the plain. He began to see more of them —seven or eight moving out in the distance, none fast but all in his direction.

— What are we going to do?

But she didn't answer.

She was in the city.

There was a rattle of dislodged stones below. He jumped back and cursed. How had he missed…? With sudden urgency, he scrambled back up the rocks behind, heading for the cave where he and Candle had been hiding. He crested a small outcrop, glanced back and saw what he feared — a human shape twenty yards below, climbing fast. He saw a dark mane of windswept hair and a lithe form, moving clumsily but with speed untamed by any human fear or sensation.

He would never make the cave. He had to turn and face it but he needed a surface, somewhere flat where the slightest swing of his fist wouldn't pitch him down the hill. He took a gamble, halting his ascent and contouring round to his right. He knew without looking that the puppet altered course to match, closing the distance smoothly and efficiently. It had a sort of lock on him; its void-black eyes weren't important anymore. As it closed, colours seemed to shift greyward and the fierce sun turned pale. A thin spinroar seeped into his ears. The groping arms of the thing were only yards below his skittering feet. He clambered up a sloping cactus rockery, over a tumble of boulders and saw the flatter area he'd gambled on. The creature, upright now, raced up the slope with bounding steps and arms aloft. Timoth reached the plateau first and hauled himself up onto it. He rolled onto the dusty surface just as the creature's hand grasped the edge.

It wheezed out a throaty howl as it leapt onto the edge.

Timoth turned onto his back and kicked hard against the ground to get away. The infested body was female with a face was etched by deep furrows, signs of a hard desert existence and its futile end. The outer sack-weave clothes hung loose but there was a layer of something else that clung tight to its body beneath. As it crouched, arms wide, and as the daylight lost all colour, Timoth began to see it as a bat, not a woman.

He clambered to his feet and growled at the bat. He knew the physical danger was only half of it but he'd seen Martoth take out two of these in the barn and it gave him confidence. He wasn't sure what role Weakjohn had played then, nor Seronin with Father Roderick. Something else would be coming at him beside fists and knees and nails and teeth.

There were tactics in his recent training. He knew he was more powerful than this dumb spin-thing if he could just work out how to attack it. He limbered up his perspective as he would to shift to *Happenstance* and began to feel the shape of the world around him, the boundaries, the materials he had to work with. Then he let his imagination fly. He cast a sheet of liquid flame between him and the puppet and pushed it towards his adversary. But as he advanced, the dark shape shrieked and leapt through it and clutched its hands tight around Timoth's throat. It fell on him and he was suddenly fighting for breath. Its wet black eyes were inches from his and the a cloying smell of rot filled his nostrils. He kicked his legs hard but couldn't throw off the bat-thing.

He was searching for ways to work with the bat-thing's body, to subvert or modify it. He wasn't sure what he wanted to do, set it alight, liquefy it, make its blood flow backwards. He knew he could find a way to do any of these if he had the time. As his chest spasmed trying to shake a breath of air into his lungs, an idea struck and he made a leap of perspective he had no right to assume would work. He became a mind that comprised Timoth and the bat-thing's body. It was a hostile overlap and it was the beginning of a vicious fight.

He wrestled to secure his perspective on the new mind. The creature's body sprung off him and staggered back, regaining its feet. Timoth's body gasped noisily, sucking air through a battered windpipe into starved lungs. He felt *both* bodies wince at the bruised throat.

There was something he could feel in the bat-thing mind, something in the intricate relationship of brain and body and perspective, a tether, a cord. And he knew how critical that tether was to the overstretched spin that was fighting for control of the desert-woman's body. The spin was barely more than a weather system. There were crude memories embedded in it, shadows of motivations, echoes of personae, but nothing approaching animal mind. Without the tether it would disperse.

With a final push, he mastered the new fuse-mind and cut the tether.

Colour flooded back into the world. For the space of a heartbeat, he controlled both bodies and pandered to a strange impulse to stare through both sets of eyes at his two selves, but the bat eyes were dead eyes and when he tried to use them he realised what pain this body was in. He was filled with nausea and realised how close he was coming to losing everything. He retracted his perspective and let the bat-thing drop dead with a thump.

He clutched his neck. Every breath burned but he felt a growing urge to vomit.

— Candle, he called weekly.

He stood and looked out over the plain. There was no sign of the specks he'd seen earlier. Surely they hadn't already reached the rocks? The vomit urge became overpowering. He bent down but was overcome by dizziness. He blacked out.

He woke in the cave. Someone was rushing about near the

mouth, casting shadows against the back wall where he lay. His throat was sore but he no longer felt sick.

— How long was I asleep?

Candle's face appeared.

— Not long. We have to go. You were spectacular, Timoth, but not quiet.

Timoth groaned.

— We've lost contact, she said, and the leys got fried. We only have one way back.

He knew what she meant. Through the city.

— I'm outside. Bring your pack.

Where next? To the others on Tiberia? Then what, the Abbey? Catch up with Martoth…

Sitting up, he heard a curious tinkling sound like shattered pottery and he remembered putting Martoth's tile in a thigh pocket. *Please no.* But as he reached into the pocket, his sinking heart knew already what he would find. Cupped in his palm were the tiny white, red and green fragments, many as fine as powder, that had been Martoth's only evidence of the strange love of her erratic parents.

Candle poked her head back in to find out what the noise was all about.

31. Playing in the Band

Timoth, Seronin

— You're going to love this! said Seronin, brimming with enthusiasm.

Lethe tried to look excited for his friend's sake. Seronin had refused the spines and was barely touching his beer. His enthusiasm was genuine but he was preoccupied. Losing Theremy? Or Martoth? Or the leys? Or their failed experiment? Something was hanging over him. Lethe guessed he'd come to an unwelcome decision. If their wandering was coming to an end, it could not end here. Surely, it must be the Abbey.

— Any chance you might not have been the most discriminating of judges last time?

Lethe pulled his hands up inside his coat sleeves and worked on not looking bored. There was activity up on stage. A team of young men dressed all in black were readying props and puppets. An energetic "Mrs Maestro" with flyaway Einstein-hair was standing, remonstrating over the lid of her piano with a ragtag group of instrumentalists who might have volunteered tonight, judging by the chaos.

— You know, I think I'm in it, said Seronin. By mistake.

Watch out for the rainbow cape.

The Fairy Castle was a shadow of its former self. Not in the numbers — there were more in tonight than ever. But they weren't all paying customers. Supplies were faltering and the fixtures and fittings were being damaged faster than they could be repaired. The patrons were burning their own small fires here and there about the floor to supplement the fires at the base of the large chimney breasts. Some had brought their own lamps for the tables. There were even dogs nosing around beneath the tables, eating scraps and sniffing at spills and spine cartridges.

The pianist banged out a low rumble in a vain attempt to grab the punters' attention. After keeping it rumbling for a few seconds while she scanned the faces in the room, she shrugged, barked out a '2-3-4 and slid both hands up the keyboard. They launched into the first number and the boys in black leapt up, twisting in mid-air to face the room and reveal their gaudy papier maché puppets.

Somebody, could have been anybody, was posted by each window facing out into the night. These were the outward guards. Two people were sat high on chairs balanced precariously on the bar itself and a handful more on chairs that had been hoisted up onto the tables around the room. These were the inward guards. Janine, an old tormentor of Seronin's from his Vigil days, was one of these, perched several feet above them a couple of tables away.

— They're here! said Lethe suddenly. At the way head. They made it!

His relief was all the deeper as he'd been unable to help this time. Candle and Timoth had done it themselves. In the swell of excitement, he found it hard to stay still. He drank from his tankard and sat back to take in the show, tolerance restored and sense of humour reinvigorated.

The outward guards were signalling to each other as

punters crossed the snowy square tower the tavern. Though Lethe knew without effort where Candle was, he found was looking up every time they signalled.

Finally he saw the signal he was waiting for. The inward guards were jumpy; two of them rendezvoused by the door and waited with stern eyes on each other. They took two paces back as the door opened.

There they were.

At twenty feet Lethe could see Timoth had changed. His face was dry and rough from the sun and a light beard had taken hold. He was moving with newfound confidence. He submitted himself to he guards' search without concern and he didn't seem in the slightest ill at ease. The guards backed off with hands up and motioned them in.

They came straight over and Timoth dropped his pack by the table.

— We have new firepower, boys, said Candle.

— Congratulations on your handiwork, said Seronin. Sit down, Timoth, and check out the show. Then your education will be complete.

He pulled a chair up to the table. Seronin saw him noticing Theremy's absence but he didn't enquire.

— Is this the thing you were telling me about? With Humpoth the Rice Magnate? asked Timoth, eyeing the stage suspiciously.

— No, no, no... this is totally, totally different. You're gonna love it.

— Any news fr—?

Janine was up and one of the other inward guards was on his feet too. Both were poised, feet firm on the tabletops amid the spillages and toppled glasses. Timoth craned his neck around to see and realised he was searching in the flux as well.

Seronin put an urgent hand on his arm and met his look of surprise with an apologetic wince. Then a shout went up — a false alarm: a harmless demonstration, some ill-advised entertainment. The inward guards exchanged irritated glances and returned to their thrones.

— Before we lost comms, said Seronin. They're with Barnabas. We have more of Martoth's visions, and some corroborating evidence we're starting to see ourselves.

Timoth nodded.

— We've seen some of that too, he said. And not just in the Dioclete spins and the puppets. Even before we entered the dead city, it was in everything around us. You can get down to it wherever you look: this "Clindor"… these pioneers… What Martoth's seeing, it's all embedded somehow in the world around us. Like you thought.

Candle had been distracted by the show but turned back to the table. The theatrical defecations and tuneless singing had not charmed her as they had Seronin.

— What *are* we watching?

Even Seronin was focused on other things now:

— Theremy said it was like some layers have been peeled back in the world. It feels like that doesn't it? Like there's a new depth, like we can dig deeper into of every particle and every occasion. But I allowed his thought to influence me too much. Our experiment failed. A context as wide as a galaxy, a legion of sparks lit, and it looks absolutely nothing like what's happening. I put everything into it.

Lethe put down his drink.

— You've changed your mind?

But Seronin seemed keener to explain himself than answer questions.

— The uncovered oracles, the memories that are coming up to the surface, the new depth. The new material is cropping up everywhere, in every pulse, in every feed, in the relics. It's so spread, so pervasive, I was looking for something universal. We know how widespread this Dioclete material is. So if that provides the coldwake context and you add in the resonance dimensions I've been exploring as an activation channel... well you could have armies of puppets and spins crawling out of the woodwork. It all seemed to fit. You don't *need* any enemy if you've got this material everywhere. At least not one who's alive now. Somehow the world was a time bomb and our time had run out. Or we'd armed the bomb.

— *Whoosh*... Timoth made a comic gesture of something going right over his head.

Candle rolled her eyes. The orchestra played on.

— Whatever, said Seronin. I was wrong.

Lethe stared at Seronin, mouth wide.

— Don't tell me you've accepted the *Vigil's* theory?

Right on cue: one rainbow-clad superhero shitting on a book.

— I forgot how universal our own legacy is. How all this..., he gestured at the stage, the tables, the giant fireplaces, the bar, ... all of it, Tenistan, Cobalt, Schiller, Fennerstoil, the entire modern diaspora and its curious cosy bed in Concreta... it is all just a dream of ours. The shape of the world is the shape of the human mind.

Timoth was lying. Even if he didn't understood where Seronin was leading, he understood the jargon. The flight through the city had not only honed his skills and allowed him to develop some devious hostile perspectival techniques. It had thrown him into a deep end spilling over with subsapient phenomena. Even when they weren't under attack, there were weather systems, chanters, teratologies and artificials spun off from the migrants and their systems. The settlers had brought hyperdense materials with them too. There were cylinxes amongst the ruins, every one fought over and infested. As Candle watched, Timoth's sprightly mind bounced in and out the chaos and touched more and more of the boundaries of reality. And though he was burnt many times, Timoth spoke with the inhabitants of the menagerie. When he reached the way head he was older.

— So…? prompted Candle.

Seronin had lost his thread.

— Oh, yes. So, he said. Yes. So Diocletian definitely *is* murdering the world.

But he was distracted again.

— Lethe, did you feel… the way head?

Lethe nodded.

— We're losing it, he confirmed. If we're not off this planet in a few hours, we're Quartzers.

The beer Seronin had been toying with for the last hour was suddenly addressed with renewed vigour.

Lethe and Candle went off for a while.

— There's something I really need your help with, said Timoth.

Seronin made a face that was meant to look open and accommodating but was ruined by his keeping one eye fixed on the entertainment.

Timoth drew a hand out of his pocket and tipped out a powdery pile of white fragments, peppered with slivers of red and green glaze.

— Oh, no fucking way, said Seronin.

Timoth pleaded but Seronin stood firm:

— Ask Lethe for a lecture on taking responsibility sometime. They're a real scream.

— Is it really so dangerous? asked Timoth, indicating the inward guards on their perches.

— We're on a knife-edge, said Seronin. Places like this…

the tiniest deviation and a darkspin seeps out of the walls. There've been rips too. There are lots of people who can deal with them here, but that's also lots of people prone to causing them. Believe me, you don't put Janine in any position of authority unless you've got a good reason.

Seronin shot a sideways glance up at his old schoolfriend and Timoth saw a troubled look cross his face. He seemed to be keen to avoid her notice although she must have seen him.

— To tell the truth, muttered Seronin, I wouldn't mind a vantage point like that. If it weren't so exposed. There are a couple of old-timers I'm looking for.

He stood up, keeping his tankard to his lips as if to hide his face as he scanned the room.

— Hmmh. Timoth. You don't play the weedhorn do you?

— One of those cheap ones you just sing through or a proper one?

Timoth caught Seronin eyeing up a trunk full of instruments tucked under the stage.

— Oh no way! You can do that yourself!

— Come on! Miranda loves it when new people volunteer.

— Do *you* play anything?

— Not so you'd notice.

— No. No. *No.* I'm not even half drunk enough.

— Ha!

Seronin snatched something from the table —a cartridge containing some orange fluid— and before Timoth could object he jabbed it into Timoth's neck.

— How about… *now*?

Timoth was too stunned to respond so Seronin dragged him and his pack off the bench and over to the instrument chest.

Seronin was confident that their lack of talent would be obscured by the general chaos and he was probably right. He was right about Miranda too: as their heads popped up in the ragtag group in front of her piano, she screwed up her face, closed her eyes, guffawed and raised her beer to them with her right hand while playing on with her left.

— What are we doing here, Seronin? asked Timoth and blew some tuneless flatulent sounds out of his weedhorn to a rhythm he'd copied from the wasted bassoonist next to him.

Seronin had picked out a sort of miniature banjo and was strumming the open strings randomly whilst solemnly swaying his hips from side to side.

— Shush. You've got to *feel* it. Just let it take over.

— You're actually talking about the music aren't you?

A music stand stood in front of Timoth with a fat sheaf of music on it. Seronin pshawed and made an exaggerated show of throwing the sheets to the floor.

— Trust your feelings! he whispered urgently under his voice.

— You know I can't read that stuff right?

But Seronin's eyes were trained on the crowd. He was looking for something or someone. A wave of fear passed over Timoth as he fought an urge to let his mind range out. How easily he could "deviate" as Seronin had put it. How quickly some things had become as natural as breathing…

— Gods. Can't leave you two for a minute, came Candle's voice in their heads.

— Ohh it was waaaay more than a minute, said Seronin. And what about you two, huh? Where may I ask are your bodies?

— We wore them out, said Lethe without regret.

— Just as I thought, said Seronin. So you can hardly begrudge me and my bandmate a little fun.

Timoth took Seronin's advice and let himself get carried away adding his own weedhorn accents to the more scatalogical elements of the finale. Ultimately the *Tetrawocky* came to a triumphant end without incident in orchestra or audience. The band relaxed while the cast regrouped. Just like Miranda, the other musicians were unperturbed by their new colleagues.

— OK bunnies, yelled Miranda over her piano. The *pageant* next…

The band groaned in unison.

— Oh, said Seronin. I forgot about that…

— What?

— You don't need to worry. Play just like before. Except when I nudge you, we all turn round and wiggle our arses in time okay?

— *What?*

— Can we talk? asked Candle.

Seronin and Timoth grimaced at each other. This was taking some concentration.

— You two could? said Timoth hopefully.

Seronin tapped Timoth on the arm and they both turned their backs on the crowd and wiggled.

— Guys. This is hardly appropriate, said Lethe. Who are you looking for?

— Sa-go. Or-any-of-the. Old. Guard, sang Seronin to the beat.

— I'm hurt!

— Just another point of view, Lethe, said Seronin. Sago was butting up against the bounds of the diaspora all that time you two were spinning your wheels at the Ab-*BEEEEY*.

…the last word being embellished by Timoth's increasingly confident hornwork.

— Come on Timoth. Fun's over. Lethe's grumpy.

They raised horn and banjo in friendly salute to the rest of the band, then ducked out and retrieved their packs. Their table was taken, but Seronin was hustling them towards the exit anyway.

— When's the last time you slept? he asked Timoth.

Days ago, thought Timoth. Before the dead city,

Seronin nodded at the outward guard and they stepped out into the snowfall.

Quartz-in-Tiberia was a beautiful town in its way, at least in the winter night. The snowfall was light, the amber glow of the lamps settled into their tracks and spilled across the squares. Up beyond the snowfall the cloudy darkness rippled in chaotic patterns. Timoth did not know whether he saw this with his eyes or his mind. Was it an effect of the wind and swirling snow? Some alien chemistry in Tiberia's atmosphere? Or was he beginning to see the tumult in the decaying Allpsyche that distressed the others so much?

Despite the riotous noise, the paranoia, and the accelerating dilapidation of the premises, the Fairy Castle had been a blessed comfort after the scorching air of New Gobi. Timoth had been on Tiberia for only a couple of hours but this breathless trek through the snowy lanes told him his visit was already over. The route Seronin bounded along with his peculiar loping gait was the same route Timoth and Candle had taken up from the way head, through the tangled forest, the strange tunnel and the lamplit streets. Somewhere by the pub door, Lethe and Candle had concresced, dressed for the weather, and they trudged along behind Timoth. Lethe was the first to ask where they were going. But Seronin wanted to pick up his earlier thread:

— Our simultaneity nets don't cut it, not on their own, he called back without slackening pace. Solving simultaneity… it's not enough to blow open rips in Semele, the Leap, the Abbey… deep space… send darkspins and puppets, across the galaxy. You couldn't do it. I couldn't do it. Sounness couldn't do it. Grace couldn't do it.

He paused to catch his breath but only for a moment. There was a new urgency in him and Timoth was trying to work out whether it had come from a change, a realisation or a decision.

— I don't believe Diocletian, Clindor… whoever… could do it. Just because you can granulate your perspective to a billion points, doesn't mean you can granulate across the known universe. So I thought… something already everywhere, pre-propagated…

Seronin wasn't really talking to them. He was explaining himself. As he set off again he kept up the monologue.

— Martoth's connection got me thinking about the architecture we've got. The Allpsyche looks like it's unravelling, but that's just the stuff we've built in the last century. When do we ever trace further back than that? We don't, we only ever hit the closed ways. It's only ever by accident, we get glimpses, insights, like all the things we're starting to see now. Clindor's face. Detail in the relics. But the *oracles*…

— All our oracles take feeds from other oracles and that goes back as deep as we can go. There are leys we stumble on occasionally that are unfathomably old. There are older ways, older connections, we just can't see them so well. Or at least we couldn't…

They were hiking fast now, towards the town's Eastern Wall, across sleety rivulets by the street edges and sleek patches of darker ice. With a heart sunk into his boots, Timoth knew they were aiming for the same dank, freezing tunnel that he had emerged from so recently. But though he was none the wiser about their destination, Seronin's monologue gripped him. This antiquity of humanity's engagement with the Allpsyche was a mystery that tugged at a cord deep inside. For Martoth, it was her reading, her thirst to understand, that connected her back into that broad river of humanity. Now Timoth was finding something similar, his own connection to a deep well. But the flame of excitement was dampened by an unshiftable guilt that Maroth, who worked so hard, who deserved this more than he, might never glimpse the things he was now able to.

— But all these things spider out like the migrations don't they? continued Seronin. So what if there really is just a single source oracle? A single source that's old enough and deep enough to have become entwined with everything we've built since. One oracle feeding the material to all the others. Wherever humanity went we tapped something that tapped something else that starts going back to the deep oracles and then ultimately, alongside all the novel stuff they throw into the mix, there's a thin lineage from this one deep, old oracle to pretty much everywhere.

— And that's what Martoth's connected to? asked Timoth.

— Yes.

Seronin went silent when they reached the tunnel mouth. The last lamp was twenty yards back into the town and thorn bushes had been left to grow wild by the side of the tunnel path. A wet film of ice had frozen around the wooden structure and a dark moss spread out from the inside. There was no light within.

All four were itching to explore with their minds and all four were holding themselves in check. But Timoth had not been so careful earlier. It was what the others would call bad weather, a century of fear and distrust that had permeated the fabric of the tunnel.

Seronin put a hand to the mossy wall and entered. His voice went thin:

— And we're wrong about the damage in the Allpsyche...

They followed him into the blackness. If Seronin was moving by touch alone he was going very fast. His voice receded and Timoth stepped up his pace, afraid of losing him.

His hand carved through the wet moss on the tunnel wall.

— It's only mush from the angle we're used to looking at it. Look at it a different way and it's not destruction at all — it's reconfiguration… In fact, I think… it's *amplification*.

Inside the chill was biting. Timoth had added some layers since New Gobi, but he wasn't dressed for the cold. There was hardly any point now.

— Such a deep, old, oracle… said Seronin, emerging on the other side of the wall. The question to ask is:

— Who built it? said Lethe.

— …yes…

— And who controls it now? said Candle.

— …yes…

— And what could they use it for? said Timoth.

— Yes!

All these ideas jumbled together in his head, like a jigsaw that he was solving by free-association and trial and error. He was horrified by this notion of an ancient, sinister, oracle pumping the stuff of thought straight into Martoth's head. Seronin thought Diocletian was using this web of oracles to send spins, cause rips, puppetise victims across the universe… well, what danger was she in? How could she survive? Where was she now?

— So, said Seronin, if we know the mechanism, we know the flaw. It's one mind with a megaphone and finally we know where the megaphone must be.

— Earth! whispered Lethe.

— …and.. for the first time in seventy years, said Seronin as they walked out into the centre of the broad clearing that Timoth had left behind only hours earlier, *we can actually go there.*

PART THREE

32. Martoth at The Abbey

Martoth

Martoth stood beneath a wall of rock. The men waited behind. She could feel their eyes on her. It was a dead end but she did not turn. She did not offer them anything but the back of her thick anorak and the wind-tangled chaos of her hair.

She'd caught a shivery cold over the last few days and her face was full of a mucoid snot that she kept coughing up and spitting out, partly for the fun of appalling the bearded brethren watching her every move, and partly because it was irritating Weakjohn too. There was a cramp-like pain behind her eyeballs and every muscle ached. The hike out of the Backshades into this hilly country had been tough. Like the Downs that lay between thIe Backshades and the Abbey, these distant hills were exposed. Even when the snow held off, a wintry chill nipped at her ears and lips. The incessant shivering was bringing on sharp pains in her neck and spine. Though she'd never show it, she and Weakjohn both knew how close she was to tears.

The rock looked bizarre to Semele-trained eyes: purple-grey, volcanic, rising near-vertically for hundreds of feet before vanishing away to an invisible summit beyond. From its base a smooth surface reached some seventy, eighty feet up the cliff, a vestigial hint of a lost portal broad enough to swallow the Crowbeck motel or the whole of Havers Hall. This vast sheet of stone met the rest of the cliff face without any seam.

She wasn't sure if she should be feeling something.

— When did anyone last enter? she asked.

— No-one's entered in my lifetime, said Abbot Barnabas.

— There's history before that? asked Martoth, catching the eye of Chin, the historian, the only woman present and the youngest of the group from the Vigil.

Chin frowned:

— You realise the *physical* locations of these things were of purely academic interest till now? she said.

— That's why you're here, grumbled Barnabas.

There was a frostiness between these two that Martoth had not got a handle on yet.

— I'm not aware that anyone ever entered, admitted Chin.

— So it hasn't been opened since the planet was settled? asked Martoth. Since the *crises*?

Chin shrugged.

— I doubt they ever were intended to be opened. It's ironic really.

Weakjohn was keeping a strict policy of speaking only to Martoth. This combined front benefited them both. It avoided marginalising Martoth, and the group's assessment of Weakjohn's power and position wasn't harmed by the necessity to speculate. Weakjohn explained Chin's irony to Martoth: a few weeks ago entering would have been as trivial as it would have been unnecessary.

— Why seal it at all?

— No good reason I can see. But these oracles were direct links to Earth and the Earth was on fire. It was a time of crisis. There was an atmosphere of fear, of distrust. There were embargoes, moratoria, forbidden books... It may look like superstition but that's how people behave when reason fails.

Her eyes were on Barnabas as she spoke and Martoth didn't miss the barb.

— Maybe they knew something we don't, said Martoth.

— No doubt, she agreed.

— And here we are in crisis again, said Barnabas softly.

For all its strangeness, halting at solid rock was the perfect antidote to Martoth's sense of anchorless drifting. When Weakjohn explained the higher strata, it was Martoth who opened Timoth's eyes to the implications. *Think Timoth! Everything we ever imagined is just the least quarter of what is really out there.* But only days later when Timoth encountered Seronin, he repaid the favour with interest. *You thought we were the bottom* he said. *But we're somewhere in the middle and it might go down forever.* There was a time, quite recently when they got a kick out of dazzling each other like this. But the dazzle was a world where they might as well be different species.

Back in a reality as solid as this —where cliff faces were impassable once again— she and Timoth might make sense.

Martoth and Chin walked back together to the campsite and Martoth learned more about the settlement of the Abbey.

The Vigil back then was still under the regime of the Earthborn Abbots and they were remote and mysterious figures. Chin could recount the events of their reigns but knew little of the men themselves even though Abbot Simon's reforms were recent enough for even Weakjohn to remember.

— How did the Vigil start? asked Martoth.

Weakjohn laughed in Martoth's head. *Abbot Cheras was entrusted with the vigil,* she told Martoth privately.

— Abbot Cheras was entrusted with the vigil, said Chin.

— I've heard that before, said Martoth. How do the visions

fit in?

— We know Cheras was born on Earth in the nineteen nineties.

Martoth waved away a cloud of midges.

— Your visions seem to be from the late thirties.

— So…?

— So it's possible that Cheras's lifetime overlapped with some of the people you've been seeing. It's always been doubtful that he was entrusted his vigil by Diocletian because we know Diocletian was active right up into Sheras's reign and there doesn't seem to have been any kind of relationship during that time.

— So you think Clindor emerged into whatever higher state of being at the end of the thirties and these *others* started some kind of vigil, passing down their customs through Cheras down to today… through Xeras, Sheras, Simon, Demeter and Barnabas?

It was a working assumption but it wasn't enlightening. As far as Martoth could tell, most of the Vigil saw their mission as a struggle to keep a flame burning, but there were so many flames in the fire: flames of scholarship, learning, kindness, cruelty, the flame of human unity, the flame of human purity.

— But what's the *vigil*? asked Martoth. Is it possible that the Vigil and Diocletian were enemies from the start? Suppose we have the Swiss group murdering Clindor but at the point of death he *emerges* seeking revenge? Then, at least, there's a bloody good reason for them to be vigilant.

— So where along the line did we get so confused? asked Barnabas, walking up behind them.

They had used help for the journey, a passionless freelancer called Mebbit who must have been Vigil once but was content to pitch in for the price of a car, a gun and some ready cash. Weakjohn was convinced she'd known Mebbit by another name but couldn't dredge it from her reconstituted memory. Between them Mebbit and Weakjohn forced a stuttering needle-trail through the leys, and they concresced at a way head in the rolling hills to the South of the Abbey buildings that the Vigil called the Downs.

If Weakjohn did most of the work, it was Martoth's body that took the backsnap. She pitched over and spewed up her breakfast then sat pale and sweating for a few minutes before she stirred again.

Mebbit recovered quicker. As Martoth's strength returned, her gaze fell on this curious woman who was staring down over the ruins of the Abbey. She was dressed for action: leather jacket and close trousers that would not restrict movement and only a tiny pack on her back that she'd packed to cylinxual density. Her hair was clipped short and while her hands were small, they were rough and rugged. She held a water bottle which she was tossing from hand to hand as she stood.

The Abbey was a smouldering smudge on the landscape a mile below. The fields that ranged out from the central complex lay under a thick grey smog. Earth and rock had been deeply scarred by whatever fires had raged and the occasional glimmer of reflected sunlight suggested flooding.

Martoth stood beside Mebbit and realised that she was struggling to take it in. She had a face like the sea floor but though her eyes narrowed as they passed over the broken landscape, they had softened too.

— There are people alive in there, said a voice behind them.

A young novice, robust and red-haired with a tentative beard, sat there, crouched against a wooden structure that looked like a provisions cache.

— …but we can't get them out now. Who goes there, by the way?

Martoth consulted internally.

— Hi, she said. Martoth Heep-Parton and Weakjohn Steeple.

She waited for Mebbit to introduce herself but Mebbit remained still, silent and expressionless.

— Weakjohn? From Semele?

The novice introduced himself as Menelaus, one of a group who'd arranged amongst themselves to wait at the various way heads in case friends showed up. It wasn't clear what friends they were expecting, nor whether it might be more prudent to expect trouble. Martoth saw it as an enthusiastic act of desperation but was grateful for it. Weakjohn observed that the whole enterprise seemed to be operating without the knowledge or consent of the Vigil seniors and drew her own conclusions.

In any case Menelaus led them away from the ruins, deeper into the countryside and off towards the forest he called the Backshades. Mebbit stowed her water bottle and tagged along a few paces behind.

Menelaus led them under the broadleaf fringes of the Backshades and in the space of a few yards it had already grown dark. This wasn't the airy larchwood of Semele or even the denser pines of the forest where she had seen Clindor's corpse. This was thick and dark and alien. The tree bark was black or purple-copper where Menelaus's torchlight shone. A black ivy swarmed the trees and strange fungi meshed threads across their path and billowed spores at the merest touch.

At one point Martoth shrieked and pulled up short. A human thumb lay on the forest floor at her feet, dirty, damp and disembodied. When she realised the thumb was *crawling* slowly, deliberately, towards her, only the dry void in her stomach saved her from being sick once more.

— Calm! said Weakjohn but Martoth backed away anyway.

The thumb crept onward, bending and straightening at the knuckle to push itself blindly thumbnail-first over the rotting leaf litter.

— They're called *Knucklings,* chuckled Menelaus. They're a type of caterpillar.

— …and racing them is a favourite game of the youngsters here, added Weakjohn privately, for those who don't prefer to burn or squash them. I haven't worked out which type our new friend is yet.

— They've been here longer than we have, said Menelaus. It gets freaky in Spring when you get hundreds of them crawling over each other looking for spots to coccoon.

The Knucklings were only the half of it. There were thin red worms that looked like entrails and beetle-sized reptiles that leapt out of the trees and gripped onto their hair. Menelaus swatted them away without noticing. Martoth picked the wriggling things out with her fingers until she remembered she had a hat in her pack.

— We have three camps in the Backshades, said Menelaus, keeping apart so we don't have all our eggs in one basket. There were some survivors in the Midshades too but we can't contact them anymore.

— Ask him *why*! urged Weakjohn.

The *why* was Barnabas's embargo — an absolute veto on mindwork that the survivors probably had to thank for their pitiful lives. No light, no travel, no contact, no probes, no changing, no shifting, no nothing. Certainly no hanging out near the way heads. And so the Vigil, once the universe's foremost expression of mindwoke humanity, of the power and potential of the human mind, had become no better than the scattered tribes of mindblind.

There was a growing swell of dissatisfaction though, amongst Menelaus's group at least, and Martoth sensed that the embargo's time was passing. There would be plenty, she surmised to Weakjohn, who'd count living a poor recompense for helpless and starving.

As they came out from under the trees, daylight returned stained amber by the gathering dusk. Tents were pitched chaotically, close together, filling the entire breadth of the clearing. There had been some new felling of trees in recent weeks and firewood and building timber were stacked in tall piles between the tents. Here and there rudimentary wooden structures poked out above tent roofs. People were lighting fires, sharpening knives, patching textiles, preparing food. Some wore Vigil cassocks but most had one practical outfit at least and had been wearing it continually since the flight from the Abbey. They were ragged and unwashed. Few looked like they'd had a decent night's sleep. Weakjohn had been silent at the way head but, seeing old friends so reduced, she couldn't stifle the cry that only Martoth heard.

Menelaus led them to a large tent on the rim. In front of it was a wooden picnic table and a cluster of collapsible plastic camp chairs. On the chairs the seniors of Barnabas's camp sat looking serious and sullen. Martoth saw them notice her from a way off and saw too that her arrival had given them something to talk about for the first time in a while.

— Be careful, Martoth, said Weakjohn. They may not look it but these people are dangerous. They are all stronger and cleverer than I am. Remember we're here to offer help and don't answer too quickly. Let me prompt you if you can.

Mebbit had slipped away somewhere between the edge of the clearing and this tent. Fair enough. She'd done everything they'd asked of her and they knew she had her own concerns about getting involved with the Vigil.

The old man who was so obviously Barnabas was sitting in a camp chair, gripping his fingers tightly around the plastic arms. He wore his black cassock and his mane of grey hair exploded out from his head both skyward and across his shoulders. His face was creased and old. In his lap rested something like a fly swat. Martoth wondered if it was intended for the leaping reptilians.

Menelaus led Martoth before him and Barnabas pursed his lips into a fat wrinkly frown as he appraised them both.

— Hi, she said. I'm Martoth. I have Weakjohn with me.

She expected him to ask where but he was old and sharp and he knew what was going on.

— Must be a remarkable story, he said, and we will have time for it, but perhaps you could relocate the punchline to the start?

So she told them of the visions: the gallery, the group, the experiments, the spiders, the lecture theatre, Clindor's death or emergence. In telling it she found herself lapsing into it again. As she told of Pierre and his heart pills she found herself in the back room watching him swallow them down with a swig of beer. As she spoke of Wojciech, she felt his presence at her side and a reassuring hand upon her shoulder. As she spoke of Dr Harrison, a strange chill settled upon her and she had the uncomfortable feeling of being watched from the shadows. Stephen drew a great deal of interest from the people in the chairs. They murmured to each other and exchanged meaningful looks.

— Weakjohn, said Barnabas. What do *you* make of this?

— Weakjohn believes it's a connection to an oracle and it is beginning to harm me. Lethe and Candle tried to remove it but they couldn't so she's inside trying to keep me alive.

At this there was uproar amongst Barnabas's committee. Amid shouts and appeals, one or two chairs were upset as some rose to approach Barnabas but he motioned them all away.

— I believe Weakjohn is right, he said. We have seen snippets of these events ourselves, in the oracles on this planet, and in the cosmic background. It might even be one of our own oracles but we cannot engage with them anymore. You are cursed, Martoth. On the one hand you are almost certainly beyond our help. On the other, you are the best source of information we have in trying to pick ourselves out of this mess and we will expect a lot of you. I am sorry.

— *Don't leave it there!* screamed Weakjohn in her head. *Make it clear you are not his. We are not his.*

Martoth understood.

— What you expect, Abbot Barnabas, is fascinating, she said, and paused to let her racing heart settle. Let's be clear: I'm offering to pool our resources but I am no more Vigil than the company I've been keeping. As soon as I saw this place, it was clear to me that you people are not going to fix this. So I won't be scurrying this way and that while your scholars try and make sense of me. You won't be getting in my way.

Barnabas raised his eyebrows but if there was anything else, any anger or amusement, it was hidden deep behind his furrowed brow.

— Weakjohn? he said, expecting some intervention.

None came.

— I'll spend tomorrow with your best people, offered Martoth, and we can try and puzzle out what's happening. Then we will go and see one of these oracles.

...and did Martoth imagine just a little adjustment in Menelaus's posture? At the start he had been a pace off to the side as if exhibiting a curiosity. Now he seemed to be standing right where she had imagined Wojciech before, on her shoulder, ready to step up and fight alongside her.

Martoth tarried as they returned from the oracle, allowing Barnabas and the others to go ahead. Chin gave her an apologetic glance and chased after them.

Along the airless paths between the two largest campsites,

candles were lit at dusk. They bore no names or pictures but Martoth knew what they were. Days earlier they had floated sombrely at head-height. As they proliferated beyond count, Barnabas introduced his embargo and the twinkling lights drifted groundward. Now the candles were anchored in their own wax on rocks, tree stumps and tree boughs. The number continued to grow but not so quickly.

— They're not used to living like this, said Weakjohn.

Martoth remembered the chaotic refugee camps starting up outside Laketown. She had left everyone behind, not just Teresa and Ma Mackelay, and Alban and Teppen, but Timoth and Theremy. It was her choice, perhaps, but what choice was it really? At best she was dying, at worst she was a ticking time bomb, a slow-motion puppetisation. If it weren't for Weakjohn, she would have been lost days ago. She knew that now.

The air was cold and Martoth's shiver had got worse. She trailed further and further behind letting her eyes lose focus in the tangle of the darkening undergrowth.

— Can we get away from them for a bit? Pleaded Martoth pausing at a fork in the way.

— Not far, cautioned Weakjohn, I'm worried about you. I want you to see Psalieri again.

Martoth mind-mumbled her acceptance and set off along a fork in the way, heading into deeper forest. The pain behind her eyes was becoming harder to bear and at times a touch of earache was getting going too.

— Is there anything you can do?

— Not without risk. Remember the thimble.

Martoth knew what she was talking about: *the easiest way is with your hands*, she had told Timoth, *and let us never forget it.*

— It's just a cold, isn't it?

— Only partly. Your mind is adapting, putting some pressure on different parts of you and me.

— I thought something would become clear at the oracle.

But there were many oracles around the Abbey. Chin could list fifty. Even if Martoth's mind *was* inextricably entangled with one of them, what good would it be if they found it? And Weakjohn had begun to fear a deeper root now, a feed direct from the dead Earth, in which case what hope was there?

As she moved away from the main path, a tram flashed by before her eyes and some alien rain splashed across her face. Then then she was back in her own skin again.

She'd been living amongst the remnants of the Vigil for two days. She'd submitted to careful inspection by some of Barnabas's best, describing her visions at length. No-one could trace their source. But more and more she felt she was really living amongst these others, these antique Europeans, and that it was an ethereal Vigil who slid in and out of view like visions. The Swiss group were rarely far from her thoughts. She had seen their early experiments, watch them fuse with spiders, watched them fumble their way into *Happenstance*, seen Clindor's use of fear and pain, Stephen's theoretic genius, Wojciech's granite pragmatism. She knew their names, their personalities, their private falsehoods. Describing their world was as easy and as impossible as describing her own. But it was a slippery reality, the oracle's narrative. There were gaping holes, mysteries that the protagonists were oblivious to. There were reruns and replays, reimaginings, rehearsals of conflicting possibilities. She was frequently left in doubt as to what had actually happened. As it became her reality, her understanding of reality broadened and softened and the two realities blended.

Even now she saw Dr Harrison, standing silent in the trees, pale-faced, his long black hair pulled tightly back beneath his hat, so solid she could have stepped under the trees to touch him. Did he acknowledge her? Bow slightly as she passed? *He* had been a figure that had piqued the interest of the specialists, not with the same focus as Monsieur Clindor, but nearly. And through Stephen, they traced a path to Professor Templeton and his writings, his dialogues and his resonant eponym, "Diocles". This sent them scurrying off in all sorts of directions. But what could they do? The libraries at the Abbey were lost except for the volumes they'd carried with them and Barnabas's embargo forbade all engagement with the oracles. Martoth was their only source. So they scurried back again and she began to call more of the shots.

A stabbing pain behind her eyes caused her to stumble and fall. She howled as a tree root jagged into the hollow of her knee and then reeled as the dizziness came on.

— *Martoth!* cried Weakjohn. Hold tight! Breathe. I'm here. Breathe! In… Out… In…

Martoth felt she was going to be sick and crawled forward on her hands. Loose hair fell around her face. Slowly she tipped sideways, hit the ground. Then the convulsions started.

— …to intervene, dear.

Where was she? Suspended in the night sky? Somewhere high, a pinnacle. She was crouched low, touching earth, but wind buffeted her and tugged at her hair. Weakjohn was *next to* her, outside here head.

Scored through the sky were the claw marks they'd left in Crowbeck but now reduplicated a hundredfold covering every part of the night sky as if a cage of slashed velvet had unfurled around the world. Was this the peak above Crowbeck? What had happened on The Leap?

Yes, this was the Crow. And The Leap. There was no moon. But something in her told her that this was long ago. This wasThe Leap as it was, *unsettled* — untouched by humanity, or by human hands and feet, at least. A darker past. The claw marks had spread backwards in time?

— Is this *Happenstance*? she asked.

— Yes dear, I had to move you.

— I didn't know I could.

— You never know what's inside you. But I've taken some big risks.

Martoth looked out across the landscape. Other fells and crags rose behind her inside the cage of claw marks. She remembered a dream in which she strode across this landscape like a giant in the night. The wind dropped and she began to find it easier to talk.

— What's happening to me?

— You had a kind of seizure, an attempt to puppetise you so I shifted you here. With your perspective here we have a little flexibility about what might happen to you in the concrete.

— What *is* happening to me in the concrete?

— You've been found. They're examining you. What they'll do, I'm not sure. Barnabas's embargo complicates things. I've breached it now but I don't know if others will.

Even here Martoth could feel her other reality interfering. The earth beneath her was solid but, when she turned her head, the fluid air at her neck seemed to congeal into white ceramic, only to melt away again as she turned back. Something gruesome lay somewhere just in front that she could neither see nor touch but she could sense through the finest of changes in sound and air pressure.

She wailed in panic.

— It's coming again! Help me!

Weakjohn held her and stroked her hair.

— I'm here. You're safe here.

It was as if the drowning dream had finally consumed her. Just as in the relic she writhed and fought in the dark water, now she writhed and tumbled amongst these long dead minds, in different times and places. Sometimes she was in Switzerland in the 1930s, sometimes elsewhere with older minds, in other towns with names she barely knew: London, Odessa, Riga…

She couldn't tell who she was any more. She seemed to merge with and travel between the characters in the visions, each moment seeing the world through their different eyes, coloured by their different hungers and revulsions. Sometimes she was Stephen, sometimes Lena, sometimes Pierre. Sometimes they *took over*.

I must stop this. I am Martoth, she told herself.

I am Martoth.

I, *Martoth*, am Martoth.

But she tumbled still further.

I, *Pyotr*, see her suddenly after all this time. Seated, eating. As if by accident but it cannot be. She has seen me. Her lips part for a breath — *in* or *out*? I should go over. No, she's coming.

I, *Martoth*…

I, *Anna*, am hiding things. He is so untarnished. How can he still be so simple and beautiful? I must hide things, I must be as untarnished as he.

— Anna…

Anna he says, not Annochka. Say Annochka, Pyotr.

— Anna, it's been…

— Pyotr…

She doesn't know how to continue. Oh god is she okay? Is she…? She's here alone, she's… independent.

— Pyotr, you never—

— I couldn't, I cannot. I cannot do any of those things anymore.

I see she didn't know. And it seems suddenly like betrayal, like we walked together into a dark cave and I crept away behind her back, leaving her alone in the darkness and she never even knew.

I don't believe him. How could that be? How could you unfurl the fingers of a hand that clutched the deepest secrets of reality. And yet. He looks so unburdened. So at ease. He has been happy. Happy without me. Happy not even knowing.

I can't tell what she's thinking. I don't know what she's doing. Is she hurt? Angry? Is she still... Could this be dangerous? My baby daughter flashes before my eyes. An impulse of mine I think. Anna could not be... *intruding*? No, there is no danger. She is not meddling; who even knows if she still can? But she is *coy*. Is it something she doesn't want me to know, or something she wants me to find out. Oh Anna, are you playing games?

I don't believe his facade. You were never one for modesty, Pyotr, why this false weakness? Is this your *style* now? This affectation. No, Pyotr, you're better than this. But is there a reason, what's the reason, it must be important, what is it Pyotr, what is it?

Be like he is. Be like he is. Be like he is.

No. Rise.

— Pyotr, you could still, if you wanted, you know. I could help. We...

...and I smell my fear for when have I ever dared say *we* since I was six and *we* was something else the weight of the world balances on the pinhead of that *we* and it teeters this way then that tugging my heart with it I have the words in me and I shoot them out like a train from a tunnel...

— ...we could do it together—

His eyes I choke on the words.

I am the useless Pyotr now. Pyotr's morbid flesh caked around a sluggish heart. I've sinned by omission, by laziness, by gravity, I've made this. But I cannot give her what she wants. My daughter flashes into my mind again, and my wife. I must escape. But I must not desert her again.

— No, it's… Anna, I'm better like this.

It stings like I've passed sentence on her. She turns her face from me. There's something heart-wrenching in the rise of her chest and her sallow cheek. I'm sinking into the floor boards. Oh God, let things be not this.

…how dare how dare he how I shouldn't I know I shouldn't I should control myself but I can't and I unveil something the biggest most awful thing…

She turns her face back and it's full of rage. I want to turn away but I can't, I have to watch her rage because it's mine and I did it. I have to watch even though something else is going on, something playing out in the corner of my eye, some fellow rising, stumbling from his table, chair knocked over. Now he's more in my line of sight, he walks with a rag-doll limp, up to us, up to Anna, she's ignoring him, no she's not, she's looking at me like this is some sort of triumph. Oh God, I see it, she's done him like a spider. He's next to us, he holds her, he kisses her, kisses her lips while her eyes are on me with the rage still a red fog between us. She pushes him away, he falls back, lost, confused, twirling about, till he's fixed in the stare of his mortified wife. What have I done?

…I have failed it is all failure.

I must escape.

I must escape.

.

A scene, yes, a vision, yes, a truth possibly, but what to make of it? What did it mean? Martoth knew something had passed in that room more than heartbreak. But even when she *was* people, she wasn't party to thoughts they weren't thinking, or any thoughts that passed too slowly to fit in her fleeting visits. Had someone decided something? Had they each resolved on something? And floating throughout it all, had she not seen the ghost of Dr. Stephen Harrison, sitting over the shoulders of these two no-longer-children, regretting his own mistakes and making his own decisions?

33. The Forest

Timoth, Seronin

Timoth hadn't expected birdsong, but he woke to the richest, most delicate, tapestry of whistles, tweets, chucks, and chirps that he had ever heard. There were tiny shrieks that melted out of airy silence and cracked into swooping calls that seemed to dive and flutter themselves. There were deep, resonating croaks that barked at each other in the treetops. There were melodies intricate and complex, staccato and legato, darting across intervals, trilling on accents. Timoth had woken outdoors on Semele more times than he cared to calculate and knew all the varied sounds of Semele's birdlife, but he had never heard the like of the chorus that greeted him on this ancient world that was supposed to be dead.

Lethe was on his knees weeping openly, gulping down the forest air like he was drowning for the lack of it, all the time saying:

— Never again. I am never leaving again. Never.

Candle went to him while the others got to their feet and looked around.

— It's the right place, said Seronin.

It was — the original Forest, the prototype of the

archetype. Just like the relic but without the symmetries. The trees, the undergrowth, everything matched, but matched in an authentic, organic way as if a life that had been missing flowed afresh in the veins of the leaves and the roots in the ground. Here and there the sun glittered through the canopy. The ground undulated unevenly in shallow hills and hollows.

— There's no oracle here, said Candle.

— No.

— Are we camouflaged? asked Timoth.

— For now, said Seronin.

Timoth could feel history in the air around him. He let his mind explore the flux. There was a density he'd never felt before as if the products of millennia of thought had accumulated on top of each other, a giant palimpsest of thought written on thought written on thought. He could feel and follow the leys. They criss-crossed this landscape and the countryside around them with such intricacy they made New Gobi feel like twice the desert it was. He wondered how Semele would feel to him now, now the eyes of his mind were open and he could look out into the world in ways he never could before.

The ley they'd come in on was left far behind. Lethe had navigated right through into this latticework without even slowing. There was no need for way heads in a world like this one. How powerful the mindwoke must have been before the crises! He felt a surge of blood course through him.

— Careful, said Seronin, reading his expression.

— It's not what I expected, said Timoth. I thought, you know, pollution, corpses, …

— …yet life survives and flourishes, said Lethe. Don't forget we don't actually know how things ended here. Those of us who escaped at the last… we didn't get to look back. There was no exploding fireball in the rear view mirror.

— You taught us they all died! said Seronin. You and your generation.

He must have been feeling some of what Timoth was feeling. Not cheated exactly, but patronised, protected from a complicated truth.

— So they did! You know they did. When I left every city was burning. Every family was starving. Scarcity turned every group into a feud, every nation a civil war. And how many machines were minds? And each mind a potential predator. There were enough causes of death to share around the last few billion of us even if we handed them out one by one. The fossils will distract us for centuries but you know it's irrelevant. You can explain the paradoxes of organisation better than I can, Seronin. Even if it takes a billion individual explanations, the maths will do it every time. You want seas of lava, or no-go plague zones, or robots run amok, or a moon turned to blood. You can have them all but the only truth you need to understand is the implacability of the maths. We crossed the threshold where these things became inevitable.

He tried to explain how it was, what it felt like to live through the end, but the obstacles were formidable. As they had prepared to flee Lethe was already an emergence, freed from his human body but not yet able to fabricate one at will or instance himself in the raw noumena. He and Candle roamed the world, shifting their minds across whatever substrates came available. The dying Earth was not short of them: the physical trappings of hardware computation, silicon and quantum, fixed and mobile; the riot of virtualisation in the country-sized data centres; the cylinxes and other hyperdense media that had begun to proliferate. Eventually they learned to embed themselves naked in the noumenal layer itself, as they would have to for their escape. Lethe spoke quickly, breathlessly, words spilling over one another as a poignant past that had been trailing behind for decades finally seemed to catch up with him. He knew only Candle understood.

— Martoth's visions, said Timoth. They're from a much older time, aren't they? I understand them better.

— That is the point I guess, said Lethe. Somewhere there at the end, we crossed too many lines. And as we came to understand the power of our own minds better, we just accelerated. The act of living became so much an activity of the mind, so divorced from what even now you think of as a normal human life. Every human became an unwitting component of the emergent mind that was our self-annihilation. Seronin, help me out here.

— I just don't get it, said Timoth but he knew he lacked the Vigil education that would have helped him understand. His burgeoning grasp of perspectivals and tetrarchy was intuitive and had become practical and powerful, but the catastrophe of Earth touched on some deep and frightening mathematics that he was years away from.

— You know sometimes I am not so convinced either, said Seronin. Every group a feud? And that just all stopped the second we landed on The Leap, Schiller, Tenistan…? We turned from raving savages back into peaceable migrants?

— Of course we didn't. Lethe was getting agitated, and Candle put a hand on his arm. The Tier Ones are littered with evidence of us getting the Earth out of our system. New Gobi was all about us coughing up the crap we'd been choking on for hundreds of years.

— …and you know what, said Seronin. Now I'm here, I'm not even sure they're all dead.

Lethe and Candle gaped at him. For the first time Timoth looked at Seronin and saw a young man, a man who wasn't even born when every event that was significant to the life he led had happened, and somehow he began to understand how Seronin's rebellion had come about.

* * *

But their hope withered as they began to move through the trees. For all the birdsong there was a chemical smell on the breeze and the blush of the sunlight was wrong for the sun's height in the sky. Lethe and Candle dissolved their physical forms and Seronin and Timoth walked together with only the occasional reassurance of their presence, an interjection or a caution. Timoth had a growing sense of something malevolent hiding just out of view, and his shivers were not all from the touch of the chill air on his skin.

Seronin's new theory explained much, even if Timoth could only follow the headlines. Diocletian had returned. Diocletian was reconfiguring the allpsyche to amplify the influence he had from the deepest oldest oracle out through the web of oracles to the edges of the universe. Diocletian was using the web to watch the world and unleash these terrifying attacks on mind-workers across the universe.

No-one seemed to be asking the obvious question: *Why?*

Perhaps the answer was to be found in Martoth's visions. From Weakjohn's last messages to Seronin, it seemed they'd been quickening. Even when there was no new insight, the older images were hitting faster and harder. They were making her short-tempered. She had been unusually forgetful. She repeated conversations, retraced steps.

Two visions that Weakjohn had related he found all too easy to imagine as he passed beneath the dark pines towering in electrified rigidity and the birches that wept leaves over their black-burst bone-white trunks: Clindor shot and Clindor mutilated.

Martoth had described both. In the first he lay crumpled in a marsh of blood and leaves, still breathing, she thought, though barely. In the second, his corpse was bound upright to a tree, its face slick with blood from its altered scalp. Its arms were suspended by twine in an odd posture that Martoth had tried to demonstrate to Weakjohn. It had meant nothing until she finally connected it with the Creed picture. In the painting Clindor had been sweeping items off the table, making way for something new. The posture of the corpse reproduced the picture too accurately to be chance.

— So what do you make of it? Seronin had asked Lethe.

— Emergency emergence.

— You're telling me he did this to himself? asked Timoth, unbelieving.

— Definitely. Well not the gun shot wounds. He was shot all right, and dying anyway, so he took his chance. He'd have been been considering it for a long time before.

It was the grotesque pantomime of the corpse that finally persuaded Timoth that they hadn't been barking up the wrong tree, that Clindor had been the architect of his old body's desecration. The spectacle was so consistent with what they had learned of Clindor and his obsessions. The human need for some kind of gesture at emergence was something to which Lethe vigorously attested. This bizarre performance would have been Clindor's.

— Hang on — what is it we're following? said Seronin. This doesn't feel right.

They stopped.

— I don't know, said Lethe. There have been other things here too. We could have latched onto anything... massacres, war graves, a plane crash.

The trees thinned a little and a grassy undergrowth sprouted where sunlight made it through. As they picked up their pace, Timoth found himself in a private conversation with Lethe's disembodied voice.

— What actually *is* an oracle?

— A record of things or events — like a book, but it propagates in the allpsyche. It's like a feed of information, but because it's a perspectival construction it's a bit more immersive than that. Oracles are a mental phenomenon — you can tap into them directly from your mind. I used to have hundreds that I was connected to. They're not hard to make. The hard part is weaving in the source material. So its very common to weave in other oracles as sources and we've ended up with a very tangled web out there. The web of oracles is one of the most important structures of the allpsyche but also one of the easiest to forget about. Because we built oracles as we migrated away from Earth, the web grows outward from there.

— I don't think I've felt anything like that.

— You have without realising it. New Gobi City will have been full of them. Before the crises, they used to make little oracles as souvenirs. Bigger ones were created at universities and corporations to disseminate texts and history, or sometimes as cenotaphs, memorials to people who died. Even now on Schiller there is a little entertainment industry churning out oracles. Diocletian's later works showed up as oracles. No-one knows how they started.

— They might have grown out of something else?

Lethe shrugged.

— This recording and publishing capability was never new. We built it on physical substrates too. We had this big amorphous thing called the internet which was once used like that. Sometime before the crises.

— It was destroyed?

— In a way. It was *completed*. By the end it stated every fact and its opposite. It was useless as any kind of medium of information. And it had grown complex. It was a fertile breeding ground for new minds and areas of it touched some deep and dangerous limits. In some ways, oracles are a quite poor version of the internet's publishing capability but they also exist in a much deeper layer of the world. When the

Earth died, so did the internet, more or less, but all the oracles are still there. At least we think so. The closing of the ways got in our way.

— I get it. If the oracles on the Earth feed into the oracles we know about and the mental smog round the Earth has thinned out, the signals have been getting stronger again.

— Exactly. And if anyone could ever count as an architect of this web of oracles, it's surely Diocletian.

— So can you *send things through* oracles?

Lethe pulled a wincing frown.

— If you ask the experts, he replied, one vanished world of billions and one nearly-dead society of thousands are united in agreeing that you can't. But you know Seronin.

Seronin felt it first — the beginning of something, the edge of something. He stopped and turned slightly, facing up a gradient in whatever it was. Timoth sensed it too. They looked at each other.

— Lethe, said Seronin. How do you think you'd expect the site of an emergence to feel? Fury…? Vengeance…?

But Lethe was lost in his own thoughts so they walked on cautiously, eyes and minds on the forest as it began to change around them. The sun held its position but the light it cast shifted to cooler shades and before long Seronin and Timoth began to feel more like they were wading inside a low-roofed sewer.

— We can't get close, said Candle. There's too much interference. We can concresce a little way back and catch up?

— Just wait, said Seronin. This isn't the oracle. We can handle it.

Soon they noticed a pale blue luminescence hanging amongst the trees ahead.

— This is it, whispered Seronin. Don't disturb *anything*.

Seronin had let the camouflage slip but he put an arm out

to keep Timoth behind anyway. They stepped into a shadowy glade.

Against an ancient tree at the centre hung a blue glass sculpture lit inside by a thousand points of flickering flame. Arms stretched out and ruined head bent backwards, it was the image of Clindor in death.

— A spin, murmured Seronin.

— This was no emergence, whispered Timoth.

— No, said Seronin. It was an execution.

As they spoke the eyes on the sculpture opened, its face crumpled and its mouth opened in the shape of a scream. But the thousand flames continued to flicker silently and the blank eyes did not turn towards them. Whatever it was, it was intent on its own suffering.

Wordlessly, Timoth and Seronin backed away then bolted down the path they had taken.

34. The Scream

Martoth, Timoth

Weakjohn had never seen anyone bleed in *Happenstance*. It didn't make sense. There was an ongoing act of construction inside the very essence of *Happenstance*. Why would anyone fashion themselves a self that bled? But then Martoth wasn't doing this all herself. Weakjohn was almost entirely responsible for maintaining Martoth's perspective here. Almost. She'd assumed that the last thrust upwards was Martoth's own, that there was some latent knack or intuition to thank. Now she wasn't sure. What if part of Martoth's construction was Dioclete? An imperative sprung out of the deadly connection? A new terror consumed Weakjohn. What if she'd unwittingly allowed the darkness in? Given the enemy unchecked access to the deepest parts of Martoth's mind?

Martoth was unconscious and bleeding from the nose. She lay on the Crow's peak, her listless squirming punctuated by occasional violent spasms. Weakjohn couldn't trace her wandering perspective. Her attention was on dreams playing in the private theatre constructed out of the fragile mentality back down in *Concreta*.

A bird's call pierced the night, the croak of a crow somewhere high above, and Weakjohn pricked up her ears. It was foreign to their construction. Nothing in Martoth's mind was creating it. It wasn't Weakjohn. Nor was it Vigil, like Chin's futile attempts to insinuate herself. This was an intrusion of an altogether more subtle character and it felt eye-wateringly remote.

She caught her breath and leapt up suddenly, trying to rouse Martoth. Martoth's eyes remained closed. When Weakjohn checked, her eyeballs were rolled up inside her skull and shuddering.

Weakjohn stumbled down off the peak and called out, waving her arms above her head.

— Up here! she yelled.

The crow croaked again and Weakjohn saw it this time, passing overhead like a jet needle through the torn velvet sky. She called again.

And then, thank the flux, *Timoth* came bounding up the slope out of the gloom.

— What's happening? he asked, a sickly pallor on his lips as he knelt over Martoth's fitful form.

There were tears of remorse in Weakjohn's eyes. She could barely force them to meet his as she said:

— I can't save her, Timoth.

— We are on the Earth, Weakjohn! We are on the Earth! We can find this thing. We can break it. And if we break it—

Weakjohn was stunned.

— You located Diocletian? On Earth? Where?

— No! Yes but no! Listen, the *ways are open*, Weakjohn, they're open again. I thought we had more time. I didn't know. We found the Forest… *Poland*, says Lethe.

He had hold of Martoth's hand but he couldn't stay still. He knelt then sat then squatted down and she seemed to become more agitated by his presence. Together they were one ball of abortive misdirected energy and Weakjohn remembered their strange togetherness the first time they'd met.

— Listen, I don't know what the Vigil are saying but *it's not Clindor*. Diocletian's not Clindor. He was destroyed. The visions, Martoth's visions in the Forest... Diocletian is someone else.

— Calm Timoth, show me.

Weakjohn touched his forehead, as much to soothe him as to lean on the symbolism, and he showed her the execution site: The Forest, the chemical smell, the reddening sun.

— We've seen more, said Weakjohn and passed some images in return. The line between memory and speculation was treacherous — she gave him everything they had. The new scenes, the theories, the fragments of the group splintering as war erupted: the climbers adrift in London, Wojciech and the Norwegians creeping across Central Europe, and presumably, somewhere lost to sight, the vulnerable Stephen and his charges, Pyotr and Anna, fleeing South or East.

Timoth had infected Martoth with his restlessness. Her neck tensed and she pointed her vacant gaze this way and that to the invisible corners of the sky.

— Timoth, you're making it worse! cried Weakjohn.

— I don't know what I'm doing, he said. I can't help it.

He let go but she was on a downward spiral now. She began to shake violently and blood bubbled at her nostrils. Timoth stared at her in shock.

— We need Candle. I can't—

Martoth screamed.

The world changed without changing. Something that had always been there became known for what it was. It was this scream, the scream that seemed to come from the failing body of Martoth-in-Happenstance but in truth came from the deepest of wells sunk into the allpsyche. A scream that had always been there but never noticed until Martoth became a living emblem of it. The scream of a child.

Her eyes blinked open.

— *Anochka*! she whispered. Anna. It's Anna. Oh my God. It's Anna.

Chin was banished from the tent but, alert in the darkness outside, she heard every word of the argument and watched their distorted silhouettes playing on the canvas.

Since they lost Sounness, Abbot Barnabas was a different man. Whatever had been between the two men no-one would ever know, but the loss to the Vigil was mirrored in what Barnabas had lost in character. He had presided over the final vanishing of learning from the world and he seemed blunted, deflated, darkened. What he'd lost in zeal he'd also lost in boldness. His deliberations were slower, more meandering. His decisions were hesitant and cautious. The embargo was the last vestige of authority he clung to and he clung to it ferociously.

That was a ferocity that no-one Vigil-trained could withstand. Chin winced for Weakjohn. However hidden she was inside that girl's skull she was taking a blast that all her Vigil history had trained her to quail at. Chin could imagine the shame and the uncertainty. The fury that had descended upon Chin for even minor infractions — it was a place she would never willingly go.

This girl though... Martoth. What was she made of? Some stuff sterner then steel. These seizures looked like puppetisation attempts, any of which should have killed her five times over. Just look at Sounness for flux sake. Vicious he may have been but he was the most powerful noumenist the world had seen barring Diocletian himself. Or Seronin, if you believed the stories… And Sounness was puppetised in one attempt. An imperious colossus in the allpsyche transformed into a stumbling black-eyed moron in the concrete, then slain by a novice like nothing more than a cockroach.

Chin had always trusted Barnabas, idolised him once. But what good was the embargo doing anybody now? They couldn't just sit here camped out in the Backshades waiting to be picked off as the Dioclete sought them out with its marauding tentacles. Or starved as the few who knew how to forage were puppetised or ripped. She imagined a future trying to swallow and keep down the wriggling knucklings and it didn't seem remote at all.

Weakjohn had taken this girl into *Happenstance* and got away with it. Discounting the ire of Barnabas which they were currently enjoying. But saying as much had got Chin banished from the tent.

Well if Martoth could be stern and if Weakjohn could be bold, then so could she.

She took a deep breath, stepped forward and tripped over a guy rope.

— You're not listening! croaked Martoth.

Barnabas was pacing around on a thick rug that lay amongst the meagre furnishings of his tent though with his tall frame and the slope of the roof, his turning circle was pretty tight. He'd stopped raging at them. Weakjohn was a numb silence. Martoth was bored and angry and sick.

— He never has, said a voice from behind her.

Martoth turned to find that Chin had stumbled back in through the doorway. She seemed drunk, reckless. Her hair was dishevelled and there were smudges of dirt on her robes. Barnabas shouted something sharp and incoherent.

— …at least not to more than a handful of people, continued Chin. He listened to Simon, Demeter, Sounness. He listened to Seronin, to Yorgen, ...maybe one or two others. You could do quite well with all those voices in your ear, but four of them are dead and one was exiled a long time ago. I'm not sure Abbot Barnabas has learned to listen to anyone else.

Barnabas's fury was beyond words and he flapped his arms comically, gulping like a fish.

— There were some, twenty years ago, she said, who expected the Vigil to pass from Demeter to *Sounness* you know. It was the danger of that selection that ensured the Vigil passed instead to Barnabas. He was Demeter's contemporary after all, hardly a fresh new face for the future.

Martoth was grateful to have Barnabas's attention elsewhere for a minute.

— What's she doing? she asked in her head.

— I think she's trying to rile him, said Weakjohn.

— It's working.

— She knows how, doesn't she?

Martoth turned her attention outwards again.

— You must know what I know, Abbot Barnabas, continued Chin. You know what things are entrusted to my care. I have an oracle of Demeter's dying thoughts. Of course you know this. What has flummoxed you is your utter inability to comprehend that I, a student of the Vigil, might break this confidence. And that, Father Abbot, is because you have forgotten the very humanity which caused you such sorrow twenty years ago.

The back of Martoth's head touched canvas and she realised she was backing herself into the wall of the tent. But though he still could not speak, Barnabas's fury seemed to be spent. His face was pallid and damp. His brush-like mane of grey hair lay flat against his head, swept with white. And his eyes were red.

— Demeter wept for you, you know, because of the burden you were forced to bear. Wept for the cruel fate that led him to die too soon, though I know how close he came to defying the precepts. He wept because he knew you never wanted it. Because he knew and you knew that Sounness must not have it. Even though you might have wished it. But mostly because he knew that the man who could have been, should have been, the future of the Vigil was still a vulnerable nine year old and that you loved him as a father.

Barnabas groaned. He shut his eyes and lost himself in a distant reflection.

— I found him, he moaned. I found him. I spoke to his mother. It was me. Five years old. I found him. He might as easily have been mine.

His despair was in the open and his rage had burned out.

— This is all done with, he said. Break every confidence you like, Chin, it changes nothing.

— Done with? Chin was amazed. Wake up Abbot! Everything's flipped on its head! Suddenly it's Seronin on the Earth trying to face Diocletian, while we're pissing about racing knucklings in the Backshades.

— Seronin's on the Earth?

Martoth gave out a wail of exasperation and almost leapt on the Abbot. Barnabas flinched and looked about as if surprised to find himself in the tent at all.

— Abbot Barnabas, said Martoth, please *listen*. My friend is there with him and if it's the hotpot of batshit everyone says it is we can kiss goodbye to all of them unless we start pulling our fingers out. Between you and Chin and me and Weakjohn we have all the pieces of this puzzle, can we *please* just put them together?

— Clindor started hurting people, said Martoth. Once he had them trapped. Finally he murdered Stephen, sadistically, in front of all of them, even little Anna.

Barnabas and Chin waited, enduring this revelation

without any of the excitement that had reanimated Martoth.

— I saw everything! she said. They were all fixed there, stuck to the benches. He was torturing *them* as well as Stephen. I saw their eyes. None of them moved. No-one left, *except Anna.*

— What happened to her? asked Barnabas. You actually saw her leave?

— No. I didn't. Because I was seeing it all through *her* eyes! It's the only time in any of the visions I've been so locked in someone's head. I know she left because I *was* her as she walked out. If the oracle is Diocletian's, I'm telling you Diocletian is Anna. Not Clindor, not Templeton, not Stephen, not Pyotr. *Anna.*

In the ensuing silence the sounds of night in the Backshades grew. Howls of monkey-things, the eerie rattles and croaks of amphibians. The murmur of the camp and the crackle of campfires.

— If you're right, said Barnabas, perhaps we should be relieved that the idol we've cherished was not the monster we feared.

— Such a comfort, observed Weakjohn.

— Martoth, Oracles aren't as simple as you suppose, said Barnabas. Your point of view doesn't prove this was Anna's memory. Nor does the integration of Anna's memories imply Anna built the oracle. And there *was* another missing from the group was there not? What of him?

— Pyotr? Martoth hesitated. I don't know.

Abbot Barnabas cursed under his breath.

— This information is no good to us here, he grumbled. I need to speak to Seronin.

— Easier said than done, said Weakjohn in Martoth's head. Timoth found you before, maybe he can again. Maybe Barnabas can do better, assuming the embargo is dead. But they already know about Anna, remember.

— What are we going to tell him? asked Martoth aloud. Maybe *I* can get a message through.

Barnabas gave her a sour look but Chin leapt in:

— The *chrysalis*…

His eyes widened but after a moment he nodded.

— Yes, he said, yes… the chrysalis.

— We're not talking about the knucklings again are we? said Martoth.

Barnabas sighed.

— Chin is reminding me about some arcane snippets from Diocletian's earlier works that might be relevant for the first time ever. The chrysalis is a theoretical structure invented by Diocletian to be a fortification in the allpsyche. You saw how our oracles were encased in rock… It looks formidable but that's just in *Concreta*. To an unembargoed adept that only stops you stumbling in by accident. To protect something across all the strata you could use a chrysalis. It is anchored in the *Apocryph* and extends through *Sanctum*, *Happenstance* and *Concreta* meaning there is no way in at all.

— You've seen one of these things?

Chin laughed.

— We thought it theoretical only. Only Diocletian has ever shifted to the *Apocryph*. We never thought that he… she… might have built a chrysalis.

— But that's not all, said Barnabas. I've got people here who know everything Diocletian published, text, broadcast, oracle. There might be hundreds of these things… who knows what Seronin might need?

He frowned and then said softly, but no longer secretly:

— He needs to come home.

35. Double Vision

Timoth, Seronin

Seronin's reaction horrified Timoth. His eyes went hard and he jutted a twitching chin forward, clutching Timoth's arms so tightly they hurt.

— Anna? *The child?*

They were still in the forest, but yearning to be free of it. Lethe and Candle were scouting. They'd found ruins of buildings, settlements, motorways nearby but they were overgrown, rife with decay and sunk in a mental cacophony that made New Gobi City look placid. Now they were pushing further, supposedly looking for safe routes to the coast but Timoth had caught a look in Lethe's eyes and knew he'd been snared by some grander ambition. Timoth couldn't tell how long he and Seronin would be waiting here.

Timoth nodded, watching his friend intently. He had more to tell but he didn't want to teach anyone to hear what he could now hear.

— I can show you, he said, but...

Even as perturbed as this, Seronin could arch an eyebrow at Timoth's reluctance.

— Okay, muttered Timoth. There is a scream. You can hear

it all the time. I think it's always been there. And when you start hearing it you realise you've always been hearing it and just thinking it's what the world sounds like. But then you can't stop hearing it. It's horrible.

— That's *Anna?* murmured Seronin.

They'd reached some ground high enough to lift them a little above the treetops and found their faces were drawn up to the rusty sunlight.

— I've been stupid, sighed Seronin.

— What difference does it make? said Timoth.

…but Seronin wasn't listening. He seemed listless. Moments before he'd been a grateful escapee from the gloom below. Now he stood like a sacrificial offering, an unresisting victim of the sun's rays.

Suddenly he bellowed in fury and cast his arms forward. A giant noumenal rip tore from his fingertips, fifty yards into the forest, slicing through trees and leaves.

— Jesus! shouted Timoth, leaping back. What the actual real-life fuck?

…but his words were lost in the spinroar, the creaking and cracking of the falling trees and the screeches of the startled birdlife. A smell of grass and leaves, of sawn wood and hot earth, rose from the wounded forest.

Gradually, Seronin's own howl began to drown out the turmoil below.

Timoth kept clear, watching the wreckage settle, and waiting for Seronin's anger to subside.

Once he'd calmed down, Seronin set about fixing the damage, without a word or even the barest acknowledgement of Timoth's presence. He spent an hour patiently salving the chaos and massaging reality back into shape before sitting on the ground with his head between his knees to accept the backsnap.

* * *

— You think that might have got us noticed?

Lethe shook his head:

— Not on this planet.

Their second evening on the mother planet beckoned and Seronin was still sitting with his head hanging and saliva glistening on his lips. Candle was off scouting.

— What have you found? asked Timoth.

— Horrors. There's no better word than *haunted*. There are places the fabric is so densely overlapped that Candle and I can't pass through. We've found a route to the coast that avoids the worst. A week's hike if we walked it but we can tic it once he's back up.

What was the point? wondered Timoth. If confrontation was inevitable, why skulk in the shadows? But the target was the oracle. If they *could* reach it without a confrontation, all the better.

Dusk was falling and tiny pipistrelles were flitting about in the higher branches. Other small creatures were learning to trust the broken trees again, and moths were darting around the small fire that Timoth had lit.

— What is it we have to face? he asked Lethe, while Seronin languished in silence.

— Destroying an oracle wouldn't be hard, said Lethe, if it was unprotected. But what are the chances of that? And if Diocletian is at the root, in whatever form…

— Would he, she… would she be like you and Candle? Invisible? Emerged?

— Of course. Her original body would be two centuries old. Maybe she has a use for a body occasionally but I doubt it. And what state is her mind in? Fragments have been shearing off her for centuries, we have traces of her mind everywhere we look. The Vigil taught that she dispersed, that she dissolved in the breeze. Spread to every corner of the universe. Touched every human mind. Became a part of humanity. Is there even a single perspective that we can fight?

— How do we fight the breeze?

— That's what we were banging our heads against. But now Seronin's come round to the Vigil's idea a single coherent Diocletian is behind everything.

— So she never dispersed at all? Where's she been?

The fire spat sparks into the falling darkness. Lethe frowned, brought back to a problem he'd forgotten.

— The evidence... to most people, it's ancient history but it was only in Sheras's time. I remember garbled publications, fragmented transmissions... Analysts concluded it was a dispersal but it could at a stretch have been a fission. A breaking along cracks into a small number of minds. And a small number of minds could live on in their own lives, or be stored, replicated, through the years, waiting for the day...

— ...the day they fused again, finished Timoth. It's all the same though isn't it. It doesn't help us.

— It doesn't help us, agreed Lethe, but it's more significant than you think. We've noticed a few fusions cropping up recently, haven't we? As if somebody out there has been making fusions intentionally. Two have come to our notice because they were inserted as children into the Vigil, both connected with one name in particular...

— *Meef Parton!* cried Timoth, leaping up. Martoth's *dad* resurrected Diocletian?

Lethe shrugged.

— It's all speculation, he said. One day she'll discover whatever was going on. Till then, we do our best to make sure it's all academic... In the meantime, let's just say, if Diocletian only fissioned, it's far from inconceivable that *somebody brought her back.*

Seronin could never explain his world. He'd been a teenage virtuoso in a pit-orchestra of jobbing musicians, blessed with a insight they could never share: a vision that passed through the music to its genesis and the possibilities of its evolution and to the means and direction of its own destruction. That destruction was a truth he'd lived with every day of his life, an inevitable entropic deterioration into blank, white noise.

Seronin knew his place in the tapestry of humanity more clearly than any of them. The Vigil's great achievements were mastery of perspective and identity amidst the fluid boundaries of mind. But he knew that future ages would steamroller these fragile redoubts in an inexorable blending of all things. The ultimate destiny of humanity was *a single thought*.

That future, that thought, was ever-present in his waking and sleeping, weak and remote, a golden shine dawning on the far horizon. He had not named it yet and the Vigil had scarcely imagined it. But it was there and it was the future of man- and womankind.

And when all is one what will be left to fight for? What point in fighting at all? Might as well... Jam. Another. Spine.

He'd thought he had seen a way clear of the fog. A right and a wrong. An evil, so beguilingly dressed up for him by the Vigil: Diocletian resurrected, pulling strings. But it was a sham he should have seen from the start. This wasn't evil. It was hurt. It was suffering so monstrous, who could not forgive the reflex?

And now he was expected to fix this?

Could they not see?

Fixing it was *exactly* what Diocletian was doing. Had been doing for centuries. This was cleansing. This was correcting a wrong turn. And in the grand story of humanity was the fix so wrong? Who's to say whether any one oneness is better than any other oneness?

The others weren't looking. Seronin fumbled in his pack, searching out the twenty orange cartridges he knew were in there somewhere.

When he closed his eyes, Timoth saw his mother. Sometimes even his father, further off. He saw the deep paddy in the wind with the floats bouncing in the choppy water and his barrows at the water's edge. He saw the mud and the rocks of his daily path. He saw the gloves he popped on the ends of tree branches. He saw the tree in the taproom yard where Alban had broken his leg all those years ago, where Mulkah kept his vicious bantams, and where the small community sent its departed on their next journey. He saw Alban, Teppen, Mulkah. He saw the book crates. He saw dancing. He saw the aunties getting drunk on saki. He saw the canvas sheets he rigged against the rain flies and heard the din as they gathered around him. He heard the raucous wail of the clarino and the blunt fart of the weedhorn. He saw the line of Martoth's collar bone, the sweep of her hip and he smelled the warmth of her.

What did Seronin see?

A home before the Abbey? Maybe not. A mother? Who knew?

It was easy to get embroiled in Seronin's drunken silliness, but it was very difficult to see where it all came from. Seronin had joined young. His childhood friends would have been novices like him. Even if it had all ended in a giant bust up, there must have been happy times at the Abbey? For all her cynicism, Weakjohn was in love with the place. It had inspired Theremy.

— Lethe?

— Yes?

— Have we lost him?

Lethe knelt down to feel Seronin's forehead and take his pulse.

— For now.

— He's giving up.

— I doubt it's that simple.

But Timoth knew it was. The things Timoth saw when he closed his eyes, the people he cared about — he knew they were his riches. They were his resources, the fuel that propelled him through the world. Take them away and he'd be as flimsy and inert as a jellyfish on the shore, without enough internal structure to keep its shape, let alone the strength to move. Seronin was surviving without these resources. He was running on empty.

Lethe? He had Candle. She had Lethe. They'd been there for Seronin forever. They loved him but maybe that wasn't enough anymore. They were the background he lived against. They were no longer sustaining him.

Seronin had given up.

— Did he have a family? asked Timoth.

— A mother once. He never saw her after he joined the Vigil.

— He's given up. He gave up ages ago. Why is he even here?

Timoth didn't pretend to understand what Seronin could do. Lethe and Candle had their specialisms. It was always Lethe who navigated the leys, always Candle who went inside minds. Both deferred to Seronin on any of these things, even when he could barely see straight. Weakjohn regarded him as a mischievous demigod, Theremy as a wayward vigilante. But barring that rip through the forest and the pyrotechnics in Crowbeck, Timoth's best evidence of Seronin's genius was the deference of his friends.

If Seronin was to be their salvation, Timoth was beginning to understand he would have to be driven forward every step of the way.

— What are we expecting of him? he asked in a hushed voice.

— Wonders, as ever.

Candle concresced behind them.

— Can *you* talk to him, Timoth?

— Me?

...but Timoth already knew, deep down, that he was the one who would drive Seronin on. Lethe and Candle were Seronin's comfort blanket and his conscience. They would not take him anywhere he wasn't already going.

Timoth wasn't proficient yet talking in people's heads. He'd had a link going with Candle as they'd toiled through the streets and alleys of the city, keeping together in mind while they lost sight of each other in *Concreta*. But to establish something with Seronin seemed harder, and in this state too.

He knelt down next to Seronin and began to open his mind.

He felt first what he could only call the "surface" of Seronin's mind. Like Candle's, and his own he supposed, it was a deeply-knotted Moebius in many imaginary dimensions. To find the place where a thought must be had, he knew he had to see it in a different way, to find the metaphor that would bring sense to the mess, that would allow his own mind to map on to the surface. Metaphor and meaning — Candle had taught him that these were the real triumphs of our evolution, the leverage that frees all thought from the gravity of the noumena.

He watched Seronin's mind transform into a world in his view. He saw the glowing cities and highways of thought, the conurbations and nexuses where the perspectival rotated through the physical, where the poverty of Seronin's brain met the glory of his mind. He swept across the world and beneath him structures of thought elaborated themselves along the dimensions Timoth had built for them.

A thing caught his view.

A thing.

— *Ha!*

He saw the thing and he knew it was what he wanted. It was there precisely for this. Seronin had put it there. He'd even signposted the damn thing.

In he flew, preparing to switch metaphors again, to fuse and have the thoughts he needed. He began to wonder just what he was actually going to say once this excruciating mechanism was perfected.

But something tripped him. It was as if his two eyes had veered off in different directions. Everything doubled, overlapped on itself. While one surface drifted left another jerked upwards. A queasiness enveloped him and he felt his stomach spasming. He rolled away onto the soil of the forest floor.

— I… don't know what I did wrong.

He felt Candle's mind on his, checking, applying a little gentle pressure.

— It's like… It was like there were suddenly two of him. And I was being pulled apart by them.

Lethe swore, and dropped down beside them, shouldering Timoth aside. Candle moved over to the other side of Seronin's prone form. Timoth was aware of urgent manoeuvrings in the flux. Something he'd said had spooked them.

There was a sharp intake of breath from Candle and Lethe yelled in anger:

— *How did we not see it?*

Candle looked at him silently. Lethe screamed again.

— *How the…?*

He jumped up and took a few paces into the forest.

— Do you think he knows? asked Candle.

— Which one? asked Lethe.

— Our one.

— Which one's our one?
— One of them's our one.

36. Whales and Minds

Timoth, Seronin

The edge of the sea was like the afterblur of a sweeping spotlight, lingering too long where it had been, leaving a ghost of itself behind. A froth, stained and thick as beerfoam, trailed it back to the depths. Timoth stepped onto the wet sand and then skipped back again as the surf rushed back at him. Despite the vile smell in the air it was good to get out from under the trees.

From here he felt he could read the true story of this planet, in the rainbow layers of the sunset, in the viscous sucking of the sea, and the shrill calls of the terns that swooped out of the twilight. Looking across the sea, he saw a cluster of tiny twinkles where fountains of water were dancing beneath the dying sunlight. Something was alive out there. Whales maybe.

Seronin was coming round further up the beach.

Candle was calling.

As he crossed banks of pebbles and seajunk and kicked the dried seaweed off his feet, he saw Seronin sit up and sink his face in his hands, but he looked tired rather than upset.

— Timoth, he said weakly, I hear I have you to thank for

this discovery.

— I don't know what it means.

Seronin stretched his legs out in front of him and poked his toes into a heap of pebbles.

— I knew something was up. Ever since the first rip. I've been trying to put my finger on it. But now you've shown me the way, I've made a few more discoveries of my own.

— It's bad?

Lethe concresced and immediately wandered off, shuffling around in the plastic rubble of the beach, searching for firewood. He gave up quickly and hopped up onto one of the uprights in a wooden groyne that ran off into the sea, and began to climb carefully along, out over the lapping water.

— Maybe, said Seronin. I am experiencing something called *overlap*. When you tried to look at my mind in the flux you found there are actually *two* human minds intersecting on this body.

— Who's the other one?

— Me.

— Both of you are Seronin?

— I am.

— Both of you can speak?

— Both of us just did.

— But which of you said that?

— I did.

As ever, Seronin's deadly serious looked like anyone else's larking about. Timoth was concerned enough for his friend to bite back his frustration. Instead he left a silence inviting enough for Seronin to fill.

— This may not be that unusual. For there to be two perspectives, two subjects of experience located in the same place, feeling the same things, thinking the same things, doing the same things... well you would never even know, short of the type of fluxual aerobatics that you pulled out of the bag. It might be quite common. It's not a tragedy.

Lethe had reached an upright distant enough that his feet disappeared under the bigger waves. As he stood, staring into the sunset, suddenly Candle was with him, balanced impossibly on the groyne behind, slipping her arms around him. Timoth had an impression of extraordinary stillness despite the rushing waves and the calling birds.

Seronin was watching them too.

— But…?

— Well, it seems like my two perspectives are quite different. They have been using my brain quite differently, realising memories differently, emphasising different aspects of the normal psychological processes, and ultimately they've been growing further and further apart. That *is* normally thought to be bad. If we were to use different parts of me to disagree… well, it's not clear how that ends up. Maybe one mind sane and one unhinged. Maybe one mind sane and one mind dead. Or maybe it goes badly for both. You can see how it could be difficult and dangerous for one mind to say something to you that the other is not also saying. Not impossible of course: one mind might not always know quite why it's saying something. Some of that is normal. Lots of that is madness.

— You can see it yourself now?

— Actually one self saw it quite some time ago. Both selves can now see it. We're getting along pretty well by the way.

— I'm happy for you.

— Well, back to where I said: difficult if one mind says something the other doesn't… Seems one of my minds has been taking a bit of a battering from the other in that regard.

— So one of them *is* the real you! The one that's always been in control?

— Not that simple.

Timoth puffed out his cheeks in irritation.

— Listen Timoth. You found Martoth and Weakjohn before. Could you do it again? I need to talk to Barnabas. One of me is a very scared ten-year old boy.

Timoth gazed out to the dancing jets of water catching the sunlight on the horizon and looked inward to his own mental resources.

They met in *Happenstance* on the Crow's Peak, over Martoth's prone body.

She and Weakjohn had fought off another puppetisation but the grey cast of her skin hinted at the spreading change inside.

This time Candle was with them.

Seronin inspected the construct: an elaboration of the claw-ripped sky on the Leap, a proto-landscape inspired by the Crow. It was shaped by Timoth and Martoth and it implied unsuspected capabilities in each. But they had guests: Lethe, Candle, Seronin, Weakjohn, Barnabas, an archivist called Chin.

Seronin was tense to the point of cramp. He didn't bother trying to control it.

Candle had not shown herself in front of Vigil minds for twenty years and Chin was visibly discomfited by her presence. Barnabas was pretending she wasn't there. That's what passed for class in his book. Lethe fixed a poisonous stare on the elderly Abbot and remained watchful and suspicious. They were taking a big gamble. What if Sounness showed up?

Candle conferred briefly with Weakjohn, keeping one eye on the Abbot. Then she crouched down to tend to Martoth.

As Barnabas approached Seronin allowed his contempt to show but couldn't mask the apprehension he always felt when Barnabas was around. If their last conversation had veered off course, this one was lost from the start. It was not a moment he could have rehearsed. How could he even start? "What have you done to me?" was impossible. Too much water had passed under this bridge — he would never expose that much vulnerability to this man. "Just who the fuck do you think you are?" *might* be useable.

But Barnabas seemed frail. His flesh was drawn tight against the bone and he seemed oddly angular as he hobbled forth.

— What's happened? asked Seronin, his voice colourless and even.

And Barnabas broke down.

Actually broke down.

He was so weak, even his groan was a theft of precious air from his lungs. Even the air around him withdrew its support. He fell awkwardly on the boulders of the Crow.

Chin came to his side to sit him gently against a supporting rock where he recovered slightly. His eyes opened and gazed through them all into the scarred sky.

Seronin saw the amazement in Lethe's eyes, eyebrows arching like rampant knucklings. Something moved deep inside Seronin and some part of him remembered a distant fondness that he had forgotten for most of his adult life. "Just who the fuck...?" was not useable after all. Seronin stood with his mouth wide and lips moving soundlessly. Why was it always a surprise when talking became the hardest thing in the world?

Then he realised a solution lay within his grasp: freewheel — allow his *other self* to open the conversation...

Child-Seronin cradled Barnabas's head in his lap.

— It was a difficult time, Barnabas sniffed. Abbot Demeter died. Diocletian was gone. Simon's reforms had survived but taken on a life of their own. There had been a hardening of opinion in the Abbey, people were beginning to see the value of cruelty again. There was a reassertion of some more regressive theory. And the succession was going to take the Vigil in that direction.

— You *did* take the Vigil in that direction, accused Lethe through gritted teeth.

— I was balance. I've always been the balance.

— You mean Sounness? said Seronin.

— Sounness is dead, said Chin quietly. Puppetised and slain.

Candle looked up sharply. Lethe made a humph of satisfaction.

— This was for my *protection*? asked Seronin. Why? Why me?

— You were a threat, said Lethe. To somebody.

— Oh come off it, Lethe, said Weakjohn. This is not some medieval intrigue. And he was, what, ten?

— I was afraid, coughed Barnabas, they'd see what I had seen... way back when I met you and your mother... on a world we hadn't even charted.

— You were afraid of the future, suggested Candle, afraid for the child you loved, so you preserved him? You took a *backup*?

— *No!* wheezed Barnabas, his irritation showering specks of spittle onto Seronin's arms. No! Don't you see? It's unfinished. I was trying to cure you.

Seronin nodded eagerly as if everything was suddenly fitting together.

— Of *course*... I was *already* a monster.

— Never in my eyes, Seronin.

— But if the others found out...

Pain creased Barnabas's face but he did not reply.

— It's okay, I understand now, said Seronin.

Chin helped Barnabas across to sit back up against a rock and recover himself.

— Well I still don't understand, said Lethe. The child is some sort of interrupted rebuild?

Seronin nodded.

— Cure what? asked Candle, disturbed.

Lethe threw his arms up in despair. He'd known Seronin as long as Barnabas, been closer to him than anyone, and never once seen what Barnabas had known from the start. Timoth was astonished by what happened next. Lethe touched Seronin's chin and tenderly raised his face so that their eyes met.

— *Seryo*, he said quietly. *Seryo*, are you there? *Seryo*, have they hurt you again?

…and a tidal wave of realisation swept over Timoth. How much more was there to this ancient friendship that hid behind the matey exterior? Barnabas was portraying himself as a father but what of this couple who'd known and cared for the orphaned, bullied Seronin from infanthood? What were they? Even if Lethe had never changed a nappy, Timoth was under no illusions that he'd done analogues of it, day after day, year on year. If there *was* a child Seronin still, it was a child Lethe knew as well as Seronin himself.

Seronin simply waved him away.

— Think! he whispered. I'm a natural birth. What could be so shocking to the Vigil?

Candle looked up sharply from where she was tending to Martoth.

— *Reincarnation*, she said.

— Uh? said Timoth.

— It doesn't exist, said Lethe, but without conviction.

— Familial? Is it your mother? asked Candle eagerly, fascinated. Your grandmother?

— Uh! Hold up now, insisted Timoth. His mother was alive when…

Seronin shook his head:

— I don't think so, I think I go back further than that, I don't know how many times I've propagated forward and I can't talk to that part of me. Yet. But I think it's ancestral. It's possible I'm as old as Diocletian.

— Can I look? asked Candle. The difference between what he excised… it could reveal who you are.

He shook his head.

— It's too late for that. Already we're not nearly as separate as we were. There's a brave boy in here who's finally given up on his childhood and he's begun to make some changes.

Barnabas was fading again, struggling with the effort of *Happenstance*. Chin was trying to coax him to downshift but he swatted at her in irritation. Candle looked over to the Abbot and raised her eyebrows at Lethe. He shook his head fiercely. Let him suffer.

Martoth was coming round, however. Chin stepped uncertainly into the ring that had developed around her.

— Martoth thinks the oracle would be at the gallery, she said. It's where everything started.

— Can you show us where it is? asked Lethe.

— I think so, she said, the general area at least.

She produced a map. In *Happenstance* it was hand-drawn on a folded piece of parchment but what libraries of knowledge it might encompass in *Concreta*, Timoth couldn't say.

— You know of "Switzerland"? she asked Lethe.

He nodded as if to say "of course" and gestured for her to continue.

— We think the gallery was tucked against the mountainside at the foot of a glacier, or where a glacier would have been in the 1930s. We don't have any surviving records that mention it but Martoth described a car journey, some rivers. It must be about here, near Grindelwald-Gletscherdorf, by the lower glacier.

Seronin took a deep breath:

— This is it then.

— What are you thinking of? asked Chin nervously. Barnabas doesn't want you going inside.

Timoth waited for a cynical snort from Lethe but it didn't come. They were all silent.

— He thinks it's suicide.

— It's not suicide, said Seronin.

And Timoth had an insight that this was what it always came down to with these two. It can't be done. You don't know what can be done. You can't do it. I've done it. You're deluded. You're blinkered. These days Seronin got his way. He had his own sort of Vigil. And Barnabas was wilting away.

Chin wasn't wilting though.

— You won't get the oracle without facing her.

Seronin and Lethe looked at each other. Till now Chin had acted the underling, voicing other people's thoughts. This was the first time she'd sought or gained their full attention.

— I can be pretty sneaky, said Seronin defensively.

— And the oracle will be protected. What do you expect to find?

Timoth suddenly understood how valuable Chin could be. That hand drawn map was more than it seemed, a token in *Happenstance* of much more knowledge and learning that passed between them in *Concreta*. Seronin became very serious.

— You suspect something?

— A chrysalis.

Seronin frowned as if confused and rubbed his temples as if trying to dredge up a distant memory. Finally a blissful grin spread across his face as some private realisation dawned.

— Chin, you've given me a ray of hope. What else?

This threw Chin into some consternation.

— What *else*?

— Sure. You know all the obscure stuff better than we do. What other clues has she left us?

— There are two tracts on oracle construction that have this barrage of weird complications that we've never really assumed to be significant.

— I remember. Do you have them with you?

She didn't but she passed on what she remembered which seemed enough to revive some distant memories in Seronin.

— And I guess, she said, you've considered using spearspins?

— Sp—?

— But just in case you are I can probably help…

— Wh—?

…and what she passed to Seronin almost toppled him out of *Happenstance*. Timoth saw him stumble and Lethe step in with some support.

— Seronin! It was Martoth's voice, hoarse and crackling. Seronin, take Timoth with you.

— I don't know if—

— You need him. I need him *at the oracle*, she said. Please.

She was agitated again, hands in the dirt, trying to push herself up off the ground.

— Okay, Martoth. I'll get him there.

A shout went up. It was Weakjohn, waving urgently.

— The *camp*! she cried. Quick!

— Lethe! said Candle urgently.

Something in the timbre of her voice conveyed an immeasurable weight:

— Lethe, I'm going with her.

— Can you even—?

…but they were already gone.

* * *

Lethe had clambered out along the wooden groyne again. The haze had cleared and the night sky was strewn with stars, satellites and space debris, some fixed firm to night's canopy like the vast sweep of the Milky Way, others tracing threads between them, wheeling ceaselessly through their unforeseen afterlife.

Timoth tiptoed along the wooden structure behind him but stopped a few yards distant.

— I wish she was still here, said Lethe, to see this.

— There'll be time now, said Timoth, after…

— We used to climb on these things. Somewhere in Scotland where the crises still felt remote. We were beginning to talk about my emergence. I used to stand there out over the waves and try to feel how it would work. Daring myself to take risks that all seem so small now. It's a big thing you know, leaving your body. It took me years and I couldn't have done it without her. But compared with leaving *Earth*…

Timoth knew without seeing that there were tears in his eyes.

— It can be healed you know, said Lethe. Slowly. It will take generations.

— Could you find the things you left behind? asked Timoth. The things you miss. If we… win…?

— Some of them maybe. Never all. But it's enough, you know. Enough to have made it back after all this time. Candle will know that, if…

Seronin and Lethe had been friends from the start. This feeling they were all sharing now, Timoth knew it was a feeling they'd shared many times, if never so intense. He was a new factor and he still wasn't sure how he was going to fit. Timoth didn't know whether he'd graduated to the big boys' league or whether he was still just a battery pack.

The thing that set him alight was Martoth's insistence that Seronin bring him to the oracle. She needed him. She wanted him. It could hardly be for his capabilities. She needed *him*. And she needed him at the source of whatever was pumping right into her very soul.

— Okay! This is where we start from, said Seronin, somewhere behind them.

They climbed off the groyne and Seronin showed them the spearspin patterns that Chin had distilled from the Dioclete background. He showed them the map. He showed them his mind. He showed them how he needed them to expand, enhance, where he would trust them to hold him up, rebuild, recycle the moving parts of his perspectives, and to take his backsnap.

— We're going to use a rope, said Seronin. A connection strong enough that Timoth can trace it to the oracle but slender enough it might go unnoticed. I'll lead the rope. Timoth, you'll be at the other end.

— Me in the middle? mused Lethe.

Seronin shook his head.

— Lethe, buddy. You *are* the rope.

Lethe closed his eyes and dropped his head and Timoth began to unpack the metaphor to understand what Seronin was asking of Lethe. Whenever they travelled the leys they risked dispersal each step of the way. It was a terrifying and painful experience. Now Lethe was to exist in some smeared half-state, performing his feats of navigation *continuously*, stretched across half the planet, holding onto Seronin on one end and Timoth on the other. It was surely a peril too extreme to demand of anybody, except that Seronin would be facing worse, and these two went back so far who was to say what either could ask of the other.

— And me? asked Timoth, starting to twig that his own role was every bit as deadly as the others.

— When the time is right, you're going to *enter* the oracle.

— Seronin! chided Lethe. You can't-!

— It *can* be done. And Timoth can do it.

Timoth did not have the first idea how to do it, or even what it meant to do it, but after the shifting currents of *Sanctum* and the flight through the dead city, he'd begun to trust his instincts. But Lethe's words about leaving his body haunted him. How different from Lethe's years-long process of emergence was this insanity that Seronin asked of him?

— … and a *chrysalis*? asked Timoth. He was sure this had baffled Lethe too and it sounded important.

— A chrysalis, if we find one, is evidence that even now, Diocletian is as hamstrung by the orthodoxy that bears her name as the Vigil. And if that really *is* true, it might be our one precious advantage.

He showed them a picture.

— She's missed *Brainslang*! said Lethe.

— She's missed *Brainslang*.

37. The Eiger Oracle

Martoth, Timoth, Seronin

The land was cold and dark as Seronin's mind was born in the sky above. Gouged by glaciers then abandoned to rot beneath ice-water pools, it turned an evil face to the murky sky. Not a soul had ventured here since the last desertions. A legendary landscape of teeth and maws, lost since the closing of the ways, it had acquired a dangerous mantle of bad weather. More, too, than the spins that settle naturally in dereliction. Evil spirits had gathered here.

Seronin dropped down into the mountainscape, drifting through its arteries and watercourses, shielded from the pressure by the constant toil of his friends: Timoth, crouched on a dark distant shore and Lethe, smeared across the thousand miles of haunted growback that separated them. Pale-frothed rivers rushed relentlessly along, breaking the banks that humans had once established and tended. The sprawling trees were corrupted offspring of their ancestors, some grown gigantic, others stunted and ingrown.

He lingered on a jutting rock island, letting old limb-knowledge settle into his freshly concresced flesh like feeling his way to the end of a shirt sleeve or a sleeping bag. Spray plastered his skin, wind tugged at his hair and the wet rock jabbed into his buttocks. This was the landscape of the drowning relic, he realised. Somewhere hereabouts was the chimney pool, the terrible cleft of that primordial memory. His own relivings of that evil plunge flooded over him and his heart quailed.

Tentatively, he pushed himself upright, reaching his arms out to keep his balance. Then he turned to face upstream.

He spoke into the deafening roar of the river: *I have come.*

Before going on he flexed the muscles of his mind. He shifted up to *Happenstance* and down to *Brainslang* and back again, fused and defused with the matter and life around him. Fish, trees, insects, lizards, the very churn of the river, dense and cylinxual. Then he leapt up and lofted his physical body into the sky to search the landscape again.

He had climbed thirty feet when the buffeting of the wind stopped the breath in his throat and he had to make changes to his own body to survive and take his search further. He took every cell into the stretch of his mind and thought into being an alteration that allowed them to survive in deathlike suspension, he expanded pores into spiracles, capillaries to sponge-vents. In physical fact, only half human and only half living, he reeled up into the gloom and cast his eyes around the valleys.

Though vegetation had grown thick, the lay of the land matched Chin's map. Soaring high in the freezing damp of the sky he could make out the ravines where the upper and lower glaciers had ground their way down the mountains. Around him the peaks of the Eiger, the Silberhorn and the Mönch towered in majesty undimmed since the twentieth century. The sunken canyon of Lauterbrünnen lay below, washed by torrential green waterfalls many times the size of their forebears.

The incessant wind twisted his spine horribly close to

breaking point. He could continue reworking the fabric of the manifold enough to survive but each second built up a backsnap debt that might finish all three of them. He searched more urgently, swooping down the carvings of the old glaciers, top to bottom.

He came down the upper Gletscherdorf ravine and knew he was getting close.

Two sheared megaliths faced each other across the void like praying hands. The mentality of the place was more mixed now. Amid the layered tumult of the darkspins were wisps of memory, resonances. Something in the weather was throwing out these ephemeral chanters with litanies of triumphs, of loves, of sorrows. He was close to *something* now, but what? The Oracle? *Diocletian*?

He settled by the shelter of some rocks on one of the prayerful hands and lay down, face to the earth, braced to accept the backsnap.

Even bolstered by Lethe and Timoth, it was pain like he had never experienced before. He worked changes across his body to ease its progress, snapping and healing his spine with the spasms that wracked it but finally he passed out.

He came to with one arm and his head dangling off the cliff edge, and with eyes fixed on the chasm floor below. Slowly he became aware of shapes and patterns in the terrain that cut across the natural contours of the landscape, that held straight where they should have meandered, that must have been man-made. He hauled himself to his feet and started picking his way down an ancient trail. Even the earth at his feet was throbbing with subsapient mentality. He couldn't tell how dangerous it all was.

Martoth pushed herself to her feet and coughed up the gunk that had settled in her throat, wincing at the pain behind her eyes. The sound of fighting came from outside but it was bathed in the beating buzzing she knew to be spinroar. She could almost smell the rips. And she could see the glow of firelight through the canvas where something had ignited the big stacks of firewood. She massaged her temples.

— Oh, Candle! Welcome to the party.

— Some party, said Candle in her head.

Martoth felt like her head was packed with explosives. Straining to lift it, she stood and reached an arm out to the canvas roof to steady herself. She knew this was a disaster unfolding around them. Who but these poor abused orphans of the Vigil would save the world? Seronin might avert its destruction, but that wasn't *saving*. That wasn't rebuilding. That wasn't the hope that had been lost. That was just carrying on. And all she wanted from Timoth was to save *her*. Who was to save these hapless children?

— I hope you two have some tricks up my sleeves.

Barnabas was struggling to his feet and Martoth let him shuffle out of the tent ahead of her. Chin trailed dutifully behind. At the doorway, he tripped and staggered forward, silhouetted against a burning wood stack beyond. Martoth had a sudden flashback — the fires, the black figures…

— *Chin*! she cried.

Chin turned and Martoth felt the spinroar build in her aching ears as the thing that had been Barnabas rose up behind Chin.

Martoth screamed and ran madly forward at it, hitting it, pushing it, driving it, forcing it back, back further, back into the fire.

As they tumbled in, it was the blinding light that Martoth was aware of, not the burning heat. She was still pushing, pushing the thing down through the flames into the white-hot embers at the core. If the thing screamed she didn't hear it. She had given herself up to the white world of light that encased her.

— Martoth! MARTOTH! ROLL!

It was Weakjohn's voice in her head. Where the will came from she never knew but she managed it. She rolled off and out and across the glow-tipped twigs onto the cold grass beyond. She was alive. Firm hands picked her up, roughly, dragging her to her feet.

When she had her balance she pushed the arms off her and recognised Menelaus in the glow of the fire.

— Are you okay? he asked, his face puffy and pale with fright, his eyes betraying a lost helplessness revealing that despite the pain, the fires and the death, these vigilants by some inexplicable enforcement of will were *still holding themselves in check.*

She clapped a hand on his shoulder then swayed past him to climb up onto the picnic table that still stood in front of the tent. From the table she could see over the tents and through the flames to the pockets of fighting around the camp. She could see shadows mustering at the edges of the clearing.

— The embargo's over, she cried. The embargo is *over*!

They heard her, she could tell, all of them — by some magic of Weakjohn's or Candle's. She couldn't tell who was doing what anymore but she knew now that the vigilants would follow her.

Chin and Menelaus clambered up onto the table with her. A figure ran past the fires below her and looked up, turning black smudge-eyes towards them. There were other sinister movements at the edges of the firelight.

She growled:

— The embargo is OVER!

...and cast her hands forward at the puppet in some vain gesture of admonishment. To her surprise, a searing blaze of light shot from her hand and smashed into the creature. It flew back and hit the turf in an ugly mockery of human motion. Though Martoth couldn't see clearly through fire and smoke and the floating scars in her vision she had the distinct sense of scorched and bursting skin. She contained her rising sense of disgust.

— What the *fuck*?

— Party, you said?

Candle sounded unnaturally energised, pumped up in a way that Martoth had never heard before.

— We can't win, Candle! One by one we're *going over to their side*!

— So…? said Weakjohn.

Martoth imagined the three of them, back in three bodies, staring wordlessly at one another, each looking for ideas in the others' blank faces.

— I take your point.

She dropped down from the table with Chin and Menelaus at her back. She checked herself, steadied her legs, took a breath and launched blazing into the fray, her fingertips fizzing with every species of noumenal weaponry that Weakjohn and Candle could imagine into being. All around, the air crackled as one by one the vigilants abandoned the mindwork embargo and began to give reality the kicking they'd been storing up. And one by one, they all fell in behind Martoth.

Seronin stood in the courtyard, shivering and drenched and pulled his hood across his face. The ice-cold rain had turned to a hail that stung his cheeks and ears. His head ached from the cold but it was no longer a time for altering himself. It was time to gather everything he had, everything of himself, everything from Lethe and Timoth, still holding on, still touching his mind from afar, fingertip to fingertip, like God to Adam.

If it weren't for the ghostly lights wavering at the

windows, the gallery would be a blunt grey megalith, a dead boulder from the past, smashed into the darker grey of the cliff behind. The stone portico had collapsed years ago. Where the door had been, blank, seamless deadspace barred the way, neither standing nor suspended but there, and impenetrable. What should have been glass at the windows was deep and pale as the arctic, if the arctic was lit below by the ghosts of gaslight.

The lights were a sign or a challenge. A flaunted imitation of welcome in the hailstorm. How long had they been lit? A century? Or these last few weeks? Was Seronin the first to stand beneath this bastion?

He felt like he could stay here. There was no menace emerging from the inside. The foul weather in the sky was not matched in the mentality of the place. There was a curious absence here, no spins, no chanters. Whatever terrors waited within could no more leave than he could enter. He could stay here. Stay here and just… *not*.

But there were two of him. And neither had much to lose.

So.

Now.

He shifted to *Happenstance*. And caught hold of himself. Nothing changed. *Nothing changed.*

The gallery, the ruined entrance, the ice floe windows, the phantom lights, the hail lashing his face.

He saw at last the genius of the chrysalis. *Nothing changed.*

Every detail, every act of recreation, every reinterpretation of the concrete world below, was a recreation of a detail of the concrete. He knew he was in *Happenstance* because of the effort of maintaining his perspective but it was like he had not shifted at all. It was dizzying.

Seronin's leaden stomach sank and he almost slipped to the frozen earth at his feet. The implication of this reproduction of one stratum in the next… it was an infinite regress, an extension of the manifold far beyond the four strata of the orthodoxy. It was the double-ended infinity in opposing mirrors. It was *his* world not Diocletian's. If the concrete reappeared in *Happenstance*, and then *Happenstance* in *Sanctum*, there could be no end of it in the *Apocryph*. The architect of the chrysalis could not have missed that. Seronin's one precious advantage began to crumble, taking all hope with it.

He could stay here and just *not*. Or… Another possibility opened up at last, a way whose entrance had tantalised him before but only at the point of death, like with the girl upstairs at the Fairy Castle. He could shortcut this pointless existence and dissolve into the future oneness that shone always over his mystical horizon. The true nature of his gift seemed to reveal itself to him now. His power, his gift, his blessing above all that others might have, was the prospect of escape.

Even as he flirted with oblivion, he heard Timoth's voice pulling him back. It was snatches of Timoth's voice, overlapping, echoing and resounding as if they'd tumbled chaotically onto a musical score. *Both of you are Seronin?* he heard. *It's Anna. There's a scream. Both of you are Seronin? It's Anna.*

He could barely make sense of it and how it drove him on he never knew but there was some lesson in it that Timoth had not once said aloud but had somehow exemplified every second they'd known each other. *Whatever the future, Seronin, whatever your blessings, whatever it is you can see, you're no better than the rest of us at knowing what's important.*

Spiral winds whipped hailstones into the tender flesh of his cheeks. The brooding monolith of the gallery loomed, filling his sight.

— What's important, he admitted, bowing bodilessly to his silent other mind, certainly isn't me.

He took a first pace forward in the *Happenstance* replica of the concrete. It was precise in every detail. The gallery glowered, the hail swept, the throat of the glacial ravine yawned. It was a formidable achievement. To Seronin it felt more magical than when first he shifted to *Happenstance*, accidentally, before even Barnabas had discovered him. Each facet of the reproduction was as beautiful and wondrous in Seronin's mind as a twinkling star. That Diocletian should have invented this construction way back in the twentieth century, developed the theory of it in isolation... There were many who thought Seronin a prodigy, but Diocletian was the genius.

Seronin would be crushed. Must be.

There was no way in.

He prepared to shift to *Sanctum* but he knew already he would find the same microscopically faithful representation of the concrete, one level loftier in the untoppleable tower of creation. At one further multiplication of effort and discomfort and many magnitudes more at odds with the nature of reality at that level.

He shifted. The gallery, the ruined entrance, the ice floe windows, the phantom lights, the hail lashing his hood. Nothing changed.

He was captivated by the glory. *Sanctum* was a fickle reality, a drifting weave of dislocated imagery. To find the construction that did *this*, that rebuilt the whole world inside it... He ripped his hood away and let the rain wash his eyes and the hail sting his cheeks.

It was as he gave himself up to the unbelievable weight of elements, each hailstone a triple-tower of ice, each gust a triple-mountain of concrete reality below, he saw the end of the construction, the escape from the regress. For though the gallery, the rock face, the glacial mouth were exact, none could eclipse *Sanctum*'s shoreline.

The tide that was forever receding. It didn't break the representation of the mountainside so much as modify it. The gallery stood as still as the rock that encased it but its very stillness was part of the ebb and flow of *Sanctum*'s shoreline. And beyond the shore… the *Apocryph*.

Hope flowed back. The chrysalis *was* a creature of the tetrarchy. And the tetrarchy was a lie.

He pulled his hood back up and smiled in the darkness.

A moment to prepare.

A moment poised.

And down, down, *DOWN…*

Xxz. Fbrrk. Memmnemnmnremnr. Xyxz. Dghtghr.

And he was inside — through the deadspace and choking in a black dusty hole. The outer lights were a lure. There nothing visible within. But the invisible world was on him in an instant: darkspins, vortices, and a dreadful choir of chanters.

Once more, he dived down into *Brainslang* and bounced up reconfigured for combat. He lashed out and fought off the demons, the part-minds, the unseated aggressions. He pushed them away and shielded himself as they receded into the darkness.

He stopped still, relaxing as much concentration as he could while keeping the shield up. He tried to judge the space around him. He listened to the echo of his footsteps. He sensed the drift of his breath. It was a hall, or a airy space. There were no imperfections in the creaseless dark. It was complete.

Cautiously he unscreened his mind and felt outwards in the flux, probing the retreating spins and vortices. The weather was an intractable murk of dread and shame, the chanters were litanies of despair, but of the more dangerous subsapients he found only a handful. It was a haunting, not a defence.

He lashed out violently, throttling, severing, crushing. A brief flash lit the rotting atrium and he saw two moss-covered stairways skirting the walls to a gallery above and wide openings to each side, on the ground floor and above. As darkness fell again, the spinroar went quiet.

Seronin relaxed his defences, trusting to his intuition in the darkness.

He could not sense an oracle. Not yet.

He contrived a weak light on the floor at his feet but where the light fell, the fetid matter it shone upon turned black under his gaze. He tried again but wherever he shone light, the gallery swallowed it.

The air was still. The only sound was a slow dripping of water.

He stepped forward, he thought, in the direction of the left hand stairway. His heart stopped. There was something else, another sound concealed in the echoes of his footsteps. He waited but heard only the droplets.

One more step. This time there was nothing. It was his imagination, or an effect of the chanters.

Another step. More confident now, he paced forward, feeling for the banister.

He found it and cautiously pulled himself up onto the stairs.

— *Cuckoo*!

He slipped and tumbled down the stairway, cracking his kneecap against the banister at the base. Fighting off a surge of panic he searched desperately about him. It had been a girl's voice. And now he heard a quiet pitter-patter as tiny footsteps raced across the gallery above. Still the darkness was complete. He strained to call to mind the patterns that Chin had developed for them, the blueprints of a Dioclete spearspin that was the only idea any of them had had.

The pain of the kneecap was too great to bear and a nausea flooded him so he crouched against the banister and took the space of several breaths to fix it. Then he crawled stealthily up the stairs poised to launch the—

— *Cuckoo!*

She lit up like a tiny angel in the darkness, a child of golden fireworks, hanging in the air by the chandelier and then she was gone again, vanished in the dark.

He launched the spearspin and howled in pain as it tore itself free of him. The spinroar was loud enough to shake his internal organs and in his mind it felt like barbed wire scoring away flesh at he wrenched it into the outside world. It reeled and tumbled into the darkness and crashed in to the chandelier and on through the walls and the rock behind and on into the mountain beyond. The sound of shattering glass and falling masonry replaced the roar as the spearspin twisted away, and then slowly the chaos settled and the sound of falling water was all that could be heard.

He held on to the banister

A whisper came, the whisper not of a child but of a grown woman in an icy fury, so terrifyingly close to his right ear:

— It's. Your. Turn.

He shot upwards, racing up the stairs and shifting up through the strata at the same time. In *Happenstance*, light flooded back into his world and he found himself weaving up the stairs through guests and waiting staff. She was near but he couldn't see where. He shoved guests aside as he flew upward, upsetting wine glasses, staining evening dresses. At each obstacle he felt her closing on him.

This way! It wasn't a voice in his mind, it was *his own* mind. A memory of his own, long hidden. He let it guide him and it raced him upward, led him through the guests, hopped him up over the final step and swerved him left. There was music somewhere, a Haydn quartet, the rattle of crockery from somewhere downstairs. He had never seen anything like this except in the snippets of Martoth's visions but it seemed so natural. He knew the layout, he began to recognise faces. Something he didn't understand was happening. Something in his history was taking over.

He knew she was almost upon him. He saw flashes of socks, flitting between the guests. A girl's heel, a running elbow, a bent knee, a swinging plait. Never a face. Not yet.

He did not want to see her face.

Through this room, along the wall, twist round the corner through the door and out into…

As he rushed into the next room he shifted upwards again, into *Sanctum*, into a swaying cubist rearrangement of the room. The pressure on his psyche was immense, maintaining this perspective, holding onto Lethe and Timoth, keeping an embryonic spearspin primed at his mental fingertips, but he knew at last where he was going. The oracle was at the Creed. Or at the wall where the Creed had once been, but not in *Concreta*, not in *Happenstance*, not even here in *Sanctum*. Diocletian had built her oracle in the one place only she had ever been.

He skidded to a halt in front of the Creed wall where a gaping blackness yawned. Two steps forward, two tripping tiptoes and he found himself on the brink of what he'd always known as the end of humanity. *Sanctum*'s shoreline, the *Apocryph*.

A childish giggle, and he felt something enormous eating up the world behind him.

He shifted. His mind, stretched to breaking point, rebuilt itself one last time, according to the pattern he was so close to letting go.

Seronin entered the *Apocryph*.

* * *

The oracle lay before him, and through the oracle, the mind of the universe, all the stars of humanity. All around him the infinite re-entwining of thought, the blissful shine of what is and what will remain. It was a centre like The Forest but not just of place, and the centre was at once the boundary and the core of all things. This stratum was the trajectory, the fate, of humanity.

What will did he have left? What strength did he have left? He faced the possibility that he was ruined. That all he had left was mute awareness. That he was a victim, a sufferance. But it was not the truth. For he was not alone.

— *Timoth*, he whispered, tugging on Lethe, the tortured rope he'd trailed from the sea shore to here. *Timoth, now!*

And as Timoth climbed the rope, squeezed through the channels that Lethe held open for him, crossed the chrysalis, scaled the tetrarchy, and poured his supple mind into the black void, Diocletian's oracle, Seronin cut himself free from the rope then he turned and beheld her face.

— Cuckoo? he whispered, his nerves cracking.

A blast of white light pushed him backward and set his skin on fire.

— BURN! cried the mind who'd owned the world like none other since the world began.

He screamed and let fly the spearspin, and then another formed in the space of a heartbeat to the same pattern as the first, and then another. He melted down each part of his mind that was not part of the spearspin machine and he fired and fired. Any of these should have been death for Diocletian. Each embodied everything the Vigil had learned from generations of Dioclete analysis. Each should have woken her fears, scalded her rawnesses, aggravated her agonies. But they were futile.

He did not see the fiery spins that Diocletian launched

back at him but he felt them and whimpered at each impact. Each was the twisted remains of a spearspin that Seronin himself had fashioned, but each returned vestiges of Seronin's own psyche that he'd leaked into it himself, now subtly reinvented as a decoy to work through his mental defences. Like boiling pitch the Seronin mind matter fused to Seronin and then delivered its payload of searing pain into his nervous system. At one blow, Seronin felt all the desperate guilt of his desertion of the Vigil, he felt his betrayal of the Abbots and with each he shrank further from his purpose. At the next, his own worth was laid bare and he despised himself.

From the far edges of the flux he heard a new growl of mockery and hatred. She had discovered the *rope*, the fraying end of Lethe's stretched mind left visible in the *Apocryph*, and in one effortless movement she lit him like a fuse and obliterated him — blew him to pieces as Seronin hung pinioned in her grasp — casting the shreds of his mind into the turbulent world like whispers in the wind.

Seronin howled and thrashed as if to throw himself to the wind after Lethe but he could not. He was incarnate in four strata, and in each one, every cell was a maelstrom of pain, each become part of an alien mind that infested him. The full force of Diocletian's cruelty was now bent entirely on Seronin, consuming him from the inside.

Even in his agony he was awed by the majesty of Diocletian's capability. What unimaginable authority over the flux, what deep participation in the phases of concrescence, allowed a being to so casually disassemble and pervert these spearspins into personalised tortures? Seronin was fighting a god and he knew it at last.

And he was dying.

— The flux, yelled the noumena with the mind of Diocletian and the voice of Anna, is *mine*.

With each impact, beneath sheets of pain, memories and opinions that weren't his began to entwine themselves into Seronin's mind. At the point of death he was not only Seronin, but Anna, Pyotr, Stephen, Clindor, Creed.

Timoth flowed through the web, out across the universe, chasing down a million madnesses and the one that he loved.

With one fibre he held onto to his body, a fibre whose strength grew from Timoth's determination that there was something still worth fighting for.

As he entered the Oracle, Candle's voice sounded its old caution in his mind — *Keep. It. Together.* — and he fought to stop his mind sprawling out of control into the forests of thought that pressed around him.

As he searched amongst the forking paths, he began to understand what this was. He was in the skeleton of the world. The structure on which the flesh of the modern diaspora was hung. There was nowhere that humans had spread that was not connected to this web of oracles.

If this was Diocletian's then Diocletian was the architect of reality. There was no serendipity. There was no surprise. Not in the habitability of Semele, nor in the landscape of the Leap or the pastures of Schiller. Diocletian had already been there. Every Oracle we'd connected to every source traced back to this one and to Anna.

As well as the works of Diocletian other sturdy boughs forked from the trunk, other lineages and traditions. The minds of the Swiss group hurtled forward into the modern day, lines that became the Vigil, and lines that became... *something else.* It was there that he found traces of Martoth's mother. Marta, who was connected thinly to the Vigil lines was building on *other* traditions too, lines that came from others in the Swiss group.

This trace of Marta was all he needed. He recognised

finally how to find what he was looking for. He tracked back to the root Oracle and looked for lines that were swollen from use, the conduits scarred by ripspins and puppet-minds. And he raced down them, choosing, every moment, narrower paths, using her visions to guide him. What had she seen? What had she not seen? So this path, that path, this path…

As the paths narrowed to a hair's breadth, he found himself at the end, on the narrowest of outcrops, facing a terrifying descent into the world of the Abbey. As he prepared to jump, to cut the fibre, to go where once on the Crow he had needed Candle's help, he looked behind and faced the greatest mystery of all.

For Diocletian's Oracle, old as it was, was *not the first.*

He looked in awe. Every hundredth stone Cheops's pyramid builders had lain in Semele and was waiting undiscovered in the forests. There were Roman walls that ran from Earth to the Leap. There were Rapanui *moai* whose heads had fallen into Tenistan. There were Tudor shipwrecks on the ocean floors of Schiller. Mindwork wasn't magic; it was just what humans did. And after all this, they had only escaped into a world they'd created themselves, and he knew that their own demons would chase them still. What had Diocletian seen of this? How much did Seronin suspect?

And what would Martoth make of it all when he told her?

Martoth swayed forward, letting Candle and Weakjohn throw her arms this way and that. She could no longer speak to them. She concentrated on leading her group forward. A crowd of vigilants followed her, blazing noumenal weirdworks at every shade that lumbered out of the trees but her army was thinning and as often as not turning their fire inward on themselves. She remembered the strange threshold that had been breached back at the Hitspeke junction and wondered if this light show would tip them over, or whether there were too few of them left now. She knew she was running to a standstill. Her face felt bloated and blocked and the pain behind her eyes seemed to extend down her neck and spine. Each step was a labour of Hercules. She felt like there were two of her now — the thing that Candle and Weakjohn were keeping going and the thing that had let go of them and was drifting away.

A puppet charged at her in the black cassock of the Vigil. Something hit it, something fast and bright, and it fell broken at her feet, but as she struggled forward, she tripped on the body and found herself face down in the mud. She had nothing left. She was spent. Anything could be happening above her. Any blow might fall. She couldn't stop it anymore.

The battle went on above. She was trampled on, kicked and burned. Howls of anger and despair rung out and in the alternating heat from the burning tents and wood stacks and cold of the gusting wind, she felt rain begin to fall. She closed her eyes and waited for some ending to come.

Heels stamped about her, shouts rang out, flames came and went, but the end did not come. Finally she became aware of a familiar presence at her side but when she opened an eye and peered across the mud surface she saw nothing but the dead.

Then she realised who it was.

— Timoth! she gasped.

The pressure relaxed behind her eyes, released her neck and limbs, freed her lungs. Air flowed in again.

— Aah, she breathed. Aargh.

He wasn't fully there. She could not see him, and what terrifying chasms he had crossed to leave his body behind she couldn't imagine. But she knew he was with her and her illness had gone.

She rolled to the side, bent a knee, pushed, bent the other. Onto her knees. Arms pushing. Head back, neck stretching, eyes to the evening stars.

— *UP!* she yelled. *UP!* They've found the oracle! They've taken it!

The child knew now he was not a spark. He was a *phoenix*, a new hand to fit adult-Seronin's glove, a surviving breath to swell his lungs, a kindling light behind his eyes.

At last he recognised adult-Seronin for who he really was.

He was the *poet*.

He was Pyotr!

But there was other material entwined around Pyotr like a vine on a trellis, the result of generations of regeneration, of accretion and evolution through which the cursed Pyotr had retreated further into passivity. No wonder Barnabas had blanched at the monstrosity of his protégé. Adult-Seronin was so barely human at all. And the growth of the vine was so thick Barnabus had been emboldened to create a new Seronin, to burn out the ancient trellis and let a new vinebush stand on it own — a child-Seronin who was no longer Pyotr.

Man-me could not speak to that deep part of himself because the poet had lost his words. They left him one by one as the years passed, as he was forced, time and again, back into a life that would not shape itself according to *her* plan. Until finally, voiceless in the dark, even she could not find him, and he echoed onward in the same cycle, diminishing further with each rebirth. The Pyotr that lived still in Seronin was mute, beaten down, surrendered.

The poet always knew what he meant but saying it got harder and harder. He made shorter verses when he lost confidence in reaching the end of longer ones. Each sentence was a risk the guillotine would fall. Ever more frequently he stopped short, breath gathered at his windpipe, mute in front of an invisible block, his lips poised, the river of his intent flooding against the dam, and the word would not come. He suffered the indignity because he believed he deserved it. What more apt punishment could there be? For his desertion of her? Not once but repeatedly, as children, as adults, as ageless ripples in the flux. All for his freedom at her expense. And for his surrender to the weakness of mind that could not encompass the horror of what she was become.

But adult-Seronin did not see it yet. He did not know who he was. He did not understand the forces that were coming to the fore, the rising tide of Pyotr's ancient guilt that would overwhelm him.

Seronin did not fear death. He no longer felt pain. But he feared her fury. The fury that consumed the *Apocryph* expanded many times over in *Sanctum*, spidered out again in *Happenstance*. What did her fury encompass in *Concreta*? Had he just provoked her? Had his "cuckoo" lit fires across thirty worlds?

She didn't need the oracle. Seronin was nothing but a meteorite burning up in her atmosphere, more wreckage to fall on the unsuspecting souls of the universe.

For a moment, that was his *Apocryph*: his death in her fires.

But then he saw a courage he never expected. The *child* shifted here with him. The child stood next to him in her fires. Seronin had not wanted this. An anger rose within him at Barnabas and his unseeing cruelty. He thrust the child back and placed himself in front but the child would not be shielded. The child turned his back to Diocletian and shone his own fiery light on Seronin.

Then... did Anna's fires relent?

Did her fury falter as the child stood to the fore? Yes, but not for the child.

Seronin stood, mind stripped naked. The deepest and oldest fibres of his being, heartstrings, roots, lay open to the sky. So much of him was now scoured away, the raw underneath that swelled in the gaze of Anna, was the wordless poet. Mute and sorrowful Pyotr. Pyotr, whose only remaining intention was to offer himself, finally and forever. For he saw at last that his every act of independence was abandonment and only that.

Her fires choked and sputtered and went silent.

They floated, the last three: Anna the monster. Seronin-Pyotr the penitent. The Child, a pale light as the others went dark in each others shade.

He bathed them in the last of his light. He kept them warm and allowed them to excavate each other. He swept away the debris that had settled on their souls. He blew the sand from the limbs of their embrace. And he laid them bare to each other, let them match their contours, hill to hollow, rock to river. Until at last they were one.

38. The New Abbey

Martoth, Timoth, Seronin

The fires were out and the air was clearing. The survivors huddled together as the dawn dew descended on them. The people from the other Backshades camps had joined them as the sun rose and now there were parties trickling in from the Midshades too. Shouts went up from time to time as lost faces reappeared out of the forest, or were found among the dead.

— Barnabas failed, said Menelaus, sitting with a few others on the picnic table by Barnabas's tent.

— Barnabas had failed before he was even born, replied Martoth. The Vigil entrusted to Cheras was just a humiliating reflex of Bastien's remorse. The Vigil in the end was an echo, a ripple, a mirage. It was a wish to protect something that was already destroyed. A mission to save Anna from Clindor when Anna had slaughtered Clindor and was anything but saved.

— So where do we go now? *Home?*

Why would they ask her?

Martoth knew the rawness that he was touching on. Most of these people hadn't seen the homes they came from since they were little more than children. A few had travelled like

Marta had or lived away like Weakjohn or Theremy but most were like Menelaus, as near rootless as made no difference, never having drawn a breath beyond the Abbey.

— It's not for me to tell you, said Martoth. You have a new Abbot.

This caused a commotion in the assembly. Martoth was enjoying the moment but found herself a little unsure how to play it. She didn't know whether to step aside or mimic a fanfare. Instead she just grinned kindly at the buzzing crowd while she waited for the big reveal.

Weakjohn hobbled out of Barnabas's tent with her walking stick, beaming at the crowd.

At first there was some silence and a little scattered laughter, but then a cheer broke out. It was a sound of relief, a well-why-the-hell-not, rather than an unambiguous triumph but it was infectious and in a few seconds the whole crowd was cheering for Weakjohn.

It didn't take much direction, thought Martoth, when people were as lost as this. She began to see tears in their eyes.

As the crowd cheered, Weakjohn walked over to confer with Menelaus and then he and his friends cleared the picnic table and hoisted Weakjohn up onto it. She gestured for silence then addressed the crowd.

— Yeah, yeah, she said. Quiet now, I have something to say. Quiet! Hey, quiet! Come now, your Abbot commands it.

They chuckled into silence, appreciating a fond and gentle mockery of Barnabas's style.

— I have something important to say to each and every one of you.

A hush descended.

— There is no Vigil. There is only the Abbey. And the Abbey must survive.

— There is a path ahead of us now and it is not an easy

path. We live in a world of mysteries and we must confront them afresh. We have to throw away our prejudices, our preconceptions and every shred of orthodoxy — many things that are dear to us all. Not all of you will want to hold with me on this path. And that's okay. I want to say loud and clear now: Everybody is free to leave. Everybody is free to disagree. Everybody is free to give up, to stop, to walk away. I am old enough to know how hard change can be. But if you join me on this path, then know this: I am here for you and you must be here for each other.

— What then is our path? she continued.

A quite murmur passed amongst them. Their path had never been clear. Their purpose had always been myriad. Each vigilant found their own in the end. To even tee up an answer like this felt like impossible daring. They waited patiently for her to diffuse the tension.

She paused and gestured up to the sky with her stick.

— There are a billion souls out there in the universe as lost and confused as we are and we must become a beacon for them. We haven't deserved our pre-eminence. We must deserve it before we lose it. We must rebuild and reform. We must be home to the brightest stars, not the purest or the most orthodox. We thought Diocletian was a luminary. She was a lost child. We should have been the home she could return to. Instead we became the crust she wanted to tear away. We tore children from their parents. We cast out those who needed our care. No more. The new Abbey will reach deeper than the old. We will be where the people are and we will be as much a force of kindness and bravery as scholarship and technique.

— Lastly, I say this: Look within yourselves. Find those resources within you that the Vigil never cared for till now. And be ready to bring what you have and nurture what others have.

— Tonight we celebrate. Tomorrow we start on the fields. By the end of the week we'll be back under proper roofs. Then the real work begins.

Back in the tent, Weakjohn burst into laughter.

— Did you see their faces? she beamed.

Candle smiled wanly.

— What are you going to do?

— You're talking about the Earth, aren't you? said Weakjohn.

— Forgive me, I heard you suggesting the Vigil shouldn't have cloistered themselves away and I couldn't help thinking you were abandoning the Abbey…

— No, said Weakjohn. Maybe one day but not yet. We'll keep our base here but spread out across the worlds, mindwoke or not. We'll send people back to Earth too but we're not recolonising.

— Others will, she said.

Weakjohn nodded.

— I'm guessing that's where you are headed?

— A funeral of sorts, she said. After that… After that, I don't know.

— I… you know we all loved him, said Weakjohn. You know I'm sorry, for everything.

Candle nodded.

— And if you find Theremy… she said, but trailed off.

— I miss him, said the new Seronin, the child grown swiftly into a man's body.

Timoth didn't know how to reply. If it wasn't enough that the new Seronin needed hand-holding through something unprecedented in the history of humanity, Martoth seemed to have jammed every circuit in Timoth's mind. He couldn't form a single thought without being distracted by this giant buzzing inside him. He hadn't known whether to expect elation or despair, so she'd come along and served up both as usual.

Maybe new Seronin didn't need much.

— I miss him too.

They were sitting in Weakjohn's tent. She'd been clear. Timoth and Seronin's home was with the Abbey. They were the future of the Abbey.

Well that was fine. The future of the Abbey was in the future and Timoth still had another life to check up on. And Seronin needed…

Well it wasn't clear exactly what Seronin needed, but Timoth's hunch was he needed a friend. So Seronin was off back to Semele with Timoth. They'd confront the mess, do things together for a while, with some luck, catch up with Alban, share a saki at the taproom, maybe join the band.

— Will we stop off at the Fairy Castle for a couple of jars? suggested Timoth.

New Seronin nodded solemnly, holding his hands in front of his face to inspect them.

— I believe that is the proper operating procedure.

Martoth followed Weakjohn away through the bustle of the tents and the serene hush of the Backshades to the glade where the candles had burned. With barely a gesture Weakjohn lit them again and Martoth cried in delight as they floated up from their stumps and hollows into the air once more. All around her the forest dusk was decorated by flickering flames and for a brief second Martoth thought she saw faces too, superimposed over these tiny memorials, faces of the hundreds of men and women that the Abbey had lost. Many, many more must have died across the other worlds.

— It'll be harder when they try to come to terms with this, Weakjohn said.

She was being oblique. On both their minds was one

passing that no-one had memorialised, a suffering so large that people would use whatever excuse they could to look past it.

— Should there be a funeral for *her*? asked Martoth.

— One day yes, agreed Weakjohn, but we're not ready yet.

Weakjohn waved an arm and hundreds of candles wafted aside to form a glittering tunnel into the heart of the glade, which they passed through to come to a large flat rock in the centre. They sat there and contemplated the souls of the departed. After a minute another tunnel opened up through the candles as a figure in Vigil robes approached from the other side of the clearing.

He was a handsome young man despite a bony clumsiness to his movements and a haunted look in his eyes. He joined them on the rock and smiled at Martoth.

— Martoth, this is Heb, said Weakjohn, one of our brightest talents. While we were enjoying our grand reveal, I had Heb enter the Abbey.

Martoth swore. She'd looked in horror on the seething turmoil of the Abbey and assumed it would be beaten back slowly from the edges by *teams*, not risked by daring individuals. She revised her initial impression of Heb.

— Tell us, Heb, said Weakjohn.

— Once I was in, I could use help, he said. There were a few of us involved by the end. We cleaned out a cylinx and fought to the archives and made them accessible and probably mostly trustworthy. We even touched a couple of the old oracles. There are no attacks any more, just what is already there.

Weakjohn's relief was visible.

— And?

— It's excruciating that we never looked for this before, he said. The Dioclete background is gone. The scream is gone. So many of our primary sources are gone.

— Chen will do the history, said Weakjohn. I want the forensics.

— It's mostly speculation, he said. There is still a lot we don't know. Some of what's in Martoth's visions is accessible through the deep background now, but the Eiger Oracle has gone quiet. There'll be more information back on Earth, if you'll permit…?

Weakjohn shook her head.

— Soon, she said.

— So. Anna Irma Wilkes was born in 1933 to Robert Wilkes and Angela Harrison—

— …about whom we know…?

— Nothing, admitted Heb. We know nothing of their deaths. We know very little of Stephen Harrison and haven't found any residue of his mind although the visions contain some correspondences with items from the Grammarian Oracle that are quite striking.

Martoth raised an enquiring eyebrow but Weakjohn waved it aside.

— *Anna*, she prompted.

— Yes, said Heb. We have documentary evidence of her living with Greta Giroud until the early fifties. So Anna was living a double life almost immediately from the moment she killed Clindor. What family life was like with Greta is quite hard to imagine — we think Anna discovered the Tier Ones during this time, a century ahead of anyone else. How much she influenced them we're not sure. She can't be solely responsible for the phenomenon of serendipity —Timoth had some rather exciting discoveries in that direction— but certainly she ranged far and wide. She was unlike any child ever in the history of the world. I suppose extraordinary loneliness on top of whatever else she had to deal with.

— She must have been a clash of warring impulses from very early on. Whatever caused this final apocalyptic breakdown, the seeds were there from a much earlier stage. In retrospect there are what might be hints of it in Diocletian's works. I think a reassessment is due in the light of our new… humility.

— Chen's got that, said Weakjohn.

— On Pyotr, we actually know a bit more from Barnabas and the boy Seronin. There was an incident Martoth witnessed between Pyotr and Anna in the fifties that corresponds to the distinction we've historically made between the early works and the later works. Sometime later when Pyotr died in Holland we believe she forced this echogenesis upon him, recycling his mind into one of his children, with what motive is not clear. Maybe she wanted to punish him, maybe she just wasn't ready yet for whatever use she had for him. Then later to one of his grandchildren, and so on. We think most of the line were daughters. Barnabas discovered Seronin on Zaaland, one of the unmapped fringe worlds. How the family came to be there will take some time to establish.

— We think that this is relevant to what happened when she returned. Imagine: she'd been propagating him forward all this time while she strode out across the universe, then there was this… painful interruption… and then out of nowhere she's back suffering the worst coldwake the universe has ever inflicted and the one thing she's been clinging to all that time… suppose she can't find him anymore, suppose she's searching frantically but she's lost him, well maybe some older impulses are going to come to the fore again. Right from Clindor we know what she was capable of.

It made sense to Martoth. Even if it wasn't a true love lost, it was a life's work ruined, no solace, no haven, only pain, maybe all that was left was lashing out.

— We can forgive her, now, can't we? said Martoth

although she wasn't sure. She knew how it felt to be carved apart by fusewounds and to teeter on the brink of death. Many others had been less fortunate.

— We can very fervently wish her eternal rest, said Weakjohn wryly. But I'm not sure forgiveness is really the province of the new Abbey. In any case I think we need to know more about what she was doing all that time. Do we know anything more about the "interruption" as you called it?

— A little, nodded Heb. Seronin said Theremy is a hexagon, a fusion of six minds into one. There are tantalising hints in the post-resurrection Dioclete samplings which might suggest hexagonality. We might assume Merrick was the same. You could take this as a sort of signature of the fusion technique employed and look for evidence of it elsewhere. If Diocletian resurrected when some of the fused strands were jointly complete enough to allow her to recover herself using elements of the Dioclete background, it certainly suggests that her destruction seventy years before was more like a fission than the dispersal we had believed. And that is much more likely to have been the result of hostile action.

— Oh my, said Weakjohn. She was assassinated?

— And you might even speculate about whether the web of oracles that she used to publish might actually have been the vector of the attack on *her,* before ever she conceived of using it to mount her own revenge. We like to think we're the only mindworkers out there but we're not.

— It's too soon for a funeral, said Weakjohn.

— Or too late, said Martoth.

— It's so frustrating, said Heb. We'd trained ourselves not to ask.

— That's got to change, insisted Weakjohn. You carry on, Heb. Use whoever you need. One day we'll have that funeral. And... perhaps you should double check all our people, sensitively you know, in case anyone else has six corners.

Heb frowned.

— Its not as easy as that, he said. I'm not actually sure how Seronin—

— And what next? asked Martoth abruptly.

There was a pause. Did the new Abbey's mission really extend to chasing this all down? Martoth was inclined to think they had neither the right nor the duty. If the French boys' vigil was a well intended failure from the start, the latter Vigil had become an instrument of suppression, a machine more likely to turn the knife in Anna's wounds than bring her the release she needed.

— Meef Parton, said Weakjohn.

— What about Marta? cried Martoth.

Meef was *her* lead and Weakjohn seemed determined to ignore problems closer to home.

Weakjohn sighed.

— Yes. We'll go through all her assignments.

Heb coughed awkwardly.

— A brief check through her assignments shows she wasn't allowed a great deal of freedom though I think we can assume she was familiar with more obvious ways of tampering with the record. She didn't introduce any other novices apart from Merrick and Theremy.

Weakjohn's cross expression suggested she was not yet ready to doubt Marta's honesty in the same way Heb was, but her look of resignation indicated she was prepared to leave the question of Meef to Marta, for now at least.

— We'll assign you someone, said Weakjohn to Martoth.

— Actually, I have an idea on that already, said Martoth.

Mebbit tossed a small wooden globe to Martoth. She caught it and turned it over in her hands. It was carved in hard wood, unvarnished and grubby. Up close, it was polyhedral, hideously precise with faces in various shapes and sizes. Burned into its surface were dark curves and dots, each dot annotated with a tiny letter or symbol. The curves crossed over each other and turned unpredictable loops around each other but each ended at a dot. Martoth understood that this was a chart of sorts. Mebbit wasn't much of a talker, but now she asked:

— Where next for Martoth Heep-Parton?

Martoth tossed the starball back at her and looked down over the ruined Abbey.

Here they were, back at the way head. Timoth would go home, for a while at least, but he'd be back at the Abbey soon. It wasn't too late to go with him. She had breathed a goodbye into their final embrace, her breath still hot and ragged. But Timoth didn't want her to go, she could still as easily go his way.

She sat down and emptied the tube into her lap and picked out the piece of paper to inspect for the hundredth time. There was nothing new to learn from it. *Parton Investigations, 35 Helicon St, Merriweather, Marston, Schiller.* The key, you would have to hope, went with the address. The ring and the shells remained an enigma.

— Schiller, she said.

In time she'd visit Marta's grave. She would learn more from Semele. Check on Ma Mackelay and Teresa. For the time being, let Timoth tug at the Jessic angle. Martoth was off to collect her inheritance.

— Seems I could be heading your way for just a while longer, said Mebbit.

— I'd be grateful of that, Mebbit.

— Call me Katya.

Each raindrop hung suspended in the infinite night. Nothing moved. Nothing warmed. Nothing cooled. Love was met with love, hunger with sweat, curiosity with candour, but there was no annihilation. What remained, remained. Fused and dispersed across a million drops of awareness that were inert, unafraid, unwilled but aware of time's passing and the dark face of forever. This forever was kinder than any forever that had been promised, but it was still forever.

The trillion drops of rain that would never splash were lit by lightning that would never flash. Each prism in eternity looked out into the world and sorrowed. What now?

But then the trillion drops were matched with a trillion fires. To each drop a tiny campfire, a soldier, a roasting animal, a blade. From the earth rose a trillion soldiers to look out into the starshine, on the shoulders of every raindrop, to raise arms to the sky, to every corner of the night, to point a trillion ways, a trillion solaces and a trillion purposes. A trillion small forevers became a trillion small forgivenesses.

Theremy smiled.

Epilogue

24th April 1955

She stood again in the roaring snarl of the world.

Back in the fierce Oberland landscape she had not seen for fifteen years, here she could become a child again, a wide-eyed wanderer apprenticed to the peaks that had woken her once before.

She had travelled by sea and by train over the course of a week pausing briefly in Bern to test her own fragility, then making her way South over two days via Interlaken to a guesthouse in Kleine Scheidegg and now she had hiked out to here, a high platform in the heart of this landscape of the gods.

She yearned for blankness, to burn away this perverse hyper-awareness that so plagued her.

For she knew now that everything she had done, she had done in hope. Each thing done for herself had been done for a self that *he* might desire. Hope that had always been as foolish as it was false. In all the ways that so pained her now she was still that five year old who heard a trillion raindrops. Why could she not now be that five year old again in all the other ways? The innocence? The faith?

But you cannot burn away your self. This... *stuff*... that was so odious, it wasn't a growth or a covering or a decoration or even a part. It was what she was and the way she had become it. It was foul and unfair and pointless. She couldn't be the only thing she had ever wanted to be.

What was left for her now? She had done things no human had ever done. She knew things she couldn't begin to explain to any other living soul. She might even be a god. She might be the meaning of the world.

So she would retreat, retrace her steps — take the journey of her life, unwind every twist, disentangle each knot, step by step, each fact to forget, each skill to unlearn, each moment to unlive. A mind growing backward from scarred adulthood, to adolesce in reverse, back to healthy beginnings, back to where it all went wrong. If she had a destiny, she rejected it. If she owed a price she would default. She would turn her back and retreat along the path she had followed to get here.

How much of the world would track back with her? she wondered.

What could she recover?

Would she see her mother again?

And if she couldn't? What if her greatest trial became her newest, greatest failure?

Well.

She stared down between the craggy rocks, into the freezing pool below. In near darkness, twenty feet beneath her, black icy water waited under heavy cold air and the reverberating echoes of a thousand drips and ripples.

There was always that.

25th April 1955

In her moment of absolute despair, she plunged, fast, cracking her head and knees against the rocks on the way down, wracked by pain she no longer feared. Twenty feet down, the fearful speed of her fall through the cold air was arrested by the impact of her body breaking against the icy water and then she sank swiftly into the darkness below, dragged by the weight of her clothes and boots. Her death wish did not flinch, but her body panicked in struggle against the first breath of water, and she thrashed her broken bones in a fight as primal as any impulse within her.

Down she went, blind in the ice-cold blackness, thrashing still. Whatever movement she made, whatever twists, whatever hopeless, agonised flapping, down she went. How deep could this freezing hell be? Would she find out before she died? She was breathing in water now. Death must be close. There was nothing now that could stop this horrifying descent. There was no purification here. No release. No escape. No burning away the pain. Just this inexorable sinking. Just a continuing, enduring end of everything.

But there was not even that.

She was not dying.

Thirty times that day she drowned herself and lived. Each time she better conceived the relationship of what is called mind to what is called body and the future where she could dissolve it. In destroying and recycling her own body time and again, in repeatedly suffering the agony of death without the release of death, she began to plot her escape from death.

She need not ever die. There were no limits anymore.

She truly was a god.

She was Diocletian.

26th April 1955

Was it vengeance she craved? She could have it.

But it wasn't vengeance. Not since Clindor.

Power? Supremacy? They were hers already.

It was still what she had always wanted.

If he lived, he must live in the world.

To become *his* world she would become *the* world.

He would not live without her. Not in the end.

He would not die without her. She would not be deserted again.

And her watchers?

Fools.

She had *been* the Eiger. And now she was the North Wall. She was the white spider. Sheer and ice-clad, built out of the very stuff of the world. She cared less for her watchers than the mountain cares for the climbers strung across its face.

Acknowledgements

Enormous thanks to those who subjected themselves to drafts, early and late, and who offered editing suggestions, insight and advice, especially Ruth Ritzema, Phil Dickinson, Anne Currie, Catherine Forbes and Tom Newman. And thanks generally for the support and tolerance of family and friends.

Thanks to Natalia Junqueira for the map of the tetrarchy.

Thanks also, and apologies, to the billions of artists and creators whose work got micropillaged by the processes that produced the AI models that went into the cover art.

Humble apologies to the memories of philosophers whose ideas I've debased, whose terminology I've abused, and whose points I've deliberately missed in the making of this book. Some may recognise, in particular, mutant outgrowths of the work of Immanuel Kant, Alfred North Whitehead and Edward Douglas Fawcett, but there are others.

9 781738 408719